Winter Wonderland

Emma Craig,
Leigh Greenwood,
Amanda Harte,
Linda O. Johnston

LOVE SPELL BOOKS   **NEW YORK CITY**

LOVE SPELL®

October 1999

Published by

Dorchester Publishing Co., Inc.
276 Fifth Avenue
New York, NY 10001

ISBN 0-505-52339-6

Here Comes Santa Claus

Leigh Greenwood

To Roxie for saving me fried chicken at Christmas.

Chapter One

Michael Wetherford pulled his car to a stop in the driveway. He had no desire to get out. Just being there put his life into reverse. The brown-shingled house looked just as he remembered it—huge, impersonal, dominating its block in the residential section of the small mountain town of Wetherford Gap. Though he knew every room, every secret corner, every hidden recess of that house, he had no desire to go inside.

He had been born in that house, had grown up there, but he hadn't set foot in it in ten years.

Closer inspection showed the paint peeling in several places, bare spots in the lawn, and hedges that hadn't been trimmed. The lawyer had said something had gone really wrong with old Nick Wetherford. Michael agreed. His father had always kept the big house and extensive grounds in perfect condition. The place had stood as visible testimony to his success.

Even more unusual—no, absolutely inconceivable—a huge, three-dimensional Santa with his sleigh and eight reindeer covered the roof, the reindeer in full stride, Santa waving, the sleigh piled high with gifts. But apparently even that wasn't enough for his father. A young man had just climbed a ladder to string colored lights from one end of the front porch to the other. The shrubs and trees that dotted the front yard had already been draped with enough lights to pose a fire hazard. The columns on the porch had been decorated in an equally lavish style. Michael had no doubt that when all the lights were turned on, they would cause a brown-out from one end of the valley to the other.

He took a letter from inside his coat, pulled out a photograph, and looked at it for the thousandth time. It showed his father in the town square, handing out gifts from a large bag to a crowd of children gathered around him. The lawyer had said his father was selling everything he owned, but Michael doubted that even a thousand bags of toys could exhaust his father's wealth. Still, the fact that his father had given away anything at all shocked him. North Carolina hadn't spawned a more tight-fisted, penny-pinching, sour-tempered, money-grubbing scrooge than Nick Wetherford. The old man wouldn't give money away with one hand unless he'd discovered a way to haul in even more with the other.

Just as disturbing, the lawyer had said Nick had been emptying his attic, giving away everything, even Michael's old toys. Michael had never had a good relationship with his father, but he couldn't believe the old man would give away his things without asking, even toys he'd obviously never use again.

Michael looked back at the photo. The camera had

caught his father smiling. Michael couldn't believe anything short of a pact with the Devil could cause his father to give up anything he'd acquired. He couldn't believe anything *at all*, including the threat of eternal damnation, could make him do it with a smile.

Then there was the girl.

Nick Wetherford exemplified the term misogynist. Except for his wife, dead more than twenty years, he didn't come within a hundred yards of a woman if he could help it. A very pretty young woman dressed as an elf stood next to his father in the photo, selecting gifts from the bag. Michael could only assume the girl, identified as Ellen Weems, had bewitched Nick. Not even an ill-fitting elf suit could hide the fact that Ellen Weems would be considered attractive anywhere, and especially in a little town like Wetherford Gap. But not pretty enough, Michael would have thought, to have slumguzzled the most notorious tightwad in Cleveland County. Michael couldn't imagine his father turning into an old fool who would fall for some young fortune hunter, but he understood even less why such a woman would encourage him to give away his money.

Michael didn't really care what his father did with his money, but he'd be damned if he'd let the old man be made a fool of by some fortune hunter, even one as beautiful as Ellen Weems.

He put the photograph back in the envelope and slipped both into his coat pocket. He opened the car door and got out. The weather commentator on the radio had remarked repeatedly about the unusually warm weather, especially for the mountains, but Michael shivered despite a sweater and a coat. He'd forgotten how cold it could be in the mountains, warm spell or not. He'd spent the last ten years developing resorts in the South Pacific and considered anything below seventy degrees the beginning of a cold wave. He'd have to buy some long johns if he hoped to stay warm until he got back home.

The boy putting the lights on the roof had dressed for a heat wave. Running shoes, cutoff sweats, and a sweatshirt. A baseball cap, bill backward, covered short, nearly black hair. Hairless legs and downy cheeks said he couldn't have reached puberty.

"Don't you think you've got too many lights up there?" Michael called out as he approached the ladder.

The boy continued his work without turning around. "Nick wants his to be the brightest house in the whole town," he said in a very unmasculine voice.

Leave it to his dad to hire a kid so immature his voice hadn't changed. He probably planned to pay him less than minimum wage. Michael wondered if his father had conned those lights out of the local hardware store owner. More probably, he'd taken old lights the town fathers had discarded from their public Christmas decorations. Michael hoped they wouldn't short-circuit and burn the house to the ground. Not that he would mourn the house. He had no fond remembrances of this huge mansion, only memories of feeling very much alone in it.

"If the strain on the transformer when you plug the lights in causes it to blow, I can guarantee everyone will see it."

The boy leaned way over to loop the lights over the gutter on the corner of the house. "If you hang around for a while, you can find out for yourself," he said. "If you just want to complain, do me a favor and go suck on a lemon."

Rude little wise-ass. Michael didn't know why parents couldn't teach their kids to have more respect for their elders. He pulled his coat tight against the breeze.

The bright sunlight had only raised the temperature to fifty-two degrees. He intended to head straight back to the South Pacific as soon as he got this business about his father straightened out.

The kid came down the ladder, then backed up a short distance to inspect his handiwork. "Pretty good, if I do say so myself. What do you think?"

He turned, and Michael came face to face with the elf in the photo.

"What are you doing here?" she demanded, clearly surprised and unhappy to see him. "And don't tell me Nick sent for you because I know he didn't do any such thing. That nosy lawyer wrote you, didn't he? Don't bother denying it. It couldn't be anybody else. Why do lawyers have to be such creeps?"

Michael didn't produce his usual snappy rebuttal. He'd seen his share of beautiful women—rich men invariably used looks as a primary criterion when choosing a second or third wife—but never had a woman effected him so powerfully. And he had no idea why. She was certainly no temptress. Her outfit and expression made her look like a truculent teen. Gray eyes, a face bare of makeup, and compressed lips did little to ameliorate that image, but the effect remained the same.

She had to be a witch. He could think of no other reason why she could affect him *and* his father so forcefully. He immediately steeled himself against her. "This is my home."

She acted like a sheep dog guarding the fold from the wolf. She probably assumed he'd come home to make sure she didn't get a penny of his father's money.

"From what I hear, your home is a grass hut filled with dark-skinned beauties blessed with even less than a grass skirt."

13

He didn't know where she'd gotten her information, but his love life looked a lot better from her perspective than from his. "The modern world has reached even the remote islands of the South Pacific. They've given up grass skirts and coconut shells for cotton-polyester blends."

"How unfortunate for you."

"When they decide to wear anything," he added, to be intentionally provoking.

She eyed him in an unfriendly manner. "Now I understand why you haven't been home in ten years."

He doubted she did, but he didn't intend to explain. She'd been hired to hang the lights and disappear, and he was anxious to see the disappearing part of her act.

"Are you finished here?" he asked.

"For the time being."

He reached for his wallet. "How much do I owe you?"

"You don't owe me anything. I did this for your father."

"You'll come out of this a great deal better if you let me pay you. That way you can get on to your next job."

She started to take down the ladder. "I put it up by myself," she said when he offered to help her. "I can get it down the same way."

"Be my guest," he said, thoroughly irritated. "Just collect your stuff and leave. I'll see my father sends you a check."

"That won't be necessary. I volunteered to do this without charge."

That didn't make him feel any better. She must know his father couldn't turn down anything he could get free. This babe had studied her subject thoroughly and mapped out an artful battle plan.

"Kind of you," he said, making no attempt to disguise his skepticism. "I've never seen you before. Have you been in Wetherford Gap long?"

"I came five years ago when my father retired here."

Lots of people have retired to the North Carolina mountains these days. Land you couldn't have given away fifty years ago could have made millionaires out of a dozen families who had grown up with wood-burning stoves and outdoor privies. It would have too, if his father hadn't been clever enough to buy most of it first.

"Shouldn't you be home with your father now?" Anything to get her away from the house.

"My father died a year ago."

He felt like a toad and resented her for being the reason for it. "I'm sorry. Why haven't you gone back to . . . where did you come from?"

"New Jersey. I haven't gone back because I like it here. What are *you* doing here?"

"I live here."

She faced him squarely. He saw no give in her expression. "You *used* to live here. Why did you decide to come back after nearly ten years?"

He didn't know why she thought she could ask such questions—or why she deserved an answer—but he refused to explain himself to her. "Are you going to put that ladder up or waste time arguing with me?"

She glared at him. Much to his dismay, he found her glare attractive. How did she do it? He ought to avoid her, but he didn't dare leave until she went home. She shrugged, picked up the ladder, and headed around the side of the house. He followed.

The house sat on a steep hillside, which made it necessary to walk up ten steps to the front door but down three to the rear of the house. It also made it nearly impossible to maintain a lawn. His father had terraced the yard so extensively that it reminded Michael of Chinese rice paddies. Ellen threaded her way though the terraces without missing a turn. The woman obviously came here frequently. Another bad sign.

"You ought to put that in the shed," Michael said, when Ellen leaned the ladder against the back porch.

"Nick wants me to put up more lights tomorrow."

He'd have to talk to his father. He didn't mind Christmas decorations—after years of theirs being the only house on the block without any, it might feel good—but he saw no reason to go overboard. Their yard would look like the set for one of those mawkishly sweet Christmas specials his guests enjoyed watching in the comfort of their tropical seventy-five-degree days and sixty-five-degree nights.

"You'd better wait until you hear from me."

"Why?" She wiped her feet and opened the door to the glassed-in porch.

"Because I intend to have a talk with my father as soon as I go inside."

She turned her back on him, entered the porch, and walked straight to the back door without hesitation. "You'll have to wait. He's taking his afternoon nap."

"How do you know?" He followed her in, glad to be out of the sharp wind. "And what are you doing treating my father's house like you live here?"

"I know he's napping because he takes an afternoon nap every day. I'm treating your father's house like I live here because I do." She unlaced her shoes and kicked them into a corner of the mud room.

He'd underestimated this babe. If she'd already moved in, he might be too late.

"What the hell do you mean?"

She removed her hat, ran her fingers through her

short hair, turned, and treated him to a *you-poor-little-fool* expression. "I thought they spoke English in your tropical paradise."

"Don't try to be funny."

"I live here," she said very deliberately, as though explaining to a great idiot, "because your father needs someone to take care of him, to do the sorts of things a man never learns to do." She pulled the sweatshirt over her head. He thought for a moment that she would treat him to a glimpse of her bra. But underneath she wore an *I ♥ Australia All Year-Round* T-shirt covered with koala bears involved in seasonal activities. Her breasts focused special attention on January and June. He jerked his attention away from her body. He had to remember she was dangerous, not delicious.

"He could hire someone."

"True, but I wanted a place to stay, and he wanted someone to keep him company."

"My father never wanted company in his life. Why should he want you?"

"He and my father were good friends. When my father died, Nick asked me to come live here."

They passed through the room his mother had used to arrange flowers, into the laundry. She tossed her sweatshirt into the laundry basket and headed toward the kitchen.

"Why did you do it?" he asked. It ought to be interesting to hear her story.

"I like Nick. He's a great old guy, fun to be around."

A bald-faced lie. Nobody liked his father, and fun didn't exist in his world.

"Besides, I didn't want to go back to New Jersey, I hate living alone, and I wanted a place to stay while I finish my book." She opened the refrigerator, took out

17

a can of V-8 juice, popped the top, and took a swallow.

"You're a writer?" He'd heard of gold diggers claiming to be nurses, even social workers, but *writer* added a new dimension to the list of acceptable occupations. "Anything published?"

"Not yet." She took out cheese and carried it to the table.

"What do you write?"

"Women's fiction."

Big surprise there. "Do you mean those little books with syrupy happy endings?"

She got a knife from the drawer, a plate from the cabinet, and crackers from the cookie bin. "Don't you like happy endings?"

"Doesn't everybody?" He'd been looking for his own happy ending for most of his life. He'd begun to doubt he'd ever find it.

"Then don't bad-mouth little books with happy endings, especially if you haven't read any." She carried everything to a large oak table centered before sliding glass doors that gave an unobstructed view of the back lawn.

"I have," he said. "Our guests leave hundreds of them at the hotel. I prefer westerns."

"Wonderful. Gunfights and dead Indians everywhere."

"Actually, I prefer to see the hero and his woman ride off into the sunset together. I just don't want him groveling at her feet, promising to do anything if she'll just love him."

She gave him a disbelieving look. "A man with a conscience!"

"Is that so hard to believe?"

"Of you, yes." She sliced a block of sharp cheddar into thin pieces.

He towered above her, letting his anger show, but she didn't appear to be intimidated. "What makes you say that?"

"You haven't been home in years. You probably wouldn't have come home now if that nosy lawyer hadn't told you your father planned to give away all his money."

He couldn't deny that. He certainly wouldn't have come during the Christmas season if he hadn't felt it was an emergency. He hoped to be on a plane to Los Angeles by tomorrow afternoon.

Waiting for him to deny her accusation, she calmly bit into a cheese-and-cracker. There was something sensual about the way her lips folded around the food, the way her teeth bit cleanly through, the slow motions of her chewing. She didn't offer him any.

Michael shook himself. He couldn't afford to let himself fall under her spell. "I don't care what my father does with his money."

She clearly didn't believe him.

"I am concerned that he's acting totally unlike himself."

"You haven't seen him in a long time. He could have changed."

His father had celebrated his fifty-first birthday the week before Michael's birth, which guaranteed they would never understand each other. Growing up had been difficult and unhappy. Losing his mother the summer before he started the fourth grade made it lonely as well.

"Not my father," Michael said. "His personality was set in stone before he stopped nursing."

As though to contradict what he'd just said, his father entered the kitchen at that moment. As far back as Michael could remember, his father had never

19

emerged from his bedroom unless meticulously dressed, tie held firmly in place by a tie tack, perfectly ironed white shirt, vest even in the heat of summer, his cheeks freshly shaved, and his hair neatly combed.

Today, his white hair flying in all directions, he wore a bathrobe over flannel pajamas and slippers run down at the heels. Still more surprising, after a startled recognition of his son, he smiled. No, he laughed. A single chuckle, almost to himself.

"Hello, Michael."

"Hi, Dad." He felt stiff, uncertain. How did you greet a man you'd never liked, hadn't seen in ten years, but who was your father?

"You going to offer him any crackers?" he asked Ellen.

"If we don't feed him, maybe he'll go away."

"Would you?" he asked Michael.

"I got something to eat in Asheville."

"We're stuck with him. Better offer him some cheese."

She gave him a measured glance, hunched a shoulder, put some cheese on a cracker, and handed it to him. "There's plenty of V-8 in the fridge if you want some."

Michael had no thoughts to spare for food or drink. His father must have lost his mind. The man dressed liked an old fuddy-duddy, smiled, and acted as if he actually wanted his son home. He could see how Ellen had been able to take advantage of him. The poor old man had lost his marbles.

"Eat that cracker," his father said. "But don't eat too much. We don't want to spoil Mrs. Hood's dinner. She's the best cook in Wetherford Gap."

"I thought Ellen cooked," Michael said.

"Ellen doesn't have time to cook."

"Or do the cleaning or the laundry," Michael ventured. He'd wondered about that.

"Mrs. Eringhaus does that," his father said. "Ellen needs all her time to work on her book. She's going to be a great author."

It pleased Michael to see Ellen blush. Some small portion of her conscience might still be alive.

"I don't claim to have the makings of a great writer," Ellen said, "but I hope to be commercially successful."

"You will be," his father assured her. "I've read your stuff. It's good."

Michael couldn't believe his father had read any book that didn't have to do with making money. Neither did he see why having a commercially successful writer for a wife should appeal to the old man, but his father beamed at Ellen as though he'd created her himself.

"Michael doesn't like happy endings," she said. "He prefers gunfights."

It didn't seem worthwhile to argue with her, especially after his father winked at her. Winked! If Michael hadn't known better, he would have sworn his father had a nervous tic.

"It usually takes men a while to figure out what's important," his father said. He appeared to be talking to Ellen, but he looked straight at Michael. "Even then, half the time they won't admit it."

Ellen took a last swallow from her V-8, capped the bottle, got up and put it back into the refrigerator. "What he does is no concern of mine," she said. She gave his father a kiss on the cheek. He beamed. "I want to work on my book before dinner. I think I've finally figured out what to do with that scene. Don't eat too much cheese."

Finally, after ignoring Michael for virtually the entire time, she turned to him. "You can eat all you

21

want. I don't care if you spoil your dinner."

She padded out of the room in stocking feet without a backward glance. Michael felt as if his power source had disappeared, as if he'd been floating, lost his buoyancy, and come crashing to the floor. He felt bruised and breathless.

"What is she doing here?" Michael asked.

"Keeping me company," his father replied. He picked up one of the cheese-and-crackers and stuffed it into his mouth. "An old man like me shouldn't live by himself."

"You always wanted to be by yourself. You closed yourself up in that office all the time. Mother and I hardly ever saw you."

"I've changed."

"Enough to ask a young woman to move in with you?"

His father grinned like a child. "She's cute as a button, isn't she?" He stuffed another cheese-and-cracker into his mouth. "She's certainly livened up this place."

"If you *liven up* any more, you'll have a heart attack. You never used to eat between meals," Michael said when his father consumed a third cheese-and-cracker. "You had a fit when I did."

"I didn't know what I was missing. If you don't want that cracker you're holding, I'll eat it."

Michael looked down at his hand. He still held the cracker Ellen had given him. He handed it to his father, who popped it into his mouth.

"Now tell me," Michael said, "what that woman is *really* doing here."

"Exactly what I said," his father replied. "Keeping me company."

"Since when did that include dressing up like an elf and helping you give away everything in our attic?"

"So you saw that picture, did you?"

"Roy sent it to me. Along with the article in the newspaper. I could understand giving presents to needy kids—at least I could understand somebody else doing it—but not dressing up as Santa Claus."

"But that's what made it fun. It wouldn't have meant much if I'd walked in looking like old Nick Wetherford and started handing out gifts. Where's the magic in that?"

The more his father talked, the less Michael understood. "When did you start worrying about magic? You certainly didn't with me."

His father had eaten all the cheese Ellen left. He moistened his finger to pick up the crumbs and put them into his mouth. He glanced at the refrigerator but apparently decided not to get more.

"Why did you give away my old toys?"

"Do you want them?"

"No."

"Do you have any kids I don't know about running about that island of yours?"

Michael thought he almost looked hopeful. "No."

"Then why do you need them?"

"I don't. I just thought you'd ask me before you gave anything like that away."

"Why?"

Good question. His father had never trusted sentiment. Decisions had been based on facts, things bought or kept according to their usefulness. Michael had made his own fortune using the same principles. Why should he care about his old toys?

He couldn't explain. He only knew he did. He hadn't enjoyed his childhood; he remembered his teenage years with anger. He couldn't even remember any specific toy except his electric trains. He hoped his dad hadn't given them away. He'd had a train station, loading docks, rivers with bridges, mountains, trees, and enough tracks to cover the floor of one whole room, a virtual slice of North Carolina. He even had a village complete with houses, street lamps, a church, and people to walk down its streets. For years the train room had been the place he retreated to when things were at their worst.

"I suppose because I considered them mine," he said finally.

"They're just things," his father said, but without the impatience or irritability he used to display when Michael disagreed with him. "They don't make a person happy. That's why I'm giving away my money."

Chapter Two

Ellen paused in the act of putting on a pair of pearl earrings. She'd been trying for the last two hours to account for her reaction to Michael Wetherford. She hadn't expected to like him, and on first sight she hadn't. But she did like him. At least, she wanted to.

She had thought about him the whole time she should have been working on her book. It wasn't his looks or his size. She was immune to handsome, tall men. The only daughter of a millionaire had to fight them off. He certainly hadn't tried to make himself agreeable. He'd been rude from the moment he opened his mouth. So why was she attracted to him? It must be her years of enforced abstinence. Her body was so desperate, it would be attracted to any man who got close.

But not Michael Wetherford. She wouldn't allow that.

She decided pearls were wrong for this evening, tossed them aside, and looked for something else. Nick had changed a lot since she'd first met him five years ago, but he still liked to dress for dinner. She didn't mind. She'd grown up dressing for dinner. Her parents had had guests almost every evening. She had chosen a wine-red sweater, a black skirt, and low-heeled shoes. She didn't like high heels. Yet, she'd considered them, actually pulled them out of the closet along with a very dressy white sweater suit with a gold belt.

Michael. It had to be. Why else would she want to dress up?

She chose some simple gold studs, an onyx necklace, her gold watch. No bracelet. When she'd decided to stay in North Carolina, she'd promised herself she would never again play a role. Moving in with Nick had been perfect. His fierce reputation kept everyone at a distance. She had finally learned to be herself.

So why was she trying to impress Michael?

Why should she give a fig what he thought? He obviously had no feelings for other people, or he wouldn't have stayed away from home for so many years. He hadn't been exactly a barrel of laughs since he showed up. More like a wet blanket. Probably hankering after his tropical sun and his willing women. She could just see him setting out to seduce some almond-eyed, dark-skinned beauty, using his good looks as a lethal weapon, his kissable mouth as—

She pulled the gold studs from her ears and tossed them back into the jewelry box. If she couldn't control her thoughts any better than this, she had better stay in her room. She'd considered it, but it seemed pointless because she hadn't gotten any work done on her book since her encounter with Michael. She kept seeing

Michael rather than Nathan, her hero. Even worse, she'd imagined herself in the heroine's place—kissing Michael, not Nathan.

After that, she'd given up in disgust.

If she'd thought it would do any good, she'd have slapped herself for being so foolish. She'd liberated herself from the two men who'd controlled her life up until a year ago. She had no intention of letting herself be attracted to anyone just as egocentric. She had her life just the way she wanted it. She didn't intend to let anybody upset the balance, and that included Michael Wetherford and his oh-so-kissable lips.

She picked up the pearl earrings, put them back in her ears, and exchanged the onyx necklace for a single strand of pearls. She kept the gold watch. Giving her hair a final brushing, she spritzed it lightly with hair spray, then dabbed perfume on pulse points at her wrists and throat.

She stood back to study herself. She'd never be a beauty, but she chose her wardrobe to take advantage of her strongest point, her figure. Sweaters, fitted skirts, T-shirts, and jeans all showed her well-sculpted form to advantage. She refused to practice false modesty. She enjoyed having men stare at her. She also occasionally enjoyed a little harmless flirtation. But she had no intention of going beyond that point. She didn't need a man in her life.

Except Nick, of course. She sat down on the daybed to put on her shoes.

She wondered again why Michael had come home. The money, of course. But somehow she felt that hadn't been his only reason. His attitude toward her had been hostile from the moment he first spoke, probably because he thought she had some scheme to marry his father. She smiled. Why would any young

27

woman of twenty-six want to tie herself to a man of nearly eighty, even one as charming as Nick?

Money. But she didn't need money. She needed freedom.

Still, there had been something else in his attitude. If he hadn't stayed away from home for ten years, she might have said he felt concern for his father's health, his well-being. But no man who had spent his adult life cavorting with equatorial beauties and steadfastly ignoring his only living relative could have a compassionate or caring bone in his body. He couldn't be interested in anything but the money.

She slipped her feet into her shoes and stood.

According to Nick, Michael owned several fancy resorts that catered to the ultra rich. If so, he ought to be too rich to need Nick's money. She refused to yield to the uneasy feeling that she had judged him too harshly. He'd be here for another day at least. She'd have plenty of time to figure out why he'd *really* come home. She hoped he didn't try to stop his father from playing Santa Claus. She didn't want to fight him, but she wouldn't hesitate on that issue. Being Santa Claus had made a new man of Nick Wetherford.

She opened the door to her room, stepped out into the hall, and nearly bumped into Michael.

Taller than she remembered, he somehow left her feeling overwhelmed and slightly breathless. He looked very nice in a classic kind of way—navy blazer, gray slacks, and a club tie. She wondered where he'd found it. People didn't wear blazers in tropical paradises. Sometimes they didn't wear anything at all.

She didn't know what to say to him, but after he blatantly allowed his gaze to roam slowly over her body, she threw out all the comments she'd been considering. "I hoped you'd moved to a hotel."

He ignored her remark. "This is an improvement on your sweatshirt."

She looked away, started down the hall. "I'm glad you approve."

"I doubt you care what I think one way or the other."

"I was trying to be polite."

"That's a turnaround from this afternoon."

She wanted to blast him, but she had been rude. She hadn't intended to be, but it annoyed her that he would come home for the first time in years just to stop his father from having a little fun. If he didn't want to have anything to do with his father, she didn't see why he thought he should have any say in what the old man did. As for his inheritance—any son who would try to restrict his father's pleasure for the sake of money didn't deserve consideration.

She turned back to face him. "I may as well tell you, I don't have a very good opinion of your motives for being here."

"You haven't the foggiest notion what they are. Nor do you have any right to know them."

"Possibly, but I like your father a great deal. He's been very kind to me. I don't want you to do anything that would make him unhappy."

He looked amused. That startled her. She'd expected him to be furious. "And I suppose you know exactly what will make him happy?"

"Only Nick knows that. But once he decides what he wants to do, I help him do it."

"Giving my belongings away makes him happy? How do you think that makes me feel? Or do you care?"

He didn't look so amused now. He actually looked hurt. Well, she supposed even heartless, thoughtless, uncaring men had a few corners of sensitivity hidden inside them. She supposed his childhood belongings could be one of them.

"I don't know you well enough to answer that question, but I wouldn't expect it to make you happy. I suggest you discuss it with your father." She started to turn away. "Do your objections extend beyond your childhood toys?"

"I don't know. What else is he figuring on giving away?"

"Lots of toys. That will be expensive."

"I don't imagine that will break him."

Apparently Michael didn't care so much about the money. At least he wouldn't mind his father giving some of it away. She didn't know. He seemed a hard businessman, one who would consider it wasteful to give anything away. Just like Nick used to be.

"I have no idea of your father's resources, but—"

"I thought you'd know them down to the last penny."

She hadn't been mistaken; he *had* taken her for a gold digger. "Let's get one thing straight right from the start."

"A little late for that."

"Okay, from this point on. I don't want your father's money. I certainly don't want to marry him. I moved in because I was lonely. So was Nick. Besides, your father encourages my writing."

"And if you make it?"

"I don't know. I suppose that depends on whether I'm barely surviving or making a decent living."

"And if you don't succeed?"

"Then I'll have to decide on another career."

"Like what?"

"I have an MBA from Princeton in finance. I suppose I can find something." She enjoyed the look of surprise on his face. Why did men always find it surprising that a woman could have an aptitude for money? "Now we'd better go down before your father comes after us." They'd been standing in the hall, confronting each other like two young toughs feeling each other out before the real battle began.

She wished he hadn't come. Their Christmas plans would have gone so much more smoothly without him. But he had come, and she would have to deal with him. That didn't seem such a terrible burden as it had a few hours ago. She ruminated sourly on the foolishness of women who let themselves be influenced by a handsome face, broad shoulders, and a tall body. Really, hadn't women made any progress since the Stone Age when survival made pairing with a big male absolutely necessary, no matter what his other attributes? Maybe other women had, but she apparently had a throwback gene. She'd have to see what she could do about ignoring it. Making Michael angry enough to go back to his island playpen seemed the best way out for her and his father. She wondered if she could do it. It wasn't easy being rude to a man she found so attractive.

Michael found himself warming to Ellen despite having made up his mind to move her out of his father's house as soon as possible. All during the meal, she had kept his father entertained with a flow of small talk. His father clearly enjoyed her company. They seemed to have a relaxed and friendly relationship, one devoid of sexuality.

Michael felt better about that. His father couldn't expect his eighty-year-old body to keep pace with a young woman. Besides, women had never interested him as much as making money. He'd never had time for them, not even in social situations. Michael couldn't understand what about Ellen had reversed his father's lifelong habit. But for a man Michael's age, Ellen posed a different problem, one called temptation.

Her appearance affected him strongly. She used a very red lipstick with the skill of an artist. Leaving everything else about her face understated—except the eyelids and eyebrows, which were the same startling shade of black as her hair—the bright red drew attention to her mouth. It had a nearly hypnotizing effect on him. Despite his best efforts, he found himself staring at her, hanging on her every word. She knew it, dammit, and enjoyed the irony.

But her lips were only secondary to her spectacular figure. He knew all about outstanding female figures. The women who patronized his resorts—actresses, supermodels, second and third wives—depended on them for their success. Despite a pair of very nice legs, Ellen in sweats couldn't compare to Ellen in a sweater and skirt. He couldn't say she'd taken his breath away, but she'd deprived him of an uncomfortable amount of it.

How could he concentrate on separating her from his father when he couldn't stop hoping she'd give *him* some of her attention?

"Don't you think so?" Ellen asked, turning to him.

"What?" He didn't pretend to be embarrassed. She and his father had excluded him from the conversation most of the evening. Only Mrs. Hood's fine dinner had kept him at the table.

"Which do you think is better?"

"Which what?" he asked, when she looked annoyed.

"Michael always did prefer his own thoughts."

"That's because I kept being told to be quiet and listen to those who had something important to say."

"Did I say that?" his father asked, apparently in genuine surprise.

"Constantly."

"I apologize."

No question about it. His father had lost his grip. He'd never apologized for anything in his whole life.

"It doesn't matter."

"It does because I've done it all over again. Ellen and I have been talking about our plans for the next few days, and not once have we asked about yours. Or invited you to join us."

He had his chance now. He could thrust himself into the middle of this nonsense and ease Ms. Weems over and out. "I'll be happy to join you. Just tell me what you want me to do."

"You can begin by smiling," Ellen said. "The scowl on your face would scare off half the children in Wetherford Gap."

He forced himself to smile. "Will this do?"

"It would do better if it looked sincere."

"I'll work on it." If she continued to snipe at him like this, he wouldn't have too much trouble resisting her allure. "Now tell me what you've got in mind."

"I wanted to clear everything out of the attic," his father said. "Your mother and a string of housekeepers put stuff up there for forty years. I don't know what we've got, but it's not doing anybody any good up there. Most of it's probably junk, but there might be things other people could use. I want to clear out the basement, too."

Their house had been built over seventy-five years earlier in the old-fashioned pattern of a full basement and an attic that could be converted to a third floor if necessary. Basement and attic probably contained enough stuff to furnish three houses.

"Where's my stuff?" Michael asked.

"In the attic, I guess."

"Do you mind if I look through it before you give it away?"

"It's yours. Take anything you want."

His father appeared to be sincere in both his apology and his willingness to let Michael claim what he wanted from the attic. Could he really have changed? If so, how much did Ellen Weems have to do with it? He found it as difficult to believe she'd moved in purely for companionship as he did that his father had made a complete about-face after a lifetime of being coldhearted, unsentimental, and completely without interest in other people.

"Tell me about your plans," Michael said, "the ones you want me to join."

"We're going to an orphanage tomorrow," Ellen said. "We're giving some furniture to the orphanage, toys to the children."

"Then I'd better gather up my keepsakes tonight. Or have you already packed them up?"

"Your father is buying the things we're giving away tomorrow," Ellen said.

"We still haven't bought the toys," his father reminded her.

"I'll do that tomorrow." Ellen turned to Michael. "Your father doesn't intend to clear out the basement and attic until after Christmas. That ought to give you plenty of time to set aside anything you want to keep."

"Will you take it back with you?" his father asked.

Michael hadn't thought about that. "I won't know until I see what's left after the stuff you've given away."

He wished he hadn't said that. He'd never seen his father look hurt, and he decided he didn't like it. He especially didn't like being the one to hurt him.

"I didn't think you wanted it."

"Why would he think you wanted anything from here," Ellen asked Michael, "when you haven't bothered to set foot in your own home for nearly ten years?"

She could think what she wanted—and she seemed determined to think the worst—but he refused to explain his relationship with his father to this outsider.

"You don't need to defend me, Ellen," his father said. "I should have asked before I gave his things away. I'm sorry for that, too."

Michael decided to say no more. He'd not only succeeded in hurting his father, he'd made himself look small in doing it. He had been the victim, yet now he found himself in the role of the villain.

"Don't worry about it. I doubt there's much up there I'd want anyway."

"I should hope not," Ellen said. "A grown man playing with children's toys isn't a pretty sight."

She didn't have to defend his father so fiercely. She acted like a daughter defending him from some interloper. She made Michael feel like an outsider in his own home.

But he *was* an outsider. He always had been.

"Take your time and go through everything," his father said. "I'll have the housekeeper pack it up so you can take it back with you."

"You'll have to ship it. I have to return tomorrow."

To his surprise, his father seemed disappointed. Even upset.

"If you meant to come back only long enough to distress your father," Ellen said, "why did you bother coming back at all?"

He looked at his half-eaten dessert and decided to leave it that way. "If you'll excuse me, I think I'll start now."

He left the table, aware of a heavy feeling of disappointment. He had almost reached the attic before he figured it out. He hadn't wanted to come home—in addition to the inconvenience, he didn't see anything to be gained by it—but once he'd decided on the necessity, he'd hoped he could somehow establish a better relationship with his father. That now seemed a forlorn hope. He ought to leave tonight.

He couldn't, not until he'd talked to the lawyer. And the doctor. Regardless of his own feelings, he had to make certain his father could take care of himself. And if not, then—well, he'd cross that bridge when he came to it.

The attic stairs squeaked under his weight. They hadn't when, as a boy, he came up here when his room didn't seem far enough removed from his father. He read then, played with toys he hadn't played with in years, or just sat and thought, dreamed about what he'd do once he finished college and could leave Wetherford Gap forever.

His college roommate used to envy him for having a whole town named for his family. Michael couldn't tell him it simply reinforced an isolation made virtually ironclad by his father's determination to wring the greatest possible profit out of every situation.

Michael opened the attic door, put on the light, and stepped inside. Almost immediately he felt himself hurtling fifteen or more years into the past. He saw the chair his mother used to sit in while she did the endless tatting that filled her days. Furniture from his mother's bedroom, the sitting room, and the family parlor had been packed into the attic until only narrow pathways remained. Huge stacks of dust-covered magazines, newspapers, and binders full of papers rested in corners or spilled out of boxes cracked with age or chewed to tatters by mice, squirrels, or other rodents that had apparently made the attic their home over the years. Michael found all of his stuff under one of the gables on the west side of the house.

He passed by the stacks of *Sports Illustrated, The Thoroughbred Record,* and *Runner's World.* He made a mental note to go through the boxes of books if he had time.

He ignored suitbags of clothes no one had discarded even after he outgrew them; oddments left over from his days in the Boy Scouts, the science club, the Honor Society; trophies from years on the track, swim, and soccer teams. He headed straight for a group of wooden boxes stacked by themselves in one corner.

His trains.

He opened one box and took out a metal case. He opened it. Inside, in velvet-lined grooves, rested a glistening back engine, three cars, and a caboose. A second and third box contained more engines, more cars. He became so engrossed in memories of the hours he'd spent with these trains that he didn't hear Ellen's approach.

"Your father said you'd look for your trains first."

He started, felt a spurt of hot anger that she had intruded on his past, something that had nothing to do with her.

"Did he send you to make sure I don't take anything that isn't mine?"

"Why are you so angry at your father?"

"If you've wiggled your way into his confidence as far as I think you have, you ought to know."

"You still think I'm trying to get my hands on his money, don't you?"

"At least you're not trying to hide it."

"I'm not hiding it because I'm not doing it. I have—"

The sound of the attic door closing and the key being turned in the lock caused them both to turn.

"What the hell!" Michael exclaimed. Much to his surprise, Ellen seemed to be trying not to laugh. "What's so damned funny? We're locked in here. Who could have done anything so stupid?"

"Your father."

"Why?"

"He sent me up to try to become friends with you. He's afraid you'll chase me away, so he locked us in."

"Of all the absurd . . ."

"Yes, but you've got to admit we have to talk to each other."

"What about? I know nothing about you except your name."

"Your trains," she said. She pointed to the cases open around him. "My father used to have at least a dozen trains. The tracks filled a whole room. He ordered me to stay out, but he stayed away on business so much that he never knew I played with them anyway. I see you have an LBG set. Daddy preferred the really big ones. I didn't. None of the pieces you could buy would fit with his set. Daddy had some things made, but of course I couldn't do that."

"What are you doing in this house? I mean, really?"

"I told you."

"I don't believe you."

"That's obvious."

"What did you expect me to believe, especially after that picture?"

She backed up, settled on the arm of a chair. "I moved here five years ago with my father when a heart attack disabled him. Like your father, he'd devoted his whole life to making money. My mother had died years before, so I decided to move him as far away from his business connections as I could. I bought our house from your father. Knowing him to be very much like my father, I asked him to visit. I hoped he would help my father learn to think of something besides making money."

"You went to the wrong man."

"That's what everybody told me—later—but they turned out to be wrong. I think your father was the first real friend my father ever had. Since Dad couldn't involve himself in business anymore, he could devote all his time to his charitable interests. He asked your father to introduce him to various groups like the board of the orphanage."

"My father never set foot inside an orphanage. He'd be afraid they'd ask him for money."

"They did, and he refused, but my father got on the orphanage board as well as several others. When his failing health prevented him from going to meetings, he asked your father to go in his stead. They'd talk about it afterward. Ultimately your father began to get interested. After my father's death, he continued on his own. Since we were both involved in many of the same things, he suggested I move in here so working together would be easier."

"I thought you wanted to be a writer."

"I do, but it takes a long time to get published. In the meantime, I like to keep busy."

"Then get a job."

"You still think I'm mooching off your father, don't you?"

"I can't imagine you paying him rent."

"If I'd known you were coming home laboring under the burden of your antiquated Puritan suspicions, I wouldn't have moved in at all, with or without rent."

"Then you can leave now."

"Absolutely not. I'm staying put to see you don't bully Nick into giving up what he enjoys."

"Are you trying to tell me my father *likes* giving away money?"

"Yes. He said he'd devoted his entire life to making money. He said he'd become rich, but in the process he lost your mother's love and drove you away. He said if he had it to do over again, he'd settle for being poorer in the world's goods and richer in family."

Michael found it easier to believe that his father had fallen into a trap set by a young and pretty fortune hunter than that he'd finally realized his obsession with money had cost him his wife and son. Nick had never cared about that before. Why should he care now?

"You don't believe me," she said.

"I find it difficult."

"He said you would."

"Then why did he send you?" If he wanted Michael to believe him, why hadn't he spoken for himself?

"He said you liked me, that you'd believe me before him."

Michael swallowed an involuntary protest. It was apparently useless to try to deny his interest. But even though Ellen might not be as bad as he thought, she was still dangerous, to him and his father. He needed to get her out of this house, but she wasn't going to leave willingly. He might have to stay longer than one day.

He quivered with pleasurable anticipation, then told himself not to be a fool. This woman might not want his father's money, but she was a manipulator. He'd been manipulated his whole life. He didn't intend to let it happen again.

Michael got to his feet. "There's no need for you to be locked away with me because of my father's fan-

tasies. If he'd ever concerned himself with the work-
ings of this house, he'd have known there's a door
leading from the attic straight to the kitchen." He led
the way through several narrow pathways until they
came to a tall, narrow door. He turned the knob and it
opened.

"It brings you out in the pantry," he said. "It ought
to give Dad a start when you show up."

"He's not going to be happy," Ellen said.

"You'd be even more unhappy if you had to sit for
hours watching me go through junk."

She hesitated, then left. Michael closed the door and
leaned against it. It had been a close call. He almost
hadn't told her about the door.

But he didn't trust himself to remain locked up with
her for hours. He might find he believed her, that he
had no reason to dislike her. He also needed time to
think, to figure out why his belongings were
untouched. His father hadn't given away anything.

Why had he lied?

Chapter Three

"Wait and have breakfast when Michael comes down," Nick said to Ellen.

"Why? He thinks I'm trying to marry you for your money."

"I'm sure he doesn't think that anymore."

She laughed. "Next time you lock two people up to force them to get to know each other, you'd better check all the doors. I know why you did it," she added, her voice softer, "but it didn't work. He doesn't like me at all."

"Nonsense. It would be impossible for any young man not to like you."

She laughed. "Not if he thinks I'm a fortune hunter."

"Michael doesn't care about my fortune. He's made a lot of money on his own."

"Being rich never stopped a man from wanting to be richer."

"When Michael left for the South Pacific, he told me he wanted to get as far away from me and my money as possible."

"What an awful thing to say. I don't know why you wanted him to come home. No, of course I do," she said, as she gripped the old man's hand. "He's your son."

"It's not just that. I want to make up for some of what I did all those years ago. It's too late for my wife. Maybe it's not too late for Michael."

"What could you have done that was so awful?"

"I never had time for him or his mother. I always had some deal cooking, some new way to make more money. I'd been dirt-poor as a kid, and I swore when I grew up I'd be the richest man in western Carolina. Well, I accomplished my goal, but I lost my wife and my son."

"He's the one who didn't come back, who didn't—"

"He didn't come back because I didn't want him back. He disappointed me, and I didn't have time for him. I was determined to make more money, to show him . . . I don't know what I wanted to show him. Anyway, he swore he'd make his own fortune, prove to me making money wasn't anything special, that anybody could do it. Well, he's done it, and it's ruined his life."

"How?"

"He's not interested in being rich. He wants the family he never had. But he's too driven to prove me wrong to see that."

Ellen had known Michael hadn't been home since he graduated from college—anybody in Wetherford Gap could have told her that—but Nick had never fully explained why. She felt sorry for Michael, but she didn't know what she could do to help him or his father.

"Have breakfast with him," Nick said again.

She didn't want to. The more Nick told her about Michael, the easier it became to excuse what he'd done, to let herself like him. That would be foolish. He clearly didn't like her. Besides, if he'd come all this way to stop his father from giving away his money—even if he didn't want it himself—he was a controlling man. She'd had more than enough of that.

"I don't owe him an explanation for my actions."

"But I do."

"Then you tell him."

"He'll believe it better from you."

"He didn't last night."

"Try one more time, please?"

She couldn't refuse Nick anything. She owed him this much.

"Okay, I'll try again, but I don't promise success."

"Good. I think I hear him coming down. I'll disappear."

Michael surprised her by coming down in a coat and tie. He didn't appear pleased to find her in the kitchen, but at least he didn't seem angry. Not much progress, but some. She didn't look forward to this. She felt like a sacrificial lamb.

"Do you always dress for breakfast?" she asked.

"I don't eat breakfast. I just have juice and coffee."

"I'm not too fond of breakfast myself, but I don't come to the table looking like I just stepped out of a Fifth Avenue shop."

He eyed her askance. "I'll take that as a compliment."

"You should. You look very nice—quite handsome, in fact. Very much like Nick did at your age, I imagine."

She shouldn't have added that last bit. His dawning smile faded quickly.

"That's what I've been told." He moved to the refrigerator and took out the juice container.

She handed him a glass from the cabinet.

"Thanks."

He didn't look thankful.

"How do you like your coffee?"

"I can get it."

"So can I. How do you like it?"

"Cream, no sugar." He downed his juice in one long swallow.

"I thought you'd be a diesel-quality man."

"I used to be, until it started eating through my stomach."

"You should eat breakfast."

"I don't have time. My job starts before the customers wake up."

"You have to eat."

"I catch something on the run or dine later with some of the guests."

"Not good for your digestion."

"I survive."

"You need to get married. Your wife would take care of that."

He stiffened. "Do you mean she'd *order* me to eat breakfast?"

"Of course not. She'd probably be one of your island beauties, lovely enough to keep you in bed mornings eating grapes from her navel."

He nearly choked on his coffee.

She felt herself blush. "Or some such thing," she added quickly.

"Is that what you think we do?"

"That would keep you in bed, wouldn't it?"

"Undoubtedly. Unfortunately, grapes have to be flown in at great expense." A light suddenly appeared in his eyes. "Is that one of the ways you'd keep your husband in bed with you?"

45

She suddenly had a picture of Michael eating grapes from her navel, and she nearly melted right where she sat. She had to stop this foolishness. Anymore of this, and she'd actually *want* him to do something like that to her. "I imagine it would work."

"Ever tried it?"

"No, but I'll keep it in mind for my wedding night."

"You'll have to leave here to find a husband."

"Why do men think every woman needs a husband?"

"For the same reason women think every man needs a wife."

"I don't."

"Neither do I."

"At least we agree on something."

He looked at his watch and practically gulped down his coffee.

"What's wrong?" she asked.

"I have an appointment downtown."

"I know this is none of my business, but would that appointment be with your lawyer?"

"You're right. It is none of your business." His gaze never wavered. "But, yes, it's with my father's lawyer."

"I want to go with you."

"Why?"

"To make sure you don't do anything underhanded, like apply for a power of attorney."

"And if I do?"

"I'll fight you every step of the way."

"You're certain if I wanted a power of attorney, I'd want it for my advantage, not my father's?"

"I don't know, but I'd like to be sure."

"And if I don't let you go with me?"

"I'll follow you and force my way in."

His gaze bored into her, but she refused to yield.

She thought a lot better of him than she did yesterday, but she didn't trust him yet.

"I'll make a deal with you. You swear you'll leave this house the minute you sell your book, and I'll let you go with me."

"It could be years before I sell a book."

"I'll take my chances."

She tried to intimidate him with her gaze, but it bounced off him like raindrops off a raincoat. "I'll probably be gone before then, but I'll agree."

He took a final gulp of coffee and put the cup in the sink. "Okay, let's go."

"I'm not dressed for a lawyer's office."

"It's go like you are or come later."

She made a quick decision. "I'll come like I am."

He grinned. "You don't trust me, do you?"

"Not one inch."

But when he grinned like that, she wished she could.

They walked along the narrow sidewalks of the small town up a steep hill toward a modest yellow-brick building. Downtown renewal had replaced many of the old hardware, feed, and five-and-dime stores with trendy boutiques that catered to the wealthy retirees. They'd even turned an empty area alongside the railroad track into a parking lot landscaped with trees, flowering shrubs, and lights on wrought-iron poles. Pedestrian crosswalks had been paved with brick. Everything looked so different, it hardly felt like tiny Wetherford Gap anymore.

Michael couldn't figure out why he'd let Ellen come with him. Regardless of how close she and his father had become, this didn't concern her. Despite his father's apparently sincere apologies, Michael couldn't imagine he and his father living together.

Maybe if his father became incapacitated, Ellen would take care of him. Nick obviously liked her better than his own son. That rankled, but he pushed it aside. He didn't care as long as she could do the job. But could he trust her?

He didn't like to think that her attractiveness could have anything to do with his decision. He hoped he hadn't become that susceptible to an attractive woman, but he had to admit he almost wished he'd forgotten about that second door to the attic. He wondered what it would have been like to spend a couple of hours with her.

"Has this lawyer known your father long?" Ellen asked as they entered the old building.

"At least forty years."

"Then he could be *non compos mentis* himself."

"His two sons share the practice with him, and they're definitely not."

Roy Shupe didn't look pleased to see Ellen, but he ushered them into a small, unadorned office. No fancy furniture, oriental carpets, or expensive art for Roy. Just shelves groaning with books on all the walls and more books in stacks around the room.

"Do you think she ought to be here?" he asked Michael.

"No, but she probably knows more about Dad's state of mind than anyone else. We ought to at least listen to her."

Mr. Shupe frowned, showed them to deep chairs covered in maroon leather veined with the cracks of age and use. He subsided behind a desk that showed signs of having survived at least two generations. He picked up a sheet of paper and began to recount, in exhaustive detail, some of Michael's father's activities over the last year. "Not only has he made serious inroads into his capital," he said in conclusion, "he has made himself an object of curiosity among his neighbors."

"If being concerned with people less fortunate than himself makes him an object of curiosity," Ellen said, her temper obviously strained, "the fault lies with the people of this town, not with Nick Wetherford."

"I don't care about the money," Michael said, "unless he's giving away so much he doesn't have anything left to live on, but I am concerned about his being able to make responsible decisions."

"Who's to decide what is and is not responsible?" Ellen asked.

"He's giving away too much money," the lawyer said.

"How much?" Michael asked.

"He recently gave a million dollars to an agency that buys farm animals for needy families throughout the world and teaches them how to care for and benefit from them."

"The Heifer Project International," Ellen said. "I told him about them."

"He gave another million to a home for needy elderly people."

"What else?" Michael asked.

"He's given smaller sums to other organizations, most of them here and in the mountains of Virginia and Tennessee. If he goes on at this rate, there won't be much left for you to inherit."

"I'm not interested in an inheritance," Michael said.

"Are you willing to stand by and see him give away everything he owns?"

Michael turned to Ellen. He knew she'd been watching him carefully. "Do you think he'll pauper himself over his charities?"

"No. Your father is just as careful about his giving as I expect he is about making money. The two large gifts were to establish endowments, which will provide an annual income."

"But his gifts exceeded his income last year," the lawyer said. "Here, look at these figures."

Michael waved the paper away. "Until he gives away so much money that he's in danger of being unable to support himself, I don't want to know anything about his finances."

The lawyer made his unhappiness quite plain. "That could happen at any moment." He directed an accusing glance toward Ellen. "Who knows when someone might introduce a new charity to his attention?"

"There are thousands of good causes," Ellen said, "all easy to learn about without any assistance from me."

"But he never gave away his money until you came," the lawyer said, accusingly.

"If you know anything about Dad," Michael said to the lawyer, "you know he never listens to anybody when it comes to money." Ellen looked surprised that he'd come to her defense. He hoped he wasn't making a fool of himself by believing her.

"Nick thinks of me as a friend's daughter," Ellen told the lawyer. "Nothing else."

"If you weren't so wealthy yourself, I'd suspect—"

"She's wealthy?" Michael asked.

"She's worth more than your father."

Relief flooded through him. As much as he'd wanted to believe her, gold-digging seemed the only rational explanation for her presence in his father's house.

"You must admit the situation looked highly suspicious," he said.

"Only to a suspicious mind."

"You're young enough to be his granddaughter and you're beautiful. What could I think?"

"I'm twenty-six, I'm not beautiful, and you could have thought any one of a thousand other things."

"Maybe, but—"

"We're here to discuss your father, not your mutual distrust," the lawyer interrupted. "I think you ought to petition the court for power of attorney," he said to Michael.

"You can't do that," Ellen protested.

"You don't have to use it, but you'd have it just in case."

"It wouldn't do me any good," Michael said. "I'm leaving tonight."

"Tonight!" Ellen exclaimed.

"This is our busiest season," he said. "Wealthy executives trying to escape the cold of New England make December through February my most profitable months. I wouldn't have come home if Roy hadn't convinced me my father had gone crazy."

"I don't say he's crazy," Roy said, "but he's definitely not responsible for himself."

"I disagree," Ellen said. "He's giving away that money because it makes him feel good. He said he'd never done anything for anybody else in his entire life, that he'd only thought of making money any way he could. One day he realized he'd soon be dead, and he had nothing to show for his life except money."

"I've known Nick Wetherford for forty years. I can't believe he said anything like that."

"When did he say it?" Michael asked Ellen.

"Just after my father died. Dad had gotten Nick interested in his charities."

"That's when I started to worry about him," the

lawyer said. "Nick always said they were leeches sucking money out of people who had the gumption to make something of themselves instead of sitting around expecting a handout."

"He's changed," Ellen insisted. She turned to Michael. "He's never said so, but I think your not coming home after college had a lot to do with it."

"He didn't want me here before I went to college," Michael said. "Or afterwards."

"He did," Ellen said.

"You didn't live here," Michael said. "I did."

"You must have misunderstood him. He's really a sweet old man. He's—"

"We've strayed from the point," Mr. Shupe said, his frustration at their discussion showing. "The question is whether your father is responsible enough to manage his own affairs. I say he isn't and that you should apply for a power of attorney. I've already filled out the forms. All you have to do is sign them."

He handed the papers to Michael.

"You can't do that," Ellen exclaimed.

Michael took the forms and stared at them. For years, whenever the relationship between him and his father dipped to one of its lows, he'd imagine what he would do if he ever got control over his father. If he had power of attorney, had his father declared *non compos mentis,* he could control his father just as his father had controlled him as a child. Only Michael didn't want to do that now. He felt as if he held a snake in his hand, one that could turn around and bite him, injecting a poison that would destroy forever any chance of a better relationship with his father. And as much as it surprised him, he realized he couldn't give up that chance, no matter how slim.

"I need to see his doctor," Michael said. "I'll get

back to you after I've had a chance to consider what both of you have said."

"I can't believe you'd even consider such a thing," Ellen said as they left the lawyer's office. "This is your father we're talking about."

"I know that. Despite the fact that I haven't been home in a long time, I still care for him. And part of the caring is making sure he's truly able to take care of himself."

"Of course he is. You can see that for yourself."

"What I see is a man who's suddenly deserted the habits and beliefs of nearly seventy years. Even though I'm not the kind of son he wanted, that concerns me."

Ellen stopped on the sidewalk, forcing the pedestrian traffic to flow around them, and under the huge green wreaths with candles in the middle that hung from the street lights. All along the street store windows were filled with Christmas decorations, and the sound of Christmas carols floated from open doorways.

"What do you mean you're not the kind of son he wanted?" she asked. "He loves you."

Michael took her by the hand and pulled her along. "Stick to what you know."

"But how can you say—"

"I grew up with his telling me exactly how I'd failed. Now, unless you want me to leave you on the sidewalk, stop arguing. We're at the doctor's office."

They didn't have to wait long.

"There's nothing physically wrong with your father," the doctor assured Michael. "If he's decided to act peculiar, and I think he's been acting *damned* peculiar, it's not because he's senile."

"See, I told you," Ellen said.

"But he may be having delusions. You may want to take him to a psychiatrist."

"What delusions?" Michael asked.

"Thinking he's Santa Claus," the doctor said. "I heard him myself. Stood right there in the town square and announced it to everybody."

"He was talking to the children," Ellen said. "He didn't mean he *was* Santa, just that the kids could come tell him what they wanted."

"Had a Santa suit made especially for him," the doctor continued. "Had an extra made in case he got it dirty or torn. Now he's having a new one made because the old one doesn't make him look authentic enough."

"He has to have a suit if he's going to give away toys," Ellen said.

"He had a sleigh built, too," the doctor continued. "Paid a fortune to have a company in Hickory make him one out of metal that looked like wood. If you don't believe me, go look in his shed."

"He wanted to help the children believe in the fantasy," Ellen said to Michael. "He said he had to look like a real Santa if they were going to believe him."

"Is that why he imported real reindeer?" the doctor demanded.

"Reindeer!" Michael said. "Where would he find reindeer this side of the Arctic Circle?"

"That's where he kept calling," the doctor said sarcastically. "The North Pole."

Michael turned to Ellen, hoping she had an explanation.

"He hired them to pull his sleigh for the Christmas parade," she explained. "He said kids in North Carolina have never seen real reindeer. He had the means to change that, so he did."

"How in hell did he handle *real* reindeer?" Michael asked.

"They come with their own handlers," Ellen said.

"It was the highlight of the parade. People came from all over the valley."

Michael decided reindeer were an extravagance but not a sign of insanity. He sort of wished he could have seen them himself.

"I can't give you a medical reason for locking him up," said the doctor, "but common sense ought to tell you he's not safe."

"I don't want to lock him up," Michael said. "I just want to make sure he's in possession of his faculties."

"Then you'd better see a shrink, because he's not running on a full battery."

Back outside, huddled inside a heavy coat, Michael thought longingly of his tropical beaches. The thermometer had barely made it to forty degrees today, and the wind had picked up.

"You can't take him to a psychiatrist," Ellen said as soon as they left the doctor's office. "There's a perfectly logical explanation for everything he's had done and everything he plans to do."

"Everything seems fairly reasonable when you explain it one thing at a time. But when you put them all together, it's hard to accept. You don't know my father like I do."

"And you don't know him like I do."

He stopped and turned to face her. "So which one of us is right?"

She pulled him along so he wouldn't block traffic. "Both. You know him as he used to be. I know him as he is now."

"Which still doesn't answer the question of whether he's capable of handling his own affairs."

"Then you can't go back to your island paradise this afternoon. You've got to stay here until you realize your father is perfectly sane."

"You make it sound like some sordid little place where I indulge in endless orgies with platoons of dark-skinned beauties."

"Well, what is it like?"

They'd reached his rental car. "Get in, and I'll tell you."

Bright sunlight had overheated the car during their absence. Despite being used to tropical weather, Michael had to roll down the windows. Ellen acted as if she'd faint.

"I own three separate resorts," Michael said. "They're designed to help wealthy businessmen relax and forget the pressures of their work and the ice and snow back home."

"So *you* provide the tropical paradise, and *they* hold orgies."

"Actually, we specialize in family vacations. We have wading pools for the little kids, a babysitting service for parents who want to go scuba diving or island hopping in one of our planes. The teenagers are a little more difficult to please, but they usually manage to entertain themselves on the beaches. We hold cookouts and outdoor dances for them five nights a week.

"We have continuous showings in two movie theaters, indoor pools, game rooms, a casino for those who want to gamble, boat rides, deep sea fishing, hang gliding—"

"It sounds like a huge theme park."

"It's better than that. I own the island. There are no strip malls, no tourist traps, nothing except my hotels. We didn't even pave the road from the airport. We aim to provide a *real* tropical getaway."

"While nestled in the lap of luxury."

"You can't expect anybody to pay ten thousand dollars for two weeks in the tropics to stay in a grass hut."

Ellen laughed. "I guess not. How did you ever get into something like this?"

Michael's cheerfulness vanished. He remembered all too well why he'd chosen his line of work, but he doubted Ellen would appreciate his reasons. "It's a long story. Do you have any errands to run?"

"Yes. I have to go shopping for the toys your father is giving away at the orphanage tonight."

"I'll drop you off."

"No, you don't. You have to help me pick them out."

Chapter Four

From the frown on his face when they drove up in front of the toy store, Ellen feared this might be a wasted effort. Nick had asked her to take Michael with her. He said it would help him unwind, ease some of his stress. Ellen wondered if anything could ease the stress that seemed to have young Mr. Wetherford tied into double knots. She'd never seen a man so afraid to smile.

Maybe afraid wasn't the right word. He had smiled several times, enough for her to know he had a truly charming smile, but the smiles had disappeared, leaving him just as tight-lipped and grim as before. She couldn't see any sense in smiling if it didn't make you feel better. You might as well announce that you liked being a Gloomy Gus, that you insisted upon staying depressed no matter how much fun others were having.

"How many presents do you need?" Michael asked.

"At least thirty-four. Your father wanted to make sure every child got at least two things."

"Let's hope the wrapping department isn't busy."

"This place is like a toy warehouse. They don't have a wrapping department."

He groaned. "We'll need an acre of wrapping paper and a mile of ribbon. You'd better call every friend you've got as soon as we get home. You'll never get that much stuff wrapped by yourself."

"We don't have to wrap everything. We can just hand the toys out."

"You can't do that," he said. He acted like she'd just committed some terrible sin. "Half the fun of presents is opening the package and being buried in ribbons and paper."

She hoped she didn't look as surprised as she felt. He couldn't mean what he said. It would mean he had a heart, some sensitivity, some element of humanity. If he had all that, she might like him far too much.

"Some of the presents are bound to be large," she said. "Others won't come in boxes."

"It doesn't matter. You've got to wrap everything."

She didn't see any point in arguing with him. They could decide what to do about wrapping the presents after they bought them. Besides, she didn't want to argue with him. Every time she thought she knew him, he slipped sideways and she had to start all over again. At the rate he was going, he might soon become someone she could admire and respect.

They entered a barn-like store with toys by the thousands stacked on seemingly endless rows of shelves. She'd never imagined there could be so many different toys. "We'll need two carts," she said.

"Probably twice that many." He enlisted a clerk to follow with extra carts. "What are their ages and sexes?"

She took out a notebook. "Girls five through thirteen."

"How many of each age?"

"Two five-year-old girls, one seven, eight, nine, eleven, two twelves, and one thirteen."

"Good. We can buy stuff in three groups. What about the boys?"

"Two six-year-olds, one eight and one nine, two tens, and one eleven and twelve."

"The age difference makes it harder."

"Why?"

"They won't all enjoy the same things." They came to a section where dolls of every description were stacked from floor to ceiling.

"How about a Barbie for all the girls?" she said.

"That's fine for the bigger girls, but the two five-year olds will want stuffed animals, something they can hug, drag around, something soft and squishy to take to bed with them. What do you think of a Happy Hugs or a Cabbage Patch doll?"

"They're so plain. Your father wanted to give them something very nice."

"They'll like this better."

"They've got to be sturdy." She might not know as much as he did about children, but she remembered her own collection of stuffed animals. Her favorite, a bedraggled-looking kitty, had accompanied her nearly everywhere she went for years.

"You can give the middle group of girls your Barbie dolls. Get the ones with lots of clothes. They'll have fun dressing them."

They took so many boxes from the shelves that they filled the first cart before they finished with the dolls.

"What about the big girls?" Ellen asked.

"Give them one of the fancy Barbies, the kind they put on a shelf to look at."

He seemed to be very sure of himself. She didn't know if she should follow his suggestions, but she had no sisters and no girl cousins. In fact, she knew very little about children.

"What's that?" she asked when he took a huge box off the shelf and put it in his cart.

"A play kitchen."

"You can't give one of these to each girl."

"We'll just give one with all the extras. You can say it's for all the girls, but just the little ones will play with it."

"What can we give the bigger girls?"

"The little ones will want the big ones to eat with them. We'll need enough dishes for all the girls. I wonder if they have enough tables at the orphanage."

He didn't wait for her. While she counted out dishes, he searched the shelves for pots, tea kettles, and every kind of cooking utensil he could find.

"Can I help you find something?" one clerk asked.

"No," Michael replied, "but you can take these carts to the front and bring us some more. We'll probably need a dozen before we're through."

The clerk's eyes grew big. Ellen was sure hers had grown just as large.

"I'll never be able to pay for that much with the money your father gave me," she said.

"Then he'll have to give you more," Michael said. "If you're going to do this, you have to do it right. What do you think about this Bed Time Baby? And how about a play doctor's kit the kids can use to check up on each other when they get sick?"

Michael had taken control of this project in less than ten minutes. It irritated her. She didn't like dictating, controlling men, but he seemed to be doing it out of a genuine concern to get things right for the kids.

"Now something for the boys," Michael said. He pulled down at least a dozen plastic dinosaurs and twice as many wild animals. "My favorite when I was a kid was the rhino," he said. She'd have thought he'd have gone for the lion. "I saw a show once where they'd cut off their horns to protect them from poachers. I felt sorry for them after that."

Hard to imagine a child feeling sorry for a four-thousand-pound animal.

He filled another cart with tool sets, an earthmoving machine, and enough cars and trucks to supply a small city.

"I think we've got enough," Ellen said.

"Nowhere near," Michael said. "This is all stuff for inside. They need to get outdoors. Bring us three or four more carts," he said to one of several dazed clerks who had started to follow them around to watch. The tale of this shopping spree would be all over town before lunch.

"What do we need now?" she asked.

"Baseballs, footballs, basketballs, soccer balls. Bats, helmets, hockey sticks. They need strenuous exercise to develop their major muscles. Watching too much television weakens more than their brains."

Giving in to Michael's infectious enthusiasm, Ellen put her list back in her purse and gave up any idea of keeping him within shouting distance of his father's budget. She didn't know what Nick would say when he saw the bill, but he had no one to blame but his own son.

Within minutes they'd bought enough sports equipment to supply a dozen teams.

"We need T-shirts," Michael announced.

"What for?"

"So you can tell the teams apart."

He bought a dozen T-shirts in assorted sizes with a vicious-looking shark on the front. It looked like it was straight out of *Jaws*. The other T-shirts had some sort of monster creature she sincerely hoped stayed in outer space.

"You'll give them nightmares," she protested.

"Kids like much scarier animals than adults. They have no fear."

Ellen couldn't accept that. "Maybe boys, but not girls."

He laughed. "Girls are worse than boys. If a boy is your enemy, you know it. A girl can smile and pretend to be your best friend while she cuts your heart out."

"You don't have a very high opinion of women, do you?"

"It has nothing to do with what I think. It's just the way they are."

No wonder he'd never gotten married. He'd probably prefer the company of spiders. Of course, working with all those high-living types, he probably got more attention than he could handle. He probably smiled for his guests all the time. No one could deny his good looks, especially when he smiled. If he looked as good in a bathing suit as he did in his coat and tie, she imagined he had to retreat to a private beach to avoid being attacked. Men who could afford his kind of resort usually had large stomachs, bald heads, and little knowledge of how to please a woman. Their wives probably considered Michael their own personal Christmas present.

She was surprised that made her feel jealous, or angry, or protective. She couldn't decide which, but all were absurd. She certainly shouldn't be impressed by his buying spree. How much effort did it take to spend his father's money?

She pulled a dozen T-shirts decorated with pink bunnies off a shelf. "The girls will want to wear something without fangs."

"It doesn't seem fair to pit the boys against the girls all the time."

"What do you mean?"

"You'll never get a boy to wear one of those T-shirts."

She put them in the cart anyway. "They look cute."

He stopped at the row of bicycles.

"The Kiwanis Club gave them bicycles last year," she said.

"Good. I didn't want to face having to wrap seventeen bicycles."

They raced through the remote-control cars section. Another half cart. He bought an armload of computer games. "For afternoons and weekends when they can't play outside."

"And have finished their homework."

He grinned. "Don't bank on it."

He surprised her when he headed toward art supplies. "I wish I knew what they had," he said.

"Nothing. I remember one of the girls saying she liked to paint, but she had to wait until art class at school."

He didn't need any more encouragement. He filled a cart with brushes, paint sets, individual little jars of paint, paper of all sizes, and several easels.

"The people who have to clean up after them are going to hate you," she said.

"Tell them I could have bought a potter's wheel and a year's supply of clay. That would have been messy."

They wandered down the remaining rows, picking up books here, a learning computer there, a train set on another row.

"If you don't stop, we'll need an eighteen-wheeler to get the stuff to the orphanage. Do you have any idea how we're going to get it to the house?"

"I'll think of something. Right now we need wrapping paper and ribbon."

"Up front," one of the clerks said.

The wrapping paper came in boxes of twenty-four rolls each. Michael picked up two boxes and put them into a cart. "You get the ribbon while I find the bows." He bought enough to fill a plastic garbage bag.

"I guess that's it for today," he said. "While they're ringing everything up, I'll see about delivery." He pulled out his wallet, withdrew a credit card, and handed it to her. "Use this for everything above budget." He disappeared, leaving Ellen with seventeen carts piled high and her mouth hanging open.

"Lady, what are you going to do with all this stuff?" one of the clerks asked. "Can't nobody have that many children."

"We're giving everything away," Ellen said.

"Looks like it would have been easier to run the kids in here and let them carry it out."

"Then they wouldn't have been surprised. We're buying for the orphanage."

"They're getting more than my kids." The clerk paused. "But I don't guess nothing makes up for having no mama or daddy, does it? You the one giving all this stuff?"

"No. Nick Wetherford is."

"That old skinflint!" she exclaimed with a look of disbelief. "I'm surprised you got him to part with a nickel, much less all this. You know some sort of secret he don't want getting out?"

Ellen laughed, but her laughter was tight, a little strained. "He's really a very nice man."

The clerk snorted. "If he'd acted half that nice to his own kid, I might believe you. The old miser must have some plan up his sleeve. Folks around here can tell you he don't give nothing away."

"What do you mean about his son?" Ellen asked.

"Everybody knows he froze his wife right into her grave, poor soul. Sent his son away to school so he couldn't get to know nobody here. Wouldn't let him have no friends home to stay. Then he did everything he could to turn his boy into a mean, stingy devil like himself. Everybody could see the boy weren't like that, but that old man wouldn't stop. Drove him away. He went off to college and never came back."

Ellen had assumed Nick had exaggerated when he told her he'd treated Michael badly. Now she wondered if she knew the half of what Michael had suffered.

"I heard tell he went off to one of those islands on the other side of the world," the clerk said, ringing up toys the whole time. "Doesn't surprise me he'd want to get as far away from the old man as he could. I doubt we'll ever see him around here again."

"You just have," Ellen said. "The man with me is Michael Wetherford."

The clerk stopped, her mouth open. "Him! Why he's downright good-looking—too good-looking to be old man Wetherford's son."

"He arrived yesterday."

"Well, I'll be. I didn't see no wedding ring on his finger."

"He's not married."

Her eyes crinkled with merriment. "Wait till the girls hear this. You'll never see so much preening in your life. And don't tell me old man Wetherford's buying these toys. I saw that man give you his card. Are you *sure* that's Michael Wetherford? He's a hunk."

"I guess he is rather nice-looking."

"I don't know what kind of men you're used to," the clerk said as she rang up the last item, stuffed it in a bag, and hit the total key. "But compared to the men we've got around here, he might as well be a movie star. Of course, being old Nick Wetherford's son is a drawback. There's some things a person can't put up with, not even for money. You want to pay for these carts one at a time or all at once?"

"Add everything up, and split it three ways," Ellen said.

She'd been so busy encouraging Nick to do whatever made him happy, trying to protect him from his son's interference, that she hadn't stopped to realize she hadn't contributed anything herself. It had taken Michael's unexpected generosity to jolt her into remembering.

His generosity had come as a shock. So had his enthusiasm. She'd begun the day determined to protect Nick from his son's efforts to get legal control over him, only to find Michael had no interest in doing that. He was just making certain his father was sound of mind and was capable of taking care of himself.

Unfortunately, that didn't relieve her mind. She didn't want to find him chock full of admirable qualities. Finding Michael attractive, wondering what it would feel like if he kissed her, made her feel too vulnerable. It had been easier when she thought he was a villain. She still had her doubts about grown men who hid themselves away on South Sea islands when they should be home looking after their aging fathers, but it was getting harder and harder to remember them. Everything he did continued to raise him in her opinion. That frightened her. She didn't want to like him that much.

She had a definite prejudice against marriage. Men were too controlling. Her father and her ex-fiancé were two perfect examples. If the clerk could be believed, Nick used to be even worse. She suspected Michael had inherited that trait from his father. He certainly had taken over the toy buying without seeming to be aware of what he'd done. Clearly the sign of a man used to controlling everybody and everything around him.

Exactly the kind of man Ellen meant to avoid.

But since Michael would be here only until the evening, there couldn't be any harm in a little flirtation. It had been a long time since she'd been attracted to a man, longer since she'd been around a man as attractive as Michael. It might be fun—if he would loosen up and smile as if he meant it.

"We've got it added up and divided three ways," the clerk said. "How do you want to pay for this?"

"With a check and two credit cards." She handed the clerk the credit cards.

"You can't sign for your mystery man. You don't think he's disappeared leaving you to pay for everything, do you? That sounds like something old man Wetherford would do."

"*Old man Wetherford* gave me a signed blank check," Ellen said, showing the check to the clerk.

"Well, I'll be damned," the clerk said, staring wide-eyed. "The old man must be senile. You ain't trying to marry him and steal his money, are you?"

"No."

"Well, what's caused the old coot to go off the deep end? Is his son here to put him away?"

"Of course not."

Apparently no one in Wetherford Gap besides herself could believe Nick *wanted* to give something away. If his behavior had been as bad as people seemed to believe, Michael must have had a truly awful childhood.

Nick had never tried to hide the fact that he'd been a terrible parent. So why hadn't she believed him? Why had she been so sure it was Michael's fault?

Maybe she'd let her fear of controlling men turn into paranoia. She couldn't see the truth because she didn't want to see it. That bothered her. How could she write a romance if she distrusted men? That might be the reason she'd been having so much trouble with her book. You couldn't write about falling in love with a man when you hated the idea.

But she didn't hate the idea, just the reality.

But maybe she'd gotten so paranoid about the reality, she'd forgotten not all men were controlling. Some were quite sensitive and thoughtful. Most were somewhere in between. She wondered where Michael fell. He seemed controlling when it came to his father, but he had shown sensitivity and thoughtfulness when it came to knowing what kinds of toys to choose for children. Maybe she ought to make an honest attempt to get to know him. It might provide insight for her book.

Who was she kidding? Getting to know Michael had nothing to do with her book. It had to do with liking him, wanting him to like her.

Michael reappeared.

"I rented a U-Haul truck," he announced. "Let's get this stuff outside and loaded up."

"How am I supposed to clean?" Mrs. Eringhaus asked when the living room began to fill up with boxes.

"You aren't," Michael said. "Put away your vacuum and dust mop. We need all the hands we can find to wrap these presents before tonight."

"You'll never get them done," Mrs. Eringhaus said, eyeing the growing stacks of boxes.

"Maybe Mrs. Hood can help us," Ellen suggested.

"We still have to eat dinner," Michael said. "Do you have some friends who could help us?" Michael asked Mrs. Eringhaus.

"Well . . ."

"I'll pay three dollars a package."

"I'll be right back," Mrs. Eringhaus said as she hurried to the phone.

"That will cost you more than a hundred dollars," Ellen said.

"I'm no good at wrapping, and Dad has never wrapped anything in his life. That leaves just you. Can you handle all of this?"

"No, but—"

"Then I guess we have to depend on Mrs. Eringhaus's friends."

If he hadn't been certain he'd make a mess, he'd have wrapped some himself. He hadn't felt so good about anything in a long time. After years of buying toys with a profit in mind, buying them to give away had turned out to be an unexpected pleasure. He'd had fun choosing toys he thought the children would enjoy, fun anticipating their pleasure when they saw the presents, when they opened them. He wouldn't have believed it if anyone had told him, but giving money away really was more fun than making it.

Ellen would never have believed it, but Michel had turned the job of wrapping presents into a party. He had assigned her the job of keeping the women supplied with paper, ribbon, tape, and cards to identify the contents of the packages. He had put his father in charge of packing the truck so the presents could be handed out in the order he wanted. Turning on enough charm to light Times Square, Michael made sure the ladies had all the coffee, tea, cocoa, cookies, and cake they could consume; he had joked, kidded, and flattered, done everything he could to keep them in good spirits while they wrapped the mound of gifts.

Six women sat scattered about the parlor, working at tables, on the floor, in their laps. They talked, laughed, and generally treated Michael like a movie star. You'd have thought each of them was his old maid aunt, and he was trying to sweet-talk her into leaving him all her money. She'd never heard so much blarney in one afternoon.

She found herself being jealous because he hadn't directed any of it toward her.

"Do you really have dancing girls at your hotels who wear nothing but grass skirts and coconut shells?" one woman asked, her eyes wide with wonder. Ellen doubted she'd ever been more than fifty miles from Wetherford Gap. Anyone who'd been to the South Pacific must seem exotic, bigger than life to her.

"That's Hawaii," Michael said. "Our dancers prefer brightly colored materials. But they don't cover very much."

"I bet you have to beat the men off with a stick," one woman said with a pleasantly horrified titter.

"We do have more requests for reservations than we can fill, but we're a family resort. The men bring their wives."

One woman hooted. "I wouldn't let my Oswald go near such a place. He'd be bound to go off with a heart attack."

"The wives really let their men look at such women?" another asked.

"Sure. Why not?" Michael asked.

"That's like showing a tomcat a pot of cream he can't have."

"All of our dancers work in the resort," Michael

said. "Our guests get to know them as waitresses, hostesses, managers of the day care—"

"You have kids in that place?" another asked.

"I told you, we're a family resort."

The women looked at each other and went off into a shout of laughter. "I wouldn't take my boys there," one woman said. "One week of your dancing girls, and they'd never come home again."

"My husband neither," another said, and broke up laughing.

"It wouldn't do mine any good to stay," another said, "not unless you've got an unlimited supply of Geritol and Viagra."

They went on like this for more than an hour, eating, wrapping, and joking in between debating aloud over what kind of wrapping paper should go with a particular gift. They spent just as long deliberating over the choice of ribbon. When they finished, Michael handed each of them their money—in cash. Six happy women left singing his praises.

"Where did you get that much cash?" Ellen asked.

"I sent the truck driver to the bank. It's always best to pay as soon as a job's done."

There appeared to be little he didn't know about handling people. She wondered if he handled his girlfriends as well. He probably had so many that they never stayed long enough to develop territorial rights.

She had no right to be thinking things like this. She certainly had no reason to think he kept a stable of girlfriends. The time had come to start judging Michael by what she saw with her own eyes—not prejudice, not hearsay.

Not jealousy.

She had to admit, regardless of how much it mortified her, that she had come down with a severe case of jealousy. Nothing rare. Nothing exotic. Plain old, ordinary jealousy. Even worse, her jealousy stemmed from his treatment of six nice old ladies, all of whom probably had sons his age.

Pathetic. She had to get a grip before she did something truly appalling like . . . well, she couldn't think of anything sufficiently dreadful just now. But considering her thoughts and feelings, she probably would at any minute.

"I'd better start getting dressed," she said. She had to get out of the room.

"Aren't we going to eat first?" Michael asked.

"Nick wants to hand out the presents early in the evening. That way the children will have time to play with them before they go to bed. We can eat when we get back."

"Are you going to dress up as an elf again?"

"Of course. Santa's little helper."

"What time will you be back?"

"I don't know. Why?"

"Mrs. Hood has to know when to have dinner ready."

"Mrs. Hood is leaving everything in the refrigerator," his father said as he entered the room. "We can heat it up in the microwave."

"Then give me a call when you're ready to leave the orphanage, and I'll have everything hot when you get back."

"Have you decided to stay another day?" Ellen asked.

"Yes."

"Good," his father said, "but you're not going to stay here. You're coming with us."

"What can I do?"

"You'll figure out something. Meanwhile, you can help me into this damned Santa Claus costume. I got a new one, and I can't figure it out."

73

Chapter Five

Michael entered the large, formal bedroom with its dark mahogany furniture and massive four-poster bed. When he was a child, that room had seemed almost like a hallowed inner sanctum. Now it was just another bedroom.

He looked at the Santa Claus suit laid out on the bed. Rich red velvet and thick fake fur made it look like something out of a fairy tale. Shiny black boots, gleaming patent-leather belt, and a luxurious beard guaranteed the children might believe Santa really had come to their orphanage. An intricately designed layer of padding would make his father appear really fat, but Michael couldn't see anything complicated about it.

"You don't need any help with this costume," he said, eyeing his father with suspicion. "What do you really want?"

"I could use your help," his father replied. "It's the devil to get into all this stuff by myself."

"I'm sure Ellen would be glad to help."

"That's one of the things I wanted to talk to you about."

Michael felt a sudden dread. Ellen might not be interested in marrying his father, but that didn't mean his father didn't want to marry her. "What's the other thing?"

His father had been in the process of undressing. Wearing nothing but a T-shirt, boxer shorts, and socks, he turned to Michael. Michael had never seen his father in his underwear. He had always appeared hard, unapproachable, invincible, too powerful to need anybody as puny and useless as his son.

The man standing before him now, slender, frail-looking, his white hair mussed, didn't look like his father. He looked like a stranger. Michael didn't want his father to appear vulnerable, mortal. Despite their differences, he admired his father. For reasons he'd never stopped to analyze, he'd always wanted his father to appear bigger than life, indestructible. Yet he felt he might be able to talk to this man, *really* talk. Michael had tried to deny that he cared, but he'd always cared very deeply.

"I wanted to talk about us," his father said. His gaze didn't waver. He faced his son just as he'd faced everything else in his life, head on. "I didn't realize it at the time—I could only see what I wanted you to do and be furious when you didn't want the same thing—but I was a terrible father. I was a worse husband, but it's too late to do anything about that. I hope it's not too late to do something about us."

Michael didn't know what to say. Despite every

75

sign of change, he'd decided his father was just getting old, maybe losing his grip.

"You're not saying anything," his father said.

"I don't know what to say."

His father smiled ruefully. "You probably think I'm senile, even though the doctor told you otherwise."

Michael felt a flush of embarrassment. His father smiled. "Nothing is a secret in this town, especially when it involves one of us. I knew you had seen the doctor five minutes after you left his office. I expected you would. I wanted you to know I hadn't lost my mind. Did Ellen tell you about her father?"

"A little, but—"

"Burt Weems was the first real friend I ever had. He got me involved in his charities—against my will, mind you."

Michael felt himself smile. "I'm sure of it."

"I'd been feeling the loss of you and your mother. My money didn't mean much without the two of you. I had turned into a bitter old man, blaming others for my unhappiness, and he dragged me outside myself. He taught me to enjoy giving pleasure to others less fortunate. I know that sounds awfully corny, but that's not what I'm getting at. I'd been feeling sorry for myself, and he made me see how fortunate I was. I was hale and hearty; he was dying. I came to see the little mistakes he'd made with Ellen. That enabled me to see the much bigger mistakes I'd made with you."

Michael felt like a stuffed toy, just standing, listening, unbelieving.

"I know we can't get back what we've lost, but I hope we can get to know each other a little better. Maybe you'll even want to come for a visit once in a while. I don't want you on the other side of the world, not giving a damn whether I'm alive or dead."

"I've always given a damn." Michael had difficulty speaking. The words stuck in his throat.

His father smiled wanly. "That's just it. You've damned me from one end of the world to the other. I want more than that." He picked up a piece of the padding and handed it to Michael. "Now, help me put this on." He held out his arms so Michael could slip it on. "Then there's Ellen," his father said.

"What about her?" Michael kept his eyes on the row of snaps that would hold the padding in place.

"Her father loved her dearly, but he was so consumed by his business and his charities, he didn't realize he didn't know her any better than I knew you. When he tried to become a part of her life, it was to find her a husband who could run his companies after he died. When she turned down all his choices, he didn't understand. Unfortunately, the man Ellen found on her own turned out to be just as controlling as her father. Now she won't even date."

"What am I supposed to do about that?" Michael picked up a second piece of padding and snapped it into place.

"Don't tell me you've spent ten years in the resort business without learning how to handle women."

"Maybe, but I started off on the wrong foot with Ellen. I accused her of wanting to marry you for your money."

His father chuckled. "She has more money than I do."

"I know that now."

"You like her, don't you?"

"Dad, I just met her yesterday. How can I—"

"I didn't say pretend you're in love with her. You're too different for that. I just meant talk to her, say nice things, maybe even take her to dinner if you're here long enough. Just enough so she'll stop distrusting all men. She's a wonderful gal. She ought to be married and raising a family of her own, not locking herself away in some room writing about love instead of experiencing it. She never will if somebody doesn't help her get over being afraid everything in pants is going to take over her life."

"After the way I took over buying the toys and getting them wrapped, she probably thinks I'm like all the rest."

"No, she doesn't. She likes you."

"You're nuts. Since I got here, she's dogged my heels to make sure I won't clip your wings."

"And will you?"

He felt himself stiffen. "I don't want your money."

"You told me that when you left here ten years ago."

He felt himself flush. "I was angry."

"You had a right."

"Maybe. Anyway, I came home to make sure you were all right."

"And to make sure I wasn't about to be bamboozled into marriage by some gold digger."

Michael couldn't help but grin. "That, too."

"I thought that picture would bring you home."

"You knew about the picture?"

"Stop talking so much and help me get dressed. I've got on so much padding, I can hardly move. I'm afraid if I pick up my feet, I'll tip over."

Michael helped his father into the Santa Claus pants.

"Tell me about the picture," Michael said while his father tried to buckle the belt to his satisfaction.

"I had a friend make a whole bunch of them. I sent the best one to Roy. He's such an old woman, I knew he'd panic and write you first thing. Just in case that picture wasn't enough, I told him I was giving away your toys."

"I noticed they're still in the attic."

"I may be an old fool, but I wouldn't give away your things without asking."

Michael could think of at least a dozen times when he'd been too overcome with emotion to speak to his father, but before it had always been anger. He'd never felt anything like the emotion he was experiencing now. He hadn't known he could. "I see you haven't lost your cunning," he managed to say after a bit. "You can still get people to do what you want."

"I wanted the chance to apologize for all the things I did, and for the even greater number of things I didn't do. I was afraid, if I didn't do something drastic, you wouldn't care enough to come home."

"I would have."

His father seemed to relax.

"I couldn't be sure," he said. "In your place, I doubt I would." With that, his father seemed to put a lid on his emotions. "Now help me with this beard. The last time I wore it, I looked like I'd backed into it by mistake."

Michael didn't know how he'd let himself get roped into going to the orphanage. He was still reeling from his talk with his father. For years he'd told himself he didn't care, that nothing his father did would ever again have the power to affect him. He couldn't have been more wrong. He felt wrung out, at a loss, unsure of what he did feel. Now his father expected him to help Ellen overcome her distrust of men. How could he do that when he hadn't entirely overcome his distrust of her?

He shouldn't have come. He should have stayed home and tried to get his mind straight. Instead, he was driving his father's Lincoln, his father in the back because the Santa Claus suit was too big to allow him in the front seat, Ellen in the front next to him, looking adorable in her elf costume. He tried to block out his father's request to pay some attention to Ellen, but it kept ringing in his ears.

"Are you sure we have enough gifts?" his father asked for the dozenth time as they pulled into the orphanage parking lot.

"More than enough," Ellen assured him. "Now stop worrying. Michael will keep filling bags for me to bring to you. All you have to do is pass them out. I've written a child's name on each present."

"I hope they remembered to keep the children together."

"Michael called twice," Ellen said. "Everything is under control."

"I just don't want to seem like a fake Santa Claus. I wish there'd been some way I could have come down the chimney."

"You'd have gotten stuck in that outfit," Michael said. "Bursting in through the outside door ought to be enough."

The large room at the orphanage looked cold and formal. The feeble warmth put forth by the small fire wasn't enough to stir the children to life. They played and talked quietly, without movement, without zest. The whole room lacked warmth and emotion, humanity. Then his father threw open the door, laughed in a voice Michael swore had to come from his toes, and announced Santa Claus had come to deliver his presents in person this year.

For as long as he lived, Michael would treasure those first few moments when the kids saw Santa Claus and his huge bag of toys. Even the bigger boys and girls stared in disbelief—and hope. Suddenly everything seemed warmer, brighter, happier. He could hardly believe it when his father started calling the children by name, reminding them of some of the trouble they'd gotten into during the year.

"How can he know that?" Michael hissed to Ellen.

"He had the orphanage send him pictures and a little information about each child. He memorized everything."

His father was talking nonstop, moving among the children, mesmerizing them until there wasn't a child in the room who wasn't convinced—at least in a tiny corner of his or her heart—that Santa Claus was real and that he was in their orphanage tonight.

"Now let's see what I've got in my bag," his father said, settling down into a chair near the door.

To Michael, his father seemed transformed. He wasn't anything like the hard, emotionless man Michael remembered. Michael saw what his father could have been had his early life been different. He felt sorry for both of them. Michael decided right then that things *would* be different. Maybe he'd move his father to the resort. These cold winters couldn't be good for him. Of course, he had lived in Wetherford Gap his whole life and might not want to leave. Michael didn't know what he'd do about that, but somehow he was determined that he and his father would spend the rest of his father's life together.

"I would never have believed that if I hadn't seen it for myself," Michael said as he brought the Lincoln to a stop in the driveway. "For a while there, I could have believed you *were* Santa Claus."

"I feel sorry for the old boy," his father said. "Only seventeen kids, and they wore me out. I don't know how he makes it around the whole world."

Michael found himself laughing as he helped his

father out of the car. It almost sounded as if his father believed in Santa Claus himself.

"He probably has thousands of people like you and Ellen helping him," Michael said. "I'll bet he's relaxing at the North Pole, a hot buttered rum in one hand and a TV remote in the other, his feet up to the fire, knowing you'll do all his work for him."

"Well, he'd better not plan on any more help from me tonight," his father said as he unlocked the door and entered the house. "I've had it. I'm going to shed this costume and go straight to bed."

"You want me to help you?"

"No. You take Ellen into the kitchen and give her something to eat. The poor girl is starved."

"No, I'm not."

"Of course you are," Nick said.

"Well, maybe I'd like some coffee."

Michael caught the wink his father gave Ellen as he went off to bed. He didn't know what the conniving old man had told her—probably that Michael was suffering from a deep melancholy and she had to try to help bring him out of it. Michael didn't mind. He had already admitted to himself that he felt a strong attraction to Ellen, and he couldn't do anything to stop it. He might as well see what could come of it.

Besides, he had to thank her for what she'd done for his father. He had been a miserable old coot when Michael walked away from Wetherford Gap ten years ago. Now he seemed to have turned into a kind, caring human being.

"Do you want something to eat?" Ellen asked.

"No. Do you want some coffee?"

"Yes."

"So do I. Where do you keep it?"

"I'll make it."

"I didn't think women made coffee anymore."

"They do when they plan to drink it."

"Suppose we make it together. I'll put the water in the coffee maker, and you put in the coffee."

"I don't suppose you have to fix anything for yourself when you're at your resort," she said as she took a can of coffee off a shelf and opened it.

"That depends. I have a small kitchen in my apartment. On my days off, I stay in the apartment and cook for myself, or I find a deserted corner of the island . . . and cook for myself."

"Do you like solitude?"

"When you run a resort, you're always on duty. There's somebody wanting something every minute of the day. I need to get away when I have free time."

"How many cups of water did you put in?"

"Two."

She measured out two scoops of coffee and turned on the coffeemaker. "Cream?"

"Yes, please. Where are the mugs?"

"In the cabinet behind you."

He set mugs on the table. She set out a creamer. Then they sat staring at each other, waiting for the coffee to brew. He wondered if she expected him to make the first move.

"I'm sorry I thought you were trying to marry my father for his money," Michael said finally.

"I guess you couldn't have thought anything else."

"I could have, but I didn't."

"It must have been a shock to find a young woman living in your father's house."

"That's putting it mildly," he said, grinning as he remembered his initial reaction to Ellen's presence. "Knowing my father's aversion to giving away anything whatsoever, it was the only explanation I could think of."

"I apologize for thinking you were worried only about your inheritance," Ellen said.

"I still can't get over the change in Dad. You wouldn't believe how he used to be."

"He told me, but I didn't really believe him until I talked to the clerk in the toy store. I figured if she told the same story, it must be right."

"And what was that?"

"That he was a terrible father, that his ambition for you, his refusal to let you do what you wanted, drove you from home."

"You know, I can't remember a single tender moment with my father, no time when he smiled at me, no time when he thought I'd done something right, no time when he was proud of me. Yet I wanted to love him. And I wanted him to love me. I think I left because I was afraid he never would."

"And now?"

"I still want very much to—"

The coffeemaker chose that moment to sound off. Michael got up and poured the coffee. They were silent while they added cream until they were satisfied with the color and taste.

"What are you going to do now?" Ellen asked.

"Go back to work. I still have my resorts to run."

"I thought you might stay here."

"And do what?"

"Run your father's business?"

Michael laughed. "He hasn't changed that much. Nick Wetherford doesn't allow anyone to stick their fingers into his business."

"But he's getting older."

"He'll die in harness, and that's fine with me. Now we've talked enough about me. Tell me about yourself."

His coffee tasted flat. He supposed he'd gotten too used to the exotic blends at the hotel that weren't available in Wetherford Gap.

"I'm trying to write a novel and not making much progress. Outside of that, there's nothing to tell."

"What do you want to do?"

She laughed. "Have some publisher buy it for a million dollars."

"Dad says you have more money than he does. Why should you want more?"

"I don't. I just want someone to think something I've done is that good. You may not think so, but it's not much fun being a rich woman who's done nothing to justify her existence."

"You've turned my father around. That's enough to warrant the Nobel prize."

They both laughed.

"I didn't think he was that difficult," she said.

"You weren't his son."

They were silent a moment. Each took a sip of coffee.

"You know he's trying to get us together, don't you?" she said.

"I figured that out when he locked us in the attic."

"I was still too mad at you to listen to a word you said."

"Same here."

"What do you think of me now?"

"I don't really know you well enough to answer that." He was avoiding the truth. He might not know a lot of facts about her, but he knew all he needed to know to like her very much. It didn't make any sense at all, but that didn't change the fact that he found her fascinating, attractive, and very alluring. And the elf costume she still wore didn't change things a bit.

He imagined she'd probably forgotten she was still in the costume, but it had an unexpected effect on him. Rather than make her look silly, it made her look adorable, far removed from the fire-spewing female he'd met that first day.

Yesterday. He could hardly believe it had been such a short time. It seemed that he'd known her for much longer. Odd how you could meet a woman for the first time and almost immediately discover you couldn't imagine what it was like not to have known her.

"I didn't mean to put you on the spot," she said. "I guess I just wanted confirmation you don't still think I'm a vamp."

"I don't."

The silence stretched between them.

"Are you still angry at your father?" she asked.

"I don't know. I've vowed at least a million times that when I have a son, I will do everything differently."

"Do you have any family?"

"No. I don't make a habit of scattering illegitimate children about the island. It wouldn't be good for business."

"I didn't mean that. You've been gone for ten years. I thought you might have married, maybe divorced. It happens so much these days." Her flush made him regret his hasty retort.

"I'm not married, divorced, or a father, but I haven't given up hope."

Ellen laughed. "I should think not. According to the clerk, now that everyone knows you've come back to Wetherford Gap, and that you're still available—she noticed you weren't wearing a wedding band—you're going to be pursued by every single woman in the area. To quote her, *You'll never see such preening in your life.*"

Michael had been pursued by many women over the years—unfortunately, most were married to his guests, which made things rather awkward from time to time—but he'd never been pursued by the women of Wetherford Gap. He'd never been home long enough.

"I hate to disappoint them, but they'd probably hate living on a Pacific island resort. It's not what women around here are used to."

"What kind of woman would like it?"

"First, she'd have to have complete faith in her husband's love. There's a lot of flirting, being ambushed in out-of-the-way places, private meetings with very beautiful women. If she weren't absolutely sure she had nothing to fear, she'd probably be consumed with jealousy."

"That doesn't sound very inviting."

"She'd also have to realize that if you own a resort, the job never ends. There's no such thing as privacy, and the customer is always right."

"I don't think I'd like that."

"She would have to like all kinds of people and be very knowledgeable, very cosmopolitan. If not, she'd probably start to feel inferior."

"You're right. No one from a quiet mountain town could possibly fit those requirements. How did *you* manage it?"

He'd never asked himself that question. When he finished college, he'd looked around for an opportunity to make his fortune in a place as far away from his father as he could get. He'd settled on the South Pacific first, on resort hotels second. The combination had worked perfectly. He'd never stopped to ask himself if he liked it.

"I was trying to get as far away from my father as possible. The work I did didn't matter."

"At least you're honest about it."

"I've never tried to hide the fact that I've spent most of my life being angry at my father. I'm just now able to admit I've spent just as long wanting to love him, wanting him to love me."

"You've got your chance now."

"I hope so."

"But surely you can see your father has truly changed."

Michael drained his coffee cup, considered whether to have another, and decided against it.

"I'm sure it all seems very straightforward to you, but it turns most of my life upside down." He got up and put his mug in the sink. "Now I'm going to bed. I have to recruit my strength in case my father comes up with some more earth-shattering revelations. Change isn't all that easy to accept, you know, not even for the relatively young."

"You'll manage."

"We'll see." He bent over and kissed her on the lips.

She reacted with startled surprise. "What was that for?"

"For changing my father into a person I could learn to love. That may not seem like very much to you, but it's something neither my mother nor I was able to accomplish. You're a very special person."

Chapter Six

Ellen stayed at the table after Michael left the room. She felt dazed, flummoxed—and all from one tiny kiss. She hadn't expected Michael to kiss her. Ever. For any reason. So why had he done it? A man couldn't go around kissing women he didn't know. That was a good way to get a black eye. He could have just thanked her for what she'd done for his father. That was what strangers usually did, and they *were* strangers.

But she didn't feel like it. She felt as though she'd known him for a long time. She found it hard to believe they had met just a little more than twenty-four hours earlier. Usually she had to know a person for several weeks, sometimes even months, before she'd be friendly. Yet she had sat still and let Michael kiss her on the lips. It began to look as if Nick wasn't the only one who'd changed out of all recognition. She hardly knew herself. Maybe her struggle to write a book about love—something she was forced to admit she knew nothing about—was driving her crazy.

Whatever the reason, she had become prey to all sorts of unfamiliar feelings. How could she have reached the age of twenty-six, met hundreds of men, dated a number of them, and never once experienced any of the sensations that were threatening to turn her inside out? She hadn't even liked Michael twenty-four hours ago. At least, she'd tried not to like him. As late as this morning, she'd followed him to the lawyer's and doctor's offices determined to block everything he tried to do.

Yet now she sat in the kitchen, too weak-kneed to get out of the chair, feeling that for the first time she could go upstairs and write the scene in which the hero and heroine met, *and this time she'd know what the heroine was feeling*.

But what was it?

Excitement. And it had nothing to do with the Christmas season. She felt awake, alert. Too awake and alert. She wanted to jump up and move around, and at the same time she felt too weak to move. Her heart beat a little faster, her breathing was a little more shallow.

She felt a sense of expectation. Something was about to happen. She didn't know what, but she believed it would be something good. She felt a heightened sensitivity, an increase in sensual perception.

She felt a little bit of fear, too. She had no way of judging, predicting, knowing what to do. She felt that things were going out of control—might already be out of control—and she didn't like that.

Yet she knew she wouldn't hold back. This had to do with Michael. And though she warned herself to be careful—anyone could see he showed signs of being everything she feared in a man—she could no more back away from him, from her feelings, than she could pack up and leave Wetherford Gap. She didn't believe in love at first sight—or in a week for that matter—but it would be foolish to deny that something had happened between them.

Most shocking of all, he'd described exactly what it would be like to be married to him, what his wife would have to accept if she wanted a successful marriage.

Why had he told her? Was he trying to drive her off, warn her before either of them went too far? Was he giving himself an excuse for not being married, or was he setting up obstacles, hoping she'd knock them down?

She didn't know, but he must have had more reason than just making conversation. Her fingers brushed her lips. She could still feel his kiss. She had said a woman couldn't accept his conditions, but could she if she truly loved him?

Would she if he asked her?

Michael couldn't decide whether he was being foolish or merely trying to recreate a childhood he'd never had. He'd gone out and bought a Christmas tree for a house that already had a huge tree fully decorated. And all because of a box of ornaments he found in the attic. The tree in the hall had been professionally decorated in blue and silver—beautiful but as cold as the entry hall where it stood. He wanted a smaller tree in the warmth of the family room, with colors, bright lights, and ornaments and decorations that reminded him of his childhood.

Some people might say he'd lost his mind. He would probably have agreed with them. He certainly wasn't acting like himself, but he couldn't decide whether it had more to do with his father or with Ellen.

There could be no doubt that his father's change of heart had generated a lightness of spirit in the house. While he couldn't rid himself of a sliver of fear that all this might disappear and his father might go back to being the way he used to be, Michael wanted to love his father. He always had.

Then there was Ellen. Now that he knew she really wasn't after his father's money, he had no reason to dislike or distrust her. He was thankful, in fact, for her part in bringing about the change in his father. It would have been all right if he'd just liked her. She was an attractive woman. But why had he kissed her?

Why did he want to kiss her again?

Why had he bought the Christmas tree for her?

Okay, he'd bought it for himself as well, but he'd been thinking of the look on her face when he brought it into the house, the laughter they'd share while they decorated it, the fun they'd have seeing their presents under the tree on Christmas morning. He'd spent half the morning buying presents for his Dad, the cook, and the housekeeper, but he'd bought even more for Ellen. He didn't bother asking himself if she might already have one of those, or if she even liked that type or style; he just bought what he wanted. The back seat of the car was stacked high with boxes. He pulled into the driveway wondering what she'd say when she realized half of them were for her.

"Where're you going to put that?" Mrs. Eringhaus wanted to know when he walked into the house with the Christmas tree. "We've already got one."

"It's going in the family room," he told her. "The other tree is too big and formal. This one is little and friendly."

"Only a man as tall as you could call a six-foot tree little," Mrs. Eringhaus muttered as she protected a lamp, two porcelain figurines, and several pictures from its branches.

"What do we need a second tree for?" his father asked when Michael dragged it into the family room and set it up in a corner he'd cleared earlier.

"Did you help decorate that monster in the front hall?" Michael asked as he set the tree down and adjusted it to his satisfaction.

"No, but—"

"You can't have a real Christmas without a tree. And you can't get into the spirit unless you decorate it yourself. Give me a hand. I've got boxes of lights and decorations in the car."

His father grinned. "Did you buy this for Ellen?"

Michael felt his cheeks grow warm. "I bought it for all of us. You've been so busy trying to give things to other people, you've forgotten about yourself."

"I don't know what Ellen will say when she sees this."

"She'll probably think I've been out in the tropical sun too long. Here, hold out your arms and I'll load you up with boxes."

"You've got enough back there for a dozen trees."

Michael felt heat in his cheeks again. He didn't know why he should be embarrassed to have his father know he'd bought Christmas presents. "I had to wait until I got here to buy your presents. There was nothing at the resort you'd want."

"I hope you bought something for Ellen."

Michael piled the boxes so high, he didn't have to look into his father's eyes. "Of course I bought her something."

"What did you get her?"

"You'll have to wait until tomorrow to see. Now take those boxes inside and don't drop them."

"I can't see where I'm going," his father complained. "You'll never get all of this under that puny tree."

Michael relented and took three boxes from his father's load. "Follow me. I'll hold the door."

"I'm not helpless."

"No, you're a cranky old man who doesn't want to decorate his own Christmas tree."

"I never said that."

"Good. I'll let you put the angel on the top. I'll hold the ladder."

Ellen opened the door for them.

"You're supposed to be working on your book," his father said.

"I can't write with all this going on," she said standing back to let them pass. "Why did you buy another tree?"

"He said the other belonged to the house," his father explained. "This one's for us."

That wasn't what he'd said, but it showed that his father understood what he felt. He guessed that was even better.

"Complain, complain," Michael said. "I thought you two were into the joy of Christmas. I'm supposed to be the wet blanket."

"You certainly have proved to be anything but," Ellen said, hurrying ahead to hold open doors. "I never know what you're going to do next."

"Turnabout's fair play," Michael said as he set his load of boxes down in the middle of the family room floor. "Now, are you going to help decorate the tree or hide upstairs working on your crusty old book?"

"It's gotten a whole lot less crusty in the last twenty-four hours," Ellen said, then blushed furiously. "But you couldn't chase me out of here. I can't wait to see what a man would buy to decorate a tree."

"Since you're so nosy, you can put the hooks on all the ornaments while Dad and I string the lights."

"Chauvinist."

He grinned. He hoped it was a wicked grin. "That's the way it is in the South Pacific. We'll start from the bottom," he said to his father as he began unfolding the first string of lights, "and work our way to the top."

"And back down again from the number of strings you've bought."

"I'll find something to do with them."

"It seems to me I remember just yesterday you were worried about causing a brown-out in the valley."

"I've decided I don't care if the whole state goes dark. I'm going to have my Christmas tree."

And that was how he felt. It was *his* tree. It was the beginning of *his* Christmas. The feeling of well-being, almost a happy-go-lucky carelessness, increased as they wound string after string of lights around the tree.

"There's no place left for the ornaments," Ellen said when they finished.

"Nonsense. This tree has a hundred limbs. You can put at least five ornaments on each."

"I thought you said you passed math," Ellen said.

"With the best grade in the class."

"The teacher must have been a woman."

"Are you implying I didn't deserve my grade?"

"Yes."

"Then you count them."

"I'll settle for handing you the ornaments."

"No, you don't. Dad and I can choose our own. You've got to hang just as many as we do. I want this to be your tree as much as it is ours."

The door opened and Mrs. Eringhaus entered carrying an armload of packages. "You left the car door open," she said to Michael. "When I went to close it, I

95

found all these packages. Mrs. Hood is bringing in the rest. Where do you want them?"

"How about on the sofa?" Ellen said, giving Michael a questioning look.

"You'll need more room than that," Mrs. Eringhaus said. "It'll take me another trip to get them all inside."

"I was going to get them later," Michael said.

"No bother. Might as well bring them in now. They want them on the sofa, Orida," Mrs. Eringhaus said to Mrs. Hood. "And don't peek. One of them has your name on it."

"I got something for both of you," Michael said. "You deserve it for putting up with Dad for so long."

Both women protested that he was being too harsh on his father, but they grinned happily as they left the room.

"A lot have my name on them," Ellen said, astonishment evident in both her voice and her expression. "Why would you buy me so many presents?"

Michael didn't have his explanation ready. He'd planned to bring the presents in after Ellen had gone back to her room. Maybe, in the excitement of opening them, he wouldn't have had to offer an explanation at all. Unfortunately, things hadn't worked out that way.

"It's easier to buy presents for a woman."

The light-hearted feeling surrounding them turned suddenly serious. "Thank you," she said. "That was very thoughtful of you."

"Not at all," he said, trying to recapture the easygoing atmosphere. "With you and Dad beating me over the head about giving stuff away, what else could I do?"

"You could change your mind about going back tomorrow," she said. "You could stay a little longer. At least until New Year's."

He had forgotten about his plan to leave Christmas

day. He'd told his staff he'd be back. They'd be expecting him. So would his regular customers. Many of them hadn't gone through Christmas in several years without him.

"I promised I'd be back. A lot of things depend on me."

"Like what?" Ellen asked. "If you've got good personnel, they can carry on without you."

"Don't pressure him, Ellen," his father said. "If he has to go back, then he has to go back. I know it's your busy season, son. I'm glad you were able to spare a few days."

"He only came home to spy on you, to cause trouble. Why should you be thankful for that?"

As though she hadn't realized what she'd said until the words were out, Ellen's hand flew to her mouth, her gaze to Michael. "I'm sorry. I didn't mean to say that. I don't know what got into me. You were having so much fun decorating your Christmas tree, and I've ruined it. I'm sorry."

She dropped the ornament in her hand and ran from the room.

Michael stared at the shattered ball on the floor. He didn't understand how his idea of decorating the Christmas tree together could have gone wrong so abruptly. "What's wrong with her?" he asked his father. "Did I do something?"

"I think maybe she likes you enough to hope you'll stay longer."

"I really can't. I shouldn't have left at all. I—"

"I know. If I hadn't tricked you, you wouldn't have."

"I wish you wouldn't think of it like that."

"I'm just glad for these two days. But I want you to find some time this summer when you can come home for a couple of weeks."

"Why?"

"It's about time you learned about my business. You're going to be taking it over before long."

Michael nearly dropped the ornament in his hand.

"I should have done it years ago," his father said. "Maybe then you wouldn't have gone away."

"No," Michael said, suddenly realizing the estrangement had been as much his fault as his father's. "It took the separation to make both of us realize what we'd lost. I regret the time we lost, but we might not have had anything if I'd stayed."

Ellen would have kicked herself around the room and down the hall if it would have done any good. Why did she have to strike out at Michael? He'd been sweet and thoughtful to buy the Christmas tree for his father, and to buy presents for her. She had no right to expect anything else, especially after the way she'd treated him in the beginning. The logical thing to have done—what any decent, polite, reasonably intelligent female would have done—would have been to thank him politely and take the first opportunity to slip out of the house and buy several presents for him.

She could only excuse herself in part by saying that if the Christmas tree had surprised her, the presents had left her speechless. Well, unfortunately, *not* speechless. It would have been better if she had been. Then she wouldn't have struck out at him like the thankless, spiteful female she was. It wasn't his fault that she'd been knocked senseless by the sudden realization that she loved him. And in the same moment, devastated by the knowledge that he couldn't possibly love her.

No sane woman would have fallen in love in one day, but she'd done exactly that. And she'd compounded her stupidity by getting angry because

Michael was leaving before she had a chance to make him fall in love with her. As if you could make any man fall in love just because you wanted him to. And a good thing. Imagine the havoc that would create!

Well, she couldn't stay in her room feeling sorry for herself, being angry at the world for letting her fall in love with a man who didn't love her, and for letting her discover how to write a love scene by being denied one of her own. As much as she wanted to run back to New Jersey, she had to go downstairs and apologize. She had to think of some excuse so far from the truth that he couldn't possibly guess it.

She forced herself to get up and leave the room. The hallway seemed shorter than it ever had before, the steps too few. Before she knew it, she stood outside the family room. She forced herself to walk in before she could change her mind.

Michael and his dad were putting the balls on the tree. They had a long way to go, but it was looking like a real tree already. For a moment she regretted the necessity of intruding. They seemed to be getting on remarkably well. Maybe they'd found themselves in agreement over her bizarre behavior.

Both men looked up when she entered the room. Nick smiled in welcome. Dear man. She could never do anything wrong in his eyes.

"I was hoping you'd come back," he said. "It's not half as much fun without you."

"I doubt Michael feels the same way."

"Of course I do." He smiled reassuringly, but she thought he had a slightly strained look around his eyes.

"I apologize for my outburst," she said. "I don't know what came over me. I've been having a terrible time with the hero in my book. I can only guess that I took my frustration at him out on you."

It was such a stupid excuse, they just might believe it.

"I'm told characters are a lot like children," Michael said. "You love them dearly but have absolutely no control over what they do."

She had to laugh. "You've pegged my hero exactly. And the heroine's not a cakewalk either. How could you know something like that?"

"Writers come to the resort periodically. The more trouble they have with a book, the more they want to talk."

"If I promise not to go off the deep end again, will you let me help decorate the tree?"

"If you hadn't come back, I'd have come after you," Michael said. "There's a whole bag of ornaments waiting for your approval."

She wondered if he really would have gone after her. He looked sincere. Still, she reminded herself that he ran a successful resort. His face was a mask for the public. She wondered if she'd ever seen the real Michael.

She had when she'd opened the door and seen him with his father, in the brief moment before they realized she'd returned. Her instincts hadn't been wrong. He was a man who could feel deeply, who could love just as deeply. She wondered if his father was right about his wanting a wife and family. He didn't seem to need anyone.

If only he were going to be here longer. But he wasn't, and she might as well make up her mind to that. Maybe he'd come home again this summer. But somehow she felt that if he didn't love her now, he never would.

She hadn't put hooks in half the second box of ornaments when Mrs. Hood came in bearing a tray that she set down on the coffee table.

"Hot chocolate and oatmeal-raisin cookies," she

announced. "If you don't like that, there's different cookies in the kitchen."

"This is just fine," Nick said. "Won't you join us?"

"Thanks, but I've got to get on with dinner. I'm anxious to get home."

"Let's finish this box of ornaments before we stop," Michael said. "Once I start eating, it's hard to go back to work."

"Maybe I'll ration out the cookies," Ellen said. "You hang six ornaments and you get a cookie."

Michael did a rapid calculation. "That's seven more boxes of ornaments with no more than a dozen in each box. If Dad gets his share, I won't get more than seven cookies."

"I should think not," Ellen said. "It would spoil your dinner. And your waistline."

"She hadn't intended to add that last bit, but with all this bending and stretching and leaning, she'd become very much aware of Michael's body. As far as she could see, there wasn't a flaw in it.

"You like my waistline?"

He was teasing her. She had put herself on the spot, and he was enjoying it.

"You've obviously kept trim and fit. But I guess that would be necessary, since you must run around in hardly anything most of the time."

Nick Wetherford burst out laughing. "She thinks you've gone native."

Michael winced. "I know. She's already made some cutting comments about grass skirts. I told her we go in for brightly colored cottons instead."

"Too bad," his father said. "You had me thinking I might make a visit to check out what goes on."

"We're a family resort. I keep away from the swinging singles set."

"That's the story he tells," Ellen said to Nick. "But can we believe him? Who would go all that way to spend a vacation with the wife and children?"

"Fortunately for me, lots of people," Michael said. "Now stop trying to give me a hard time and open another box of ornaments. I'm hungry for some more cookies."

Instead of a new box, Ellen reached for a box discolored and made fragile by age. She carefully removed the top and lifted out an ornament. "This is made of glass," she said. "It must be very old."

"It is," Michael said. "It's—"

"It's one of the ornaments Michael's mother bought the Christmas before she died," Nick said. He reached out and took it from Ellen. "She found them in a catalog. She ordered them all the way from England."

"I didn't think you'd remember," Michael said.

"Is that what made you think of the Christmas tree?" he asked.

Michael nodded.

"Maybe I won't empty everything out of the attic," Nick said. "There might be a few more memories up there I'd like to keep."

Ellen felt as though she were intruding on something that should have been shared by Michael and his father alone. But they seemed unaware of her. For a moment they simply looked at each other, each with a softened expression.

"I'm coming home this summer," Michael said. "We can look for them together."

Ellen wiped a tear from her eyes. Stupid men, she thought to herself. Here they were having a magical moment, and she was the only one crying.

Chapter Seven

"We thought you were going to miss dinner," Michael said when Ellen's car came to a stop in the driveway. He didn't have to see the packages in the back seat to know she'd been out buying presents.

"Not a chance," she said, getting out of the car. She started gathering up packages.

"Here, let me help you with some of those."

Ellen loaded him down with boxes.

"Hey, I need to see where I'm going!" The pile had reached his nose.

"I can handle the rest."

"Good. Tell me if I have to step over something. I can't see my feet."

"Just follow me."

"Is that an invitation or an order?"

He didn't know what could have prompted him to make a leading statement like that. He'd said it in jest only to realize it meant a great deal more than that.

"Which do you want it to be?"

A tricky question. He couldn't be sure. Considering her outburst this afternoon, he couldn't expect it to be an invitation. He wished he could see her expression, but she kept walking and didn't turn around. He'd hardly stopped thinking about her since he had kissed her last night. It hadn't been much of a kiss, just a brushing of her lips, but it had galvanized him to such an extent that he'd lain awake until well after midnight.

"It's going to take another kiss before I can be sure about my answer."

"Is that an invitation?"

"Do you want it to be?"

She turned around. For a moment her expression looked guarded, as though she weren't willing to take him seriously. Then she smiled. "I think so. There's a step coming up, so watch out."

A good thing she had warned him. He'd have fallen flat on his face. Mrs. Hood held the back door for him.

"You all keep this up, and you're going to need another tree."

"I know it looks like a lot, but it's not," Ellen said.

"Mr. Wetherford's been on his portable phone half the afternoon. While Michael was seeing about firewood, he was ordering enough stuff to fill a warehouse. It's been arriving in fits and starts all afternoon."

"Firewood?" Ellen asked.

"For us and the orphanage," Michael said. "The children looked cold. The weatherman predicts snow and freezing rain for the next week. I want you and Dad to be warm after I leave."

The reminder of where he'd be going in a few days didn't brighten her spirits.

"Give me some of those packages," Mrs. Hood said. "You'll be falling over your own feet in a minute."

Michael followed the two women into the family room. The mound of presents supported Mrs. Hood's contention that his father was buying too much.

"At least now you won't be able to complain about my giving you too many presents," Michael said. "Dad will outnumber me two to one."

"Most of them are for you," Mrs. Hood said before leaving the room.

"And they should be," Ellen said, apparently pleased at the shocked expression she was certain was on his face.

"But what could he be giving me?" Michael asked.

"You'll find out tomorrow. That's what Christmas morning is for."

"I could just as well ask what you're giving me."

"You'd have to answer that question for me first."

"Let's put everything under the tree. Then we can argue over who's given whom too many presents." Michael stepped across a mound of presents. "If you'll hand them to me, I'll put some behind the tree."

"Don't hide them. We don't want to miss them tomorrow."

"Don't worry. I never forget presents or invitations."

"What?"

"Invitations."

"Oh."

"Regretting it?"

"No."

"You look like it."

"Look out with that present, or you'll knock the ornaments off the tree."

"You've got me off balance. I can't help myself."

"I prescribe aspirin and a nap."

"I'd like a different prescription."

"Such as?"

"You could offer to put your arms around me to help me keep my balance."

"If you act like this with all the women you meet, I'm not surprised your resort is a resounding success."

"I've never felt this way about a woman." He hadn't meant to be quite so frank about his feelings, but he'd let a game of tit-for-tat get out of hand. He settled the last present into place and stepped from behind the tree. "I need to know if you feel anything for me."

She appeared unprepared for his frankness.

"It's a little soon for that, don't you think?"

"Not when you've been hit by an avalanche. If I were prone to infatuations, I wouldn't pay any attention, but I'm not."

"Me either."

"Did an avalanche hit you?"

"It felt like it."

He put his hands on her shoulders. She didn't move away. "Don't you want to know what that means?"

She nodded.

He stepped forward and, gathering her into his arms, clasped her body tightly to his. Then he kissed her. It seemed surreal, standing in his father's house kissing a woman he'd known less than two days. It was also something that now that he'd begun, he couldn't stop. He didn't want to stop. His hands locked against her spine, bringing her closer. When she slipped her arms around him, he wanted to lose himself in the sweetness of her lips.

He felt a tight knot inside himself begin to unravel. It baffled him until he realized the knot had been wound tightly around his heart, protecting it from hurt by keeping love out, telling him he didn't want love, that it only brought pain.

But kissing Ellen, holding her in his arms, was a balm powerful enough to erase decades of denial. This wasn't infatuation. He loved her. He knew it just as surely as he knew he would never grow tired of the feel of her in his arms, never grow tired of kissing her. She had opened his father's heart, giving them both a love they had thought permanently beyond their reach. Now she'd loosened the fetters on his own heart and cast them aside. It would be impossible to love her too much.

Ellen hadn't been prepared to be swept up in Michael's embrace and ruthlessly kissed without warning or prelude. The intensity of his kiss left her breathless, wanting more yet wondering if her own feelings were a match for his. He had rushed past circling the prey, ignored exploration and discovery, and gone straight to pursuit and capture. She didn't know if she could keep up, wasn't certain she wanted to be in the race.

Then he crushed her to him, reclaiming her lips, and her doubt was swallowed by the hunger of his kisses. They sent spirals of ecstasy through her, set the pit of her belly into a wild swirl. Standing on tiptoe, she returned his kiss with passionate energy, shocked by her own eager response to the touch of his lips.

His lips left hers to nibble at her earlobe, then sear a path down her neck. Then his mouth recaptured hers. Casting aside any lingering doubts, she returned his kiss with reckless abandon.

Maybe rational people couldn't fall in love in one day, but she could. Maybe the average woman couldn't be happy living in a resort hotel with her husband the focus of so much female attention, but she could. She could endure anything as long as, when they were finally alone together, he would hold her just as he was holding her now, kiss her as he was kissing her now.

He planted a tantalizing kiss in the hollow of her neck, scattered kisses along her jaw, anointed her eyelids with them. A nagging voice warned her that he was a masterful man, but she reminded the voice that masterful was quite different from controlling. She didn't mind masterful. In fact, she liked it quite a bit.

Their idyll was interrupted by a hoot and the sound of clapping hands. They broke apart and turned to see Nick standing in the doorway, his hands clasped together, his face wreathed in a huge smile.

"I knew you were perfect for each other," he crowed. "I knew if I could get you together, you'd know it, too."

"We were just kissing, Dad," Michael said, his arm still firmly around Ellen's waist.

"That's all you'd better think about doing for the time being, young man. I stand in place of her father."

"You can't be the father of the bride *and* the groom."

"Who said anything about brides and grooms?" Ellen asked.

"I only meant . . . well, after what Dad said . . . forget it."

"I don't intend to forget it," Ellen said. "I want to know what you meant."

"I'll tell you when long ears isn't around."

"You can't tell her without this," his father said. He took something out of his pocket and dropped it into Michael's pocket. "I've been carrying it around for two days just in case," he said to Michael. "Now I'm going to see what Mrs. Hood has left us for dinner. I'm starved."

"Your father's never starved," Ellen said. "I usually have to coax him to eat."

But Michael wasn't paying her any attention. He had put his hand in his pocket to see what his father had put there, but he didn't draw it out. As she waited, a strange expression spread over his face. Startled bewilderment was as close as she could come to describing it. Then gradually it turned into a smile.

"What is it?" she asked.

"Close your eyes and hold out your hand."

She cocked her head.

"Don't you have faith in me?"

"Yes." She closed her eyes and held out her right hand.

"Your left," he said.

A weakness attacked Ellen. She wasn't sure she could stand up any longer without holding on to something. This couldn't be what she thought. It was too soon. He couldn't possibly—

She felt a ring slip on her finger. Her eyes flew open. The ring Michael had just put on her finger was mounted with a perfect sapphire surrounded by at least a dozen diamonds. She raised her gaze to meet his. "What . . ."

"It's my mother's engagement ring," he said. "Apparently my father couldn't wait for me to find one of my own."

"But . . ."

"You're going to have to learn to finish your sentences."

"You can't mean . . ."

"It's worse than I thought. Maybe this will clear your head." He kissed her gently. "Will you marry me?"

"I don't know if I should. I'll probably make a terrible wife. I can't promise not to be jealous of all those beautiful women."

109

"I've decided to sell the resorts."

"You can't do that because of me."

"I'm doing it for myself. I've finally realized that everything I've done for the last ten years, I've done because of anger. I don't want to do that anymore. I want to spend time with Dad, help him with his business. And I don't want to have to snatch moments from work so we can be together. I think we've both seen enough of that in our parents. The best way to change is to come home and start over. After a while, we can decide together what we want to do."

"Are you sure?"

"Quite sure."

The tension inside her relaxed. "I have one condition," she said.

"What's that?"

"That you put in a standing order for grapes. I think I'd like very much for you to eat them from my navel every morning."

Silver Bells

Amanda Harte

Chapter One

"Look, Mom, gridlock!"

Ignoring the cabby's low muttering, Karen Lang smiled at her daughter. Jill was staring raptly at the snarled traffic, a grin lighting her face as her eyes moved from the sight of pedestrians darting between stopped cars to the grandeur of New York's skyscrapers, their upper stories shrouded in clouds. "That's gridlock, all right. Of course, it's probably worse than usual today because of Christmas and the rain."

"You can say that again," the driver groused. "Worst time of the year."

Karen repressed a sigh. She should have arranged a limo, but Jill—for reasons that made sense only to a 14-year-old—had been adamant about wanting to take a taxi. "Limo are for geezers," she had informed her mother with a toss of her long brown hair. "Taxis are fierce," she had added, using what appeared to be the latest term of teenage approbation. And so they sat in traffic outside the Lincoln Tunnel in a dented yellow cab, listening to the blare of horns rather than being ensconced in luxury, watching TV or enjoying the contents of a mini-bar.

It was far from Karen's preferred way to travel from Newark airport into Manhattan, but the sight of her daughter's rare smile told her the taxi's rough ride and torn upholstery were part of Jill's dream. And dreams, Karen knew all too well, rarely came true. If a battered cab was what it took to make her child happy, a few jolts and a pair of ripped stockings were a small price to pay.

Jill rolled down the window and leaned out, sniffing the moist, exhaust-laden air. "I don't care about the rain," she announced. "It's romantic."

The cabby snickered, and Karen bit back a smile. It seemed like a hundred years since she had been as young and excited as Jill, and she wasn't certain she had ever considered rain romantic, not even when she and Alex . . . Refusing to continue that thought, she touched Jill's shoulder. "I thought you wanted snow."

"Oh, I do, but . . ." Jill gasped as the clouds lifted. "That's the Empire State Building! Fierce!"

Karen laughed. It was good, so unbelievably good, to see her solemn daughter happy again. As tears pricked the back of her eyes, Karen forced them away. There was no point in thinking about what might have been, of regretting that she had waited so long to bring Jill to Manhattan. They were here now, and that was what mattered.

The light changed, and the cab inched forward, its windshield wipers chattering on the glass.

"This is so cool," Jill said as she settled back in the seat. "Wait 'til I tell Matt."

"You can wait until the rates go down before you call him," Karen said with mock severity.

"Oh, Mom!" Jill rolled her eyes. "Like I didn't know that." She pressed her nose against the window, apparently entranced by the sight of a dozen dueling umbrellas. A moment later, Karen heard a small sniff.

"What's wrong, honey?" she asked.

Though Jill refused to face her, Karen heard the tears in her voice. "I wish Dad was with us."

"Me, too."

They rode in silence for a few minutes until they reached Times Square. "Fierce!" Jill declared, her eyes widening as she looked at the neon and glitter of the New York landmark. "Just like on TV." She chattered brightly, and Karen, realizing Jill was trying to banish her blues in the only way she knew, joined in, pointing out the garlands that draped a storefront, the oversized ornaments that filled another window, and the Sidewalk Santas who stood next to members of the Salvation Army, ringing their brass bells and appealing to the pedestrians' generosity.

But when the cab at last swung south onto Fifth Avenue and pulled up in front of a building with an ornate European façade and a burgundy-and-gold awning stretching from the door to the street, Jill was suddenly silent. "Is this it?" she asked.

"You said the Burgundy, didn't you, lady?" the cab driver demanded as he pulled the trunk release.

"That's right." Karen added a generous tip to the fare. "Checking in," she told the doorman, whose black top hat, black gloves, and burgundy formal coat with gold-and-black trim had caused Jill's eyes to widen again.

"Oh, Mom, this is awesome!" Jill whispered as they entered the lobby.

Though the hotel Karen had chosen was only five

years old, its dark wood paneling, polished marble floors, and traditional furnishings gave it the appearance of a European mansion of far greater age.

"If you would have a seat, madam." The doorman gestured toward a small Louis XIV desk, where a perfectly groomed young woman sat, apparently waiting for Karen and Jill. As she looked around, Karen saw other similar desks, all staffed with attractive men and women in burgundy blazers and white shirts. This, it appeared, was the Burgundy's answer to long registration lines.

Within minutes, she and Jill were escorted to their room.

"Awesome!" Jill repeated, her eyes widening as she explored the spacious suite. Karen smiled. She had chosen the Burgundy for its unique atmosphere and had crossed her fingers that Jill would approve.

Jill tugged on the drapery cord. "Look at the crowds," she said, gazing down at Fifth Avenue.

Karen joined her daughter. From their vantage on the top floor, the pedestrians and cars looked like toy figures, smaller even than the miniatures she had once bought for Jill's dollhouse, while across the street, Central Park promised a respite from the city's bustle.

"It's not quite like Wyoming, is it?" Karen asked, picturing the vast open ranges of their home, where cattle and antelope outnumbered humans.

Jill shook her head, apparently mesmerized by the sight of so many people in one space. The storm had intensified, with rain lashing against the window, leaving the sky so dark it could have been early evening rather than mid-afternoon. "I hate rain," she complained.

"I thought you said it was romantic." This was the old familiar Jill, with her mercurial mood changes.

"Not anymore. How are we gonna go shopping in this rain?"

Karen forbore mentioning that the hotel probably supplied umbrellas for its guests. "The concierge said there are fifty shops in the arcade," she said. "We can check them out, and maybe by then the rain will have stopped."

"Cool."

Karen gave her hair a quick brushing, thankful that the short style which was so practical in the Wyoming wind would not wilt in New York rain. The curls Jill had inherited from her father had tightened in the moisture, a fact she was currently bemoaning.

"Wear a hat," Karen suggested.

"Oh, Mom . . ." Hats, it appeared, were not "fierce."

The elevator bore them swiftly to the lower lobby, where a myriad of specialty stores beckoned shoppers to explore the wonders of designer chocolates, handmade sweaters, delicate lingerie, and toys gathered from every corner of the world. Identical garlands of evergreens dressed with shiny balls and red velvet bows draped each of the doorways, giving the arcade a uniformly festive air, though no two windows had similar displays. And everywhere they walked, their steps muffled by the thick carpet that lined the halls, they heard the soft sounds of Christmas carols mingling with shoppers' voices.

Karen hummed as the haunting sounds of "White Christmas" filled the arcade.

"Will we have a white Christmas?" Jill asked her.

"I wouldn't count on it." Though not impossible, snow at Christmas was far from guaranteed in Manhattan. Even when the suburbs had a dusting of the white stuff, the city's streets were frequently bare.

"Look!" Jill pointed at a sweater with an appliqued

117

reindeer that sported an oversized red nose. "Do you suppose Matt would like that?"

"To wear?" Karen could not imagine her daughter's boyfriend in such a whimsical garment.

Jill laughed. "No, silly. Would he like it on me?"

Before Karen could answer, Jill had rushed to the next window and was considering the merits of two pairs of running shoes. Karen followed at a slower pace, smiling at three women whose enormous shopping bags were overflowing with wrapped and beribboned boxes. She stopped to retrieve the tattered teddy bear a young boy had tossed out of his stroller. As his obviously frazzled mother murmured her gratitude, the music changed.

Karen's heart faltered, then began to race as if she had chased Tom's horse around the paddock too many times. "Silver Bells." Only a naïve woman would have thought she could escape the song, especially here in New York, the quintessential setting for the melody that had once been Karen's favorite Christmas carol. It was only a song, she told herself. In two and a half minutes, it would be over. There was no reason, no reason on earth, to remember what the melody had once meant to her.

"Mom, look! Aren't these the fiercest earrings?"

Grateful for the distraction, Karen followed her daughter into the elegantly decorated jewelry store. Perhaps the music was piped only into the hallways. Perhaps Jill's voice would drown out the tinkling notes.

"So, where are these perfect earrings?" she asked, looking into the glass-topped display case.

"Right there, second one . . ."

Before Jill could finish her sentence, a man called out, "Karen? Karen Stevens!"

* * *

Alex Bradford was not having a good day. In fact, he was not having a good week. The last ten days before Christmas were always hectic, trying to finish the custom pieces that positively, absolutely had to be ready for Santa to place under the tree. This year, as he had every year since he had taken over the business, he had agreed to make more jewelry than any sane person ought to. He would work literally night and day to complete them, using the special orders as an excuse to avoid the seemingly endless parties and dinners that were part of the holiday season. It was better that his employees believed he was driven by greed than that they knew the real reason he turned into Scrooge each December.

His schedule was ambitious, aggressive, insane—but doable. Until this week. Why couldn't that new strain of flu have waited a mere seven days? But no, it had made its appearance early enough to wreak havoc on Alex's life. Not one, not two, but six employees were home sick, with two more looking as if they wouldn't last the day. Even if he had wanted to hire temporary staff, there were none to be found this close to Christmas. And so Alex had promised his remaining clerks enormous bonuses if they would work double shifts in the main store, while he manned the boutique in the Burgundy's arcade.

"I'm sure your daughter will like the bracelet, Mrs. Flannery," he said as the attractive blonde slid the wide gold bangle onto her arm for what had to be the twentieth time. Three other women waited patiently for him to ring up their purchases, while a man crossed and uncrossed his arms as regularly as a metronome.

Mrs. Flannery looked dubious. "Are you sure this is what girls her age wear?" she demanded.

Alex nodded. The woman had brought him a magazine ad showing the same bracelet. Her daughter had apparently dog-eared and circled it, then left it lying open for her mother to find. And still Mrs. Flannery was uncertain!

Saying a silent prayer of thanksgiving that he had no children, Alex smiled at his customer. "Shall I wrap it for you?"

As he handed Mrs. Flannery her charge slip and the carefully wrapped box, the music that the hotel piped into all the stores changed. Not that one! Alex clenched his jaw. That one ought to be outlawed. "City sidewalks . . . " He fixed a smile on his face and turned to his next customer.

"May I help you?"

After all this time, a stupid Christmas song shouldn't turn his brain to mush. He was thirty-six years old, for God's sake. He ought to be past that. It was nothing more than a sentimental tune that brought thousands of people into the city each year looking for the Christmas spirit. An outworn melody shouldn't have the power to remind him of a tall girl whose brown eyes sparkled every time she heard it, a girl who had once told him "Silver Bells" was their song.

"I'd like to see the emerald necklace in the window," the next woman in line said.

Grabbing the large key ring, Alex followed her, his eyes moving around the store, assessing the other customers. The arm-folding man was annoyed, but he would wait. The older woman who had been eyeing the pearl earrings was visibly tired; Alex would find her a chair. The dark-haired woman and her daughter . . .

Alex felt the blood drain from his face. No! It couldn't be! It was that damned song again, making him think of her. There was simply no way she could be here. And yet . . .

"Karen?" She turned, and her eyes widened in surprise the way they had all those years ago. The odds were a million to one. Make that a billion to one. She was supposed to be thousands of miles away, and yet here she was, in his store while that infernal stereo played their song. Who said miracles didn't happen?

"Karen Stevens!"

Chapter Two

Karen spun around so quickly that her shoulder bag bumped Jill's arm.

"Alex!" Her cry was involuntary, wrenched from somewhere deep inside her as she saw the face that had haunted her dreams for so many months.

It couldn't be Alex. She was tired. She had jet lag. It was that damned Christmas carol. There had to be a logical explanation why her eyes and ears were deceiving her, making her think the dark-haired man whose eyes crinkled behind his stylish glasses was Alex.

"Do you know him?" Jill wore a worried expression.

Did she know him? Oh, yes! His hair was a bit shorter now, making the waves that had been the bane of his youth less evident, and a few strands of silver threaded through the brown. There were lines on what had been a smooth face, and his shoulders looked as though he had carried through with his threat to invest in—and use—a home gym. Did she know him? Without a doubt.

Karen put her hand on Jill's shoulder, not sure whether she was reassuring her daughter or drawing strength from her.

"This is Alex Bradford," she said in a voice that sounded amazingly normal. "He was one of my friends in college. Alex, I'd like you to meet my daughter, Jill."

As Jill winced, Karen realized that she had tightened her grip. She let her hand drop to her side, then extended it to Alex. Old friends shook hands, didn't they?

He took a step forward, clasping her hand between both of his. "I can't believe it," he said.

"Sir." A middle-aged woman who had been standing next to Alex raised her voice. "The emerald necklace." She pointed toward the display case behind Karen and Jill.

Necklace. Of course. As she looked at the glass-fronted display, Karen saw the stylized lower-case *b* that had been a Bradford tradition for three generations. The font was different now, more modern, but the logo and the name remained the same. Karen had once teased Alex about the store's name, accusing him of reverse snobbism. After all, the items his family sold were hardly the trinkets the name 'Bagatelle' implied. "That's the point," he'd argued, insisting that their designs appealed to customers with a sense of humor. "We're not your typical jewelers." She had never disputed that fact. Nothing about Alex was or ever would be ordinary.

"I thought your shop was in the Diamond District," she said. How absurd! She hadn't seen the man in half a lifetime, and the only thing she could talk about was his store's location.

"The main store is," he agreed, and Karen was suddenly aware that he was still holding her hand. She ought to pull it away, yet her muscles refused to execute the commands her brain was sending them. Instead, she noticed that though he was wearing a large ring on his right hand, his left was bare. That meant nothing, of course. Many married men did not wear wedding rings.

"We have branches here and in the Trade Center," Alex continued.

The middle-aged woman touched Alex's arm. "Sir!"

Karen flashed the woman an apologetic smile. "I'm sorry we interrupted," she said. Then, turning back to Alex, she drew her hand from his. "It was nice seeing you again." The music had changed. Now the stereo was playing "Here Comes Santa Claus." Thank goodness! She did not want to hear another verse of "Silver Bells," especially with Alex Bradford at her side.

She started to move away. Alex's eyes darkened. "You can't just disappear," he protested. Glancing at his watch, he said, "The store closes at eight. Can I take you and . . ." His gaze moved to Jill, and Karen sensed that he was trying to recall her name. ". . . Jill," he said confidently, "to dinner?"

Karen turned to Jill. Her daughter was twisting a lock of hair between two fingers in a nervous gesture Karen thought she had outgrown. Even if she wanted to have dinner with Alex, which of course she did not, she would not spoil Jill's trip to New York. "It's our first day here," she said in a voice that somehow did not reveal her turmoil, "and I promised Jill a meal of street-vendor food."

The woman at Alex's side sniffed her disapproval. This customer, it appeared, lacked the sense of humor that was supposed to characterize Bagatelle's shoppers.

"I see." Though he continued to smile, Karen recognized the disappointment clouding Alex's eyes. "Maybe another day."

"You can come with us, if you want." Karen turned, as surprised by Jill's offer as the smile she flashed with it.

For the first time, Karen regretted the etiquette lessons she and Tom had given Jill. Why did her daughter have to be so polite? Now there was no way to avoid spending the evening with Alex.

How could it have happened? In a city of seven million people, why was she with the one person she most definitely did not want to see? She had been so careful, choosing a hotel that was far from both his store and his home so there would be no chance encounters. Though Jill loved jewelry, Karen had prepared an arsenal of reasons why they weren't going to the Diamond District on this trip, because that would have taken them too close to Bagatelle. There should have been no chance, no chance at all, of meeting Alex Bradford; yet here he was.

"So, is Alex an old boyfriend, or what?"

Jill sprawled on the couch in their hotel parlor, pointing the remote at the TV. Though Karen had agreed to her daughter's request for a taxi, she had refused to back down on her hotel choice and had insisted on a suite. Jill was the dearest girl in the world, but a week was more time than Karen wanted to share a room with her, and so she had reserved one of the Burgundy's executive suites. Designed for entertaining, it boasted a living room with a big-screen TV and a fully stocked bar, and two bedrooms, one on each side of the parlor.

When they had checked in, Jill had eyed the phone in her room with approval, and Karen knew she was thinking of the privacy she would have when she called Matt. Now, however, she was regarding her mother with an expression that said, while Jill might value her own privacy, she owed her mother none, especially not on the subject of a strange man who appeared to have shared part of her past.

"So, was Alex one of your boyfriends?" she repeated.

Karen raised one brow. "His name is Mr. Bradford."

"Okay," Jill agreed with a wrinkle of her nose. "So, did you and Mr. Bradford . . ."

"You know your dad and I started going steady in high school." That much was true. "Alex was one of my classmates." That was also true. If it wasn't the whole truth, well . . . there were some things Jill did not need to know.

"Art class?" Apparently accepting her explanation, Jill moved on to the next question. When Karen nodded, Jill pushed the channel-advance button and considered which of the hundred-plus stations she wanted to watch.

"Do you suppose Alex . . ."

"Mr. Bradford."

Jill grinned. " . . . designed some of that jewelry in his store? It was fierce."

They were on safe ground again. "I'm sure he did. Alex's father and grandfather were jewelers—very good ones, from what I've heard—but even in school, our professors said that Alex had a special talent." Though Karen had enjoyed her art classes, she had had no illusions about her talent. She could be a competent artisan, creating beautiful pieces from someone else's designs, but she would win no awards for her own creations.

"That is so cool." Jill leaned back, narrowing her eyes as she watched a popular musician perform his rendition of "Joy to the World." "Maybe he'll show me his shop. I'll bet he's got some really great tools."

Karen had no intention of seeing Alex again after tonight, and there was no way she would allow Jill to visit him, but she knew the allure of the forbidden, and so she said only, "Honey, it's the busiest time of the year for a jeweler. You don't want to impose on him."

With a click, Jill changed the stations. "Oh, Mom, I'm not a kid. I know that, but if Mr. Bradford offers . . ." She let her voice trail off.

Karen nodded. She would make certain Alex offered no invitations.

"Well, ladies," Alex said when they met him in the hotel's lobby, "I don't know how you arranged it, but it's stopped raining."

He put a hand on the back of Karen's waist to guide her toward the door. It was ridiculous, of course, to think that she could feel the warmth of his hand through all the layers of clothing. It was equally ridiculous for her pulse to race. That was what fatigue did to a person. Either that or being back at sea level after living at 6,000 feet for so many years. It had nothing to do with the man whose brown eyes sparkled with mischief as he ushered her into the revolving door, making her wonder whether he was going to squeeze in with her and . . . Of course he wasn't going to do that!

"Okay, Jill," he said when they stood on the sidewalk. Evening had fallen, and while the rain had indeed stopped, the mist formed halos around the street lights. The doorman, though too well trained to say anything, looked askance when Alex told him they were walking. "What do you want to eat—hot dogs, sausage, pretzels, roasted chestnuts, ice cream, Italian ice?" Alex tipped his head to the side in a gesture that brought back heart-wrenching memories. "The kiosks in the park," he said with a nod in that direction, "have sandwiches, pound cake, and gourmet coffee."

"Everything." Jill did not hesitate.

"Everything?"

Karen laughed. "You obviously don't have a teenager, Alex. She means that literally. The good news is, we don't have to keep up with her."

Jill shook her head in apparent disgust. "You guys are no fun. Now, are we eating or not?"

As they crossed 59th Street and headed south on Fifth Avenue, the crowds thickened, and the cacophony of horns and sirens rose to an almost deafening level.

Alex shot Karen a conspiratorial look as he paid for their hot dogs. "Somehow, I think Lutece or Le Cirque would have been better."

Jill was not convinced. "This is fierce!" she declared and swallowed her first bite, then smiled as if she had eaten ambrosia.

"Fierce?" Alex's glasses winked in the streetlight as he raised a questioning eyebrow.

"Better than 'cool,' " Karen explained.

Though Jill seemed eager to continue walking, Karen guided them to a raised planter in front of an office building. Here foot traffic was less intense, and they could use the concrete blocks as a table, eating while they admired the beautifully decorated lobby. A huge tree draped with thousands of white lights dominated the three-story entrance, but it was the founder's statue that made Karen's lips curve. Someone with a sense of humor had placed a Santa's hat and red bow on the bust of a man better known as a robber baron than a benefactor.

Relaxing for the first time since she had seen Alex, Karen took a swallow of soda and smiled at him. "This actually tastes good," she admitted as she bit into her hot dog.

"Fierce," he corrected her.

Jill wrinkled her nose. "Food doesn't taste fierce," she explained. "I guess you don't have any kids, or you'd know that." In a roundabout way Jill had asked the question that had been nagging at the back of Karen's consciousness since she'd noticed Alex's ring-free left hand.

"Nope," he agreed in a tone that made it clear he had no regrets. "No kids. Not even a wife anymore. Celia and I were divorced five years ago." He crumpled his wax paper into a ball, then looked around for a trash can.

So Alex had married. She shouldn't have been surprised; after all, she had married Tom. Karen tried not to picture Alex with a woman named Celia, sliding his ring onto her finger, kissing his bride, and then later exploring every inch of her body with those long fingers that could turn the simplest touch into a blood-boiling caress. She would not—absolutely would not—think about that.

"Ready?"

They walked slowly down Fifth Avenue, stopping to buy Jill another hot dog and a sack of roasted chestnuts. Though Karen had expected crowds, the reality exceeded even her most extravagant flights of imagination. Throngs of tourists filled the streets, moving shoulder to shoulder in what appeared to be a sea of smiling faces. They waited patiently at intersections, and when the lights turned green, the results were predictable.

"It's gridlock, Mom. Human gridlock."

Karen laughed as much at the joyous wonder she saw on her daughter's face as at Jill's description. It was an accurate one, for when the two opposing waves of humanity met in the center of the street, neither could move.

"Want to try Park?"

Jill would not consider Alex's suggestion. "Fifth is . . ."

"Fierce?" he asked.

Jill grinned and kept walking, her eyes darting from one beautifully decorated store window to the next. "Tiffany's, Trump Tower." She murmured the names, obviously still awed by seeing the city of her dreams.

Karen felt tears prickle the back of her eyes. No matter what heartache she suffered, what bittersweet memories this visit evoked, she could not regret coming—not when she saw Jill's happiness.

And there was no doubt Jill was happy. She ooh'ed over the store window filled with eight-foot-high gingerbread cookies, ah'ed over the fifteen-story building that was tied with a gigantic red ribbon, and sighed over the hundreds of colored lights whose twinkle turned even ordinary shopwindows into a wonderland.

"Oh, Mom! That's the most beautiful tree I've ever seen." They had reached Rockefeller Center. Though Karen would have thought it impossible, the crowds were even more dense here. Fathers lifted children onto their shoulders to show them the country's most famous tree, while mothers pointed out the white angels standing among the evergreens, and couples, their arms wrapped around each other's waists, patiently queued for the skating rink.

"Do you want to skate?" Karen asked.

"By myself?" Jill's eyes clouded, and Karen was suddenly reminded that her daughter, for all her seeming poise, was only a teenager, unaccustomed to crowds and city life.

Karen shook her head. "If it's not too uncool . . ." She smiled when Jill grimaced at the word. ". . . I'd like to skate, too."

Jill nodded, her relief tangible.

"Want to watch an old man wobble on the ice?" As Alex mimicked an unsteady gait, Jill's smile turned into a full-fledged grin.

"Cool!" she announced. "But don't expect me to pick you up when you fall."

"He won't," Karen cautioned her daughter. "Alex used to be a pretty good skater."

"A hundred years ago!"

"Sure!"

Her skates pinched, the rink was crowded, her ankles buckled at the most inopportune times, and it was magic—pure magic. As the PA system began to play "God Rest Ye Merry Gentlemen," Alex, whose ankles seemed to be made of steel while hers were definitely rubber, skated to a stop in front of her, then held out his hands.

"Come on," he encouraged her, skating backwards and pulling her along.

Jill flashed her a smile, then turned her attention to the teenager who had deserted his parents a few minutes earlier, seemingly content to skate in Jill's wake.

For a moment, as Alex smiled at her, Karen forgot that she was a thirty-six-year-old mother who hadn't been on skates in five years. Instead, she was transported back to the last time she had skated with Alex, holding hands as they'd glided around the rink in Central Park, smiling at the crescent moon. A light snow had been falling, landing on her eyelashes, coating Alex's glasses, turning the park into a winter wonderland. Half blinded, they had continued to skate, laughing as the music changed to a faster song, challenging them to keep up the pace.

Karen blinked. It felt like a lifetime since she had been so young and carefree.

"Something wrong?"

She forced a smile onto her face. "Just getting old, I guess." It was as good an excuse as any for moving away from Alex and those unwanted memories.

He crooked a finger at Jill. "Can I interest you in some hot chocolate?" He could use something stronger, and he bet Karen could, too.

Jill shook her head with the same fluid motion that her mother used. At times Jill looked so much like Karen that Alex wanted to call her by her mother's name. "I'm not thirsty, but you and Mom can go." Jill rolled her eyes. "I know how old folks have to rest."

Karen laughed and straightened Jill's collar. "The rough translation of that is, she wants to skate with that guy who's been following her around the rink."

"Oh, Mom!"

"Oh, Jill!"

She sounded so much like her daughter that Alex couldn't help laughing as he led Karen from the ice. "I figured Jill wanted some time alone with young Romeo. Not that anyone is really alone out there." Strangely, his memories of the times he and Karen had skated together did not include anyone else. Had New York been less crowded fifteen years ago, or had he forgotten?

"What brought you to New York this year, or is this an annual event?" he asked when they had ordered their drinks. It was stupid asking the question when he didn't want to know the answer. He didn't want to think Karen had been here every year and hadn't called him, but then, why would she? She had made it clear enough fifteen years ago that he was not a permanent part of her life. A passing fancy, she had called him. Odd, how that had hurt.

"No." Karen shook her head, and the small gold hoop earrings she wore bounced against her cheeks. "This is the first time since . . . " She broke off her sentence, then changed the subject. "From the time she was old enough to watch the tree-lighting on TV, Jill has been pestering me to come here. This year I finally agreed."

She looked so beautiful sitting across from him in the crowded restaurant—more beautiful even than she had in college. Her hair was still as short and shiny as he remembered, and if there were faint lines at the corners of her eyes, they only added to her beauty, telling Alex that she was no longer a girl, but a mature woman. Still, a hint of sorrow that hadn't been there before now clung to her, and when she didn't think he was watching, she would twist her wide gold wedding band. Was she missing her husband? Alex didn't want to think about that.

"How long are you staying?" he asked. Most tourists came for a couple of days, then headed home for the actual holiday.

Karen's answer surprised him. "Until the twenty-seventh." She took a sip of the coffee she had insisted was strong enough for her, holding the mug in both hands. Alex couldn't help smiling as he remembered the nights they had studied together, drinking pots of coffee to stay awake, and how he had teased her about being a two-fisted drinker.

"Jill's got a list a mile long of things she wants to do," Karen continued, her smile chasing the shadows from her eyes, if only momentarily. "I swear she's planned every minute of our stay—shopping, museums, shopping, sightseeing, shopping . . . You get the idea."

Alex shuddered. "It sounds like a dream for her, but more like a nightmare for you. As I recall, you don't like crowds."

Karen refused to meet his gaze, and he realized that she was unwilling to indulge in a game of "remember when." Wise woman, for that game led to "if only," and that one always ended in heartache.

"It's Jill's trip, and I want it to be perfect for her. So far, there's only been one hitch: I couldn't get tickets for her number-one choice of a play." When she named the show, Alex nodded. Since it had opened on Broadway, *Jane Eyre* had played to capacity audiences, and the only tickets to be had were at scalpers' exorbitant prices. Now that the holidays had arrived, even the scalpers had no tickets.

Alex drank the last of his coffee. "Jill doesn't look like someone who'd pout over missing a show." From their spot next to the window, they could see Jill as she skated by, her face glowing with enthusiasm over something her companion said, her smile no longer looking like Karen's and yet seeming somehow familiar.

"She's not a pouter," Karen confirmed, then looked at her watch and shook her head when the waitress offered refills. The skating session was almost over.

Alex rose and held Karen's jacket for her. "You must be very proud of Jill." He knew he would be, if he were her parent.

"Oh, I am!" Pure pleasure lit Karen's face. Good lord, she was beautiful when she smiled like that! He should never have let her go. But, Alex reminded himself, he hadn't let Karen go. He had done everything he could to keep her, and it hadn't been enough. She had left him for another man.

Alex clenched his hands, then forced himself to

relax them before he asked the question that had haunted him all evening.

"Your husband . . ." Alex searched for his name. "Tom? Why didn't he come with you?"

There was a moment of silence, and Alex knew he had asked the wrong question. For a second, he thought she would refuse to answer him, but as a wave of pain swept over her face and moisture glinted in her eyes, she said, "Tom died the day after New Year's."

Karen wasn't married!

Chapter Three

He hadn't been this tired since he was in college, pulling an all-nighter before an exam. It was foolish, of course, working such long hours, but what choice was there? He had to finish the pieces that he had promised. Bagatelle's reputation was based on three generations of quality and commitment. Alex wasn't about to jeopardize it now, and so here he was at five AM, opening the door to his condo, his eyes bloodshot from too many hours of painstaking close work, his fingers cramped from holding the calipers too tightly, his heart . . . The less he thought about his heart, the better.

Alex slid his arms out of his jacket, tossing it in the direction of a chair. When it slipped to the floor, he shrugged. At this point, who cared about a wrinkled coat? All that mattered was that Karen Stevens—Alex shook his head, mentally correcting himself. What mattered was that Karen *Lang* was back in his life, if only for the next week.

He kicked off his shoes, then padded across the Persian carpet, his eyes fixed on the middle of the three bookcases that lined the far wall. Pushing the concealed latch, he pulled the shelves forward to reveal his safe. Seconds later, he held a small box in his hand. The cardboard was no longer as white as it had once been, and the stylized 'b' was the one his father had chosen, not the one that currently graced Bagatelle's boxes and bags. Though his mind told him to shove the box back into the safe and slam the door, his heart urged him to open it.

His heart won. Alex lifted the lid, letting his forefinger touch the contents. A second later, he drew his hand back, recoiling as if from a flame. What a fool he was! He should have tossed the box years ago. Celia had told him that, the day she had found him staring at a piece of jewelry she considered tawdry. Instead, he had kept it with a few other treasured mementos, opening the box on increasingly rare occasions when something—call it nostalgia, perhaps hope—drew him to the safe.

Cradling the box in one hand, he walked the few steps to his stereo cabinet and pressed a button. As the strident beat of a rock band filled the room, Alex sank into one of the deep leather chairs. At least this music held no memories of Karen, not like that damned Christmas carol. He had heard the refrain of "Silver Bells" echoing in his mind all evening. "Soon it will be . . ."

Morning, he told himself firmly. Forget the holiday. Forget Karen. The problem was, he could not forget.

Celia was right. Opening that deceptively simple cardboard box was like loosening the lid on Pandora's box. It released demons that by all rights ought to have been exorcised years ago. Yet here he was, looking at the precious metal, remembering the day he had placed it in the box, thinking about the boy he had been. How foolish could one man be? He was an adult now, yet he was acting like a lovesick teenager, mooning over a memento of his lost love, when what he ought to be doing was catching some much-needed sleep.

It was stupid, plain and simple. Why was he torturing himself? Karen had made her feelings clear fifteen years ago.

Alex frowned as he remembered the last time he had seen her. He had traveled to that godforsaken place she called a home in the naïve belief that he could convince her to change her mind. How wrong he'd been! Gone was the carefree girl who had smiled in delight at the crowded sidewalks of Manhattan, telling him they were romantic reminders of "their" song. In her place was a white-faced woman whose eyes brimmed with tears. Tears, she had insisted, that had nothing to do with him.

Though it was the middle of winter and the wind sweeping across the prairie was bone-chilling, she had refused to invite him inside the house. Instead she had leaned against the paddock rail, her hands thrust in her coat pockets, her face somber as she told him she loved Tom and was going to marry him. Alex hadn't thought anything could hurt more than that, but he had been wrong, for Tom had come outside, putting his arm around Karen's shoulders, drawing her close to him to comfort her as Alex longed to do. The simple, loving gesture was as painful as a jagged cut.

"It's over, Alex," she had said in a flat voice so different from the melodic trill he'd heard a month earlier.

It was over. Perhaps it had never begun.

A wise man would ignore the feelings that the mere sight of Karen Stevens Lang roused. A wise man would walk away, pretending yesterday's chance encounter was nothing more than that. A wise man would remind himself that she had made her choices. But then, a wise man would never have kept the box.

With hands that were suddenly shaky—surely the result of too little sleep and too many hours holding tools—he placed the box and its precious contents back in the safe, switched off the stereo, then walked toward the bedroom, his step lighter than it had any right to be.

He was tired, both physically and emotionally, and he ought to know better, but—try though he might—he could not repress the tiny seed of hope that had begun to grow. Maybe things would be different this time. Karen seemed different, and it wasn't only that they were both fifteen years older. Though there was no denying the faint air of sorrow that clung to her, it was far different from the sadness he had seen on her face that day on the windswept Wyoming prairie. Then she had looked as if her heart would break; today she seemed resigned. Perhaps it was only his imagination that wanted to believe it true, but he thought he had seen a glimmer of hope in her eyes.

And then there was Jill. She looked so much like her mother that at times Alex had wanted to call her Karen. At other times there was no doubt she was also Tom's daughter, for she had inherited his curly hair—hair that made Alex's own waves look straight in comparison. And the way she tipped her head to one side reminded Alex of Tom's own mannerisms. Odd. He hadn't liked Tom the two times he had met him—and he had no doubt that the antipathy was mutual—but the same mannerisms he had scorned in Tom seemed endearing in his daughter. Jill was one intriguing girl, with Karen's face, Tom's hair, and her very own smile.

Alex pulled his turtleneck over his head, grinning.

He suspected that every eligible young male within reasonable driving distance of Golden Spur, Wyoming, was going to have his heart broken by Jill's winsome smile. The Western Mona Lisa. Wyoming Juliet.

Sleep. He needed sleep. Maybe then his brain would function properly and stop feeding him such fanciful images. When he woke, he would remember that what he and Karen had shared was in the past. It was over.

But as he drifted to sleep, Alex's last thought was of the future, a future that held a disturbingly beautiful dark-haired woman.

"No!"

The sound reverberated in her ears, waking her from a deep sleep. For an instant, Karen was not certain where she was or what had roused her. Then she heard Jill's sobs.

"What's wrong, honey?" Karen switched on a lamp in Jill's room and sat on the bed beside her, trying to keep her voice calm. It had been months since she had heard such despair from Jill. Drawing her daughter into her arms, Karen began to stroke her hair in the one gesture of comfort that had never failed to soothe her.

For a few moments, there was no sound other than Jill's ragged breathing as she tried to control her sobs. At last she spoke. "It was awful!" Jill said, her voice still thick with tears. "I saw Dad. He was so close, I could almost touch him." She shuddered with remembered pain. "Then I ran toward him, and he disappeared." Jill buried her face in Karen's shoulder as sobs once more shook her slender frame.

"It was only a dream, Jill. A nightmare." Karen continued to stroke Jill's hair, wishing there were some way she could take away her daughter's pain.

"Oh, Mom, I miss him so much!"

"Me, too, honey." Tom's death had left a gaping hole in their lives. Though the immediate pain had subsided, there was a void that Karen knew would never be filled. She and Jill skirted around the hole, but there were times, like tonight, when the abyss was too wide and too deep to avoid. All they could do was share the pain and take comfort from the fact that they were not alone in their sorrow.

An hour later, when Jill was once more sleeping, Karen walked slowly into the parlor and opened the mini-bar. Alcohol might not solve anything, but that packet of incredibly sinful chocolates would go a long way toward soothing her troubled thoughts.

How different it would have been if her own father had lived a long and normal life!

Karen slit the cellophane wrapper and took out a chocolate-covered cherry, then let her mind drift back to the last time she had been in New York. Was it only distance that made her think those were the most perfect three days of her life? She had been young—so young and so in love that she had believed in happy endings. She had planned to spend five days with Alex's family, then she would go home for Christmas, and Alex would join her on the ranch for New Year's. And when the holidays were over and they had both met each other's family, they would make their engagement official. They had planned it all so perfectly, a fairy-tale romance. The start of "happily ever after." Unfortunately, their ending had been anything but happy.

Karen bit into the chocolate, hoping its sweetness would overcome the bitterness of her memories. She had not eaten duck since that night, for just the thought of the succulent bird turned her stomach, reminding her of the phone call that had interrupted the Bradfords' traditional pre-Christmas dinner and changed her life forever.

"Your father's in the hospital." Even now she could remember the strain in Tom's voice as he explained that Ralph Stevens had suffered a massive stroke and had an uncertain prognosis. The dreamlike three days she had spent with Alex ended, and the nightmare began, as Karen begged her way onto a flight to Denver, then spent a week by her father's side in the Cheyenne hospital, not knowing whether he would live. When he was moved from the ICU and the tests were complete, Karen had faced the reality that her father would never again be able to ranch, that both of their lives were changed forever.

"Stay with me, Karen," he had implored in the slurred speech the specialists had told her was the best she could expect. "You're all I have."

And so there had been no New Year's engagement, no wedding the week after she graduated, no year in Europe while Alex studied with the world's finest jewelry designers. Instead, she had married Tom Lang in a quiet ceremony at her father's bedside, and they had built a life together.

It wasn't what she had planned, and yet how could she doubt the wisdom of her decisions? Karen pushed the box of chocolates away as she remembered the joy on her father's face when he saw his granddaughter for the first time and the pride he had shown when Tom found a new oil field on the ranch. She and Tom and Jill had brought happiness to her father's final years. And if it wasn't the life she had once dreamed of . . .

Stop it! Karen rose and headed for her bedroom. She could not change the past. It was over, done, immutable. And the future . . . There was no future.

Chapter Four

"Oh, Mom! You ate the chocolate!"

Karen wakened to the sound of her daughter's plaintive cry. Though Jill had been sleeping soundly by the time Karen returned to bed, she had left her door open in case Jill had another nightmare. But this morning, it appeared, she was back to normal. Jill stood in the doorway, her hands fisted on her hips in the classic pose of exasperation.

"I'm sure they restock the mini bar every day," Karen said as she thrust her feet into her slippers. "Besides, young lady, I don't recall telling you chocolate was an acceptable breakfast food." She tied the belt of her robe and walked toward the window, wondering if the weather would be as sunny as Jill's mood.

"You know I was only razzing you," Jill said, "but

honestly, Mom, I thought you were gonna sleep all day. I had breakfast hours ago."

"And now you can't wait to count Macy's windows." Karen opened the drapes and let the sun stream into the room. The previous day's rain had disappeared, leaving in its wake a beautiful, clear blue sky. It would be a glorious day to spend outdoors, doing the sightseeing and shopping Jill had put on today's agenda.

"Matt doesn't believe there are really fifty windows."

"So you plan to be the only person in the city who actually counts them." Knowing Jill, she would do it.

As Karen dressed, her gaze was drawn to the window and the view of Central Park. With its huge rock outcroppings, duck ponds, and whimsically styled buildings, it provided an unexpectedly bucolic counterpoint to the bustling city that surrounded it. As if to underscore the slower pace of the park, the line of horse-drawn carriages had begun to form. Karen turned away abruptly. She would not think about the carriages.

"Ready?" she called to Jill a few minutes later.

"You bet!"

When they reached the lobby, the doorman greeted them. "Shall I call a taxi for you, Ms. Lang?"

Karen shook her head.

"That was fierce!" Jill whispered as she pushed the revolving door. "He knew our name!"

Karen gave her daughter a quick smile. "The Burgundy is known for its personal service."

"That must be why Alex . . ."

"Mr. Bradford."

Jill wrinkled her nose and continued, ". . . has his store here."

Although Karen did not doubt that the Burgundy's reputation was one of the primary reasons Alex had opened a branch of Bagatelle there rather than in another hotel, she preferred not to think about Alex in any context. Denial might be the coward's approach, but it did minimize heartache.

"Look at all the decorations!" Jill gestured toward the garlands that festooned light posts and the wreaths that one shop had hung on its trash cans. "Matt will never believe it when I tell him. It's just like that Christmas carol, 'Silver Bells.' You know, 'city sidewalks . . .' " She started to sing the words that had haunted Karen for so many years, raising memories that she had tried desperately to bury. It was odd, though. This morning the hurt seemed less intense, the memories more sweet than bitter.

"Most people think that song was written about New York," she said mildly as she motioned to Jill to turn left. "I thought we'd take the subway."

"Fierce!" Jill's enthusiasm increased as they descended the stairs. "Look at that wall!" Instead of the graffiti that had once characterized subway stations, this one was adorned with mosaic murals, including three whimsical butterflies. "This is so cool."

As they boarded the train, Karen watched Jill's eyes widen in delight. Though there were empty seats, she grabbed one of the poles and remained standing.

"I liked Al . . . Mr. Bradford." She corrected herself. "He seems cool."

That was not a word Karen would have used to describe him. When she thought of Alex, her own temperature skyrocketed, for Alex was anything but cool.

Jill's new term, "fierce," was far more appropriate. But that was one of many things she had no intention of telling her daughter. "Would my friends be anything other than cool?" she demanded in mock outrage.

"Oh, Mom!" Jill rolled her eyes and appeared to study the advertisement for a Spanish TV station, while the train rumbled toward the next stop.

When the doors opened, Karen glanced at the people standing on the platform, and her heart skipped a beat. It couldn't be! Surely the tall man with the curly hair was not Alex. Surely there was no reason for her pulse to accelerate at the thought of seeing him again. He turned, revealing an unfamiliar face. How foolish of her to imagine Alex in every stranger. It wasn't as though she wanted to see him again. Hadn't she already decided that if she stayed out of the hotel's shopping arcade for the rest of their stay, she could avoid him completely?

"How come you never talk about college or go to your class reunions?" Jill's question startled Karen.

Because I was afraid to. Because your father didn't want any reminders of my life there. Because I knew the dull ache that never quite disappeared would become unbearable if I went back. Of course she could give her daughter none of those reasons, and so Karen said only, "We were always too busy to leave the ranch." It was not a lie. The reunions were normally scheduled in the summer, when she and Tom were preparing for Frontier Days.

"Matt and I agreed we won't get married before we graduate."

"That's probably a good idea." Karen tried to keep her voice noncommittal. It was disturbing to think that her fourteen-year-old daughter was already planning marriage, when she had yet to go on a real date. She and Matt were allowed to see each other only at home or at parties.

Jill shrugged. "We'll have plenty of time to settle down and have a family later on. Matt and I don't want to miss out on things."

Unlike the dull ache that accompanied thoughts of Alex and her college years, the pain Jill's words produced was like a razor cut, more painful than she could have dreamt. Karen jumped to her feet and strode toward Jill. "Is that what you think?" she asked, gripping the pole with far more force than was needed to remain standing. "Do you think that your father and I missed out on good things because we married young and had a baby right away?"

Though her face flushed with embarrassment, Jill nodded slowly. "Maybe not Dad as much as you. You gave up more."

As the subway jolted to a stop and the doors slid open, Karen touched Jill's shoulder. "This is our station," she said. It was only when they were on the platform and walking toward the stairs that she turned to Jill. "Don't you ever think I regretted having you," she said, trying to blink back her tears. "I wouldn't have traded anything on earth for you!"

"Oh, Mom!" Seemingly oblivious to the crowds that surged around them, Jill gave her a quick hug. "I love you." And to Karen's surprise, her normally calm daughter's eyes looked suspiciously moist.

A minute later, Jill's face was wreathed in a smile as she stared at the first of Macy's fifty display windows. "Awesome!" she declared. This year's theme, it appeared, was seasonal songs with a whimsical twist. As mechanized horses pulled an antique sleigh and traditionally clad carolers sang the familiar words to "Winter Wonderland," the couple in the sleigh showed off their very modern holiday finery. In the next window Santa climbed into a chimney to the tune of "Up On the Housetop," his sack brimming with household gadgets rather than children's toys.

"Fierce," Jill announced as she scampered to a smaller window, this one featuring wise men whose camels plodded solemnly through the desert to the music of "We Three Kings," bearing fancy soaps, bath salts, and a loofah instead of the traditional gold, frankincense, and myrrh.

By the time they had seen each of the windows, Jill's camera was empty and Karen's ears were cold. "Inside," she said, gesturing toward the main doors. "I need to thaw out."

"And I need to buy Matt a present."

An hour later, when Karen had begun to think Jill would never find what she considered the perfect gift, her daughter cried, "This is it!" and held up a sweatshirt with a collage of New York skyscrapers emblazoned on the front.

"Nice." From the corner of her eye, Karen saw a tall, dark-haired man place a shirt on the counter. It wasn't Alex. It couldn't be Alex.

"Want one, Mom?"

For a second, Karen wasn't sure what Jill meant. Did she want Alex? Oh, yes. Then she shook her head. The sweatshirt. Jill was asking about the sweatshirt. "I don't think so." It would be difficult enough to forget this trip without any tangible reminders. She had tucked the few mementos of her last stay in Manhattan into a box that she had relegated to the back of the attic. A prudent woman would have thrown them away, but—despite everything—Karen couldn't force herself to take that step.

Though a different doorman stood in front of the Burgundy when they returned, he tipped his top hat to them and greeted them by name. Jill flashed him a brilliant smile, then turned to Karen. "Do you think they'll have restocked the chocolates?"

"As if you need any more chocolate." At Jill's insistence, they had bought a pound of fudge and had sampled several pieces during the afternoon.

When they reached their floor, Karen fished the card key from her purse, opened the door to their suite, then stopped. Two floral arrangements sat on the console table, and though they were still wrapped in green cellophane, their sweet scent had begun to fill the parlor.

"Wow! Who are they from?" Jill dropped her shopping bags.

"Probably the hotel manager. They sometimes send flowers when you stay for a long time." Karen walked closer. The larger arrangement combined red and white carnations with evergreens, while the smaller . . . She could feel her pulse begin to race as she recognized the flowers. It couldn't be coincidence. Only one person in New York knew that she loved snowdrops.

With a sense of anticipation that she told herself was completely out of proportion to the occasion, Karen reached for the card.

"This one's for me!" Jill squealed as she read her name on the other card. She opened it, read the message, and began to laugh. "Oh, Mom! How cool. Listen to what Alex wrote."

Alex. Who else would have been thoughtful enough to send flowers to both Karen and her daughter? Karen forced herself to listen to Jill as she read, " 'Wishing the next Olympic hopeful a joyous Christmas.' There's even a skater on the pot. Isn't that fierce?"

"Fierce," Karen agreed.

"What does yours say?"

With fingers that somehow refused her brain's command to stop shaking, Karen slid the card from its envelope. What had Alex written? Could she read it to Jill? She could always invent something innocuous, but there was no need. "It says, 'Welcome back to the greatest city on earth'."

"It is that, isn't it?"

Karen laughed. "At least at this time of the year." A lifetime ago—or was it only fifteen years?—she and Alex had laughed when a radio broadcaster referred to New York in those terms. They had considered it hyperbole. Today she wasn't so sure it was an exaggeration.

When the phone rang, Jill grabbed it. "Oh, Al . . . Mr. Bradford, the flowers are fierce!" Jill smiled at Alex's reply, then handed the receiver to Karen, grabbed her shopping bags, and headed for her room.

"I won't call them fierce," Karen said, smiling at the sound of Alex's voice, "but the flowers are beautiful." She held the snowdrops to her face, inhaling their fragrance.

He chuckled, and Karen could feel warmth rush to her cheeks. How could any one man be so sexy? It wasn't fair that she needed nothing more than a laugh to make her pulse race. Karen sank onto the couch and began to unlace her shoes. Perhaps the mundane act would help her return to reality.

"I know you were planning to take Jill to Chinatown tonight," Alex said, "but I wondered if you'd consider a change of plans."

He wanted to see her again. It was, of course,

impossible. She and Jill could not spend another night with him, for it would be far too dangerous.

"I promised Jill."

Alex chuckled again and Karen could feel her resolve begin to melt. Perhaps a couple hours—for old times' sake. "I think I have an offer Jill won't refuse," Alex said. "I got tickets to *Jane Eyre*."

"That's impossible."

"The three pieces of cardboard I'm holding in my hand say otherwise. Why don't I pick you up at seven-thirty and we'll have dinner afterwards?"

"We shouldn't."

There was a moment of silence, and Karen could almost feel Alex's disappointment. "Didn't you say that you wanted to make Jill's first visit to New York perfect?" he asked at last.

There was only one possible response.

If she was not the most beautiful woman he had ever seen, she was without a doubt the sexiest. She was wearing a dress the shade of his best emeralds, but while emeralds were cool, Karen was not. Most definitely not. The shimmery fabric hinted at the curves it covered, while the short skirt displayed an expanse of long legs that set a man's pulse afire. Alex swallowed deeply.

"The car's outside."

"Is this for us?" Jill asked as a chauffeur opened the rear door of a white stretch limo. Her expression combined surprise and wonder, and for a moment she looked so much like Karen had on their first date that Alex wanted to wrap his arms around her.

Instead, he shrugged and said, "I didn't think you'd want to walk two miles in high heels." He never had understood how women could walk on those teetery things.

The interior of the car had deep leather seats along the back and one side, while the other side held a TV, a refrigerator, and a cabinet filled with glasses and snacks. Jill slid to the side, leaving the back seat for him and Karen.

"This is fierce!" Jill announced.

To his surprise, Karen raised one brow and said severely, "I thought limos were for geezers."

"Oh, Mom!" Though Jill ducked her head quickly, Alex saw the flush of embarrassment color her cheeks. "Not now!"

"Let me guess. It's a private joke."

Karen nodded, sending another wave of her perfume toward him. She had changed fragrances since college. This was a bit more mature than the one she had worn fifteen years ago, but just as alluring—like the lady herself.

"There's soda in the refrigerator and snacks in the top drawer," Alex told Jill.

As Jill opened a can and stared out the tinted windows, Karen said softly, "This is wonderful, Alex. Jill was so excited when I told her about the play."

And you? he wanted to ask. *Were you excited about spending the evening with me?* Instead he said only, "I'm glad."

Jill rummaged in the snack drawer. "I can't wait to tell Matt." Matt, Alex surmised, was her boyfriend. "How'd you get the tickets?"

Alex felt Karen stiffen at his side, as if she considered Jill's question a *faux pas.* "A friend owed me a favor." He wouldn't admit just how many phone calls he had made to arrange three orchestra seats for the hottest show on Broadway.

"It must have been a big favor." Karen shook her head when Jill offered her some cashews.

"He thought it was," Alex agreed. "I attended an estate sale in Normandy to get an antique locket for his wife."

"What a hardship!" Karen's voice was laced with the mild amusement he remembered so well. If it weren't for Jill, munching nuts only a few inches away from them, he could have imagined himself still in college.

Jill leaned forward, her eyes gleaming with interest, her question bringing him firmly back to the present. "You've been to Europe?"

Alex wondered what Karen had told Jill about him. About her. About him and her. Not much, it appeared.

"I studied in Europe for a year after I graduated," he said. The limo had turned the last corner and was now inching its way into the theater district, bumper-to-bumper with battered taxis, other gleaming luxury vehicles and cars sporting license plates from most states east of the Mississippi. "Now I go over for auctions and shows three or four times a year."

"Wow!" Though he had kept his tone matter-of-fact, Jill was obviously impressed. "Mom always wanted to go to Europe," she said.

Alex knew that. Oh, how he knew that. And if things had been different, she would have gone. Instead . . .

"I learned a lot in Europe," he told Karen's daughter. And the most important lesson was that hearts could mend. They might never be the same as before, but the pain diminished and life continued.

Despite the heavy traffic, they arrived at the theater a few minutes before curtain time, giving Jill the opportunity to admire the ornate woodwork and the gilded boxes that made this one of Broadway's finest small theaters, while her mother sat back in her seat, apparently content to watch her daughter's excitement. She was quieter than usual, and Alex wondered if she too was remembering the past.

When the curtain rose, the two women leaned forward, immediately entranced by the story, giving Alex the bittersweet pleasure of sitting between the woman who had once meant more than anything on earth to him and the young woman who, if things had been different, could have been his daughter.

As Jill sighed over Jane Eyre's misfortunes and grew intent at the sight of the troubled Mr. Rochester, Alex could not help remembering the play he and Karen had seen together. He knew the name only because he had kept the playbill, but if anyone had asked him who had starred in it or what the plot line was, Alex would have admitted defeat. What he recalled of that night was the way Karen had nestled close to him, leaning her head on his shoulder while he wrapped his arm around her. He remembered that they had whispered endearments, stealing kisses when they hoped no one was watching, eventually leaving the theater at intermission so that they could spend the rest of the evening alone together.

So much had changed! Tonight they sat in the middle of their seats. Karen's hands were folded primly in her lap, while he rested his on the chair arms, careful not to touch her. They could have been a married couple who had no need for clandestine kisses, knowing they were going home to a house and a bed that they had shared for years. Instead, they were more than strangers but less than friends. The years still formed a barrier between them, and so Alex forced his attention to the stage, trying desperately not to think of the woman who sat beside him, separated by fifteen years and a chair arm.

It was agony, pure agony, being next to Karen in the

limousine, feeling the soft brush of her hand against his as she pulled her coat closed, then sitting across the dinner table from her, watching her spear a piece of food and place it in her mouth, remembering other, more pleasurable uses for those luscious lips. Supper at Antonio's had seemed like such a good idea. A small, intimate trattoria with some of the best food Alex had ever eaten would give Jill a different view of New York from the street vendors they had frequented yesterday. But he had reckoned without the torture of being so close to Karen, of remembering other meals they had shared and the way those nights had ended.

"This was wonderful," Karen said as the limousine stopped in front of the Burgundy. "Can I offer you a drink?"

Only a fool would prolong the evening, knowing it would never end the way he wanted. Though Alex had every intention of refusing, what he said was, "Sure. Are you going to join us, Jill?"

She shook her head. "Thanks, but I want to call Matt before I forget anything. Tonight was incredible!" She fished her card key from her purse and headed toward the elevators.

There was a moment of awkwardness as Alex waited for Karen. Though he knew where he wanted to go, it was her invitation. She had to choose.

"Our mini bar has a pretty decent selection," she said at last. "Want to come up?" Though her voice was calm, Alex saw the faint shadows in her eyes and realized she was uncomfortable with her suggestion.

"Why don't we give Jill some privacy for her call? If you haven't tried it, the Merlot Room is excellent." Karen's quick smile and the unmistakable relief in her eyes were all the reward Alex needed.

The small bar off the hotel's main lobby was dark,

and far more intimate than the well-lit parlor of her suite would have been. Though there were other patrons, the booths were designed for maximum privacy, giving the illusion of separate rooms. It was a spot for assignations, yet one that would not disturb Karen's sensibilities.

"This was a marvelous evening," she said when they had given the waiter their order. "I don't know how I'll ever repay you."

Alex shook his head and placed his hand on top of Karen's. Though he half expected her to pull her hand away, she left it there. "I didn't expect payment," he told her honestly. "I know it's a cliché, but the pleasure was mine." His initial thought had been to find a way to spend more time with Karen. Jill hadn't factored into the equation, but there was no denying the pleasure he had found at spending the evening with Karen's daughter.

"I'll never forget the expression on Jill's face at the finale," Karen said, smiling at the memory. "I haven't seen her that happy since Tom died."

Alex took a sip of his drink, then shook his head. If there was one thing he did not want to discuss, it was Tom Lang. "There is something you could do for me," he said, deliberately changing the subject.

Karen turned, and in the flicker of candlelight, he could see the question on her face. "I'd like you and Jill to spend Christmas Day with me."

Her eyes widened in surprise, and she hesitated for a moment before she said, "We can't do that." Karen shook her head, as if to emphasize her refusal. "I don't want to intrude on your family."

It was Alex's turn to shake his head. "You won't be intruding. Mom and Dad are in Australia. They've been talking about this trip for twenty years, and since this is the last year Dad can rent a car there, they've finally gone. So I'll be all alone on Christmas." Alex feigned a pleading pose. "Have pity on me."

As he had hoped, she laughed. "The last thing on earth you need is pity, Alex."

"You're right. I need companionship. Yours and Jill's."

She wasn't convinced. He could see that as clearly as if she had taken out a billboard. "There are no strings attached. I just want you and Jill to have a happy day."

"I don't know."

Alex pulled out the big guns. "You drive a hard bargain, lady, but I'll agree. No raisins in the sweet potatoes."

For a second Karen was silent; then she laughed. "How did you remember that I hate raisins?"

Alex squeezed her hand. "Haven't you figured it out? I remember everything about you."

Chapter Five

It was magic. That was the only way to describe it. She could lie to herself and say that she didn't want to be there. She could be truthful and admit that, no matter how she felt, she should never have come, never have given in to the wild, irresistible urge to spend a few more minutes with Alex. But the simple fact was, it was wonderful being with him. The whole evening had been magical, a night worthy of Cinderella, and Karen, who knew all too well that there was no such thing as fairy godmothers and happily-ever-afters, wanted to enjoy the last moments before her coach turned back into a pumpkin.

It was foolish, of course. For years she had refused to let herself think about him. Whenever the memories surfaced—and surface they did—she would force herself to think of something else, anything else. She had tried desperately to forget just how wonderful the time she and Alex shared had been. And she had succeeded. Or so she had thought. Tonight had proven how badly she had lied to herself. She had not forgotten Alex, not for a single moment, and he, it appeared, had remembered her.

"Do you remember?"

Karen wasn't certain who spoke first. All she knew was that their words came out together, as if they were singing a duet.

She laughed, and for a moment the years disappeared, and she was once again Karen Stevens, young, single, and in love.

"Do I remember what?" she asked. Alex shook his head, then carried her hand to his lips and pressed a kiss on her fingertips. Did she remember the first time he had done that, when she had thought it the most romantic gesture imaginable? Of course she remembered! What woman could forget?

But those were dangerous thoughts, paths she dared not walk again, and so she said, "I was thinking about the night we wanted to take a carriage ride in Central Park, but the line was too long."

"And so we rode the subway downtown and went to an Afghani restaurant." He continued the story, his eyes sparkling behind his glasses, his lips curving in the smile she had always loved.

"And I didn't want to admit that I'd never eaten Afghani food, so I let you order your favorites and tried to pretend I knew what they were." They had fed each other turnovers filled with spiced pumpkin, sizzling kabobs, and eggplant with mint yogurt, all washed down with traditional Afghani tea spiced with cardamom and rose petals. Was it only in her memory that it was the most delicious meal of her life?

She should pull her hand away, finish her drink and

end the evening. Instead, Karen said, "I shared my memory. What was yours?" Though she might be opening Pandora's box, she wanted to know what had brought that impish grin to his face. While the lines at the corners of his eyes were deeper than they'd been fifteen years ago, the way they crinkled was endearingly familiar.

"I was thinking about the afternoon we went to the top of the World Trade Center and how I kept wishing we were the only people on the elevator."

"When in fact it was packed like sardines."

Alex chuckled. "Remember that one man's hair oil?"

She couldn't help it; she laughed. "It was so heavy, you called him a human sardine."

"A bit cruel, but true. Of course," Alex admitted, "I wouldn't say that today."

"That's because you're older and wiser."

"Actually, the man might have decked me. That never even occurred to me that day."

"That's what I said—you're wiser now."

A wistful expression crossed Alex's face, and his brown eyes were momentarily serious. "Sometimes I just feel older. You, on the other hand . . ." He paused for a moment, and the mischievous sparkle she loved returned to his eyes. "I won't lie and say you haven't changed, because you have. Now you're even more beautiful."

Karen blushed. Lord, she hadn't blushed this many times in all the years they'd been apart. "No, I'm not."

Alex squeezed her hand, then entwined their fingers. "You know what they say about the eye of the beholder. This beholder says you are beautiful."

"And this middle-aged matron says you're a born salesman."

"I take umbrage . . . whatever that means."

Karen laughed again at the memories Alex evoked. It felt so good being with him! She had heard people speak of reliving their childhood, and it had always sounded somehow sad, as if the present could not compare to the past. She didn't feel that she and Alex were doing that. Instead, they were building on their shared past, finding the present more enjoyable because of what they had experienced together.

"Do you remember how we used to count the number of times Dr. Sawyer said 'take umbrage'?" she asked.

"I think the record was . . ." He stopped, raising his eyebrow in an unspoken question as the waiter appeared at their table, ready to refill their glasses.

Karen glanced at her watch. "I can't believe how long we've talked," she said. "Jill's probably wondering where we went."

Alex signed the credit card receipt, then slid out of the booth, extending his hand toward Karen. "Let's go reassure Jill." He slid his arm around Karen's waist.

It felt so natural, so good, and yet she knew she should move away. Today was over, and there was no point in pretending tomorrow would ever come.

"Good night, Alex," she said, forcing her lips to curve into a smile.

He shook his head and drew her closer as they walked out of the nearly empty lounge into the lobby. "You're not getting away so easily. Don't you know that a gentleman always walks a lady to her door?"

Karen raised a brow and matched his bantering tone. "Alert the media. Chivalry is alive and well in Manhattan!"

"Laugh all you want, my dear, but the simple fact is, I don't want tonight to end—even if I do have two pieces of jewelry to finish by Friday noon."

As they walked toward the elevator, Alex kept his arm around her waist. Surely it was only by chance that her arm seemed to have a will of its own and moved to encircle his waist. Though it had been fifteen years since they had walked together, their steps synchronized as if they did it daily.

"Not quite like the Trade Center," Alex said when they entered the empty elevator and Karen pushed the button for her floor.

"No sardines," she agreed.

The doors slid closed and the elevator began to rise.

"Remember that ancient elevator in your dorm?" Alex asked.

Karen nodded. "The first time I rode it, I couldn't figure out why it wouldn't move."

"And then we realized what a great thing that was!"

The elevator had been so old that, in addition to the automatic outer door, it had an inner iron gate that the passengers had to close before the cage would rise. She and Alex—like many other students—had quickly discovered that they could stop the elevator mid-floor by unlatching the gate, giving them a private place to share a kiss.

Alex grinned. "No gate here. I guess I'll just have to be inventive."

He wrapped his arms around Karen and lowered his mouth to hers. At first his lips moved slowly, softly tracing the outline of her mouth, feathering kisses at each corner, then moving toward the center.

"Sweet, so sweet," he whispered. And then, with a groan that seemed to come from deep within him, he moved his hand to the back of her head, running his fingers through her hair as he pulled her closer, deepening the kiss, demanding access to the sweet recesses of her mouth.

The languorous warmth from his kisses turned to a conflagration that threatened to engulf her as Alex drew her body to his. Karen reached her arms around him not knowing, not caring whether she was pulling him closer or supporting her suddenly weak knees. Nothing else mattered. For a long moment, there was no one else in the world, no worries, no responsibilities, nothing but the wonder of Alex's embrace. His kiss was the magic carpet that transported them to a universe for two, a place that had no past, no future, nothing but the joyous present.

And then the elevator stopped.

Karen blinked as she opened her eyes. Had it been only a few seconds, or had the elevator ride lasted half a lifetime? She couldn't say. All she knew was that somehow Alex had once more cast a spell, and she had fallen under it.

As if by tacit agreement, neither of them spoke as they walked toward her room. Perhaps Alex feared, as she did, that the spell would shatter. When she handed him her card key, he stopped and once more pulled her into his arms. This time the kiss was brief, almost chaste, yet the sensations it raised were anything but monastic.

"Dream of me," he said as he opened the door.

As if she would have a choice!

Her hair was disheveled, her lips swollen, and her eyes—she could only guess that they were wide and starry, filled with the look that Alex had always said was love, making its way out from her heart. She couldn't let Jill see her this way.

As Karen walked into the parlor, she heard Jill's voice in the distance. Thank goodness! She was still talking to Matt. Karen slipped off her shoes and hurried into her bathroom. She brushed her hair and hastily removed her makeup. Then, when she was convinced she looked fairly normal, she returned to her bedroom and unzipped her dress. Drawing it over her head, she made the mistake of inhaling. Alex! Her dress bore his scent, that light citrus fragrance that he had always worn, the one she had refused to buy for Tom, even though Jill had insisted it was the best of the men's colognes. Karen hung the dress in the back of the closet, trying to keep it from touching her other clothes. If there was one thing she did not need, it was another reminder of Alex Bradford. He was already unforgettable.

Wrapping the hotel's plush terry robe around her, she walked into the parlor to wait for Jill. Karen switched on the radio, changing stations the instant she heard the first notes of "Silver Bells." It was difficult enough to banish memories; she would not encourage them by listening to that song.

When Jill emerged from her room a few minutes later, Karen saw tears sparkling in her daughter's eyes. Unbidden, her pulse began to race.

"What's wrong, honey? Did something happen at home?"

Jill shook her head and slumped onto the other end of the couch, drawing her legs onto the seat and wrapping her arms around them. "No." She refused to meet Karen's gaze. "Everything's fine. It's just . . ." Jill's voice broke. ". . . I miss Matt so much."

Karen knew all too well how painful young love could be. "We'll be home in a few days," she told Jill, "and you'll see Matt then. Or, if you want to, we can go back sooner." At this time of year, it would be difficult to change their flights, but somehow she'd manage.

Jill shook her head again, and this time she raised

164

her tear-stained face toward Karen. "Matt said I had to stay here. He doesn't want me to miss anything."

Karen bit back a smile, remembering her daughter's brave declaration that she and Matt planned to experience all life had to offer before they married. Had that been only this morning?

"That's probably good advice," she said, keeping her voice nonjudgmental.

The radio started playing "Angels We Have Heard on High," one of Jill's favorite Christmas carols. Tonight it appeared she was immune to the beautiful music. Her eyes blazed, and she brushed back a tear. "You don't understand!" she cried. "You think it's so easy, but you've never had to be away from someone you love. You just don't understand!"

As Jill raced to her room, closing the door emphatically behind her, Karen gripped the edge of the sofa. So Jill thought she didn't understand. How wrong she was!

Though it had been fifteen years and the pain had subsided, Karen knew she would never forget the nightmare of those first few weeks after her father's stroke. Dealing with his illness, making decisions about the ranch, and trying to cope with the reality that her life had changed forever had been difficult enough. But through it all, she had felt as though she were wounded, as if part of her body had been torn away. She had expected emptiness, a void caused by saying good-bye to Alex. But it had been far, far worse. Instead of emptiness, she had experienced almost unbearable pain, as if she had an unhealed wound, one that broke open with the slightest movement.

And then there had been that scene in the paddock. To this day, Karen did not know how she had mustered the courage to tell Alex she didn't love him, didn't need him, didn't ever want to see him again, when every fiber of her being shrieked that the opposite was true. She had watched his face whiten with pain, seen his eyes reflecting the misery she knew must have shone in hers. Yet she had continued to lie, to tell him he had no part in her life.

Oh, how it had hurt!

Stop it! Karen commanded herself. It was the right decision, the best one for everyone. She knew that. That was why she had prepared her words so carefully, making certain that Alex held no false hopes, that he would never again come to Golden Spur.

And he had not. They had gone in different directions, lived separate lives, just as she had planned.

It was right.

Tonight had been magical, wonderful, a glimpse at what might have been. But it was nothing more than a moment out of time, a night that never should have happened and could never, ever be repeated.

She knew that. Why, then, did she feel as if the wound had been reopened and that this time there would be no healing?

Chapter Six

It was getting to be a bad habit, this working until dawn, pretending he was once again a teenager with unlimited energy. Alex knew that sooner or later he would crash, but this morning he couldn't argue with the results. He had completed the last two pieces that he had promised for Christmas delivery. And they weren't just finished, they were the best work he had done in years. The cufflinks Amy Franks had ordered for her father had precisely the right touch of tradition without looking old-fashioned. It had been a brilliant move, setting the diamond off center, balancing it with Chuck Franks's initials. Difficult-to-satisfy Chuck would be pleased. Hank London would be more than pleased when he saw his wife's ring. That swirled setting was perfect, even better than the original design.

Alex wasn't sure how either of the changes had happened. He'd been making jewelry for close to twenty years, and he had never, ever deviated from a design once the customer had approved it. But tonight was different. Perhaps it was fatigue. Perhaps serendipity. All he knew was that he had been thinking of Karen, remembering the way her lips curved when she smiled, and he had found himself putting that same curve into Hank London's ring. That delicate swirl was exactly what the piece needed to take it from good to great. And he owed it to Karen.

As he opened the door to his condo, Alex knew there was no sense in trying to sleep. The adrenaline that coursed through his veins would keep him awake. Pure excitement was a heady drug, and he had more than his share of that.

Karen. He wanted to talk to Karen, to tell her how much he had enjoyed their time together, how even now he could taste her kisses, how she had inspired him. But it was five o'clock, and he doubted that she would appreciate a phone call. Karen, he knew, was not a morning person.

He glanced at his watch again, then did a mental calculation. Perfect! It was early evening in Australia. His parents would be in their hotel room, having a pre-dinner cocktail. Alex pulled the neatly printed itinerary from the top of his desk and began punching numbers. A minute later, he was talking to his father.

"The most incredible thing happened," he began. As Alex listened to his father's story of the sights they had seen down under, he paced the length of the room, still too keyed up to sit. He stopped in front of a mahogany bookcase and picked up the most recent photo of his parents. They stood arm in arm on the deck of their seaside home. Their hair was slightly mussed by the breeze, and his father's nose bore signs of too much sun, yet neither seemed to mind. His father beamed happiness, while his mother tipped her head up to smile at him.

Damn! That smile looked familiar. Alex held the picture at arm's length, considering. It was his mother's smile, but he had seen it on another face. He knew he had. Whose? Alex closed his eyes for a second, trying to remember.

"Jill." Of course. Her smile looked exactly like Mom's.

His father's words brought him back to reality. "Sorry, Dad. I was woolgathering." He must be more tired than he had realized, seeing Karen and her daughter every time he turned around. That's all it was. Fatigue. An over-active imagination. That was all.

"Mom!" Jill burst into her room, switching on the light. "Alex is on the phone, and he wants to take us to Windows on the World for lunch. Is that okay?"

Karen forced her eyes open and tried to remember what day this was and what Jill had planned. Sunlight streamed through the windows as Jill yanked the drapes open, her tears of the previous night obviously a thing of the past. Had she ever been that young and resilient? Karen wondered.

"What about Chinatown?" she asked. According to Jill's agenda, today's lunch was supposed to be hot and sour soup followed by chicken and broccoli.

Jill shrugged. "We can go there some other time. Please, Mom."

Karen frowned. She had promised herself that this would be Jill's trip, that they would do whatever Jill wanted, but how could she agree to spend more time with Alex? It was so dangerous. If she had any doubt, last night had proven just how susceptible she still was to his charm. She ought to refuse. She had to refuse.

Only Scrooge would refuse.

"Let me talk to Alex." Karen pulled herself to a sitting position and reached for the phone. When Jill remained by the bed, Karen added, "Alone." There were some conversations her daughter did not need to overhear.

"Good morning, beautiful," Alex said when she picked up the phone. "Did you sleep well?"

Her lips curved into a smile at the warmth she heard in his voice. "Actually, I did." Karen had been surprised at how easily she had fallen asleep. Between Alex's kisses and Jill's tears, she had believed herself too keyed up to sleep. She had been wrong.

"Then you must have dreamt of me."

She had, though she had no intention of telling Alex about the wonderfully warm, disturbingly erotic dreams that had heated her blood, leaving her craving his touch.

"It was either you or a pepperoni pizza," she retorted.

She could hear his chuckle, and the thought of how his lips moved as he laughed sent a shiver of excitement through her body.

"You've wounded me to the quick!" he declared. "There's only one cure. You have to have lunch with me."

It was silly to enjoy their bantering so much, to remember how they used to laugh at the slightest provocation, to recall how much fun everything had been when she and Alex had shared it. But oh, how she missed that fun!

"Are you sure you can afford the time? What about those pieces you need to finish?"

"They're done!" She heard the satisfaction in his voice. "I want to celebrate with you."

How could she refuse?

* * *

"Where's the limo?" Jill looked both directions as they walked out of the hotel. A flock of tourists clustered in front of one of the booksellers' kiosks at the edge of the park, and a taxi cruised slowly down Fifth, but there were no limos in sight.

"Jill!" Karen's admonishment sounded sharper than she had intended, and she saw the look of surprise on Alex's face. Though he probably thought she was overreacting, she couldn't let him think her daughter was a spoiled brat who demanded limousines.

Alex gave Jill a conspiratorial glance. "Hate to disillusion you, young lady, but I usually ride the subway. It's the quickest way to get downtown."

"I don't mind," Jill announced with a toss of her long curls. "The subway is fierce." She led the way toward the station, leaving Alex and Karen to exchange amused glances as they followed her. When the train arrived, Jill rushed inside and grabbed a pole, while Karen and Alex took seats.

"There's plenty of room," Alex told Jill.

Karen had selected a bench that sat four so that Jill could join them, if she chose. Not that Karen expected that. "She likes standing," Karen said as she pulled off her gloves. "I think she wants to tell her friends that she was a strap hanger."

"And she'll tell them all that it's fierce."

Somehow he managed to capture Jill's inflection perfectly. Karen smiled, but the chuckle that Alex's words provoked died as he took her right hand in his and began to caress each of her fingertips. A brightly lit subway car with orange and yellow plastic seats was far from a romantic spot, yet Alex's touch ignited flames that shone brighter than the lights in Rockefeller Center. It would be easy—so very, very easy—to fall in love with him again.

"You have the most graceful hands," he said softly.

Karen shook her head. How could he consider them attractive? Her fingers were not long and slender like his, and she had short, blunt nails that she didn't try to camouflage with either polish or acrylic tips. "They're ordinary," she protested. "What you see are the hands of a working ranch owner. There's nothing glamorous about them."

Alex's eyes darkened. "Haven't you figured out that I'm not looking for glamour and pretense? Your hands are honest, like you."

Honest? If only he knew how wrong he was. She had not been honest with him, and her lies had changed both of their lives—four lives actually, since Tom and Jill's lives would have been very different if Karen had told the truth that day in the paddock. Perhaps she should admit that she had lied, but a subway car with Jill standing only two feet away was not the right time or place.

As Karen pulled her hand from his and began to chatter about inconsequential things, Alex appeared to accept her change of subject. She was safe, or so she thought. But when they reached the World Trade Center and boarded the elevator for the top floor, Alex stood behind her. As the elevator soared upward, he pressed his lips to the nape of her neck.

Karen turned, startled.

"I've always loved your neck," he said softly, so that Jill would not overhear him. If the people who stood on either side of them noticed his gesture, they gave no indication, merely keeping their eyes fixed on the elevator wall, watching the floor numbers increase. It was only Karen whose face flushed and whose pulse accelerated.

"My ears popped!" Jill swiveled her head, and

Karen hoped Alex had moved far enough away that her daughter wouldn't realize he had been nuzzling her neck. Parents were supposed to set good examples, weren't they?

"You think this is bad," Alex said dryly, "wait until we go down."

Jill's eyes widened. "Have you been here before, Mom?"

"Just to the observation deck. Not the restaurant."

When the elevator stopped, Jill scampered out, then turned and waited for Karen and Alex to emerge, an impatient expression on her face. "Hurry up, you guys," she said.

Karen smiled. It had been a long time since she had seen her serious daughter looking and acting so light-hearted. Whatever else this trip brought, no matter how much personal heartache she suffered, she could not regret anything that turned Jill back into a normal teenager.

It was obvious Alex had called in another favor when the maitre d' escorted them to a table next to the window. With unspoken agreement, Karen and Alex gave Jill the chair facing directly outside, while they took side seats.

"The view is fierce!" Karen heard a note of awe in her daughter's voice. Though she had accepted the elegant surroundings with aplomb, as though fine restaurants were part of her daily routine, the magnificent view—one that had always reminded Karen of being in an airplane—impressed her. "This is like being on top of Pike's Peak," Jill gushed.

Alex grinned. "I'll take your word for it. Now, are you going to read the menu, or should your mother and I order for you?"

Jill, who had been peering intently at the view of

New York Harbor and the Statue of Liberty, turned to Alex, her eyes wide with surprise. Ignoring his question about food, she said. "You mean there's someplace I've been that you haven't?"

"I imagine there are lots of places, especially if they're west of the Mississippi." He shook his head when the waitress appeared, ready to take their orders. "Do you suppose I could talk you into being my tour guide when I come west?"

West? Alex had said nothing about planning a trip. Karen's heart began to pound at the thought of seeing him again, this time on her home turf. It was impossible, of course. In all likelihood, he had no intention of doing any such thing but was merely being polite, making conversation with Jill.

"I'll have the clam chowder and a spinach salad," Karen said when the waitress returned. It seemed that she was spending the day changing the subject, trying to steer the conversation in less dangerous directions. The ploy had worked with Alex; maybe it would succeed with Jill.

"When are you coming?" Jill asked when the waitress left. Not for the first time, Karen regretted her daughter's single-mindedness.

"I haven't decided," Alex said in all apparent sincerity, his words and tone destroying Karen's hope that he was not serious about a trip. "When would you suggest?"

"Summer!" Jill replied with no hesitation. "Frontier Days is . . . "

"Fierce?" he suggested.

Jill's smile was blinding in its intensity. "Yeah. If you came, you could see Matt ride. He's terrific."

Karen's heart began to thud. This was getting out of control, turning from a typical party conversation in which people made promises they had absolutely no intention of fulfilling into a serious discussion. She could not encourage it and risk having Jill hurt. As for her own heart . . .

"Did you see the weather report this morning?" she asked in another blatant attempt to change the topic. "Two different channels forecasted a white Christmas. Do you think it's going to happen?"

Alex gave her a conspiratorial smile, as if he knew why she had changed the subject. He couldn't, of course. There was no way he could guess why she was so reluctant to have him in Golden Spur.

"Spoken like a true skeptic," Alex said. "Although, considering the weatherman's record, I don't blame you for being skeptical." When Jill looked crestfallen, Alex continued, "I read somewhere that this is the season of miracles. Maybe it's true, and we will have a white Christmas."

"Really?"

Alex nodded solemnly. When the waitress set their platters in front of them and he swallowed the first bite of his burger, he continued, "This storm is coming up the coast. Those are usually our worst—and most predictable—storms, so I'd say there's a good chance. If not"—he shrugged—"I'll spray some of the fake stuff in my condo."

"Yuck!" Jill wrinkled her nose at the prospect of aerosol snow.

The two of them continued their bantering, and although they included Karen in the conversation, it was clear to her that Alex had planned this lunch for Jill. He told her amusing stories of the building of the Trade Towers, and the two of them speculated on the reaction New Yorkers would have if someone decorated the Statue of Liberty for the holidays, draping tinsel around her shoulders, putting a green light in her torch.

Karen wasn't surprised at Alex. The man was charm personified, and if he set his mind to fascinating a woman—or in this case a teenage girl—he would succeed. What surprised her was Jill's reaction. It was unusual for her to be so open with a stranger. Normally Jill was slow to give her friendship, though once committed, she was steadfast in her loyalty toward her friends.

Karen repressed a sigh. She should never have agreed to see Alex after that first night. Though her instincts had told her she was risking heartache, she had thought it was only her own. Not once had she considered that she might be putting Jill's heart in jeopardy.

When he and Jill had finished their hot fudge sundaes, Alex failed to stifle a yawn. "What are your plans for the afternoon?" he asked Karen. He gave Jill another one of his conspiratorial grins. "You can tell what I plan to do."

She laughed, but it was Karen who replied, "The Metropolitan. I've always wanted to see their Christmas trees."

"And I heard that Egyptian temple was cool," Jill added.

Alex rose and pulled out Karen's chair. "They also have a great exhibit of musical instruments," he said.

"Yuck!"

As Karen raised an admonishing brow, Alex chuckled at Jill's reaction, which appeared to equate musical instruments with aerosol snow. "I see your daughter inherited your lack of appreciation for fine music."

Karen shrugged and pressed the elevator call button. They must have just missed a car, for although she had seen other patrons leaving the restaurant only seconds before them, the hallway was empty.

"Let's just say you won't find a harpsichord in my house," she said. Though she faced Alex, from the corner of her eye, she watched Jill's reaction.

Her daughter's eyes widened. "Does Alex have one?" she demanded.

"He even plays it."

Karen bit back a smile at Jill's response. She stared at Alex as if he had suddenly sprouted a third ear. "Really?"

Alex held the elevator door open for them, and Karen could see that he was enjoying Jill's amazement. "Guilty as charged."

As he pressed the ground floor button, Jill gave his hand a long, appraising look. "Playing the harpsichord must be like making jewelry," she said at last. "You need talented fingers."

Karen felt her cheeks flush as she thought of Alex's fingers and just how talented they were. The man used them to make beautiful jewelry, exquisite music, and heart-stopping love.

"You were right, Mom," Jill said three hours later when they had completed their whirlwind tour of the Metropolitan Museum and were back at the main entrance, surrounded by some of the most beautiful trees Karen had ever seen. "These trees are great." She fished through her backpack to find her camera. "I want to take a couple more pictures."

After Karen had posed in front of the tallest tree and a friendly visitor had taken Karen and Jill's picture, Karen gestured toward the museum shop. "Meet me in there when you've finished the roll of film." She wanted to buy a gift for Jill. Though they had left the majority of their presents at home, agreeing to bring only one to exchange on Christmas Day, Karen hoped to find something special for her daughter's first holiday away from home.

She wandered through the aisles, glancing at the books, note cards, puzzles, and jewelry reproductions, listening as other visitors discussed their favorite items, hoping to find one perfect gift. But, though the selection was excellent, nothing caught her eye. Until she entered the last aisle.

Karen laughed aloud when she spotted it. It was perfect. Absolutely, positively perfect. He would love it. She pulled it from the rack, then waited in line at the checkout counter.

"A very popular item," the clerk said as she took the gift and Karen's credit card. "I believe this is our last one."

Talk about timing! If she had come an hour later, she wouldn't have seen it.

Karen nodded when the woman asked if she wanted the gift wrapped. "The silver paper," she said, pointing to a simple foil roll. By the time Jill entered the shop and made her way to Karen's side, the box was wrapped and Karen was signing the credit card slip.

"Is that for Alex?" Jill demanded as she eyed the package with what could only be called suspicion.

Karen nodded. She wouldn't tell Jill what was inside the box or what it would mean to Alex, but she would not deny that she had bought the gift for him. There had been far too many lies.

Jill's face darkened, and her mouth turned down into a pout. "How can you?"

She turned and looked as if she wanted to run, but the crush of the crowd restrained her. Alarmed, Karen gripped her daughter's arm. "How can I what?" she asked as she led her out of the shop. As she had told Alex, Jill was not a pouter. Though she had been more serious than normal this past year while she dealt with Tom's death, she had a naturally sunny disposition. That sunny disposition had just disappeared.

"I've seen the way you two look at each other," Jill said, her voice laden with venom. "It's disgusting." She clamped her lips together, their trembling telling Karen she was trying not to cry. This was not like Jill. What could have happened to change her mood so completely? Surely it wasn't Alex's present.

"Jill, what's wrong?" Karen asked, keeping her voice as calm as she could. Though it hurt to see Jill so upset, she could not let her petulance continue. "I bought a gift—a simple gift to take to the man who's cooking Christmas dinner for us. That's called common courtesy. Now, what's wrong?"

Jill was silent for a moment, and then the tears that had been welling spilled from her eyes.

"I loved Dad," she said. "I don't want a new father."

Chapter Seven

"I thought you liked Alex." Karen was perplexed by her daughter's reaction. Though Jill, like all teenagers, had been subject to hormonal mood swings, she seemed to have stabilized over the past year, and the unpredictable outbursts of tears followed by brilliant smiles had been replaced with steady calmness.

"I do like him," Jill admitted. "Alex is cool. I can talk to him."

"Then why were you crying?" Keeping a firm grip on Jill's arm, Karen led her toward the door. A crowded museum, filled with happy, harried visitors, was no place for a serious discussion. "All I did was buy Alex a gift," Karen continued as they zipped their jackets and walked outside the museum. "I buy Mr. Sweeney one every year, and that doesn't seem to bother you."

Jill wrinkled her nose. "Alex isn't Mr. Sweeney."

No, he most certainly was not. Jared Sweeney was their neighbor, a fifty-year-old widower who had been one of Tom's closest buddies and the father of Jill's best friend, a man who—one month to the day after Tom's funeral—had approached Karen and suggested that since they were both alone now, they should marry. It made sense, Jared had explained. They could operate their ranches more efficiently if they combined them, their daughters were already friends, and he and Karen would be less lonely. Love, it appeared, was not one of Jared's requirements for marriage.

Karen could not imagine Alex approaching marriage as if it were a business proposal. He would . . .

Stop it! She admonished herself. It was absurd to be thinking of Alex and marriage in the same sentence. Oh, she wouldn't deny that she wished they could have a future together. The last couple of days had shown her a glimpse of how wonderful that would be. But it wasn't possible, and she needed to remember that. They would have only a few more days together, days of pure happiness that would take on the air of a dream when she returned home.

No matter how much she wished otherwise, their brief idyll would end, and reality would intrude as surely as winter followed autumn. Only a miracle would give them a happy ending. And, while Alex might call this a season of miracles, Karen knew all too well that there was no such thing. What there was was reality, and right now reality was an angry daughter.

"Jill, something upset you back there, and I think it was more than Alex's present."

As they walked toward the street, Jill ducked her head into her collar, and Karen heard her sniff. "Oh, Mom, I saw a family come out of the shop together; there was a mother and a father and two kids, and they looked so happy, and I wished it could be us." She strung the words together in one long sentence. "I want Dad back!"

Heedless of the crowds that surged by, Karen put an arm around her daughter and drew her to the edge of the sidewalk. She tipped Jill's face up and, brushing a tear from her cheek, said solemnly, "Me, too, honey. But we both know that's not going to happen, so we've got to try to be happy with what we have." *And I need to realize that Jill's brave front is nothing more than that—a front. She's still a young girl who hasn't fully accepted her father's death.* "You know Dad wouldn't want you to cry," she said.

The afternoon had turned cold and damp, the morning's blue sky replaced with a leaden gray one that seemed to match Jill's mood. She was silent for a moment, then said softly, "Can we take a taxi back? I want to call Laura."

Karen nodded. If anyone could talk Jill out of her funk, it was Laura Sweeney. Now, if only someone could talk Jill's mother out of her silly belief in happy endings.

"Can we have room service?" Jill asked an hour later, when she emerged from her room after talking to Laura. Her face was blotchy, proof that she had been crying, but she managed a brave smile.

"Sure." The weather was so raw that Karen had no desire to go outside again. Still, Jill had planned each meal so carefully. "What about Little Italy?" she asked, remembering the schedule that Jill had reviewed with her no less than a dozen times on the flight from Denver to Newark, the schedule that had changed so often since they arrived. Since they met Alex.

Jill shook her head. "Laura told me there's a great movie on TV tonight."

A movie. That didn't sound like Jill's idea of how to spend one of her New York nights, but then, this afternoon's outburst wasn't typical, either.

"Laura could record it for you," Karen suggested.

Jill gave Karen one of her "you don't understand" looks. "I want to stay inside tonight," she said. "We can put some popcorn in the microwave and watch the movie. Okay?"

"Okay." If it turned out to be one of the horror movies that Jill had favored for the past year, Karen could read or watch another channel in her room.

She handed Jill the room-service menu. "What sounds good?"

While Jill debated the relative merits of a pastrami sandwich and a stuffed pizza, Karen switched on the TV. "Record sales boost economy. Details at six on seven."

The muted bell of the parlor phone interrupted her reverie. "Hello." For once, Jill did not jump to answer the phone. "Oh, hi, Alex." Karen couldn't help it. Just the sound of his voice made her smile. Though it might be cold and damp outside, the knowledge that Alex was in the same city made Karen's temperature rise.

"The trees were great," she said in response to his question. Though Jill appeared to be studying the menu, Karen knew she was listening to her side of the conversation. "I hope you're sitting down for this. Jill insisted we go to the instrument display." From the corner of her eye, Karen saw Jill redden, though she kept her eyes on the menu, as if fascinated by the description of salmon mousse and Maryland crab cakes.

"They're predicting snow tonight," Alex said, and Karen could tell that he was smiling. "I wondered if you and Jill would like to take a ride in the park."

The gray, damp weather no longer sounded so unpleasant. Snow in the park was always magical. And snow with Alex . . .

"We can't." Karen hoped her voice did not betray her disappointment. This was Jill's trip. They would do whatever Jill wanted. "Jill and I are staying in tonight, watching a movie."

Jill shifted her legs and gave up all pretense of reading the menu. "What does Alex want us to do?" she asked.

"Take a carriage ride in Central Park." Karen murmured an apology to Alex and laid the receiver on a chair. She raised an eyebrow, letting her daughter know the decision was hers.

Jill wrinkled her nose, as if the thought of a ride was distasteful. "You go. You wouldn't like the movie, anyway."

It was tempting. So tempting.

"I don't want to desert you," Karen said. "Besides, I might like the movie."

Jill's snort told Karen just how likely that was. "I'm not a baby, you know. I can stay here by myself."

Jill might not be a small child, but Karen was still a mother, and this mother remembered how upset her daughter had been only a few hours ago.

"Are you sure you don't mind?"

"Go!" Jill picked up the menu, as if everything were decided, and Karen reached for the phone. "What time?" she asked Alex.

Two hours later, the waiter had retrieved their empty dinner dishes, and Karen had dressed in her warmest clothes, while Jill curled up on the couch, apparently waiting to greet Alex. Karen couldn't help smiling at the role reversal—her daughter letting *her* date.

When she opened the door, she saw that Alex was

wearing a down parka similar to the one she planned to wear, and he held a wrapped box in one hand.

"I always thought this and movies went hand-in-hand," he said as he gave Jill the candy. "And I wanted to say 'thanks' for letting me take your mom away for the evening."

"No problem," Jill said, sounding so sincere that Karen could almost believe she had imagined her earlier tears.

She and Alex took the short walk over to Central Park, then stood in the carriage queue. Though the majority of the people in line were families, Karen saw several other couples, including a young one who wore a courting glove, one large mitten designed for two hands, and a silver-haired couple in matching fur coats.

"The least I could have done was get us matching 'I Love NY' hats," Alex said.

"I'd settle for some hot chocolate." The predicted snow had not arrived, and the dampness had begun to penetrate Karen's clothes, making her wish she had worn another layer.

"With or without marshmallows?"

Karen raised an eyebrow. "You mean you don't remember?"

"Just testing you. It's possible you've outgrown your youthful indulgence in eight miniature marshmallows on a single cup of cocoa."

While Karen held their place in line, Alex made his way to the food vendors' kiosks, returning with two large cardboard cups.

Sipping the warm liquid, they inched their way forward in the queue until they were first. To Karen's surprise, when the next empty carriage arrived, Alex gestured toward the family behind him.

"I thought we were taking a ride," she said.

"We are." But he offered the next coach to another family and the one after that to a young couple. Then, looking down the line of approaching carriages, Alex said, "Here he comes."

"Who?"

"Frederick, our driver. You didn't think I'd let you ride in just any carriage, did you?"

Though the coaches were all similar, Karen had noticed differences that went beyond the color of the upholstery and the horses' harness. A number of the carriages were decorated for the holidays, with tinsel outlining the landau roofs, and while some of the drivers opted for practical, puffy jackets like hers and Alex's, others wore formal garb. The majority of the drivers were men, but one woman was resplendent in an elaborately embroidered cloak and kerchief that appeared to be of Russian design, while another wore a fur coat and a Davy Crockett style cap that made Karen smile.

Alex, it seemed, had surveyed the carriages and chosen one in advance. Though not ostentatious, it was one of the most elaborate and most beautiful. The coach body was shiny black, while the seats and roof were of sky-blue leather with silver trim, colors that were repeated on the horse's harness. Frederick, in his tall top hat and formal black coat with long tails, looked as if he belonged on the cover of a Regency novel, an impression that was strengthened by his London accent.

"Good evening, madam, sir," he said as he helped Karen climb into the coach. When they were seated and Alex had arranged the blue blanket around their legs, Frederick cracked his whip with a flourish.

"Showmanship," Alex murmured as he slid his arm

around Karen's shoulders and drew her closer to him. They settled back on the padded seats as the carriage made its way around the park.

"It's wonderful." Karen wasn't sure what was most wonderful, the lights of the city sparkling through the tree branches, the beauty of the park, or the joy of being part of the stately procession. But she was certain that the greatest pleasure was sharing it all with Alex.

"I've dreamt about this for years," he said softly, his lips so close to her ear that she could feel the warmth of his breath caressing her skin. "I always wished we had been patient enough to wait for a carriage the last time."

Karen turned, and their lips were only a fraction of an inch apart. She could smell the sweetness of chocolate on his breath and saw a speck of cocoa on the corner of his mouth. "If there's one thing I've learned, it's that we can't change the past." Regrets accomplished nothing other than marring the present.

"But we can create a future." Alex's lips curved into a smile so brilliant that for a second Karen forgot to breathe. When her heart began to beat again, she saw the smile reflected in his eyes.

"Oh, Alex," she whispered.

Wordlessly, he leaned forward, closing the tiny distance that separated them, and pressed his lips to hers. Karen sighed with pure pleasure as his lips moved softly, teasing her, tantalizing her, giving her a glimpse of the heaven they had once shared. Though it started as a gentle kiss, soon he deepened it, threading his fingers through her hair as he pulled her head closer. For a few moments, the outside world faded away, and nothing mattered except the fact that they were where they should be, in each other's arms.

When at length they broke apart, Karen heard bystanders cheering. She smiled a little self-consciously, but Alex shook his head. "That was worth cheering about," he said, feathering kisses on her lips.

"Everything is so beautiful," Karen murmured. "I feel like we're in a winter wonderland, where everything is perfect. All it needs is . . ." She broke off, astonished when one wet snowflake landed on her nose, followed by another. "How did you do that?" she demanded, for the forecasted snow had begun, as if on command.

Alex chuckled and drew her head onto his shoulder. "Didn't I tell you this was a season of miracles?"

"Yes, but . . ."

"No buts. Until this week, I didn't believe in miracles, either." He wrapped his arm around her waist, pulling her closer. The ragged sound of his breathing was oddly comforting, telling Karen he was as shaken by their kiss as she, though his voice was low and even.

"I hated the whole holiday season," Alex continued. "All those happy people. Most of all I hated 'Silver Bells.' Every time I heard it, I'd think about you, and that would remind me of what could have been."

Karen smiled, remembering her own reaction to the song she had once loved. "If it was playing on the radio, I'd switch stations," she confessed. "Jill used to call me the Christmas grinch when I did that."

"My employees called me Scrooge," Alex said with a grin. "They weren't far off." He kissed the tip of Karen's nose. "That all changed this week. I used to think it would take a miracle to bring you back into my life, but there I was, coping with six absent employees, listening to 'Silver Bells,' and getting even more disgusted because this time I couldn't turn off the music.

I was in a really rotten mood until I looked up and saw you standing in my store. If that's not a miracle, I don't know what it is."

The snow had intensified, falling so thickly that Alex's dark hair was frosted with white. It *was* a miracle. This whole evening was a miracle, but—like the snowflakes—it couldn't last.

"Coincidence? Chance?" she suggested, forcing a light tone to her voice.

"A miracle," Alex insisted. Under the cover of the blanket, he took both of her hands in his. Though snow had landed on his glasses, Karen could see the happiness shining in Alex's eyes. "It's been incredible having you here," he told her. "I can't explain it except to say that everything seems different—better. Why, you've even inspired me to do the best work of my life."

She couldn't let him continue. "That's all very flattering, Alex, but . . ."

"Didn't I tell you, no buts?" Alex tightened the grip on her hands. "Karen, I love you. Even when we were apart, I always loved you, and now that I've found you again, I don't want to let you go." His voice was earnest, so filled with the love he was professing that tears rose to Karen's eyes. Oh, how she loved him!

"Please say you'll marry me."

Karen closed her eyes, fighting to hold back the tears and the pain. She took a deep breath, then another, as she tried to gather the courage to speak. "I can't," she said at last.

She felt rather than heard Alex's gasp. "Can't or won't?" he asked in a low voice. The tremor he could not hide told Karen how deeply she had hurt him.

"Is there a difference?"

He nodded, and she saw the pain her words had

caused. Alex's eyes, which had gleamed with joy, were now dulled with agony. "I think there is a difference," he said. "The only reason you *couldn't* marry me would be if you didn't love me, and I won't believe that. You might not admit it, but I know you love me."

Karen tugged one of her hands free and touched his cheek, brushing away one of the fat snowflakes. "I do love you, Alex. So very, very much." Was it only this morning she had thought it would be easy to fall in love again? The truth was, she had always loved him—and she always would.

"Then marry me."

"I can't." Karen heard the misery in her voice. If only she could have given him another answer! If only the past didn't stand between them. If only . . .

"You're not making sense, Karen. How can you say you love me and then refuse to marry me?" Alex demanded harshly.

"Jill's not ready for a new father," she said at last, giving him the easiest part of her explanation.

He recaptured her hand. "I won't try to take Tom's place," he said, his voice once again gentle, loving and oh, so very dear. "I wouldn't expect her to call me 'Dad.' "

Karen closed her eyes, wishing she were anywhere else.

"It wouldn't work. Jill would be miserable living so far from her friends, and you can't leave New York." Both of those were true. Only she knew that she was grasping at excuses, trying to avoid telling him the truth.

But Alex would not accept her excuses. "I know you love Jill and want to do what's best for her," he said, forcing Karen to look at him. She saw love and something else in his eyes. As he continued, she realized that what she saw was fear. For some reason, Alex feared for her. "You need to think about yourself, Karen. Do what's right for you . . . and for me."

On the seat in front of them, Frederick flicked the reins, keeping their carriage the proper distance from the next one. The snow continued to fall; pedestrians applauded as another couple embraced. Nothing had changed; everything had changed.

Karen shook her head. Alex made it sound so simple, when her decision was anything but easy. "If Jill were in college . . ."

It was Alex's turn to shake his head. "I don't want to wait that long," he said, his voice once more intense. "Karen, I've waited for you for fifteen years. I don't want to wait any longer."

"But Jill . . ."

"You don't have to worry about her." As the carriage turned, Alex shifted his weight, drawing Karen even closer to him. "Jill's a kid, and they adapt faster than you think. Within a couple of months, she'd love New York."

Karen shook her head slowly. He didn't understand. He hadn't guessed. "It's not just that."

"I know," Alex agreed. "You're her mother, and you're worried about giving her a stepfather. I promise it'll work out."

"But, Alex . . ." He was making this so difficult. Now she had no choice. She had to tell him.

"I love Jill," he said, "and not just because she's your daughter. I love her for herself."

This was better—and worse—than she had ever dreamed. The wonder and the pure, simple love she saw shining from Alex's eyes made Karen want to cry. Why, oh why, had she come to New York? She should have stayed home, but she hadn't, and now there could be no turning back.

Alex gripped Karen's hands. "Karen, I couldn't love Jill more if she were my own child."

"She is."

Chapter Eight

It took a moment for the pain to register. It had been
like the time he had received a serious injury playing
soccer. First there had been shock, then disbelief, then
horrible, gut-wrenching pain. And that pain was nothing at all compared to what he now felt.

Dimly Alex realized that the carriage was slowing,
that Frederick was closing the distance between their
coach and the one before it. The ride was over. *How
fitting,* Alex thought. The ride had ended just as he and
Karen had come to the end of the line. For there was
no doubt that this was the end. He could delude himself no more.

Moving mechanically, Alex pulled a folded bill
from his pocket, handing it to Frederick with what he
hoped looked like a genuine smile. The fact that he
could force his lips to curve upwards was nothing

193

short of incredible, for the pain was so intense that all he wanted to do was grimace.

Brushing the snow from his glasses, he took Karen's arm and propelled her across the road, away from the queue of holiday revelers. Had it been less than an hour since they stood there, sipping hot chocolate while they waited for their carriage? Surely it had been a lifetime ago that he felt so happy, so carefree, so convinced that he and Karen would have a future together.

"You lied to me," he said, and if she flinched at the anger he made no attempt to disguise, Alex didn't care. How did she expect him to react to the news that he had a daughter? A flicker of warmth settled in the pit of his stomach as he realized that lovely, gutsy, *fierce* Jill was his child, conceived that magical night fifteen years ago when love and desire had overcome common sense, and they had made love without protection.

"You lied," he repeated. "We knew there was a chance you might be pregnant, but when I asked you, you said you weren't."

Snow swirled around the streetlights, the big flakes dancing as they fell to the ground. Just minutes ago, Alex had thought the world a beautiful place. Now he knew better. Karen, the woman he had loved so deeply, was a liar. She had deceived him about the single most important thing in his life.

Karen shook her head slowly. "I told you I was safe, and I was."

Semantics! "Now you sound like a lawyer, splitting hairs." He tightened his grip on her arm. Though Alex hated confrontations, this was one time when—regardless of how unpleasant it was—he would not stop until he had all the answers. "No matter what words you used, you wanted me to think you weren't pregnant, and that was a lie."

"That's true," she admitted. Though her voice was solemn, he heard no apology in it. Had she no shame? His daughter was fourteen years old, and he'd just learned of her existence. The pain swept through Alex again, threatening to buckle his legs.

"What about that day at your ranch when I asked you? You lied a second time." When Alex had arrived in Wyoming, Karen had looked so pale and drawn that he had been afraid she was ill. Once again she had insisted she was fine—merely exhausted from the long days at the hospital with her father—when in fact she was probably suffering the miseries of early pregnancy.

Alex slid his hand into his pocket, then recoiled when his fingers touched the small cardboard box. What a fool he was! He should have thrown it away when she left the first time. But no, he had carried that box all the way to Golden Spur, and even after she had denied she loved him, he had kept it, bringing it with him again tonight. He would carry it no more. Even a fool learned his lessons eventually.

"Were you ever going to tell me the truth?" Oh, how it hurt, realizing he might have gone through life never knowing he and Karen had made a beautiful baby that night.

As she shook her head, her gold hoop earrings bounced against her cheeks. "It was better you didn't know."

Better! How could she say that? "Better for whom?" he demanded, his voice harsh with anger and the pain that could not be denied. "Better for you? Better for Jill? It sure as hell wasn't better for me!" When Karen refused to meet his gaze, Alex tipped her chin so she was facing him. Tiny diamonds of snowflakes landed on her lashes, then melted as swiftly as his hopes had disappeared.

"Don't you think I would have wanted to raise our daughter?" The pictures of a chubby child teetering as she took her first steps danced before his eyes, wrenching his heart and filling him with a deep sense of loss.

"Alex, be reasonable."

"Reasonable! Is this some kind of joke?"

Karen started to tremble. It was surely from the cold. Alex wouldn't believe he had frightened her. "Let's get indoors," he said and headed toward her hotel.

"Try to understand," she said as they walked, and her voice mirrored some of the pain he was feeling. "Lying to you was the hardest decision I've ever made." Her eyes darkened, and though he tried to harden his heart, he could not. This was Karen, the woman he had loved for half his life. Surely when he heard her explanation, he would understand.

"My father was so ill that I didn't know when—if ever—I'd be able to leave the ranch. College was over for me, but I didn't care about that. All that mattered was you and the baby."

"Then why didn't you tell me?"

They stood at the street corner, waiting for the light to turn green. On the opposite corner, a sidewalk Santa rang his bell, while shoppers juggled packages to reach for their billfolds. It was Christmas time in New York; only Alex had lost his holiday spirit.

"Why?" he asked again.

She looked up at him, and he saw tears welling in her eyes. "I knew you'd marry me if I told you about the baby, but I couldn't let you do that."

"What are you saying? Didn't you want to marry me?" The pain that he thought couldn't worsen did.

Karen's smile was bittersweet as she brushed tears and snowflakes from her face. "Of course I wanted to marry you. I loved you, and I was having your baby.

But I knew it wouldn't work. I couldn't leave home, and you wouldn't have been happy moving to the ranch." She shook her head slowly. "I couldn't let you give up studying in Europe and coming back to run Bagatelle."

As if that mattered! The pain was so intense that Alex wanted to shout. Instead he kept his voice low, through there was no disguising his anger. "So you made the decision—a decision that affected both of our lives—without telling me."

Karen winced and tried to back away from him. As the light changed, Alex took her arm and guided her across the street. "Don't you understand, Alex?" she said, her voice choked with emotion. "I did what was best for you. I didn't want you to give up your dreams."

His dreams. He'd built a life many would envy, with a successful business, trips to exotic locations, a beautiful home in one of the world's most exciting cities. To some, it would seem every possible dream had come true. And yet, despite all the tangible rewards, his life felt empty, for the most important dream—a life with Karen—had eluded him.

"What about you?" he asked. "You gave up your dreams." The Karen he had known fifteen years ago had dreamt of a June wedding, a year in Europe, then a career as a teacher. She had had none of those.

Her eyes were bleak, and the smile she managed was hollow. "I made my father's last years happy," she said, nodding mechanically when the doorman greeted them by name.

She still didn't understand. "I asked about you, Karen. Were you happy?"

This time she didn't try to smile. "Tom and I were happy," she said quietly as they entered the hotel lobby. "We had a good marriage."

197

As his anger began to dissipate, Alex took comfort from Karen's statement. He would not have wanted her to be unhappy. He would never have wished her the loveless marriage he and Celia had shared.

A bellman approached them, then turned away without a word, as if he realized that he was unable to provide what Alex and Karen needed. At this time of the night, the lobby was virtually deserted, the only sounds the soft music from a harpist in one corner and the staff's muted conversation.

Though it was like probing a wound that ought to be left to heal, Alex couldn't stop himself from asking, "Were you and Tom happy the way we would have been?"

Karen shook her head, setting her earrings to bouncing again. "I won't even try to pretend. There's no one like you, Alex. No one else could make me feel so happy, so alive."

"But that wasn't important to you." Alex didn't understand how she could profess her love when she had deliberately walked away from it. "You told me to leave. You said you didn't love me."

Her gaze met his, and Alex saw his own pain reflected in her eyes. "It was the right decision."

He had thought his anger was starting to subside, but he was wrong. "No, that was not the right decision," he insisted, "and you know it." He drew her to a secluded corner of the lobby where they would not be overheard. "What I don't know is why you repeat the same mistake." She kept her gaze fixed on him, and Alex knew she was listening. The question was, did she hear what he was saying?

"You persist in making decisions that you think are right, because you're sure you know what's best for other people. Tell me, Karen, have you ever considered what's right for you?" Her expression was confused, as if he were speaking a foreign language. He had been afraid of this. Somehow, though she was an intelligent woman, she didn't understand. "You probably think you're being unselfish, but look at the results. You've robbed me of fourteen years with my daughter!"

Though her face was ashen, Karen continued to meet his gaze. "You don't understand."

He didn't understand? "Yes, I do," he said firmly. "I know you think you're right. That's why you want to wait until Jill's in college before you'll give us a chance at happiness." She nodded slightly, and he knew that this far she followed his logic. "In your mind, that's the right decision. But I'm telling you, Karen, it's *not* the right decision. It's not right for me; it's not right for you; and it's not right for Jill."

"But . . ."

"No buts. This is one time I'm making a decision, and it's a simple one. I will never again ask you to marry me."

Fortunately, the suite was quiet when Karen entered it. Instead of the sound of the television that she had expected, the only noise was the ticking of the clock. The door to Jill's room was closed, with a hastily scrawled note on the console table providing the explanation. "Boring movie. See you in the morning." *Thank goodness!* She could not have faced anyone just then.

Karen tugged off her gloves, then ran one hand through her hair as she walked toward her room. She unzipped her parka and placed it on a hanger, straightening the sleeves until they hung evenly. Maybe if she concentrated on meaningless details, she would be able to keep the pain at bay. Maybe she would be able to forget the anguish she had seen in Alex's eyes and the knowledge that she had caused it. Maybe she could pretend that tonight had never happened.

But Karen had never been good at pretense. Tonight had happened, and the pain that even now was rushing through her with the force of a high-speed train was real. All too real and worse than any she had ever experienced. At the time, she had thought that nothing could hurt more than standing in the paddock, lying to Alex, telling him she didn't love him. She had been wrong. That pain had been tempered, if only marginally, by a glimmer of hope that refused to be extinguished, the hope that somehow, somewhere, sometime she would see him again, that they would have the happily-ever-after of her dreams. Now that hope was gone, and the emptiness deep inside her told her it would never return.

Her dreams had ended.

Karen paced the floor, as if the activity could marshal her thoughts. Instead, when she looked at the soothing watercolors that hung on the walls, all she saw was Alex's face, contorted with pain. Pain that she had caused. The fact that it wasn't deliberate, that she had had no intention of hurting him, made no difference. What mattered was that she had hurt him horribly.

Karen picked up the truffle the maid had centered on her pillow and tossed it into the wastebasket. There were some things that even chocolate could not help.

Alex was right. She had cheated him. Her lies had deprived him of years with Jill. And more. She had kept his parents from knowing the wonderful girl who was their granddaughter. Karen and Tom had lavished love on Jill, but who could say that she wouldn't have been happier with her biological father and his family?

When the radio began to play a Christmas carol,

Karen lunged at it. She would not—absolutely would not—listen to holiday music. What she needed now was a requiem mass.

Alex was right. She had deliberately denied herself, trying to convince herself that making others happy would make her happy. It hadn't worked. Oh, she and Tom had had a good life. She hadn't lied to Alex about that. But it wasn't the kind of breathtaking, heart-stopping happiness she and Alex would have shared.

What a fool she was! She had mortgaged her happiness and Alex's for the hope of a future, and only now did she see what that future would be: as bleak as a November day, devoid of love, devoid of hope.

Suddenly unable to bear the solitude of her room, she walked toward the wall of windows and opened the drapes. For a moment she stood, transfixed by the beauty outside. The snow that had started earlier was still falling, soft flakes that covered the paths and blanketed the grass. Tree branches were frosted white, while the snow formed halos around the streetlights. It was the same view she had seen that morning, yet it looked totally different. The park, which only hours before had been a study in grays and blacks, had been transformed into a winter wonderland, fresh, clean, and white. If only she could remake her life so easily!

Karen tugged on the cord, as if closing the drapes could shut out the mess she had made of her life. There was no future. Alex had made that perfectly clear. And yet . . .

She scribbled a note for Jill; then, before courage could desert her, she grabbed the silver package and ran to the elevator.

His expression was wary as he opened the door.

"What's wrong?" Alex asked when they stood inside his condo.

Karen shook her head, refusing to give up her coat. If he rejected her, as he had every right to do, she wanted to be able to leave quickly. She glanced at the elegant foyer. The marble floor and fine Chinese carpet were so different from her own home that she wondered if she was mistaken in thinking they shared more than a child. This was a bad idea. Another of her misguided decisions. She clenched her fists inside her coat pockets and started to turn.

Alex stopped her with a touch to her shoulder. "Did something happen to Jill?" His voice was harsh with an emotion she could not readily identify. Fear, anger, perhaps something else. "What's wrong?"

"Jill's fine," she said. "It's me. I'm what's wrong." She saw the subtle change in his eyes as wariness warred with concern.

"Come on, Karen," he said, taking her arm and gently propelling her toward the living room. "Let's sit down. Then you can tell me what brought you out in the snow."

The room was as elegant as the foyer, with traditional furniture, fine carpets, and Alex's antique harpsichord in one corner. Tonight the room was decorated for the holidays. A small tree, exquisitely trimmed with silver tinsel and red balls, stood in front of the window, while three stockings hung from the marble fireplace.

Karen sank into one of the wing chairs and waited until Alex sat in the one next to her before she spoke. "You were right," she said, willing her voice to remain calm, though her body trembled with emotion. What would she do, how would she bear it if Alex refused to listen? "I should have told you the truth about Jill." Odd, she couldn't use the impersonal term "pregnancy."

Karen leaned forward, placing her hands on her knees in another attempt to calm her nerves. "I would give anything not to have hurt you. If I could, I would undo the past. But I can't do that; all I can do is tell you how sorry I am that I hurt you."

As Alex moved his head, light glinted off his glasses, obscuring his eyes. "Is that why you came here, Karen? To apologize?" His voice was husky, as if he too were battling some deep emotion, and when he moved again, she saw pain in his eyes.

"Partly," she admitted. "I couldn't leave New York without telling you that." He nodded slightly. Karen closed her eyes for a second, trying to muster every ounce of courage she possessed. "I had to apologize," she said, "though I know there's no way I can take away the pain. That's part of why I came. But mostly I came because I love you, and more than anything on earth, I want us to have a future together."

The tall grandfather clock chimed twice, marking the half hour. Though Alex's dark eyes were solemn, he said nothing.

Karen swallowed. He wasn't making this easy. "I love you with all my heart," she said, hoping he could see that love shining from her eyes. "I love you, and I want to spend the rest of my life making you happy." Still he made no reply. She swallowed again, then cleared her throat. Everything—their future, her happiness, even Jill's—depended on his answer to her next question. "Will you marry me, Alex?"

She had thought he would answer, but instead Alex reached forward and took her hands in his. His gaze met hers, and his eyes were serious as he asked, "Are you sure this is what you want?"

She nodded. "I have never been so sure of anything."

The corners of Alex's mouth started to turn up, and the blossom of hope that had started to grow deep inside Karen began to open. He loved her; she knew he did. And maybe—just maybe—he could put the past aside. Karen waited for his response, but once again Alex surprised her. Instead of an answer, he posed another question.

"What about Jill?"

Karen had thought of little else during the taxi ride from the hotel. She knew Alex was right, that they couldn't continue to put their happiness on hold, but she couldn't bear the thought that her daughter would be unhappy. "It will be hard for her at first. I know that." There was no doubt that Jill would find it difficult to move from their ranch to Manhattan, leaving her friends behind. And yet she would gain something incredibly important, something that would make the temporary pain worthwhile. "I thought we might be able to spend summers on the ranch," Karen explained. "That would make it easier for Jill. But if you don't want to do that, I'm sure she'll adjust." Karen took another deep breath. "I want Jill to know her real father. You're much more important than her friends."

Alex nodded as he pressed her fingertips to his lips. "I want to be with you when you tell her," he said softly.

The blossom was fully open now, a beautiful flower of hope, but still she needed to hear the words. "Does that mean you'll marry me?"

Alex's smile was all the answer Karen needed. It was so radiant, so full of love, that she could have believed the sun was shining. He rose and pulled her to her feet in a single fluid gesture. "Yes, my darling. I'll marry you and help raise our daughter. Did you honestly doubt it?"

It would be easy to deny it, but Karen had resolved there would be no more lies between them.

"Yes," she said simply. "I thought the hurt might have been too deep."

Alex smiled again, his dark eyes sparkling with the same joy she felt welling in her heart. "I love you, Karen. I always have, and I always will." He shook his head slightly. "I won't deny that I tried to stop. When I left your ranch, I told myself I was every kind of a fool, that you had made it clear you didn't love me. But my heart wouldn't listen. It just wouldn't stop hoping."

Alex slid her coat from her shoulders, then led her toward the fireplace, where three stockings hung from the mantel. "Let me show you how long I've been hoping." He pulled a small box from the middle stocking and handed it to her. "This was supposed to be your Christmas present fifteen years ago," he said. "I won't tell you how many times I've wanted to throw it out, but I couldn't, not even after you told me that you didn't love me."

Karen looked at the box, seeing the slightly rounded corners and the elegant *b* of the older Bagatelle logo. It held jewelry, but not a ring. That much she knew.

"Open it." She heard both impatience and nervousness in his voice, as if he worried that she would not like the gift.

Surprised that her own fingers were trembling, she lifted the lid, then touched the contents. How could he have doubted she'd love his gift? "Oh, Alex! You made them!" She smiled, a foolish, happy grin that captured only a fraction of her pleasure.

He nodded, and the smile she saw on his face mirrored the joy she felt bubbling through her veins. Only

Alex could have designed this jewelry. Only Alex would have known what it would mean to her, how many wonderful memories it would evoke. For he had fashioned earrings shaped like silver bells. That alone would have made the gift special. But Alex—wonderful, creative Alex—had made them unique, for instead of ordinary clappers, he had used their initials. Their song, their initials, their past, their future. Karen couldn't stop smiling.

"Oh, Alex!" As she pulled the earrings from the box, they tinkled softly.

"Oh, Alex," she repeated and replaced her gold hoop earrings with the silver bells. She tossed her head, reveling in the bells' song. "It's the most beautiful gift I've ever had."

"I hoped you'd like it."

"Oh, I do!"

When he opened his arms, she shook her head. "I have something for you," she said. "This was supposed to be a Christmas present," she told him as she reached inside her coat pocket and withdrew the present she had bought that afternoon, "but I think you should open it now."

Alex pulled her onto the sofa next to him and wrapped one arm around her shoulders as he tore the paper from the box. When he had pushed the tissue paper aside, he laughed, for inside was a dark green tie patterned with tiny silver bells.

"You couldn't forget our song either, could you?"

Karen shook her head and knotted the tie around Alex's throat. If it looked incongruous against his black turtleneck, she didn't care.

"There's only one thing missing," Alex said and rose to press several buttons on his stereo. He held out his arms. "May I have this dance?"

Even before the music started, Karen knew which song he had chosen. She moved into his embrace, smiling at how right it felt to be held by Alex. They swayed in each other's arms, softly humming the song they had made their own. When the haunting refrain of "Silver Bells" began, Karen raised her lips to his, and soon their bodies moved to a different melody as past and present disappeared, and the future began.

Merry Gentlemen

Emma Craig

Chapter One

"God rest ye merry—"

Thump.

"—lemen. Let nothing you dis—"

Bam.

"Remember Christ our—"

Whack-whack-whack.

"—was born on Christmas—"

Crash!

"I can't stand it!" Gina Sullivan slammed the off button of her cassette player, stormed over to the front window of her shop on Main Street, and glared out.

There it was, the source of her troubles: construction. Noise, dust, ugliness, big hairy men, scaffolding—and no customers.

How *could* there be customers with all that commotion going on? How could anyone inspect the lovely Christmas window display she'd set up if he had to risk his neck to do it? How could the discriminating buyer with taste and wealth at his or her disposal ever linger to contemplate the uniqueness and wonderfulness of Gina's merchandise if he or she had to scale a heap of rubbish and slog through a jungle of construction apes and scaffolding to do so?

Not that there were many such rich and discriminating creatures residing in the smallish southeastern New Mexico town of Roswell. Most of the locals couldn't care less about unique and wonderful crafts and artworks, and most of the visitors to the area were seeking extraterrestrial aliens and poring over exhibits at the UFO museum. Still, there might be one or two parties interested in Christmas-present-buying, if only they were allowed to see the merchandise.

But no. Fighting the rubble to reach her shop was too much trouble. People might as well go to Wal-Mart rather than brave the rigors of getting to Gina's shop, thanks to those wretched men building that wretched set for that wretched TV movie.

And if anyone *did* manage to maneuver his or her way through the construction, the gorgeous Christmas music, played to cheer people and inspire them to part with their money, couldn't be heard for the thundering noise of the blasted set-building operation.

And then there was the simmering cinnamon-and-apple potpourri Gina had so lovingly chosen for its effect in softening Scroogelike hearts. Ha! That delightfully Christmasy scent was being completely overwhelmed by the smell of dust and newly cut wood. Okay, so newly cut wood smelled nice, but it wasn't the same as sniffing Christmas potpourri. It was more likely to inspire a person to go camping than to buy jewelry or artworks.

"Go out there and bite those guys, Henry."

Henry Wadsworth Longfellow, Gina's sixty-pound, sad-eyed basset hound, opened an eye halfway and wagged his tail once before resuming his nap. Gina stared at him sourly, thinking it was just like a male to sleep while she was throwing a tantrum.

This wasn't fair, and she resented it. Of all the seasons of the year, and of all the years in which the season arose, why did it have to be *this* season in *this* year that the powers that be in Hollywood's television industry decided to film one of Theodore Hawkes's gruesome horror stories—and in front of her shop, of all places?

It wasn't as if her gallery was a hotbed of business activity, or so well-established that it could withstand the vagaries of a street clogged with messy and dangerous construction projects. Far from it. So far, in the two months the shop had been open, she'd managed to attract a grand total of fifteen customers, only three of whom had bought anything valuable enough to keep her dog in Kibbles. If it wasn't for the itsy-bitsy inheritance Gina had received from her grandmother's estate, she wouldn't have been able to stay open this long.

She sniffled miserably, thinking she'd much rather have her grandmother back than a booming business.

Lord, she was becoming positively maudlin.

Henry took that opportunity to crook his other eye open, yawn, and slurp her shoe. She nearly burst into tears. She swooped down to Henry's level and began petting him lavishly. He rolled over onto his back and basked. Henry, unlike the human population of the earth, knew what to do with life, and he did it well.

"Thank God for you, Henry Wadsworth, or I'd never survive Christmas. I miss everyone so much."

Henry opened both eyes this time and kissed her

cheek, which almost made life worthwhile—but not quite. Gina was in a funk the likes of which she'd never experienced.

"It's because I'm here in New Mexico and the rest of my family's in California," she told her dog, who whined in an appropriately melancholy tone, although his dewlaps had flopped backward to uncover his teeth and he looked silly. "If only I'd waited to move out here—but how could I?"

Henry evidently didn't know, so he allowed his eyes to drift shut once more.

"But honestly, Henry, I couldn't fail Grandma, could I?"

Henry kept his own counsel and began to snore.

Gina sighed. "And now I have the shop, which I love to death, but that stupid movie crew is preventing me from making any money in it. And everyone tells me that if I don't make money at Christmastime, I won't make any money at all. Oh, Henry, I wish I knew what to do." Gina plumped down next to her dog, feeling miserable.

"My goodness," came a gruff, imperious voice from the front door of her shop. "The woman's having a financial consultation with her dog."

Leaping to her feet and spinning around, Gina beheld a person she'd never imagined meeting face-to-face. Handsome, urbane, silver-haired, dressed and shod to perfection, every inch the dapper gentleman: the villain of her life.

What's more, he was perfectly in character. Smirking and looking superior, there he stood, the master of horror himself, Theodore Hawkes, richest writer in the universe. The author of a score or more novels crammed full of mayhem, bloody gore, murder, and all sorts of other yucky stuff, he'd recently signed a one-book contract for well into the millions of dollars. He was also, at present, the author of Gina's miseries. If he'd written a horror story expressly for her, he couldn't have done a better job.

Her mouth worked uselessly. The tip of her tongue was packed solid with things she'd love to spit at him, but she'd been brought up to honor the Golden Rule, which inhibited her a good deal—especially when she was mad, as she was now. She sometimes wished she wasn't such a nice person.

"What's the matter?" Theodore Hawkes sounded superbly sarcastic, as if he'd practiced his snooty tone for decades—which he probably had. "Dog got your tongue?"

"No." The word burst out with more force than was strictly necessary, and Hawkes lifted an eyebrow.

Henry, startled, woke up and barked, although he remained on his back. Friendly dog that he was, he blinked several times in an effort to figure out what was going on, then rolled onto his feet. He waddled over to investigate Mr. Hawkes's left shoe, tail wagging amicably the whole time. The dog had no discrimination. Gina didn't generally mind Henry Wadsworth's egalitarian attitude, but today she resented it almost as much as she resented Theodore Hawkes.

She cleared her throat. "Actually, Mr. Hawkes—"

"Ah, you know who I am." He sounded smug. Gina wouldn't have been surprised if he'd taken to buffing his fingernails on his lapel. Except that he didn't have a lapel. Actually, he was wearing a cowboy shirt and a tooled leather vest. Good grief. He actually looked good in them.

"Indeed, I suppose everyone in Roswell—"

"Ah, yes. Roswell's not exactly a hotbed of cultural excitement, is it? Notable only for alleged alien land-ings at your Air Force base some years back, no? I suppose a world-famous author coming to town would create a stir."

Gina bridled but again held her pique in check. He might be in here to buy something, and she couldn't go around snapping at what few customers there were in her world. "No, Mr. Hawkes—"

"Theodore, my dear. Call me Theodore."

She sucked in about a bushel of air. "I won't be able to call you anything at all if you don't allow me to finish a sentence." She smiled when she said it.

He chuckled. Even his chuckle was smug. Gina itched to slap his well-shaven cheek.

"You see, Theodore, I was trying to listen to Christmas carols, but the noise of the construction outside rendered them inaudible." Her heart took that opportunity to give a tremendous throb of loneliness, and she felt her smile go crooked.

"Christmas carols?" He pronounced the two words as if they either were meaningless or ought to be.

"Yes. I love Christmas carols." She felt defiant in the face of his manifest scorn.

"Why am I not amazed to discover that?"

He walked to a display of silver-and-turquoise jewelry made by a woman named Sylvia Tossa, who lived in the mountains not far to the southwest of Roswell. Gina held her breath as he fingered a bracelet she wished she could afford for herself. After lifting it to his bespectacled eyes and inspecting it closely for a moment, Hawkes put it down and dismissed it with a flick of his finger. Gina wanted to scream at him that Sylvia Tossa had more talent in her big toe than he had in his entire body.

But, of course, that was spite doing her thinking for her. After all, lots of people admired blood-soaked fiction more than they admired gorgeous, handcrafted silver jewelry. If they didn't, Sylvia Tossa would be rich and Theodore Hawkes wouldn't be. Which, if Gina ran the world, was the way things would be.

To prevent herself from saying anything nasty, she clicked her tongue to Henry Wadsworth in an attempt to call him back to her side. He immediately plodded to the door, snuffled loudly, wagged his tail even harder, and ignored her. It figured.

But Henry hadn't been merely disobeying a command. Gina realized that a second later when the door opened and a junior edition of the famous horror writer entered her shop. Oh Lord, there were two of him! He must be a relative, she supposed, because he had the same tall, well-tailored elegance as the older man, and they had the same imperious nose. He was very handsome—except that he looked as if he was suffering from terrible indigestion, probably from reading too many Theodore Hawkes novels.

Wonderful. Just what she needed. Not only was she two states away from her family at Christmastime—it was the first Christmas the family had been separated—and her newly opened shop was going bust before it had even been given a chance to succeed, but she now had not one, but two awful men with whom to contend.

She reminded herself that they probably hadn't come to Roswell solely to make her life miserable, and she forced a smile for the newcomer.

She might as well not have bothered because he didn't look at her. He brushed past the happy Henry and walked up to Theodore Hawkes.

"Come here, Henry Wadsworth. I'll give you a cookie." She didn't want her dog's feelings hurt by these insensitive men.

"Henry Wadsworth," Theodore Hawkes said, ignoring the newcomer and giving Henry a haughty half-smile. "That's a good one for a basset hound."

She turned and might have said "thank you" but for his next words.

"Trite and conventional, but good."

"Cut it out," said the new arrival. "You don't have to demonstrate your famous obnoxiousness to the provincials."

His famous obnoxiousness? To the provincials? Gina goggled at the two men.

"If I weren't obnoxious, what would you have to talk about, Alex?" Theodore Hawkes's voice had taken on an even more cutting edge, which astonished Gina, since it had already sounded as sharp as a honed blade. "God knows, you make no decent conversation on your own."

"To hell with decent conversation. I have plenty to do without chatting you up, thanks."

"Writing your paltry, sappy love stories. Of course."

Gina recoiled from the older man's tone which seemed to drip venom.

"Can the barbs, Father dear. They need you outside. You were supposed to stay on the set, if you'll recall, to answer questions the producer has."

Father? That ghastly man was this good-looking guy's father? Gina's goggling intensified.

"*Supposed?* I'm *supposed* to stay there?"

If any man had been crafted to be uppity enough for a ducal coronet, Theodore Hawkes was he. Gina would have liked to run him through with a ducal sword.

"Me?" the elder Hawkes continued. "I'm the writer of the piece. I'm the one with the money and the fame, remember?"

"How can I forget? Not that I wouldn't like to," Hawkes the younger rejoined.

For that matter, this other person, who Gina presumed was Alex Hawkes, son of Theodore, sounded pretty royal himself. They flung acid at each other with the ease and agility of long practice. Her insides winced. Since Gina would give pretty much anything to be within talking range of a member of her own family at the moment, everything in her rebelled against the open hostility between this father and son.

Without pausing to consider what she was doing, she propped her fists on her hips and said, "Will the two of you hush up? You sound like a couple of squabbling schoolchildren, and it's very unpleasant."

Theodore and Alex Hawkes, who had been squaring off to battle some more, turned and stared at her. Gina felt like an idiot.

"Good God," Theodore said in his supercilious tone. "I do believe the natives are getting restless."

Alex sighed, patted his shirt pocket, and reached inside. Withdrawing a roll of white tablets, he peeled the wrapper back, separated one from the roll, and popped it into his mouth. "Yeah. Looks like it. Listen, they really do need you outside."

"Do they?" Theodore Hawkes sneered magnificently.

"Yeah. Jordan needs to consult with you about the blood."

The blood? Gina's nose wrinkled.

"Which blood?" the elder Hawkes queried.

"The human blood. They have the bat blood rigged up along with the guts."

"Good grief. I think you're both crazy," Gina declared.

"Not crazy, my girl. Very creative and very rich, but not crazy." Theodore eyed his son askance. "Of course, I'm speaking only for myself. Alex has his mother's genes in him, so I can't vouch for his sanity. I already know he has no creativity in his soul."

"Give it up, old man," said his dutiful son. "Nobody cares about your problems with my mother." He popped another tablet into his mouth and chewed furiously.

"I had no problems with your mother, Alex."

"No. Nor with any of your other wives, according to you. I don't know why I put up with you."

"For the money, of course."

Gina had heard enough. "Why don't you both get out of here," she said through clenched teeth. "Your film has already caused me enough grief. I won't have you fighting in my shop. Take your spat outside."

"Spat?" Theodore turned to Alex. "The female thinks we're having a spat." He laughed.

It was a horrible laugh, tainted with sarcasm and vindictiveness. It gave Gina the shivers.

Alex ran a hand through his thick, gorgeous hair and looked harassed. "Listen," he said to Gina, "I'm sorry if you don't like us, but the fact is, the producer has a question for you too, if you'll give me a minute to explain it to you." He glared at his father. "If I can ever get the old man to get out of here and do his job."

"My job." Theodore scoffed. "*My* job is writing those nonsensical stories, Alex. *Your* job is to see to the filming of them."

"I wish nobody had ever thought about filming one," Gina said bitterly. "Especially at this time of year."

"This time of year?" Theodore lifted an eyebrow. He'd probably practiced that, too. "What does the time of year—Ah, I see. You don't approve of horror stories at Christmastime. Of course not. I'm sure you wouldn't." He nodded, as if it all made sense to him now, and tapped his son's arm. "This must be the buckle on the Bible belt, Alex. You'd best watch your tongue or they will run you out of town on a rail. Tarred and feathered."

"Get out of here, Dad." Alex sounded as if he couldn't take much more. "Go talk to Jordan. I'll be there in a minute."

"Don't rush, Alex. I'm finding life in Roswell tedious enough without you hanging on to my coattails."

Gina stared after the elder Hawkes as he left her shop. She turned to Alex, who also watched his father's back. He looked as if he'd like to heave something at it—preferably something sharp and lethal. Gina almost didn't blame him, although she did feel the first faint stirrings of compassion for the two men, which confused her. Why should anyone feel compassion for a pair of rich and spoiled Hollywood hotshot crybabies?

Nevertheless, the animosity between father and son seemed sad to her. It wasn't right. Family members needed one another. Families were precious—at least hers was. She missed them so much she could hardly stand it.

On the other hand, if she'd had a father like Theodore Hawkes, she might have a different attitude toward families.

It didn't matter. That detestable man and his detestable horror stories were ruining her life, and she was sinking rapidly into total despair.

Chapter Two

Alex read the bewilderment on the shop girl's face and sighed. Yet another of his father's messes left for him to clean up. He wondered if anything would happen to him if he downed another antacid tablet, and decided he'd better not. He didn't think you could overdose on the things, but he wasn't sure. God, his stomach hurt. Even his heartburn had heartburn.

Which was scarcely to the point. Trying to sound friendly, he said to the woman, "Don't mind the old man. He likes to think of himself as a literary Huston and tries to be as offensive as possible whenever possible."

She stared at him blankly, and he remembered that the name might mean different things to different people. She was probably thinking of Sam Houston. "I mean John Huston. The film director. Angelica's father. Not the guy from Texas."

"Oh." She turned, clicked her tongue to summon

her silly-looking dog, and went to the window.
"They're really making a mess out there. And an awful
lot of noise. I can't even hear my Christmas tapes for
all the hammering and pounding."

To hell with it. Alex unwrapped another antacid
tablet and stuck it in his mouth. Pressing a hand over
the pain in his stomach, he walked to the window and
stood beside her and her hound. "Yeah, well, it won't
last too long. A couple of months, maybe."

"A couple of *months?*" she screeched.

He winced. Even though his nerves were crackling
like live wires and he had too much work to get done
in too little time, he tried to moderate his own tone.
"No more than that, I shouldn't think."

She backed away and looked up at him as if he were
a monster out of one of his father's books. "In a couple
of months, if your crew is still blocking the entrance to
my shop and making that terrible racket, I won't have
any business left!"

The dog growled. Alex eyed it and decided it didn't
mean it. "Good doggy," he said. He didn't mean it
either.

The woman flounced away from him. "Don't speak
to my dog!"

Jeeze, she was really in a snit. "Listen, Miss . . ."

"Sullivan. My name is Gina Sullivan." She glared at
him. "I suppose you're a Hawkes if you're that miserable man's son."

He nodded. "Alex. Pleased to meet you, Gina."

"Well, I'm not pleased to meet you. Or your awful
father." She wiped an angry tear away.

Lord, he didn't need this. "I'm sorry if he upset you,
Gina. You're right. He is an awful man. And he was an
awful father. Still is, for that matter. But he's also
right: he's rich and famous, and you're not, and

they're going to make a movie out of one of his stories whether you like it or not. Which means the film crew is going to be working outside your shop for a while yet. I'm very sorry if it's disrupting your business, but—"

"*Disrupting* my business?"

She'd started shrieking again. Alex sighed and wondered if there was any Pepto-Bismol in the trailer.

"I have no business at all, thanks to that mess out there." She pointed a trembling finger at the set.

"Listen, maybe we can make it up to you, if—"

"Make it up to me! How can you make up customers? How can you make up the Christmas season? I can't even smell my potpourri or hear 'God Rest Ye Merry, Gentlemen!' " She burst into tears, sank down onto the floor next to her dog, and hugged the critter hard. The dog seemed to be sleeping.

This was just what he needed, Alex thought sourly. It wasn't enough that he had to deal with his bastard of a father. Oh, no. Now he had to try to bend a hysterical female to his purposes. He wasn't cut out for this, and trying to do it anyway was about to kill him.

"Uh, Miss Sullivan . . . "

She scowled up at him ferociously and wiped tears from her cheeks. "What?"

Alex tilted his head to one side as he observed her and tried to figure out what to say now. She was cute, he'd give her that. Short dark hair, big brown eyes. Her eyes actually looked kind of like her dog's, in an endearing sort of way. And it was probably the fuzzy pink sweater hugging her curves that had started him thinking fondly of Pepto-Bismol.

He shook his head hard, wondering if he was losing his mind. "Miss Sullivan, the producer asked me to talk to you about letting the crew use part of your shop. They'd like to set up their coffee and snack tables in here, if you have room and don't mind. They'll pay you, of course." He smiled one of his you're-about-to-become-a-Hollywood-insider-if-you-play-your-cards-right smiles at her. "They pay a fortune for stuff like that."

"I don't want anything to do with your stupid movie." She bowed her head over her dog and wouldn't look at him. She reminded him of a waif from one of those bleak Masterpiece Theatre productions of a Charles Dickens novel.

He wanted to go to his trailer, down a bottle of Maalox, and take a nap, but he knew where his duty lay. Hell, Alex had been officially running interference for his father for a decade now. Unofficially, he had been since he was ten years old. Not that the old lout deserved such dedication—but he did pay well these days. More and more lately, however, Alex wondered if being paid lavishly made up for the crap he had to take.

Gina sniffled and peered up at him with those huge eyes of hers; they made him want to feed her milk and cookies or something.

"I'm sorry, Mr. Hawkes, but—"

"Please, call me Alex. When anyone says Mr. Hawkes in my presence, I think they're referring to my father, and I get indigestion."

She didn't continue, and Alex wished he'd kept his fat mouth shut. Dammit, this job was going to kill him. He reached toward his pocket, decided that even if you couldn't overdose on antacids, eating ten of them in ten minutes probably wasn't a good idea, and dropped his hand again. "You were going to say something? I'm sorry, I interrupted you."

If his nerves got pulled any tighter, they were

going to snap. Alex wondered if, when nerves snapped, they made a bloody mess. His father would probably know. Probably wrote a book about it. He passed a hand over his eyes and told himself to calm down. Deep breathing was the ticket. Mantras. Stuff like that.

Although her dog protested—at least Alex presumed the whine the creature gave was a protest— Gina rose to her feet.

"No, *I'm* sorry, Alex. You probably think I'm an idiot, falling apart like this."

He gestured with the hand that wanted to unwrap another antacid tablet. "Not at all. My father's disagreeable enough to make the Rock of Gibraltar crumble."

She tipped her head to one side and gazed at him solemnly. He wished she wouldn't do that. She looked too wise. He got the feeling she was on to him, yet she couldn't be. She didn't even know him. So how could she know he'd spent his entire thirty-five years to date trying to get his old man to respect him? He'd given up trying to get the bastard to love him about thirty-four years ago.

"That's the saddest thing I've ever heard."

He jerked upright and forgot his antacid tablets. "What? What's the saddest thing you've ever heard?"

"That thing you said about your father."

Good God. She couldn't mean that. Could she? "You don't know him." He used his hardest, most sarcastic voice, which reminded himself of his father and made his ulcer throb.

"I'm not saying you're wrong, Alex. I'm only saying that it's sad when families don't get along."

"Yeah. I'm sure you're right." He didn't know what the heck she was talking about. He'd never met a family yet that did more than tolerate one another. Hell, when doing some magazine writing he'd even interviewed one of the Menendez brothers, and he'd done more than—Alex decided to hold his cynicism in check for the moment.

"No, you're not. You're not sure at all. And that's probably even sadder." She shook her head, walked dejectedly to the window, and stared out again.

Alex watched her, squinted, and took in the scene outdoors. It actually did look kind of pitiful out there. Not that Roswell was a garden spot to begin with, but she had a point about her shop. It was certain that no customers had come inside it since he'd entered the place.

Wonderful. The filming of his father's story was going to ruin this woman's business and, probably, her life. Which meant, of course, that he was going to have to slather on the charm to get her to cooperate in her own destruction.

If he had any charm left. Lately he'd been getting as short-tempered and testy as the old man. It was because his life was so stressful. He was so busy looking after Theodore Hawkes that he hardly had time for himself and his own writing anymore.

Not that anyone but himself cared about his writing, which was nowhere near as popular as Theodore's. Hell, no. Alex Hawkes didn't write about supernatural beasts who drank their victims' blood, or monsters who raped women and impregnated them with quasi-monster babies and took over the world. He just wrote stories and screenplays about relationships. Stories and screenplays he loved. About relationships he'd never experienced but secretly longed for. His stomach gave a hard spasm, and he decided to concentrate on Gina Sullivan. She was much prettier than his thoughts.

"Gina, will you please talk to me for a minute?"

She turned her head and peered over her shoulder at him. She'd taken to hugging herself, and Alex had a sudden, fierce impulse to draw her into his arms and try to comfort her. The impulse was totally alien to his background and experience. What the hell did he know about sympathy and comfort? What the hell was the matter with him?

"What do you want to talk about? Ruining my business?" This time she gave him a little gamine half-smile, and his impulse returned. Great. Just what he needed.

He cleared his throat. "We don't want to ruin your business. In fact, maybe we can help you along some. If you'll allow us to set up in here, the company will pay you a fortune." He tried for a boyish grin. It had been so long since he'd grinned boyishly that he wasn't sure he could still do it.

Gina gave no indication as to whether he'd succeeded or not. Nor did she respond to his statement.

He tried again. "I'm sure you'll make more money with us than you would with your regular Christmas customers."

"What about after Christmas, when I have no business left?"

Since she wasn't smiling back, he canned the grin and continued resolutely pursuing his goal. "It's been my experience that movie crews, even TV movie crews, draw people like flies."

"What a delightful image. Garbage dumps draw flies, too."

Now she was being deliberately contentious, and he didn't appreciate it. Thanks to his father, he had enough contentiousness in his life already. Still, he persevered, knowing somehow that if he got mad at her, he'd have to find another, less convenient spot for the crew's refreshment area. "You know what I mean, Gina." This time he tried for a sweet smile. His stomach, unused to sweetness, protested. "People flock to see movies being made. They want to see the stars."

"The stars. How appropriate for Christmas. Do you suppose the three wise men would have followed the stars to Hollywood?"

Was she going to get hysterical? Alex pressed a palm over his ulcer and would have prayed if he did such things. "They might have." He couldn't take much more of this stress. "Listen, Gina, I'm sorry if we're making a mess in front of your shop, and I'm sorry if you think you're losing business because of it, but the production company's not going away. Not until the film's in the can. About the only way we can make any of your lost revenues up to you is with rent, and the only way we can pay you any rent is if you allow us to use your shop. All right? Will you talk to Jordan? Please?"

She eyed him for a long time. So long, in fact, that his nerves twitched, and if he'd been more like his father than he was, he'd have picked up something breakable and flung it through the front window.

Just as he was about to crack, she said, "All right. You can use my shop. On one condition."

He sucked in a huge breath and stuffed his hands into his pants pockets. He wouldn't fling anything. He wouldn't. He'd behave like a civilized human being. Like his mother. He'd be damned if he'd become more like his father in any way, shape, or form. "What's the condition?" He tried to smile but couldn't make himself do it.

"You and your father have to come to my house for supper."

He stared at Gina Sullivan—and couldn't make his mouth form words.

229

Chapter Three

For the life of her, Gina didn't know why she'd said that. Or maybe she did. She could hear her mother's voice clear as day telling her, "*Feed* them, Gina Marie! *Feed* them! It's *Christmas!*" Her mother thought generous offerings of food and drink could solve all the world's problems—and so far, Gina hadn't found that belief to be unfounded. She sighed deeply and wished her mother were here to fix dinner for the Hawkes men.

Alex Hawkes cleared his throat. His right hand lifted to his shirt pocket, but he dropped it again.

Gina would bet money those pills he kept popping were antacids. Obviously, the man had problems, not the least of which was his father. And, while she was upset about all the problems Theodore Hawkes's stupid movie was causing for her business, she'd just experienced the most alarming sense of enlightenment. Even an epiphany. She realized she understood the unhappy man who stood before her, longing for his stomach to stop hurting.

What he needed wasn't a handful of antacid tablets. What he needed was a whopping dose of the milk of human kindness, a commodity Gina was relatively sure he seldom received. Who could, with a father like Theodore Hawkes? She blessed her mother for being such a saint. Now *there* was a woman who knew how to celebrate Christmas.

"I beg your pardon?"

He sounded awfully polite. Actually, he sounded as if he were trying to humor a lunatic. His tone struck Gina funny, and the weird notion she'd begun to entertain about showing the Hawkes men some honest-to-goodness Christmas cheer started to solidify. She grinned at him.

"You and your father have to come to my house for supper. And you have to allow me to show you the local sights. Call it a little holiday cheer. Christmas is only a few weeks off, and you don't seem to be in the spirit yet." If ever an understatement had passed her lips, that one was it.

He eyed her for a moment or two, clearly trying to figure her out. Her grin broadened. If his frame of reference was life with Theodore Hawkes, he'd never figure her out in a million years.

"Uh, holiday cheer?"

She shrugged. "Christmas has always been my favorite time of the year."

Alex hesitated. "Until this year." He gestured. "The film crew and everything."

"Oh, Christmas is still my favorite season. I was doing pretty well getting into the spirit of things—you know, with my music and potpourri and window decorations—until all that hammering began, but I think it's getting better again."

"Getting better again? I don't—uh, think I understand."

"No, I'm sure you don't." She experienced another twinge of sorrow on Alex's behalf. "How could you?"

His eyes were getting narrower and narrower, as if he were puzzling something out in his head that didn't want to be puzzled out. "Uh, how could I?"

"Right. With a father like yours, I'm sure Christmas was as hideous as every other day."

He hesitated again. Then said simply, "Hideouser."

"Hideouser. Interesting word."

The lines beside his eyes smoothed out a little bit. He even offered her a small smile—a genuine one this time, which Gina considered a step in the right direction.

"We writers like to make 'em up as we go along. Saves time looking in the dictionary," he offered.

"I see."

Henry got up and yawned. He glanced at Alex and did a double-take, as if surprised to find the man still hanging around. He wagged his tail. Good old Henry.

"Uh," Alex said, eyeing the dog, "why do you want us to come to supper? Wouldn't you prefer it if we took you out to dinner or something?"

She thought about it, then shook her head. "No, I don't think so. It has to be at my house. It's actually my grandmother's house. Or it was. She died recently, and it's mine now."

"Oh," Alex said softly.

"You see, I came from California, just like you." She smiled brightly.

He nodded. "I see. Uh, *why* does it have to be at your house?" He held up a hand. "I'm not complaining, just curious, is all."

She debated with herself for a couple of seconds before she decided to tell the truth. What did she have to lose? Heck, she was already going to lose her shop if business remained as bad as it had been. "I think you both need it, is why."

"We *need* to have supper at your house?"

"And you need to let me show you the sights." Showing a body the sights around Roswell struck her as funny, since there weren't any obvious ones to speak of, and she chuckled.

"You want to show us the sights."

"Incredulity rather suits you, Alex Hawkes." She laughed. Henry wagged his tail harder. "It suits you a good deal better than indigestion."

"Uh, if my father and I come to your house for supper, the 'holiday cheer' you're looking for will be sure to degenerate into arguments and awfulness."

"I'm sure it will, at first."

He pressed a hand to his middle. "I don't think I understand," he said weakly.

"No, I'm sure you don't. But the fact is"—she stalked right up to him and poked him in the chest—"the two of you are pathetic. I've never seen a father and son go at each other the way you do. You need help."

She knew to the second when he took in the significance of her words, because his blank look hardened, his forehead creased, his eyebrows dipped, and he got mad. "Oh, no. Don't tell me you're aiming to make things sweetness and light between my father and me." Contempt oozed out with his words. "Don't even think of it, Gina. Trust me on this. Stronger people than you have tried before and lived to regret it."

"You mean you both cling like barnacles to your grievances?"

He said nothing, but his lips got tighter.

She shrugged and went back to her window. "It doesn't matter whether the two of you reconcile. What matters is that I need Christmas, because my family's in California, and I'm here, and I miss them, and neither you nor your father have apparently ever had a decent Christmas, and I want to make a Christmas for you whether you want one or not, because that will make Christmas for me."

"God." He ran a hand through his hair again and made an agitated turn around the shop.

He had nice hair. It was so dark and glossy. Briefly Gina wondered if he dyed it. He did, after all, work in La La Land. But she quickly dismissed the thought. Somehow he didn't seem the type to while away hours with a stylist. Besides, she too, hailed from Southern California, so she shouldn't throw stones at him on that account.

"Listen," he said, coming to a stop in front of her, "isn't it bad enough that I have to work with the bastard? I try very, very hard not to have to take meals with him, too."

She smiled up at him, plastering on the geniality. "I'll stock up on milk of magnesia, just for you."

"I don't need milk of magnesia!"

"No?"

"No. Dammit, this is insane."

"Is it?"

"Yes."

She shrugged. "You want to use my shop, don't you?"

"Yes."

"Well, then . . ."

"You really mean this, don't you?"

"Yes, I do."

He made a frustrated gesture with his stomach-patting hand. "All right. I'll try to talk Father dearest into it."

"Thank you. This should be fun."

"Fun?"

She laughed again. "Sure. I'll enjoy it, anyway."

"That'll make one of us. When do we have to do this?"

"Tomorrow night. For the first time anyway."

"The *first* time?" He was plainly horrified, but Gina wouldn't back down. He walked out of her shop a few minutes later, muttering to himself.

Gina watched him go and wondered if she'd lost her mind entirely. Probably.

"It doesn't matter, Henry. My mind is about all I'll have left to lose if business doesn't pick up."

Henry snored his response.

When she called her mother later that evening, she got all the approval for her plan that she'd hoped for.

"Kill 'em with kindness, Gina Marie. If they don't enjoy it, you will, and that's what life's all about."

Gina really, really loved her family.

Chapter Four

"I'm sure the girl is hoping I'll seduce her," Theodore Hawkes said.

Alex stared at his father until he had to return his attention to driving down the street. Not that *street* was a word he'd use to describe it, exactly. The city fathers of Roswell, New Mexico, didn't go in for heavy-duty paving, or signage, or even curb-painting. Hell, a minute earlier he'd nearly run the car into a tree when a road had divided in front of him without even a traffic light as a warning. Obviously, Roswell hadn't been built for the automobile as L.A. had. Although his father's provocative comment made him feel slightly ill, he opted not to respond to it.

For one thing, he didn't know if Theodore was in earnest or if he was only trying to start an argument. But that was silly. The man was always trying to start an argument. The bastard thrived on discord. And

Theodore, unlike his son, never had to resort to antacid tablets.

For another thing, Alex worried that the old goat might be right. Gina Sullivan wouldn't be the first innocent female lured into an affair with the infamous Theodore Hawkes. Alex couldn't figure it out, unless they were enticed by the old man's money and celebrity. He couldn't imagine their being enticed by anything else after they got to know him. Maybe it was true that women were attracted to difficult men. Still, there was a big difference between difficult, and Theodore Hawkes, who was impossible.

"Don't you think so, Alex?"

Dammit, he wasn't going to let it drop. "Think what?"

Theodore laughed his cynical, sadistic laugh and smirked his cynical, sadistic smirk. "Don't you think that's why she invited me to her home for dinner?"

Alex discovered his jaw was aching from clenching his teeth, and he made an effort to relax. "She invited both of us, Dad. Unless she's into some pretty kinky stuff, I don't think she expects to be seduced. At least not tonight."

"Ha. Perhaps she only wants to bask in the reflected glory of a world-famous author."

"Yeah. Right."

Theodore laughed again, a smug, self-satisfied laugh that made Alex's gut tighten. He wouldn't take an antacid tablet in front of his old man, though. Not tonight, he wouldn't. No matter how much the bastard made his stomach ache. He'd sooner die an agonizing death. Which was probably next on the agenda.

He squinted at the first road sign he'd seen, a yellow thing with a black cross on it. He presumed that meant a crossroads ahead. They'd evidently left the main part of town, because now only a few isolated houses dotted the landscape here and there. He even spotted cows and horses in roadside pastures.

He'd seldom been in a town with actual outskirts. In Southern California, you exited one city right into another one. You could drive from L.A. to San Diego without ever leaving urban congestion, for God's sake. Not here. Here, you drove for ten minutes and were in the middle of nowhere. He kind of liked it.

Theodore, obviously, did not. He shuddered. "This place gives me the creeps. It's a perfect setting for one of my novels."

Theodore's son didn't like to consider a place housing Gina Sullivan and her basset hound ending up in one of his father's gruesome stories. He said nothing. Didn't even grunt. His father had become adept at interpreting his grunts over the years.

"You say this place belonged to the girl's grandmother?"

Thank God the old sinner had changed the subject. Alex pried his teeth apart far enough to say, "That's what she told me."

"God, I can't imagine how anyone could live in a place like this. There's nothing here."

"At least you can see the stars."

Alex braced himself for one of his father's sarcastic rebuffs and was relieved when he didn't get one.

"Yes, I suppose you can." Theodore rolled the window down, and a blast of cold air rushed into the car. Alex didn't protest; he knew that if he did, the old man would probably turn on the air conditioner. Theodore was like that.

Theodore stuck his head out the window and stared up at the stars long enough for Alex's arms to sprout goose flesh. Still, Alex didn't say a word. Theodore kept his head out the window another minute or so, then drew it inside and rolled up the glass.

"People make too much of nature." His voice was as supercilious as ever.

"You think so?" Alex said with forced calm. Ah, there was Gina's street. He hung a right, then realized it wasn't a street after all, but a dirt road. With a sigh, he resigned himself and his stomach to a bumpy ride.

"Anyone who needs to frolic out of doors obviously doesn't have enough useful work to do." Theodore shuddered again.

"Right."

"Good God, this is the middle of nowhere."

"Yeah."

The car's headlights picked out two ruts in the road that looked as if they'd been driven over for decades, if not generations. The dirt road was packed solid, but Alex took it slowly; he didn't feel like listening to his father disparage his driving.

The house was charming. Alex found himself not at all astonished. Hell, Gina was charming, her dog was charming, her shop was charming. It stood to reason her house would be charming. A small Victorian with a big porch and gables, it must have been built in the late 1800s or early 1900s, although Alex didn't know where people around here had found lumber to build wooden structures back then.

Roswell had an abundance of trees today, but they weren't native to the place. The only native flora Alex had been able to discover were creosote bushes and yuccas. Even the tumbleweeds, which blew like crazy in the wind and scared the bejesus out of him when they flew across the road in front of his car, were imports. They'd come all the way from Russia, back when it was Russia the first time. He'd learned that bit of trivia earlier in the week. His education was growing by leaps and bounds—much like the rest of him was doing right now. In fact, if his stomach leaped and bounded much more, it'd probably kill him.

"The girl obviously goes in for sentiment."

When Alex turned his head to peer at his father, he wasn't surprised to observe his mouth squinched up and his nose wrinkled in blatant scorn as he gazed at a big quilted wreath decorated with holly berries hanging on the front door of Gina's house. As near as Alex had ever been able to figure, there was only one thing Theodore Hawkes hated more than sentiment—and that was his son.

"Looks that way." He kept his tone mild, unwilling to give the old man fodder for argument. Alex himself appreciated sentiment. In small doses. It beat the hell out of the manipulative antipathy he fielded every day from his parent. Sometimes he wondered how his mother, a long-suffering female if ever there was one, had managed to make so massive a mistake as to marry the bounder.

He pulled up in front of the house and parked in a circular drive that looked as if it had been designed for horses and buggies. For that matter, the porch seemed to be bounded by old-fashioned hitching rails.

Alex rather liked the notion of galloping up to the place, throwing his horse's reins over the railing, and bounding up the porch steps in high-heeled cowboy boots. He almost laughed at his straight-out-of-the-movies fantasy, but he knew laughter would spark comment from Theodore, so he didn't.

"Good God, I didn't know people actually lived like this." Theodore stepped out of the car and looked around with distaste.

"Like what? I think the place has charm."

"Charm?" Theodore snorted. "You would."

Alex didn't comment. He climbed the porch steps and discovered an old-fashioned door ringer one had to twist. He twisted it. Before the sound had stopped, the door opened and a wash of warm amber light flooded out from it. His breath caught for a second.

Damn. If Gina Sullivan didn't look like something straight out of one of his better dreams, he didn't know what did. Simply but alluringly clad in Levi's and a Christmas sweatshirt—a tasteful one with a pretty tree on it—her dark hair gleaming in the light, she was smiling as broadly as one of Santa's elves.

"Come on in, you two."

Her voice was cordial. Didn't she know what lay ahead of her for the evening? Hell, she'd been given a dose of Theodore Hawkes already, hadn't she?

"Thanks," said Alex, as he crossed the threshold. He looked around with interest and sniffed the air. Whatever she was cooking smelled good. He only hoped it wasn't too spicy and that his stomach would behave for once.

"Good evening, Miss Sullivan." Theodore left off staring balefully at the boot scraper beside the door, walked inside, took Gina's hand, and kissed it.

She smiled amiably at his gallantry, as if men kissed her hand every day and she didn't find anything unusual in the courtly gesture. Alex grinned inside, glad his father hadn't disconcerted her yet. He knew the time would come, and probably soon, but he was pleased to see that Gina Sullivan wasn't easily flummoxed.

"I'm really glad both of you could come. Let me take your coats."

"Thanks." Alex shrugged himself out of his leather jacket and handed it over.

His father, who wore not only a dramatic, western-style duster but also an Indiana Jones-style hat, removed both and did likewise.

As Gina hung the items in her coat closet, Alex glanced about at the interior of her house. The front door opened into a small entryway with a polished hardwood floor. Several sepia-tinted portraits hung in the tiny hall. He wondered if they were Gina's ancestors. Somehow, he wanted them to be. His own family, so to speak, was so screwed up that if he ever decided to hang their pictures on a wall, he'd have to get more walls to accommodate all his grandparents, step-grandparents, step-parents and ex-step-parents, and countless half- and step-siblings.

A braided rag rug on the foyer floor fit the old house to a T. He wondered whimsically if one of Gina's great-grandmothers had made it out of her family's worn-out old clothes.

Surprised at the direction of his thoughts, he tried to shake off his mood of nostalgia for things he'd never experienced, but it didn't want to be shaken off.

Gina led them into her living room, which also gleamed with old wood and polish. A fire burned merrily in a fireplace lined on either side with bookcases. Cozy furniture of no particular vintage completed the room. The dog, Henry, got up from his spot by the hearth and wagged his way over to Alex and Theodore.

Theodore looked down his imperious nose at the canine, but Alex squatted to pet it and received a friendly slurp from the dog and a sweet smile from Gina for his effort, which made the pain in his stomach almost worth it. He stood and glanced around some more.

A tall Christmas tree stood in one corner, decorated

to within an inch of its life with ribbons and balls, pop-corn and cranberries, and cut-tin things that looked like the kinds of ornaments folks used in the 1930s. On top of that, the tree made the room smell deliciously of pine, and Alex experienced a fierce urge to close his eyes, inhale the scent of Christmas, and let his mind drift off into utter nostalgia. He wouldn't, of course. A drifting mind in the vicinity of Theodore Hawkes would be dead meat in no time. You had to keep your wits about you with Theodore or end up fodder for his viciousness.

Therefore, Alex kept his eyes open when he murmured, "Nice place you have here." He meant it sincerely. Gina's house touched something in his chest—unless that was heartburn starting up in anticipation of Theodore's expected performance.

"Thank you. It's been in the family since 1902. My great-great-grandfather built it. This was way outside of town back then."

"Isn't it still?" Theodore asked with a deceptively gentle smile. Alex squinted at him, hoping he wouldn't attack before dinner. Hell, the girl deserved a chance, didn't she?

Gina laughed. "It's kind of outside of town, but not *way* outside. This used to be a cattle ranch."

"Hmm. Very Wild West-ish." Theodore arranged himself in an overstuffed chair.

"Yes, I guess it was. They bred Texas longhorns at first, then switched to Jerseys. I understand Jerseys have gone out of style because their milk is so rich." She sighed. "Rich milk used to be good for you. Now it seems it's death in a glass."

Theodore actually, honest to God, chuckled. Alex tried not to gawk. He settled himself on a rocker in front of the fire. Now this, he decided in that moment, was what a home should be.

"Would you like a drink? I have wine—burgundy and a chardonnay—or there's tea or coffee. There's also vodka and some scotch I got as a present, if you prefer. I'm afraid that's it. I'm not a big drinker and don't keep much in the house."

"Do you, by chance, have any tonic water on hand?" Alex posed his question without much hope in his heart.

"Sure do."

He beamed, wondering if life could get much better.

"Alex will take the tonic, and I'll take the vodka," Theodore pronounced. "With ice, please. You can leave the ice out of Alex's. The boy suffers from terrible indigestion, poor thing." Theodore smirked.

Gina eyed him thoughtfully. Alex could tell, because he knew his father so well, that the comment had been intended to let Gina know how unworthy Alex was to be Theodore Hawkes's son.

"I imagine anyone who has much to do with you might end up with indigestion, Mr. Hawkes." Gina sailed out of the room to fetch the drinks.

Alex didn't catch himself in time to prevent a snort of laughter from escaping. His father eyed him coldly.

Chapter Five

Gina wondered if she should have challenged Theodore Hawkes so openly, then decided she didn't care. He wouldn't be in Roswell forever. She could tolerate anything for a month or two.

Her favorite Christmas carol lilted through her mind. Merry gentlemen, her foot. She'd never seen any two men *less* merry than the Hawkes duo, and the notion of giving the two unfortunate specimens of humankind a merry Christmas had taken possession of her.

She laughed at herself. As if she, Gina Marie Sullivan, a half-Italian, half-Irish expatriate from California, a nobody among nobodies, could have any sort of effect whatsoever on Theodore Hawkes, as celebrated for his acerbity as he was for his ghastly books. It would take acid to cut through his hide, and acid was a commodity she'd been lacking all her life.

She shrugged happily. It didn't matter. Doing something that might benefit those two alien creatures—and how funny that they'd come to Roswell, home to all manner of UFO legends—now sitting in her living room made her feel better than she'd felt since she left California. She set the drinks on her prettiest tray—a flowery porcelain number she'd picked up at a flea market in Pasadena—and sashayed back out to the living room. She visited Theodore's chair first.

"Here you go, Theodore. Hope you like it. I put poison in it."

Without skipping a beat, she went to Alex and handed him his tonic water. She was proud of herself for her timing; timing was, after all, the essence of comedy, and surely comedy was balm for a bitter soul. She didn't look at Theodore again until she sat in the chair next to Henry, who'd resumed his nap, and smiled at both men. She lifted her own glass of wine. "Cheers."

"Cheers," said Alex.

She could tell by the twinkle in his really quite beautiful eyes—why was it that men always got the prettiest eyes, anyway?—that he'd appreciated her humor.

Theodore was squinting at her. "I do believe that was an insult, Miss Sullivan."

"Please, if I have to call you Theodore, Mr. Hawkes, you have to call me Gina. And it wasn't meant as an insult, actually. It was meant to be funny."

He nodded uncertainly and downed a gulp of his vodka.

"How long does it take the poison to work, and why didn't I ever think of that?" Alex asked after he'd swallowed some of his tonic.

She smiled at him. "I don't know why you never

thought of it, and I don't know how long it takes because I've never used it before. It's a special kind of poison. It turns mean people nice."

"Good God," said Alex, sounding amused.

"Good God," said Theodore, sounding horrified.

"I know," said Gina. "Shocking, huh? How could you make a living if you had to write nice things?"

Theodore shuddered. "I couldn't."

"Bet you could if you tried."

"My dear child," Theodore began, clearly disgruntled, "you have no idea what you're talking about. No one who isn't part of the publishing world knows anything about professional writing, although everyone thinks he has answers to everything."

"Actually, I don't think I have answers to anything. I'm only trying to make your stay in Roswell a pleasant one."

Theodore snorted and downed more vodka.

"That's very nice of you, Gina," Alex said. He smiled his gorgeous smile at her, and Gina's heart took to palpitating. How silly she was being. She took another sip of wine to stop her palpitations and rose from her chair so abruptly that she disturbed Henry, who grunted. Dear Henry.

"I'll get supper on the table. I hope you like it."

"I'm sure we will," Alex said politely adding as if in afterthought, "Is it spicy?"

Gina gave him a sympathetic smile. "I left out the chilies, Alex, just for you. My family calls it Italian pot roast. My mother—she's Italian—gave me the recipe."

"Talented family," Theodore muttered.

He had clearly intended his remark to offend her, but Gina had set a course for herself, and she didn't leap to his bait. Instead, she offered him one of her most winning smiles and said, "Indeed, we are. My mother is a wonderful cook. And my father can fix almost anything. My brother's a disk jockey in Santa Barbara, and my sister is a third-grade teacher in Anaheim."

"My, my, and you're a shopkeeper in Roswell, New Mexico. Intrepid of you, to leave such a snug little family to brave life on your own." It sounded to Gina as if Theodore had dipped his tongue in venom before he'd offered his observation.

Again, she didn't react. "It was, rather. My grandmother was ill, and it was easier for me to help her than for anyone else in the family."

"My God, the girl's a martyr."

Gina laughed, although his comment stabbed a little. Her grandmother's illness had been a dreadful blow, and coming to Roswell to look after her had been anything but martyrdom. It had been an act of love. She was sure Theodore Hawkes would never understand, so she didn't bother explaining.

Alex, shooting a scowl at his father, got up from his rocking chair. "May I help you, Gina?"

"No, no. You sit there and enjoy the fire. It will only take me a minute or two to set everything out."

It did. Before she went to the living room to call her guests to dine, she proudly surveyed the results of her handiwork. The table, a huge oak thing that had been in the house for longer than Gina had been alive, gleamed in the candle glow, and pretty quilted mats—which Theodore Hawkes would undoubtedly stigmatize as provincial, classless, and schlocky—sat at each place. She'd used her best wineglasses and the flowered china her grandmother had left her. The stuff was old and had been inexpensive even when her grandmother received it as a wedding gift, but Gina loved it dearly. There had always been an abundance of love in

Gina's family, even if there'd never been much money, she reflected. And, judging from the specimens of wealth sitting in her living room, she considered herself fortunate.

The silence resounding from that room echoed louder than voices when she stepped to the doorway and assessed the scene. Alex was avoiding even looking at his father—afraid, Gina suspected, of triggering one of Theodore's sardonic put-downs. He was leafing with evident interest through a copy of a book called *The Love of Roses,* which Gina had found in London.

The Great Author himself stood contemplating the books in her bookcases with a wrinkled nose and an expression of contempt on his face. He obviously deplored her taste, which ran toward historical fiction and nonfiction.

"Everything's ready," she said into the heavy silence. "Come on in and have a seat."

"Settle in at the trough, as it were," murmured Theodore silkily.

"If you choose to think of yourself as a pig, it's all right with me," she replied, cheerful in spite of him. "Do you like that book, Alex? I've always been fond of old roses myself."

"It's interesting." He sounded as if he meant it. "I'd never thought of roses in history before."

"Oh, my, yes. In fact, I had myself a little War of the Roses garden back in California before I left. Don't know if they'll like the weather here, but I might try it again."

"A War of the Roses garden? Whatever do you mean, child?" Theodore had apparently forgotten to be sarcastic, because his interest sounded unfeigned.

"I had a *Rosa Gallica Officinalis* and an *Alba Semi-Plena* and a *Rosa damascena 'Versicolor,'* which is supposed to be a cross between the two."

"Have you *any* idea what the woman is talking about, Alex?"

How interesting. Theodore Hawkes didn't like not knowing something. Gina was intrigued, but she wasn't about to rub his nose in her roses. It might kill the poor things. "I'm sorry. I forget sometimes that not everyone loves historical roses the way I do. *Rosa Gallica* was supposed to be the red rose of the Lancasters. *Alba* was supposed to be the white rose of York. Of course, nobody knows for certain, but it's fun to think about."

"Is it."

"I think it is," Alex said in response to his father's dry comment. "What's the other one, the *Versi-whatever* thing?"

"That's supposedly the cross-breed, the uniting of the two families, as it were. It's also called the Tudor rose."

Gina gestured the men to the table. She was proud of the centerpiece she'd made out of yucca pods and other dried plants—it looked elegant and rustic at the same time—and she was sure Theodore would say something to disparage it. "Please sit wherever you like," she invited.

Theodore chose the head of the table, a state of affairs Alex had both expected and begrudged. Henry whuffled in, looked from one person to the other, and ultimately decided that Alex, to his father's right, would be the softest touch.

Theodore gave the dog a malignant glare. "I trust that animal won't bite anyone in pursuit of food."

"Good heavens, no. He's much too lazy to bite." Gina laughed. "I suppose your favorite character in the Wars of the Roses was Richard III, Theodore."

Alex snickered. "You're probably right."

"Richard III was much maligned by Shakespeare, as I'm sure you know." Theodore snapped open his napkin and settled it in his lap. Henry woofed softly, startled by the noise.

"Don't be alarmed, Henry dear," Gina cooed at her dog. "It's just another alien come to Roswell. He won't stay long."

Theodore transferred his malignant glare to her. She passed him the big ceramic bowl containing the meat and sauce and gave him a sweet smile as a side dish. "I'm hoping I can persuade you and Alex to go sightseeing with me one of these days, too, Theodore."

He lifted an eyebrow in a gesture of superb incredulity. Gina was rather impressed; he had his act down to a fine art.

"Sightseeing? Are there actually sights around here?"

Alex looked for a moment as if he'd take his father to task for being a snob. Gina was glad he didn't.

"Indeed there are. Some."

"You must be joking."

"Heavenly days, no. Surely you want to see the UFO Museum and Research Center."

Theodore rolled his eyes. Gina laughed.

In something of a rush, probably to prevent another barbed comment from his father, Alex said, "Aren't the Carlsbad Caverns around here somewhere?"

She turned from Theodore to the more congenial Alex. "Only about seventy-five miles off. They're definitely worth seeing. Then there's Lincoln, where Billy the Kid did his thing."

"Billy the Kid. My God." Theodore sounded as if the very notion pained him.

"Billy the Kid," said Alex, sounding neither bored

nor pained. "You mean there really was one?"

Gina stared at him. "Of course there was. Haven't you heard of Emilio Estevez?"

"What, pray, does Emilio Estevez have to do with a Wild West outlaw?" If Theodore's eyebrow went any higher, he'd lose it in his hair.

Gina shrugged. "He played Billy the Kid in a movie," she said logically.

"I'll be." Alex spooned some salad onto his plate. Gina didn't serve the meal in courses. That sort of thing was for folks with servants, according to her mother, and Gina approved of her mom's common sense. Made life easier.

"Or was it his brother?" she mused aloud.

"Whose brother?" Theodore gazed at her as if she were a rare and unique—and perhaps poisonous—specimen of reptile.

"Emilio's." Gina thought for a minute and shook her head. "I can't remember. But it all happened in Lincoln, which is only about seventy-five miles in the other direction from Carlsbad. Then there's Bitter Lake, which is a wild bird refuge, and the Bottomless Lakes, which are interesting in their own right."

"Why do they call them bottomless?" Alex looked honestly interested.

"The cowboys on John Chisum's ranch—"

"John Chisum?" Theodore sneered.

Ignoring his sneer, Gina nodded. "Yes. He had a big spread to the east of Roswell. I can take you there, too. Anyway, the cowboys on his ranch used to tie ropes together and lower them into the water with a weight at the end, hoping to hit bottom, but they never did. They, of course, assumed it was because the lakes were so deep as to be bottomless. Actually, it was because currents caused by underground water sources kept moving the ropes."

"Good Lord, I had no idea the area had so much to offer."

Was she imagining something she wanted to see, or did Theodore actually have a gleam of interest in his eyes?

There was no doubt at all about Alex's interest. She couldn't squelch a tiny hope that his interest was due to more than the purported scenic attractions to be found in the vicinity of Roswell, New Mexico.

Chapter Six

"You actually expect me to go into that pit and then walk three miles underground?" Theodore Hawkes stared at the mouth of the huge cave with what appeared to be real revulsion, although Gina was beginning to suspect him of being something of a fraud.

"You can wait for us up here if you prefer," she suggested kindly. He frowned at her. She smiled back.

"Come on, Gina. Let him figure it out on his own." Alex took her hand and tugged her down the steep, switch-back path to the entrance of the cavern.

Gina was happy to comply. Even though she'd made it a condition of cooperating with Alex's film crew, she was genuinely glad that the two Hawkes men had so readily taken her up on her offer to show them the sights.

For one thing, she looked upon shepherding the two

of them as a mission of mercy. For another thing, dealing with their problem took her mind off of her own. By closing her shop for the day, at least she wouldn't be there gnawing the inside of her mouth and wondering whether any customers would find their way to her door.

"What's that vile smell?"

She looked over her shoulder at Theodore, who had condescended to follow them down the path and into the cavern. "Bat poop," she said cheerily.

He wrinkled his nose in disgust, and Gina decided the day was really quite wonderful. Oh, sure, her business was going down the tubes faster than Drano cleared a clog, and Theodore Hawkes was a beast, but she was having fun. Since her move to New Mexico, her life had been short on fun, and she appreciated it today.

Besides, beast or not, Theodore Hawkes was a world-famous author, and how often in one's life did one get to entertain a world-famous author? Even the knowledge that when he went back to Los Angeles, if he spoke of Gina and Roswell at all it would be only to disparage both, didn't bother her. The people who knew him would draw their own conclusions—and Gina didn't know any of *them* anyway.

Not only that, but she truly enjoyed Alex's company. He was a very nice man, which rather confounded her, since his father was so awful. On the other hand, maybe he'd been reared by his mother. She decided to thrust politeness and reserve aside and ask him about it.

"You know, Alex, I can't even imagine having a famous parent. It must have been kind of hard on you."

"Hard?" Alex laughed and shot a glance over his

shoulder to ascertain if his father was within hearing distance. "I don't think the old man's fame would have mattered if he'd been a decent guy. But, as you've had ample opportunity to note, he's not. Never has been. Prides himself on his toxic tongue and doesn't give a rap about anyone else."

"And he didn't soften his disposition for his children?"

"Good lord, no. He used us to sharpen his claws on."

"Nonsense!" grunted Theodore, sounding out of breath. "I never sharpened my claws on you, Alex. What would be the point of trying to sharpen one's claws on a marshmallow? I only used worthy targets."

Alex grinned at Gina. "See what I mean?"

"Indeed."

Theodore huffed indignantly. "It's black as a pit in here."

"It *is* a pit," said Alex.

"Don't whine, Theodore," Gina advised. "Nobody likes a whiner."

"Nobody likes him anyway," Alex pointed out.

Gina whacked Alex's sleeve, but she laughed. Theodore didn't.

An hour or so later they made their way to an underground eatery. Gina recommended the chicken-strip box lunch, and Alex graciously bought one for her and one for himself.

Theodore gazed down his nose at the proffered fare. "This all looks abominable."

"It is," Gina responded cheerfully. "We're a mile underground, and this is a national park, not a five-star restaurant. It's fun to rough it every now and then, Theodore."

"God." Theodore gave an eloquent shudder.

"Come on, Dad. Stoop for once."

"Join *you,* you mean?"

Alex's lips tightened.

"You two are pathetic," Gina said.

"Nonsense. My son is pathetic. I'm a genius."

"The only pathetic thing about me is my lousy digestion, and that's only because I've had to put up with you for ten years," Alex retorted.

"Ten very profitable years, I might remind you."

Before Alex could say anything else to his father, Gina tugged him by the shirtsleeve and led him to a picnic table. It seemed to take a bit more effort, though, to wrench his mind away from his grievances with his parent and employer. He cast a hostile glance at Theodore, who seemed to be arguing with the cashier over the price of a slice of pizza. "I wonder if he'll incite that poor girl to murder."

"Don't worry about your father, Alex. He's a big boy. He can take care of himself."

Alex's eyes seemed to snap with anger. Gina was sorry to have provoked him.

"That's the trouble, Gina. He *can't* take care of himself. Hell, he was wallowing in debt when I took over his affairs. But he won't admit that I've saved his career. He won't even admit that I've helped him at all. He persists in demeaning me at every turn. It drives me nuts."

She eyed him curiously. "Why do you put up with it?"

He threw out his arms in a gesture that spoke eloquently of his frustration. "For God's sake, he's my *father!*"

"So what? That's not your fault."

Alex looked startled. "You're right."

"And I don't see why you should sacrifice your sanity *and* your digestion if he doesn't appreciate you."

"He pays me well," he admitted.

"You sound kind of defensive."

Alex's eyes flashed again. "Dammit, I am defensive. That's because I know I'm a fool to keep working with the bastard."

Gina sighed. "But you still want your father to love you. I understand."

"He's never loved anybody." Alex bit viciously into a piece of cold chicken, chewed for a moment, and glared at the remaining chicken in his fingers. "My stomach will probably hurt for the rest of my life after eating all this."

"Your stomach will hurt for the rest of your life anyway, Alex," a cutting voice said. "You're weak." Theodore had joined them.

Gina gazed up at him and sighed again. Maintaining her Christmas spirit in the company of these grinches might turn out to be a tougher assignment than she'd reckoned on.

"Hell," grumbled Alex. He attacked another bite of chicken.

"It's your mother's genes. I always told her so."

"I'm sure you did. I think she took it personally— until she realized you treated all your wives like shit."

Gina's ears perked up. "Oh, how interesting. How many wives have you had, Theodore?" She, being a peasant by nature, loved the cold fried-chicken strips and was having a good time with her lunch.

Theodore gave her a haughty sneer. "You mean you don't know? I thought *tout le monde* kept abreast of my personal affairs."

"*Affairs* is the right word," muttered Alex, who was patting his shirt in search of his roll of antacid tablets.

Gina shook her head and felt a little sorry for him. It must be hard on a person not to be able to enjoy junk food.

"Nonsense. When one marries, one is hardly carrying on an affair."

"You were." The look of loathing Alex visited upon his father would have withered a lesser being. Gina hoped he'd never look at her that way.

"Not with my wives."

"Of course not. That's why they didn't stay your wives."

"Oh," said Gina, interested. "So you were unfaithful, were you?"

"Unfaithful." Theodore pronounced the word as if it tasted as bad as his pizza. "My, my, what an old-fashioned little prude you are."

"I suppose I am," Gina agreed happily. "Life's much easier when you follow the rules."

"Rules." This word evidently tasted even worse. "Rules are made for fools."

Gina shrugged. "I don't know. I sort of enjoy knowing the rules. If nothing else, they give you a place to start."

"That's a very good point." Alex smiled at her, and she was glad of it. He had a wonderful smile.

Theodore snorted and nibbled delicately on his pizza, and conversation lagged for a while. Gina started it up again once she'd thought about where she should take the Hawkes lads next. She decided they needed to visit Lincoln.

Alex was all for it.

Theodore was not.

"Who wants to visit a crumbling western town that has nothing to recommend it but a history of violence?"

"Why, Theodore Hawkes, how you talk." Gina laughed. "I thought you thrived on violence. I thought you'd gotten rich from it."

He sneered. "I invent my own transgressions. I don't need to rely on other people's ancient misdeeds."

"I'm fond of history myself," Gina said, easily.

"Nostalgia," Theodore spat contemptuously. "The reason you're sentimental about all that claptrap is because you think life was somehow better or less hectic back in the olden days. You're wrong, you know. Life without telephones and antibiotics might sound like a swell idea until your child is ill and you can't call a doctor, and even if you could there'd be no medicine to cure him. Those old cemeteries are filled with dead babies. Is that something to be nostalgic about?"

Gina found it interesting that, contrary to the image he projected, Theodore's first thought had been of a helpless child. She declined to point it out, though, and risk his disowning the hint of tenderness. "You know, Theodore, it's absolutely fascinating to hear how your mind works. When I think of the pioneers, I don't immediately think about dead babies. I think about strength and gallantry and a certain grandeur of purpose."

"Hogwash. Sentimental hogwash. Ask one of those poor women who were made to tramp across the country with no creature comforts how much they enjoyed it."

Again Gina discerned a hint of caring Theodore customarily went to great lengths to conceal. It heartened her, and she threw back her head and laughed. Both Theodore and Alex watched her, plainly startled. When she caught her breath, she managed to speak again. "You're priceless, Theodore Hawkes. Absolutely priceless. I'm so glad I had a chance to meet you. Even if you are ruining my business."

Theodore scowled at her and bit violently into his pizza.

By the time they'd finished their tour of the Carlsbad Caverns, Theodore was in a towering grump, Alex had a world-class pain in his gut, and Gina was developing a greater understanding of both of them.

Her mission was going to take a lot of work. And she wasn't sure a single Christmas season would do the trick. But she planned to give it her best shot.

She called her mother again that night.

"Keep it up, Gina Marie. If anyone can make those two gentlemen merry, it's my little girl."

Both women laughed, and Gina decided life was worthwhile after all.

Chapter Seven

Despite the usual chaos generated by the film crew and his father, Alex had never spent a more enjoyable week. Which seemed sort of odd, since he'd never been much of a tourist. But Gina closed her shop early each day—she said she might as well, since there was no business anyway—and dedicated as much time as possible to showing him and his father the local sights.

There were actually quite a few of them, which amazed him. If one looked only at the rather monotonous landscape, one wouldn't suspect that there were bottomless lakes or wild bird sanctuaries or old lava flows anywhere in the vicinity. The capper, though, was when she took them to see Smokey Bear's grave in the mountain town of Capitan.

"I can't believe this." Theodore was aghast when Gina told them where she was driving them.

Alex, on the other hand, was charmed. "I'd always believed Smokey was a fictitious creature," he said.

She zipped down the road and swung into a small parking lot. "Nope. He was a bear. Or a *bar,* as they say out here, if you prefer. Come on, you guys. We have to visit the Smokey Bear Museum."

"The Smokey Bear Museum!" It was obvious that Theodore had about reached the limit of his endurance. Alex wondered cynically if the old man would get so mad that he'd bust a blood vessel and croak. But, of course, he didn't. Theodore Hawkes would never be so obliging. He merely became more and more sarcastic as the tour continued.

It didn't matter. Gina not only dragged them through the museum, but she made them have lunch at the Smokey Bear Cafe. She even bought Theodore a Smokey Bear cap and presented it to him with a flourish.

He looked at the cap dangling from his fingers and then at Gina, as if he believed she were some strange alien being sent to earth to plague him. He didn't say a word. As far as Alex was concerned, anybody who could put that look on his father's face and shut his mouth at the same time was a jewel of rare and precious quality.

In fact, every day he was finding more to admire about Gina Sullivan. Still, her finest quality, so far, was her easy tolerance of the intolerable Theodore Hawkes. He didn't understand how she did it. The old man didn't deserve her.

When Alex entered his father's hotel room the day after their adventures with Smokey Bear, he found the old man in a hideous humor. Theodore looked as if he hadn't slept all night, and his thunderous frown was a classic. Ordinarily, seeing him in that state would have brought on an attack of ulcers. But that day Alex merely tilted his head and asked, "What the hell's the matter with you?" It was more polite than his customary greeting.

"I've been writing all night."

"Oh? Many people ripped apart by bears in this one?" He imagined that Theodore's muse—if such a malign talent could be called by so gentle a name—might have been prodded into action by yesterday's trek to Capitan.

"None."

Theodore's scowl tickled Alex, which was a more good-humored reaction than he usually had to his father. "Hmm. Are you going to join us today when Gina shows us Fort Sumner?" Because he knew it would annoy Theodore, he added blandly, "Fort Sumner is where Billy the Kid is buried, you know."

"*Damn* you!" Theodore threw his pen at him. It missed. Alex watched, unruffled, as it bounced off a wall and rolled under a sofa.

Bounding from the chair in front of his computer screen, Theodore madly paced the hotel room. He stopped abruptly a few feet away from his son. His hair was as wild as his eyes. "I can't be interrupted, dammit! Get out of here, for God's sake, and take that idiotic girl and . . . and . . . Billy the Kid with you!"

It was the perfect opportunity to start yelling and continue their usual grudge match, and Alex normally wouldn't have passed it by without taking advantage of it. Today, however, he simply shrugged. "I'm sure Gina will be disappointed."

"And I am supposed to care?"

"Yes, well, of course, *I'm* not disappointed that you

won't be along to spoil the day. I always have a better time without you."

"Get out!"

"Yes, sir." Alex gave Theodore a friendly smile and departed. He could hardly believe he hadn't blown up at the old goat. Testing his emotions, he discovered he really *wasn't* mad. How odd.

He chalked up his relaxed mood to his association with Gina Sullivan and prepared himself to enjoy another day in her company. Soon he'd have to get back to work full-time because the set would be completed and they'd need his attention.

His stomach gave a spasm to remind him how little he was looking forward to it.

When Gina loaded Henry Wadsworth Longfellow into her ancient Toyota the day after her trip to Fort Sumner with Alex Hawkes, she found herself in a surprisingly dreamy mood. She didn't dodge Henry's affection quickly enough, and he gave her a huge, sloppy kiss on the cheek. She wiped the dog spit away on her sleeve. "Yuck, Henry." She laughed. On the other hand, he brought her back to reality with a thump—or a slurp.

It was becoming difficult for her to continue thinking of Alex as nothing more than a Christmas project undertaken to lighten her own soul because she missed her family. On the other hand, she had no business getting interested in a Hollywood hotshot. She'd have to disabuse herself of any such notion. Unfortunately, she hadn't yet discovered anything about Alex that she didn't like, except for his relationship with his father, and she couldn't honestly fault him for that. If she'd had a father like Theodore Hawkes, she'd probably have killed herself before now. Still, Gina understood how complicated familial relationships could be, and she supposed Alex wouldn't appreciate any input from her, although she'd love to give him some.

She sighed heavily as she guided the car into a parking space in the alley behind her shop. The catering crew was already there, champing at the bit to get inside and set up their coffeemakers and snack bar in her back room. They were polite about it, though, and they were also paying her handsomely, which mitigated her annoyance just a bit at having her storage space usurped for the purpose of further interfering with her shop's business. Nobody would come in to buy with all the commotion going on outside.

Given her vexed musing regarding her business prospects, her astonishment was acute when she got to the front of her shop and saw three people waiting at the door. Were those people *customers*, of all rare birds?

"Of course they aren't," she chided herself. "They're probably involved with the filming." Nevertheless, she smiled her best shopkeeper's smile as she opened the door. What the heck, even movie people bought stuff from time to time.

They weren't movie people. Gina almost dropped her teeth when the first one through the door, a beautifully coiffed, blue-haired septuagenarian with gorgeous white dentures, clasped Gina's upper arm and hissed, "Where is he?"

Gina's first thought, which made no sense at all when she thought about it later, was that the woman was asking about Henry. She pointed. "Over there. In the corner."

The old lady gazed with avid eyes at the corner and frowned. "There's nothing there but a dog."

Henry didn't even lift an eyelid or wag his tail at her. He knew when he wasn't wanted.

Obviously, she'd been wrong about the woman's interest. "Uh, I beg your pardon. Where is who?" Or should that be whom? Well, never mind; it didn't matter.

The woman straightened and gaped at her. "Why, Theodore Hawkes, of course! My granddaughter and I have come all the way from Hobbs to watch the movie being made. Isn't it exciting?"

All the way from Hobbs? That was a good hour and a half away! Gina was attempting to collect her thoughts and respond to the woman's query when a delighted cry interrupted her.

"Oh, Grandma! Look at this!"

"What?" The blue-haired female swirled away from Gina and headed toward the younger woman who'd spoken.

"This bracelet. It's beautiful. It's kind of like the one you bought for Mom last Christmas."

"Let me see it."

Gina watched, fascinated, as the old woman lifted the bracelet and eyed the workmanship keenly.

"It's a Tossa," she pronounced, turning to Gina in wonder.

Gina, who had thought the older woman merely an aging star-worshiper, dared to hope. "Are you familiar with her work?"

"Am I *familiar* with it?"

The lady lifted her right hand, displaying the ring on her middle finger. It was magnificent. "Oh, my! It's a Tossa. How beautiful. Where did you get it?"

"In Santa Fe. I bought it at a gallery there, but when I went back to buy more of her work, they told me they had no more on consignment. How did you get these?" She swept her hand over the display.

Gina cleared her throat. "Actually, I met Ms. Tossa

267

in Mescalero last summer. We got to talking, and she agreed to let me show her work when I opened the shop. I'm glad to find someone else who's an admirer of her. I think she's an especially talented artist."

The woman didn't comment on Gina's assessment of Tossa's work. She did, however, say, "I've got to have this," which more than made up for it.

Gina had barely recovered from the sale—which amounted to more than all the other sales she'd made since her shop opened—when another group came in. *These* were movie people, there to secure drinks and snacks from Gina's back room. Still, she was gracious when one of them, a bearded fellow with a huge gold hoop earring, brilliant blue eyes, and the most gorgeous red hair she'd ever seen, swished up to her.

"Sweetheart, I've *got* to have that painting."

She blinked at him. "Which painting? I mean, you do?" Lord, shock wasn't supposed to make you stupid, was it?

"It's that one on the back wall that I'm interested in buying."

He had a good eye. But a conspicuously gay Hollywood film crew member craving a painting of a pasture full of Texas longhorns? "That's my favorite, too. I'm glad you like it."

"My significant other is a cowboy, and he'll die for it," he said.

"Oh." She guessed that was reasonable. Except . . . "Uh, does your significant other live in California? *Southern* California?"

Her new customer laughed gaily. "Yes indeed. Rialto, darling. He rides on the gay rodeo circuit."

"My goodness."

"One simply never knows, does one?" He winked at her.

"No. I guess one doesn't."

He bought the painting, and even before she'd finished writing out the receipt, several more people had entered the shop. They weren't from the film crew. They were locals interested in seeing a movie being made and wanting to mingle with the film crew spending time in Gina's shop. Still, one of them bought a Mexican tin-ware Christmas tree, another bought a crèche made by a local artisan, and yet another bought a birthstone necklace.

The day got even better from there. Alex Hawkes came in, bearing food from McDonald's.

Chapter Eight

Alex eyed his Big Mac. "My ulcers may never forgive me if I feed them this. Do you have any Maalox on hand?" he asked hopefully.

Gina swallowed a bite of her own Big Mac before answering him. "I'm sorry, I don't have any stuff like that in the shop," she said, in a tone of infinite sympathy.

She dipped a french fry in catsup, popped it into her mouth, and chewed thoughtfully. "Working in the movie biz sure seems to aggravate your stomach, huh?"

"It's not the movie biz that does it," Alex ground out. "It's working for my father that's killing me."

"I'm sorry."

"So am I. Do you know what he's up to today?"

She shook her head.

"He's busy *writing* today. He's busy *creating*, so he can't be bothered to come to the set. They need him there, but does he care? Hell, no. He says I can take care of it."

"Can you take care of it?"

"Oh, sure." He threw his hands in the air. "I can take care of it. I *will* take care of it. And then the old man will ride me for doing it wrong. He can't be bothered, so he leaves it to me, and then crabs at me for it. He does it all the time."

"Hmm." She sipped her Coke and reached for another fry.

"It's always been like this. He leaves stuff up to me, then vilifies me for doing it my way. Mind you, he gives me no hint of how he wants things handled in the first place. It drives me nuts." He raked his fingers through his hair, frustrated beyond reason.

"Why do you do it?" she asked again, softly.

It was a simple question, and she'd asked it in a manner that showed she was only interested, not passing judgment. It irked him anyway. "Why do I do it?" His voice had risen. "Because if I didn't, my father would flounder."

"Can't anybody else work for him?"

"Nobody else could stand it."

"It doesn't look like you're standing it very well, either."

"Dammit, it's how I earn my living."

"Well, but why do you put yourself through it? Why not do something else? Why not focus on your own writing?"

He looked at her. "Why do you *think* I do it?"

She shrugged. "I thought it was because you were trying to win your father's approval."

He stared at her, his anger chewing at his gut, and didn't know what to say.

She smiled at him. "Guess I was wrong?"

She wasn't wrong. Dammit. He stood, leaving his hamburger on the counter. "I've got to get going. You can feed that thing to the dog."

Henry perked up his ears and opened both eyes.

"Okay."

Alex stomped toward the door.

She called after him. "Thanks for the burger and fries. They really hit the spot. Henry Wadsworth thanks you, too."

He snarled "sure," and made sure he didn't slam the door on the way out.

"Oh, there you are."

Alex stopped in his tracks and almost groaned aloud. If there was one thing he didn't need right now, it was a confrontation with his father. "I'm busy."

"You're not too busy to talk to your father, Alex. I'm the one who keeps you in antacids, remember?" Theodore gave one of his most corrosive smiles— the kind guaranteed to set Alex's stomach to aching if it hadn't been aching already, which it had.

"What do you want?" he asked ungraciously.

"I finished my story and sent it to Eddie today." Eddie Fazio had been Theodore's editor for eons.

"Good. Now you can pay attention to business."

"Business." Theodore's voice reeked with scorn. "What would *you* know about business?"

Alex couldn't stand it any longer. If he didn't get away from Theodore, he'd explode. "Right." He turned and stalked away without another word.

"Come back soon," Theodore called after him sweetly. "I'm sure *somebody* needs you."

Gina had gone to the window to watch Alex leave. The man was in quite a state today. She saw the confrontation with his father and frowned.

"Why does Alex do it, Henry? I mean, I understand

272

how a bad relationship with your parents can hurt a person, but why would you want to perpetuate it?"

Recalling that she was in her place of business, Gina looked around quickly and for once was glad the shop was empty. It had been crammed with customers all morning long.

Henry didn't even bother to lift his head and look at her when she asked her question. He was too busy scarfing up Alex's abandoned Big Mac.

"Right. What would you know about bad relationships?" She grinned at her dog. Her grin faded when she watched Alex bolt from his father. Shaking her head, wishing she could do something more than just be nice to the two Hawkes men, she wandered back to the counter.

Because it was her favorite Christmas carol, and because the music was no longer drowned out by the noise of construction, she put "God Rest Ye Merry, Gentlemen" on the cassette player. Before long, she was singing along with the tape and feeling a bit merrier herself.

She realized that being nice to troubled people wasn't a half-bad way of sharing the milk of human kindness; and, if that was all she could offer Theodore and Alex Hawkes, she might as well.

"You know, of course, that most people put the comma in the wrong place."

Gina almost dropped her dust cloth. She'd been trying to get construction residue off the merchandise.

"Good grief, I didn't hear you come in."

Theodore Hawkes huffed. He looked to be in a bad mood. No shock there. Gina had yet to see him happy, unless the sadistic pleasure he took in being mean to people counted. Her mind finally registered what he'd said. "What comma?"

"The comma in the title of the song." He pointed a slender finger at the cassette player. "It's 'God Rest Ye Merry' comma 'Gentlemen.' The ignorant masses think it's 'God Rest Ye' comma 'Merry Gentlemen.' It's because they're illiterate barbarians."

She blinked at him. "Does it matter?"

His face assumed an almost ferocious expression. "Yes, it matters! You're always rattling on about history. What good is history if you don't take language into consideration? That song illustrates a lost form of salutation."

"Oh." She still wondered if it mattered but decided it would be prudent not to say so.

"Anyway, it's the principle of the thing that irritates me."

Near as she could figure, everything irritated him. She didn't say that either.

"The English language is dynamic. It's constantly changing. I take that as a given. What I object to is having it change due to the illiteracy of people who can't be bothered to learn proper form. Do you know I heard a news reporter on your local television station ask his *compadre* 'Where's it at?' yesterday? *Where's it at?* Now I ask you, what kind of grammar is that?"

"Poor grammar," Gina said promptly. She refused to admit to the irascible old guy that she'd always been annoyed by that particular phrase herself.

"Poor? Abysmal is more like it!"

She shrugged and continued dusting.

Theodore marched through her shop like a panther longing to leap on something, rip it to shreds, and feed on the bloody chunks.

The tape ended, and Gina decided to play it again. Wherever the stupid comma went, she loved that Christmas carol.

"Most people are abominably stupid."

Since that didn't call for an answer, Gina proffered none. Theodore was in a state though, and she wished she knew how to get him out of it. Not that she cared much for her own sake. He'd be gone soon, and she'd be rid of him, and eventually she could look back upon these few weeks as merely an interesting—if somewhat aggravating—episode in her life.

She did, however, care about Alex and how his father's miserable mood would affect him. No matter how little she wanted to care, she did.

Theodore launched into a grammar lesson, sprinkling it liberally with caustic comments about the general idiocy of the public, the stupidity of trying to deal with anyone at all, and the particular impossibility of getting people to think for themselves. Or to think at all, for that matter.

Gina listened with half an ear. She was trying to concentrate on the Christmas music, since it was so much lovelier than anything Theodore Hawkes had ever said or likely ever would say.

Again she wondered why Alex put up with him. Even if he was subconsciously trying to win Theodore's approval, it made no sense to sacrifice his health and happiness on the miserable old crank's altar of scorn. Heck, even she, who'd come from a close and loving family, knew that much.

"And then there's my son."

Gina stiffened, dust rag in hand. She really didn't want to hear a litany of Alex's defects, mostly because she didn't think he had very many. "I like your son," she said.

"Of course you like my son. What's not to like?"

She peered over her shoulder at him. "*You* don't seem to like him much."

Theodore shrugged. When he did that he looked like a peevish schoolboy. "I like him all right. But he treats me like dirt."

She stopped dusting, turned, and gaped at him, sure she'd heard him wrong. Theodore didn't notice. He'd resumed pacing.

"Why, only this morning I told him I'd finished a story and sent it off to my editor. And do you know what he said to me when I told him about it?"

"Uh, no, I don't."

"He said, 'Good. Now you can pay attention to business.' Business! I tell you, that's what he said."

"And that hurt your feelings?"

Theodore spun around, gaping in his turn. "Hurt my feelings? What are you talking about? I swear, you're as stupid as Alex. Hurt my feelings, indeed."

"Then why did you object so strongly?"

"What do you mean, why did I object? Because it was a nonsensical thing to say. As if the words I put down on paper aren't business enough. Why, they're his very bread and butter!"

Gina eyed him for a moment. "Have you ever considered that the way you speak to Alex might have something to do with the way he speaks to you?"

"Bosh! I'm famous for my venomous tongue. Without it, I wouldn't be me."

She wanted to ask him why he thought that would be a bad thing, but she knew such a question would be contrary to her desire to feed him and his son the milk of human kindness during the holidays. "Perhaps that's so, Theodore, but you must realize that sharp words provoke sharp words in return, and a soft answer turneth away wrath. Or something like that."

He looked at her as if she'd sprouted a pinafore and Shirley Temple curls and had started tap dancing to

"The Good Ship Lollipop." "Good God, not you, too?"

"What do you mean, *not me, too*? It's the truth. You treat people like dirt, they'll treat you like dirt. It stands to reason. I'm surprised you hadn't figured that one out on your own. You're the famous writer among us. Anyway, it's the season of good will to all mankind. I suppose all mankind includes even poison-tongued beasts, so you're not going to rile me, Theodore Hawkes." She smiled and kept her voice genial, determined not to let him get to her. Hoping to teach him a lesson in kindness—or drive him out of her shop—she pushed the replay button on her cassette player and "God Rest Ye Merry, Gentlemen" began again.

Theodore threw up his hands, muttered, "The girl's gone mad," and stormed out of the shop, thereby achieving one of Gina's goals.

Chapter Nine

Gina watched the film being made for the rest of that day, when she wasn't busy with customers. She noticed with some interest that as his son's mood got blacker, Theodore's own disposition lightened. It was as if the author's temper improved as he made those around him suffer.

"Fascinating," she muttered to Henry, who went so far as to open both his eyes all the way and wag his tail twice before he recommenced snoring.

Alex came in during the afternoon, looking frazzled and in pain. Gina spoke kindly to him, as she might to a sick child or a wounded grizzly bear.

"Thank you," he murmured as he took the glass of ginger ale she offered him and slugged it back. "Ginger ale helps the pain sometimes."

She nodded. "My mom always gave us ginger ale when our tummies were upset."

"My stomach's killing me. I had to get away for a while."

"I thought they discovered ulcers are caused by bacteria. Have you talked to a doctor? Maybe antibiotics will cure it."

Alex swallowed more ginger ale, then shook his head. "No time."

No time. It was the story of the entire world right now, near as Gina could tell. People running themselves and their bodies ragged. It sounded like no fun to her. She took the empty glass from Alex and put a hand on his arm. He peered down at her, surprised by the gesture. He looked tired and unhappy, and her heart hurt for him.

"There's nobody in the shop right now," she said gently. "Why don't you come to the back room and lie down for a while. It might help your nerves and your poor stomach."

"Can't. Too much work to do."

"Alex, you can't drive yourself without ever taking a break. You'll do yourself in. Here, eat something. You didn't eat lunch." She handed him a paper plate loaded with crackers and cheese from the snack room.

"Thanks." He took the plate and smiled at her. "You're very kind, Gina."

"Nonsense. I just don't like to see people killing themselves. If you won't lie down in the back room, at least sit down." She drew up a pretty wrought-iron chair she'd taken on consignment from a local craftsman.

"Can't." He stuffed a cracker into his mouth, pacing much as his father had done earlier in the day.

"Why in the world not?"

"If the old man saw me resting now, he'd be on my case for a week and a half, calling me lazy and worthless. That's why."

279

She cocked her head. "He thrives on your discomfort, you know."

"Yeah, I know."

She sat in the chair he wouldn't take and gazed up at him. "I'm not sure you do. Not really."

He stopped pacing, stacked a slice of cheese on a cracker, and before popping it into his mouth asked, "What the hell does that mean?"

Henry had managed to wake up from his Big Mac-induced slumber when he smelled the cheese and heard the crunch of crackers. He moseyed over and began peering up at Alex with an expression Gina recognized as a frown. Henry didn't care for people walking as they ate because it made his job as canine vacuum cleaner more difficult. Henry appreciated stability. Gina understood completely.

"It means that I've been watching both of you today, and it's clear to me that your father becomes happier and happier as your mood corrodes. It's as if he wants to know he can have some kind of an effect on you, and if the best he can do is make you sick—in your case, literally—he'll do it."

Alex stared at her as if she'd lost her mind—which she might well have done. What did she know about these two men, after all? She'd first met them only a few weeks ago. They'd known each other all Alex's life. Still, she guessed her observation was as valid as anyone's.

She expected Alex to snap at her as he'd done earlier, and she wouldn't have blamed him. She had no business telling him what was going on his life, what games his father was playing, what he should or should not do about it, or anything else. She should butt out of his life because his life was none of her business.

He didn't snap. Instead, he walked over to the window, still munching, and gazed out. Henry gave him a black look, heaved a huge doggy sigh, and followed. After Alex swallowed another cracker and slice of cheese, he turned around. "Do you really think so?" He finally noticed Henry and dropped a piece of cheese for him. Gina realized in that instant how very much she liked Alex Hawkes. Very, *very* much.

"It's what I see when I watch the two of you interact. Every time Theodore gets your goat, he looks pleased with himself."

Still chewing, Alex began to frown, more in thought than in anger.

"Don't get mad at me, Alex, but I honestly—really and truly—don't understand why you put yourself through this. You know darned well you're smart enough to make it without him. Is it because your father can't make it without you?" she asked quietly.

He uttered a sarcastic snort.

"Even a few members of the crew have told me that you'd be better off—and more successful—writing scripts for TV, but you say you can't because you have to help your father."

"Hmmm," was all Alex said.

It wasn't much, but at least he didn't seem inclined to pace any longer. Gina was glad. She was also glad for Henry's sake when Alex tossed the dog another piece of cheese. It was such a natural gesture, and Gina approved. She thought Alex would make a fine dog owner. With an internal start, she wondered if he already was. That was among the other things she didn't know about him.

"Do you have a dog of your own?"

He'd been staring out the window. Her question made him turn around. He glanced down at Henry, who wagged his tail obligingly. "No. I've always liked dogs, but I never had one."

"Have any, uh, kids?" She wasn't sure she wanted to know the answer.

"No. Not that I wouldn't like to have a family, but I'll be skewered on a spike before I ignore a family the way my father ignored his. His *several* families, as a matter of fact. I don't think it would be fair to have a family or even a dog, since I'm on the road so much."

Her heart suddenly felt lighter. She was sure that was a bad sign, but she couldn't seem to help it. "Oh. Do you like being on the road?"

"Hate it."

Gina rolled her eyes. "I'll never understand why people put themselves through hell for the sake of money. I mean, how many Ferraris can one person drive at a time, anyway?"

"Ferraris?" Alex scoffed. "I drive a Volvo."

"Ha!" Gina laughed, diverted. "At least you can afford a Volvo. I guess the hassles might be worth the money after all. I mean, when you crash in your Volvo, your ulcers will be protected."

"I'm not sure that's funny, Gina."

She pressed a hand over her mouth. "I'm sorry." She guessed she'd said enough. Then again, how many more chances would she get? "But, honestly, Alex, I really wish you'd rethink your working situation. From where I sit, you're killing yourself for no good reason." She held up a hand to ward off objections. "I know it's none of my business, but I—well, I care."

There. She'd said it. And it was true. She'd come to care a good deal for Alex Hawkes. Sometimes she thought she ought to be locked up before she hurt herself. The notion of being locked up for love made her grin.

"Do you really?" Alex sounded as if her confession astounded him. He also sounded as if he didn't believe it.

Puzzled, Gina said, "Of course I do. Do you suppose I'd have put up with Theodore and Alex Hawkes for the last couple of weeks if I didn't care about at least one of them?"

Henry slapped a paw on Alex's shoe, and Alex glanced down at him. Henry good-naturedly wagged his tail and grinned up at him. "And here I thought you were just being kind to a couple more dumb animals."

"Well, that, too."

He walked over and looked down at her for a long time. He appeared terribly solemn, excruciatingly serious, and she smiled weakly, feeling foolish. "What? What are you staring at?"

"You."

Because his scrutiny disconcerted her, she brushed a hand over her hair, then wished she hadn't. "Well, stop it," she said at last. "You're making me nervous."

He shook his head and said, "Thanks for the food and the ginger ale. And for caring." Then he turned and left the shop.

Gina stared after him, wondering what his problem was. Then she heard Theodore Hawkes bellow something obnoxious at him, and she stopped wondering.

Henry wandered over and laid his head in her lap, hoping, she knew, to be allowed to finish the crumbs from the paper plate. Gina stroked his silky ears. "If I give you the plate to lick, you have to promise you won't eat the plate, Henry."

The look he gave her was so soulful, she shook her head and laughed. "Well, I don't suppose paper is as bad for dogs as some stuff." She set the plate at Henry's enormous feet, and he attacked it happily.

To the sound of her hound licking crumbs, Gina wandered to the window, wondering what would become of her and Henry. And Alex Hawkes. As she gazed out, the names somehow jumbled together in her mind, becoming Gina and Alex and Henry Hawkes.

With a start, she turned and glared at Henry. "Did you make me think that?"

Henry's head lifted, his tail wagged, his expressive eyes reminded her what a wonderful companion he was—and a half-eaten paper plate dripped from his mouth.

The Hawkes men came to supper again that night. Gina asked them late that afternoon when they both came raging into her shop. Actually, it was Theodore who was raging, and Theodore who snapped an acceptance. Alex, who looked fairly calm, seemed to accept the invitation with pleasure.

Gina was baffled by this apparent shift in the Hawkes men's relative positions—until Alex winked at her. From his wink, she deduced that he'd taken her words to heart, and her own heart melted like so much chocolate in the sun.

She had a dreadful feeling she was losing it to Alex, told herself she had to guard against falling for a Hollywood hotshot, agreed with herself, then asked them both to supper.

"There's no hope for me, Henry," she muttered after they'd left the shop and she tried to think of what to serve that night.

Henry, his belly still full of Big Mac, cracker-and-cheese crumbs, and two-thirds of a paper plate, didn't even lift his head.

Chapter Ten

"I'm taking you to see the luminarias tonight," Gina declared as she loaded the dishes into the dishwasher.

Alex helped her.

Theodore had stomped to the living room and begun rattling through the Thursday edition of the *Roswell Daily Record*. Gina had told him the name was inaccurate since the paper wasn't delivered on Saturdays.

Theodore had told her he wondered why they bothered to deliver it at all, since there was so little in it.

Gina said she'd sometimes wondered that herself.

Alex told Theodore not to be nasty. Then he'd laughed, astonishing not merely his father and Gina and Henry Wadsworth Longfellow—who opened both eyes and woofed—but himself as well. Hell's bells, his father had been ragging him all day long. There was no reason in the world he should be happy this evening—except that he was in Gina's cozy little home, with her cozy little self, and her cozy little dog, and he'd just partaken of a cozy little dinner and was now being assured of a cozy little jaunt out of doors to see the luminarias. Whatever they were.

"I thought luminarias were bonfires. What do they do, set old buildings on fire?"

"Those luminarias are in Santa Fe. The ones I'm talking about are paper bags filled with sand and a candle. Folks around here line their walks with them at Christmastime. When whole neighborhoods are lit with them, its a delightful sight."

"You're right. I've seen them in L.A., actually, only the guy who'd set them out called them *farolitos*."

She nodded and stooped to put another pot in the dishwasher. She had a cute butt, Alex had noticed, but he didn't think he'd better say so, political correctness being what it was.

"Some people call them *farolitos* here, too." She laughed. One of the newsmen from Albuquerque said he'd solve the argument by calling them *lumilitos* or *farolarias*."

Every time she laughed, the sound went through Alex like rays from the sun. He felt that somehow her laugh was healing him, which was ridiculous, but there it was. He had long since lost track of the conversation, too busy watching Gina and soaking in whatever it was about her that made him happy. Her warmth? Her kindness? Whatever it was, he'd never encountered its like before, and he felt like a parched plant being given a soaking.

"Okay, we're done here," she said. "Let's go." She glanced at her dog. "Henry, wanna go for a ride?"

Alex had never seen the hound so excited about anything. It opened its eyes, yawned, wagged its tail, heaved itself to its feet, then trotted to Gina and jumped up to put its paws on her shoulders. She staggered and almost fell over backward.

Alex caught her. Gina laughed again, and he joined in, again astonishing himself. He was pretty sure that if Gina knew how seldom it was he found something to laugh about twice in one evening, she'd be astonished as well. Which just went to show that money didn't mean everything.

Henry gallumphed to the floor and waddled to the front door, where he sat and wagged his tail. Gina grabbed her jacket and went to the living room. Theodore was still scowling at the newspaper. It *was* a fairly skinny paper if one were accustomed to the *Los Angeles Times*, which required a winch and crane to lift on Sunday mornings.

"Any reviews of your books in there?" Alex teased.

Theodore thrust the newspaper aside. "Surely you jest."

"I've told you before not to call me Shirley." Alex grinned at the old man.

Theodore's eyes narrowed, as if he were in pain. Gina giggled. Henry wagged.

"God, I wonder if your mother was unfaithful to *me*. I couldn't have sired anything that trite, could I?"

Alex's good humor nearly fled. He took a deep breath and reminded himself that this was exactly the reaction Theodore wanted of him. He'd never gone in for meditation, but he imagined the principle was that two things couldn't occupy the same space at the same time. Maybe if he filled his mind with "Ohm," there'd be no room for anger and frustration. Maybe.

"Come on, Theodore, we're going to look at the luminarias."

Gina's pleasant voice interrupted Alex's bitter thoughts, which might have proved his point. He frowned, musing that perhaps there was a more permanent solution to his problem.

Alex watched Gina deal with his father and wondered if he, Alex Hawkes, son of the great and miserable Theodore Hawkes, would enjoy life in southeastern New Mexico. Sans the hateful job that had bound him to his father and Southern California for the past ten years.

Why not? He didn't really like Southern California. He couldn't stand his old man. Gina's question about why he put himself through what he put himself through was becoming ever more cogent as the days and weeks of this latest ghastly project progressed. And New Mexico was looking better to him all the time. Especially one particular resident of Roswell.

Of course, if he wanted to partake of Gina's cozy world on a permanent basis, he might have a bit of cajoling to do. Would he prove up to it?

"I will not drive around looking at silly Christmas lights, whatever you want to call them, Miss Sullivan. Christmas lights, indeed." Theodore's shudder was almost as eloquent of his disgust as his tone of voice.

"Okay. We'll drop you off at the hotel first." She said it without a trace of indignation, frustration, anger, or anything but good cheer.

How did she do that? Alex wondered.

Studying her pink cheeks, her shiny dark hair, her blithe smile—and observing the way Theodore gritted his teeth when she refused to take the bait he dangled in front of her—Alex came to a decision. He *was* up to it. If it took him all the cajolery he had in him—hell, if he had to borrow some—he was up to it. He needed the woman. Sort of like he needed air and Maalox.

Gina grabbed the tape of "God Rest Ye Merry, Gentlemen" before she went out the door. She popped it into the car's tape player, and Alex could hear his father grind his teeth over the Christmas carol as she drove to the hotel.

The luminarias were beautiful—what Alex saw of them. He was too preoccupied with the new and amazing thoughts that had taken possession of what was left of his mind to pay much attention, although he got the impression they were actually quite lovely. As lovely, almost, as Gina Sullivan, who tooled her little Toyota around a part of the city called Enchanted Hills, although where the hills were Alex couldn't say. The whole place looked flat to him.

"If we go out a little farther, you can see the stars, too. I mean, really *see* them. Not like in L.A., where the city lights drown them out. Of course, even around here they don't look as bright as they used to."

Alex really didn't care about the stars right now, either the Hollywood or the New Mexico variety. He cared about Gina Sullivan. Henry yawned, and he decided he cared about the dog, too. And he listened to Gina because he loved the sound of her voice.

"My grandmother told me that when she was a little girl, the stars would be so bright, she used to think she could reach out and grab a handful of them. And if it was cloudy, the nights were as black as tar, too. No electric lights or anything. She said some nights were so dark, she literally couldn't see her hand in front of her face. She had to deliver milk to the neighbors before sunup and would sing at the top of her lungs to keep herself from being scared."

Alex nodded, because he thought he should, but what he wanted to do was grab Gina and never let her go. He wondered if he could work that one out in the limited time he had before the filming was completed. He didn't just want to go to bed with her, although he wanted to do that, too. A lot. What he wanted, he realized though, was *her*. Forever and ever.

Good God, that meant marriage! Did people still get married these days? He had a feeling they did, in places like New Mexico. Although he had an intellectual understanding that life in the rest of the United States wasn't necessarily lived as it was in Tinsel Town, he had no recent experience of anything but L.A., where marriages were temporary arrangements at best. Maybe Gina could teach him about that, too.

"I'd like to see the stars," he said, meaning it and not meaning it at the same time. Hell, he wasn't sure what he meant any longer. All he knew was that he wanted to remain in Gina's company for as long as she'd let him.

"Okay. We'll drive out to Picacho. I'll show you where Peter Hurd lived." Her wonderful laugh curled through him again. "That is to say, I'll point to where his place would be if you could see it, which you won't be able to do because it's nighttime."

"I'd like that."

She glanced at him, her piquant face alight with a new thought. "Would you like to visit his gallery? It's in his home, and it's quite lovely. I wouldn't mind living in the Hondo Valley, although it's kind of far from grocery stores and stuff like that."

"I'd love to see his gallery. Can we go tomorrow?"

Hell, what was he thinking of? He had to work tomorrow. So did Gina. He was sorry when her smile turned upside down.

"I'd better work tomorrow, Alex. How about Saturday or Sunday? That's only a few days off."

He sighed soulfully. He was beginning to remind himself of Henry. "All right." But he still felt unsettled. He didn't want to wait until Saturday or Sunday to be alone with Gina again. "Uh, will you have dinner with me tomorrow night, though? Without my father?"

Her perplexity was obvious. He sensed a slight withdrawal on her part and wished he knew what to say to put her at ease with him again. Should he say he didn't plan a seduction? Did people still use that word? Even if they did, was it the truth? He didn't think so. Should he say he wanted to get to know her better? She'd never go for that. She used to live in Southern California. She surely knew all the lines. Maybe he should just tell her the truth.

Good idea, if he knew what the truth was. If he told her he'd begun to look upon her in light of his salvation, she'd probably run for the hills. Damn. He grumbled, "I'd appreciate it. I enjoy your company, and I'm so sick of my old man, I'm about to shoot myself."

"Oh, please don't do that!"

Good grief, she thought he meant it. "I'm sorry. Didn't mean to get melodramatic on you." He heaved another sigh. "Dammit, I want to be with you. Is that so hard to understand?"

As a lover, he probably ought to write himself a better script. He also probably ought to whack himself upside the head.

After waiting entirely too long for his comfort, Gina said, "Do you really? I mean, you're not just saying that?"

He turned in his seat and stared at her hard. The night was dark, and he couldn't see her very well, but he could discern her troubled mien. "Listen, Gina, I know I'm from L.A. And I know you're probably used to all the bullshit that people sling at each other out there, but I do mean it. I've had a better time—a more peaceful and happy time—with you than I can ever

291

remember having with anyone. I want to get to know you better." Because he wanted her to know he was sincere, he held up both of his hands. "No strings. Honest to God. I'm not saying I don't want to go to bed with you, because I do, but I won't press it. I just want to be in your company for as long as I can be."

If that wasn't the stupidest thing any man had ever said to a woman he was trying to impress, Alex didn't know what was.

"And—and maybe, if you like me as much as I like you, well—God, I don't know. Maybe we'll decide to make it permanent." *If you like me as much as I like you?* Instead of banging his head against the window, as he felt like doing, Alex held his breath.

He damned near turned blue, because it took Gina a long time to answer him. When she did, his breath left him in a rush.

"Really?" She sounded as if she couldn't believe it.

"Really." He, on the other hand, sounded the way a lovesick puppy would have sounded if lovesick puppies could talk.

Another pause. Longer. Thank God he didn't try to hold his breath for this one.

"Okay. Sounds like fun." She smiled one of her glorious Gina-ish smiles at him.

Alex wondered if she'd take it amiss if he got down on his knees in her Toyota and thanked the good Lord for small mercies.

Chapter Eleven

Alex was on his best behavior for the next two weeks. He was so concerned about keeping Gina Sullivan in his life that he didn't even notice Theodore's incessant attempts to incite him into fury and indigestion. He did notice that his father seemed to be getting more short-tempered as the time passed, but he chalked that up to normal behavior on the old man's part and basically ignored it.

He had a wonderful time with Gina. Every minute he wasn't needed on the set, he was in her shop. The movie crew seemed to attract customers, and it was annoying that she was so busy selling things, but he didn't let that get to him either. He couldn't recall another time since he'd grown up that his stomach had given him so little trouble.

Maybe Gina was magic.

Whatever she was, he wanted it. He wanted her. His

determination to win her strengthened as Christmas Day drew near.

On December 23, Theodore received a call on the set from his literary agent. Gina was there; she'd come outside with Alex to watch a particularly gruesome scene being filmed.

"It's actually kind of fun to watch stuff like this being arranged and filmed," he'd told her.

She wrinkled her nose. "I hate blood and guts."

"Trust me." They were now on a touching basis, if nothing more, so he hugged her. "You'll find it hard to keep from laughing hysterically when you see how they do all the gory stuff."

He was right. In fact, she had to muffle her giggles with her hands when the blood-squirting guns went into action. Since she was there, and so was he, and he loved her madly, he pulled her into his arms and let her muffle her adorable giggling mouth against his chest. He'd seldom felt so at peace as he did in that moment.

Maybe this was what that song she loved so well meant. Maybe this is what resting merry meant. Alex didn't know. He only knew he wanted the moment to last.

It didn't, of course. Moments never did. This one's end started inauspiciously, with the telephone call from Eddie to Theodore. It continued uncertain when Theodore, an odd look on his face, approached Alex and Gina, who struggled loose from Alex's grip, even though he didn't want her to.

Alex wasn't alarmed that his father didn't seem to notice the changed relationship between his son and his son's lady friend. Unless it concerned him directly, Theodore seldom noticed anything.

Gina pulled away and went to Theodore and laid a hand on his sleeve. Alex frowned after her.

"What's the matter, Theodore? Bad news?"

She sounded as if she was worried about the man, which irked Alex. If there was one human being on the face of the earth who didn't deserve her good will, it was Alex's father.

Theodore glanced down at her, and even Alex felt a twinge of something. Concern? It couldn't be, could it? Naw. "What's the matter? Didn't Eddie like the story?"

"No, Alex." Theodore gave his son a sarcastic grimace. "Eddie loved the story."

"Then why are you looking so . . . weird? I thought you expected raves for all of your work."

"I do."

Alex was genuinely bewildered now, although he didn't want to admit it. Fortunately, Gina was there.

"Tell us, Theodore. Why the befuddled look on your face?"

God, he loved her! Alex decided she'd been out of his arms too long already and drew her back. She looked at him, startled, but he only smiled and held her closer.

Theodore glared at the spectacle of his son hugging the woman he loved, but he didn't say anything nasty. Instead, he said, "Eddie told me it was the best story I've ever written. He said it—" Theodore stopped speaking, swallowed, and took a deep breath. "He said it had tenderness and heart, two commodities he'd never read in my work before, which lifted this story from the commonplace to the outstanding."

Both Gina and Alex stared at him. Gina asked, a tentative quality in her voice, "Uh, that's a good thing, isn't it? I mean, tenderness and heart are good, aren't they?"

Theodore looked at her as if she'd asked if gangrene and AIDS were good things. "We're talking *my* work here, Miss Sullivan."

Miss Sullivan? Good God, Alex thought, he was

mad at Gina! He gawked at his father. "Hey, Dad, it isn't Gina's fault that Eddie liked your new style better than your old one."

"No, perhaps it isn't." His voice rose. "But it's her fault that I've lost my edge."

And he stalked away from them.

Gina whispered, "My goodness."

Alex threw his head back and laughed until the tears came.

When Alex proposed to her on Christmas Eve, Gina burst into tears of happiness and accepted on the spot. Then she called her mother, and father and brother and sister, all of whom were gathered at her parents' house, and told them. She had Alex talk to them, too, even though he was nervous.

"For heaven's sake, Alex, you deserve them! They're wonderful. They're my family, and they're going to be your family. I'm so happy!" She threw herself at him, he hugged her hard, and she knew she'd never want for anything again.

"It'll be nice to have a family," Alex admitted after Gina's Italian mother had nearly talked his ear off about how wonderful Gina was, and how happy she was for both of them, and when was he going to bring Gina out to see her family, and when could they meet his family, and did his father really write those awful stories, and how did he turn out so well with a father like that, and— He lost track halfway through the phone call, but it didn't matter.

When he finally hung up, his ear was red, and he knew, without the slightest doubt, that he'd been accepted. Hell, he'd been around his father for thirty-five years and hadn't been accepted. He'd talked to Gina's mother once—*once*—and now he was her son.

He liked it. He liked it a lot.

Then he gave Gina her Christmas present, which was a white-gold engagement ring made specifically for her, at his request, by Sylvia Tossa, whom he'd contacted two weeks before when he'd decided he was going to marry Gina or die trying.

Gina looked at the ring, looked at Alex, swallowed, and ran into his arms. He knew exactly what to do then. So did she. They were progressing marvelously when a knock came at the door.

Henry woofed.

Alex groaned.

Gina sighed, buttoned her blouse, tucked it into her green velvet Christmas slacks, decided she didn't need to put her shoes on, and went to the door, after first making sure Alex was decently buttoned.

"God Rest Ye Merry, Gentlemen" was playing softly in the background when she opened the door. Theodore Hawkes stood there.

Gina heard a sound from Alex and glanced at him to make sure he was all right. She cleared her throat. "Merry Christmas, Theodore. Won't you come in?"

"Thank you." No sarcasm. Just *thank you*.

Theodore walked into her house. He looked at his son. He didn't sneer. He said, "You look happy, Alex."

Alex had stood and done a fairly good job of rearranging himself into a semblance of respectability. He nodded. "I'm very happy, actually. Gina's agreed to marry me."

Both of Theodore's eyebrows went up. When they worked together that way, he didn't look sardonic or cynical, but only mildly disarmed. "Really?"

"Really." Alex's voice had an ill-at-ease quality that Gina recognized as one he often had with his father. Because he couldn't trust the man who had sired him

297

not to stab him in the heart with a verbal dart. She shook her head.

"You two. Listen, I'm going to get some eggnog, put some brandy in it, and serve it to both of you. You're going to drink it. Together. While we open presents and listen to Christmas carols. Then we're going to have pie, and I'll take you back to your hotel room, Theodore. I hope Alex will stay here with me tonight, but you can come here for Christmas breakfast if you promise to be nice."

Theodore didn't even snap at her. He nodded. "I promise."

While Alex goggled at his father, Gina pressed the replay button, and "God Rest Ye Merry, Gentlemen" repeated as she went to the kitchen. She heard son and father talking as she mixed the eggnog.

"I love her, Dad."

"You're wise to, Alex."

Gina didn't know if Alex was astounded, but she sure was. Theodore didn't even sound cynical.

"I'm giving up my job as your assistant, too, although I'll find someone qualified to replace me so I don't leave you in the lurch."

"I'm not surprised." Theodore heaved a deep sigh. "I know it's been hard on you, Alex."

"*You've* been hard on me, actually."

Another deep sigh. "I know. I'm sorry."

Gina could hardly believe her ears. Theodore Hawkes had apologized to his son. Talk about the miracle of Christmas.

"I was pretty sure the two of you were going to pair up. Even get married." He sounded as if marriage was a nonsensical institution, although he himself had married at least five times. "I've been thinking about a wedding gift for you."

"You have?" There it was again, that note of caution in Alex's voice. Gina hoped it wouldn't be there forever.

"Yes. I'd give you a house, except I have a feeling you and Gina will want to live here."

"We do."

"Then it'll have to be money. A lot of money." Evidently being nice for any length of time was hard on Theodore, because he added caustically, "I'm sure you'll need it if you're going to try to earn a living writing."

Alex ignored the sarcasm and said simply, "Thanks, Dad. I am going to move here. I can write here as well as I can anywhere, and I like it here."

"Yes, well, an author can starve anywhere, I suppose."

Alex let that one pass. Gina was proud of him. "And I'm sure Gina will be happy to have you visit us any time you want to."

"I doubt it."

That was enough for her. She'd already loaded the eggnog glasses on the lovely Christmas tray she'd picked up at Pic-N-Save a few months back—she took advantage of bargains wherever she found them—so she toted the tray to the living room. Henry wagged at her happily, and she tossed him the Milk Bone she'd brought out especially for him.

"You don't either doubt it, Theodore Hawkes. You're only trying to make something happy into something miserable, and you aren't going to be able to do it. Heck, even your *editor* knows you've changed."

"God," Theodore muttered, "it can't be true."

Alex sat on the sofa and pulled Gina down onto his lap. "I don't know if it's true or not, but I'm willing to keep an open mind."

Theodore cast him a glance, and Gina knew he was thinking of something nasty to say about a vacant mind—but he didn't say it, and she was proud of him, too.

"At any rate, I wish the both of you happiness. I suppose." Theodore lifted his glass.

Alex and Gina lifted theirs. Alex said, "Thanks, Dad." Gina said, "Thank you, Theodore."

Henry chewed, ignoring them all.

"You know," Gina said after they'd sipped their eggnog, " 'God Rest Ye Merry, Gentlemen' has always been my very favorite Christmas carol, but it has taken on a special meaning for me this year."

Alex hugged her.

Theodore said, "Why?" He was back to sounding sardonic.

"Because," said Gina, "I now have two—three, counting Henry Wadsworth—merry gentlemen of my very own."

Alex kissed her.

Theodore muttered, "My God."

And his tone reassured Gina, because it confirmed that, under his present veneer of civility, Theodore Hawkes remained a beast, even if a slightly fraudulent one. And that was good news for his future financial stability, and thus for Alex's healing ulcer, and thus for her own peace of mind.

Henry, finished with his Milk Bone, happily went to sleep and began to snore.

Up on the Housetop

Linda O. Johnston

Spectacular holidays and
a wonderful new millennium
(whether you believe it starts in 2000, 2001 or otherwise)
to all!

Special thanks to Paige Wheeler.
And, as always, to Fred.

Chapter One

Thud!

"Oh, no!" Carrie Ritenour had been hanging Christmas lights around the front dormers of her house. Now she scooted toward the rear of the sloped roof. Or at least she crawled fast, clinging to ledges and trim with bare, scraped fingers. She had a healthy respect for heights. That was what she called it.

She refused to admit to terror.

Now she looked down. The ladder lay askew in the unblooming daisy patch two long, long stories below.

Carrie's breaths grew quick and short, synchronized with the thumping of her heart. Before her head could spin too crazily, she looked straight ahead. A crow on the neighbor's overgrown yucca cocked its head mockingly, then flew away.

She stared after it, wishing for wings. Or Santa's

sleigh and reindeer—the real one, not the wonderful decoration of lights she had yet to bring up here.

Even her little Santa sleigh pendant, the one she had lost up here five years ago—the one that she'd thought brought her luck—would have made her feel better. She needed a little luck about now. *Good* luck.

But she hadn't found the pendant. One of the reasons she had come up here was to look for it.

"Joey," she called. "Help!" Where was her brother? "Joey!" she shouted. Nothing.

Steadying herself, she looked down toward the sloping back yard, then over at the grove of orange and lemon trees at the side. No sign of her brother, drat him. He was supposed to be holding the ladder. Her mother was braving the day-after-Thanksgiving crowd at the mall, and Carrie didn't expect to see her till half-past closing. Nor had Carrie sighted any neighbors today. Was she stranded? "Joey!" she shrieked. "Get me down!"

"Hello?" The unfamiliar voice seemed to come from the front of the house. "Are you all right?"

"I could use some help," she called. Gingerly, she picked her way forward.

If only Elliott could see her now, shaking, on all fours in her most worn blue jeans . . .

But of course Elliott would never have allowed her to climb up on the roof in the first place. "Too dangerous, darling," he'd have said. "I'll take care of it." Oh, Elliott . . .

Not now, she ordered herself. Besides, she had made it. Holding on to the chimney, she forced herself to sit cross-legged, then peered down.

Down? Oh, my, the ground was far away!

A man in a suit stood on the front walk, looking up. "Hi," he called. "Do you need help?"

"Yes," she croaked. "My ladder fell. If you could just go around back and stand it up for me . . ."

"Sure. Can I get through the gate?"

Steadying her shaky voice, she explained how to unhook the latch. In a few minutes, she had positioned herself at the rear of the roof. She watched the man lift the ladder, heard the metallic rattle as he steadied it against the house. She was saved! She hadn't finished hanging the lights but, darn it all, she had to get down! Right now. She'd finish later. There was still plenty of time to prove she could do it.

"Thanks," she called. She crawled to the edge of the roof, where the end of the ladder rested. She turned, thrust one leg behind her—and froze.

Now, she commanded herself. *Just get on it, very carefully, and climb slowly down.*

A great thought. But her body did not obey.

"Would you like me to come up and help?" her rescuer called.

"No, thanks. I'm fine." She had to be. She just needed to catch her breath.

In a moment, she tucked in her chin, inhaled deeply, and made her leg reach out once more toward the ladder. Her extended limb stopped in mid-air, then settled back down on the roof. "Drat!" she muttered. *Okay, Carol Cornelia Fells Ritenour,* she told herself. *You've got a way down. Take it!*

But the only thing that moved was her lower lip. It began to quiver. She was going to cry.

No, she wasn't, she insisted to herself. But neither, just then, was she going to move.

"I'll be right there," the man called. She had nearly forgotten him. The ladder shook beneath his weight as he climbed.

She couldn't try to get down while he was coming

up. That made her smile. She had an excellent reason to stay where she was. She turned. She sat. She waited.

In a minute, a man's face peeked over the edge of the roof. He had longish black hair. A strong, sturdy jaw. Smooth, hollow cheeks shadowed by dark beard and the brightest blue eyes Carrie had ever seen. She blinked. The man looked familiar, but she couldn't quite place him for a moment. . . .

And then . . . "You're . . . you're," Carrie stammered. "You're . . . Your Honor!"

Chapter Two

She had recognized him. Damn! thought Sam DiGregorio. He hadn't intended even to let the woman see him.

Nor, of course, had he intended to rescue her from her rooftop. But she obviously needed rescuing.

He gave her one of his brightest political smiles. "You know who I am." He pretended to sound pleased.

"Everyone in Calridge knows you, Mr. Mayor."

He hoped the voters did. Still, most people in this small Los Angeles County town cared more about what went on in its huge neighbor to the southwest than about the local political situation.

But this was no time to quibble. For a moment, he studied his quarry. She did not look particularly formidable—hardly more than a schoolgirl in her Cal State Calridge T-shirt. She sat hugging her legs, her small chin resting on her blue-jeaned knees, her dark hair breeze-blown about her face. Her brown eyes were huge and fearful, but curious. She was surrounded by green strings of unhung Christmas lights.

She did not look especially responsible. And, reacting the way she had to being stuck up there, she certainly did not act like a mature, capable—

"Is everything all right, Mr. Mayor?"

"Sam," he automatically corrected.

Her lips appeared to attempt a smile. "Sam," she repeated. "Are you all right?"

Funny thing for her to ask. She was the one stranded on the roof. "I'm fine. Now, why don't we get you down?"

She blinked. "Great idea." But she did not move.

He had made certain that both wide shoes of the extension ladder were now set firmly on the ground. It should be stable enough, if he was cautious. He had taken his suit jacket off before beginning his climb, so the worst he could do to his clothes was to ruin his good shirt and trousers. Now, as long as she didn't do something foolish that might injure them both . . .

"If you can come back to the ladder, I'll help," he said.

"Oh, yes, of course." She crawled a little closer. At the edge of the roof, she looked down. Her softly pink complexion paled.

"Tell you what," he said. "I'll get on the roof and steady the ladder while you climb down."

"Sure." But she did not move any closer.

"Would you rather I help you climb down?"

A huge grin lit her face, only to be replaced by a frown of consternation. "Is that safe?"

Not entirely, but what else could he do? Leave her there? That was the kind of thing the media would love: "Mayor Abandons Stranded Citizen." He could go call for help, but she looked too scared to be left alone.

"We'll be careful. Here, turn around. I'll guide your feet onto the ladder, and then we'll go down. Slowly."

Good! She obeyed. This time, she crawled backward toward him. As he touched her slender leg to help her find the ladder, he was treated to a most pleasing view of her rounded and firm derriere beneath her tight denim pants.

Get a grip, he told himself. *And not just on the ladder; on your mind.* This woman was not merely a damsel in distress; she was the object of his investigation. And if things were as he expected, she was meddling in something that could only hurt someone very dear to him.

How bizarre! Carrie thought as she slowly descended the ladder. Here she was with the mayor—she, who knew no one of consequence, for she was of little consequence herself. Why had he been there in the first place?

She knew the ladder was a good one, yet after its fall, she now worried about its stability. But it felt good to have Mayor Sam's strong hand at her waist, steadying her. Guiding her. Making her feel certain she would be all right.

It had been more than a year since she had last felt a man's arms about her. She had lost Elliott just before Thanksgiving last year. Now she had just survived her second Thanksgiving without him. How would she do at Christmas?

No. She would not think of Elliott now.

They finally reached the bottom. "Thank you," she said breathlessly to the man who had rescued her. She reveled in the solid ground beneath her unsteady legs.

"Any time. Just be sure to vote for me in the next election." The mayor certainly had a killer smile.

She could not help smiling back. "Count on it. Would you like a cup of coffee?" Where had that come from? She didn't really have time. Not now. She had to be somewhere soon. Somewhere important.

No harm done. The mayor would hardly agree to come into one of his most insignificant constituent's homes for a cup of—

"I'd love one."

"Oh. Great. Please come in." Was her house clean enough to entertain someone of his stature? Even with her mother living with her, without Elliott's gentle reminders to pick things up, Carrie just never quite got around to dealing with the clutter.

Sam picked up his suit jacket from where he'd hung it on an outdoor chair. He'd been all dressed up, yet he had still come to rescue her. Now, this was a politician who really got down and dirty to help people! Though fortunately, now that they were down, he did not appear to have gotten dirty.

She led him through the back door, straight into the kitchen. It was one of the homiest rooms in the aging California cottage-style house, full of deep cabinets in warm wood, with a round, inviting table at one end. On the table, there were a couple of stacks of mail that she whisked quickly aside. She urged Sam to sit while she ground some fresh beans and set a pot to brewing.

Yesterday had been Thanksgiving, so she had some leftover pumpkin pie. She offered it to the mayor, glad she had something to serve. She hadn't baked cookies since—

"Nice house," he said. Was there surprise in his tone? She glanced at him, but his expression was bland.

"Thanks. It's been in my family for a while."

"It looks like a big place. Do you have a large family?"

"No. Just my mother and I live here." One more

person would live here soon. At least Carrie hoped so—for it would bring an end to her crushing loneliness. "My brother has his own place about half a mile away." She shook her head. "I'm ready to kick him in the shins. He was supposed to be holding the ladder for me."

"Not very responsible, is he?"

Carrie glared. Joey was, after all, her brother. And what did it matter to this man? "He usually does just fine. I only hope nothing happened to him."

She was glad her coffeemaker worked quickly, for in just a few minutes she placed a wedge of pie and a full cup on the table in front of the mayor, then took some for herself.

"This pie is excellent. Did you bake it?"

Why was this man so full of questions? "Yes, I did."

He wasn't through yet. "You were up on the roof hanging Christmas lights?"

She nodded. "I'm not good at it. It's something I . . . used to do, even though I'm a little nervous about heights. I didn't have to do it for a while, but now it's up to me again." She glared at him, daring him to contradict her. Or to ask why she hadn't had to hang lights for four years. Four wonderful years with Elliott, who had taken such good care of her. She hadn't had to do anything she hadn't wanted to. And even some things she had wanted to do by herself, he had considered too dangerous. Or things his wife did not need to concern herself about.

Then there had been last year, when she had not wanted to hang Christmas lights at all. There had been nothing to celebrate.

This year, if all went well, things would be different. First, despite what had happened, she was going to hang the decorations. Without help, without a doubt. It was a promise she'd made herself, to show herself that she could do it.

And by Christmas, she would have reason to believe that the bleak, desolate, empty spot inside her would soon be filled.

She hoped.

If only she had found her lucky Santa sleigh pendant on the roof. Then she would have had a sign . . .

"Well, maybe you'd better think about having someone else hang those lights," Sam DiGregorio said. "You didn't seem to like being up on that roof."

"I didn't. But I can handle it." And she would. She only hoped she didn't sound too belligerent. The man had, after all, helped her. And if his impression was that she was incompetent, she had only herself to thank.

It was her turn to ask a question. "I'm glad you were here, but what brought you to this neighborhood?"

Was that hesitation? If so, it was followed by a smile that, if it hadn't seemed a touch false, would have looked wonderful on the mayor's handsome face. His reaction seemed strange. She hadn't posed a particularly offbeat query.

"I like to get around in my constituency now and then," he said. "Meet people, answer questions, that kind of thing."

He was here to answer questions? Carrie wasn't sure how he'd done with the one she had just asked. But why else would he be here?

Still, since that was his purpose, she searched for something else appropriate to ask. "What is the status," she finally said, "of the parents' request for a new traffic light on Live Oak near Orangeblossom, by the Calridge Elementary School?"

His rather nicely formed lips made a small, rueful grimace. "Sorry, I don't know."

Carrie could have kicked herself; no matter what, she hadn't wanted to embarrass him. She glanced at the clock on the kitchen wall and nearly gasped aloud. Speaking of kicks, what was the protocol for kicking the mayor out of her house? "I'm afraid I have a meeting this afternoon, so I can't invite you to stay very long."

"That's fine." He finished his pie, then excused himself, saying he had to leave too. She saw him down the hall and to the front door.

"Thank you again for coming to my rescue." She held out her hand to shake his. His grip was as firm as the way he had supported her on that dratted ladder. A politician's grip? Not being of a political persuasion herself, she didn't know, but she liked its decisiveness.

"Any time," he said. She knew that his grin was the same one he would give to any constituent for whom he'd done a favor. Even so, she basked in it as she went upstairs to change her clothes.

Chapter Three

"How are you, Leanne?" Carrie smiled at the pretty blond teen who slouched in the straightest-backed chair in Dr. Lewis's Christmas-cheery waiting room.

"Fine."

But she didn't look fine. Oh, there was nothing wrong with the way she carried the baby—not visibly. She wore a voluminous tiger-print smock over black leggings, and though she'd gripped the chair arms to ease her way down, she looked no more uncomfortable than the other three expectant mothers in the doctor's office.

The problem was, she wouldn't meet Carrie's eye.

"I've talked with a lawyer." Carrie kept her voice low so as not to embarrass the girl. "He doesn't think there should be any problem about my . . . our . . . arrangement."

"I don't know," Leanne began. Confusion swept

over her face as her blue eyes looked directly at Carrie for the first time that afternoon. "It's my—"

"Leanne Dutton?" a woman in a white uniform called from the inner doorway. A look of apology—tempered by relief—replaced the earlier expression on Leanne's face.

"I'll wait," Carrie said with a smile, praying that not even the teensiest bit of desperation was evident in her tone.

She had met Leanne in the doctor's office two weeks earlier. Carrie, there for her annual checkup, had begun a conversation with the obviously pregnant girl. The poor thing had been eager to confide while she cried. She told a common tale of young love gone sour and botched birth control. She and the father had met in college, both students in pre-med. Neither was ready to drop everything to deal with an unexpected family, and as a result of the pregnancy, the father had dropped Leanne. Leanne already loved the baby she carried, and that was why, for its sake even more than her own, she planned to give him—or her—up. She had already spoken to the appropriate local adoption agencies.

An idea had come to Carrie as she commiserated. A blockbuster, earthmover of an idea.

Not a brand new idea, though. She had been considering adoption ever since Elliot's death. They had wanted babies together but had thought they had time. Now, it was too late to have Elliot's baby—but not too late for one of her own. Since she never intended to marry again, adoption seemed the ideal solution.

Carrie checked her watch every thirty seconds, watching the door through which Leanne had disappeared. In twenty minutes, she returned. Carrie walked out of the office with her.

"I don't think I can do this," Leanne finally admitted as they got into the empty elevator together. It smelled of the fragrant pine boughs fastened along its mirrored walls.

"What? Have a baby?" Carrie said teasingly.

Leanne laughed, too, but without much humor. "No, I've no choice about that now. But about your adopting—"

"I'll be a wonderful mother," Carrie interrupted.

"You'd be a *great* mother," Leanne agreed. "I was sure of it after the way you mothered me when we first met. But whether you're right for this baby . . ."

Carrie felt herself blanch. "Of course I am. I can prove it. I'll—"

"You don't understand. It's my brother, Greg. He thinks my baby deserves two loving parents. I don't know that he's wrong. We grew up in a single-parent home, and it was tough. I told him about you, though, how nice you are and how much you want a baby." Her tone grew desperate, as though she begged Carrie's understanding. "He's my big brother. He practically raised me. He cares about me and my baby. I don't know what to do, but he's seeing me through this, so . . ." Her voice trailed off, dragging Carrie's hopes with it.

No. Even without Elliot to go to bat for her, she was not a quitter. She kept her tone calm. "I'm sure Greg has your best interests in mind. And the baby's. He sounds like a wonderful brother." But she wished he'd butt out all the same. "I want to talk to him about how well this could work for all of us. Tell you what, Leanne. Why don't you both come to my house for dinner tomorrow?"

"Well . . ." Leanne hesitated.

Carrie reached into her purse for pen and paper. "Here's my address. See you at six."

* * *

"Hey, Sis, want me to set the table?"

"Yes, please." Turning from the oven, Carrie gratefully pointed out to Joey the flatware and dishes she'd already chosen.

Her twenty-two-year-old brother had dressed for the occasion—by his standards. He wore a blue denim shirt with his shredded blue jeans. His short hair was the same deep brown as hers, but his was moussed into soft spikes.

"You remember how to arrange them, don't you?" their mother asked. Maude Fells, in a Christmas apron over a good dress, stood at the stove, stirring the pot.

"Sure. Carrie and you have told me often enough." Her brother grinned engagingly, then took the dishes and disappeared into the dining room.

Joey was on his best behavior, Carrie noted. He should be; he owed her, big time. It turned out he had gotten a call on his cell phone when he'd stranded her on the roof. A girlfriend had run out of gas and had cried to him hysterically about how scared she was parked along the freeway at rush hour.

But, Carrie had patiently explained to him later, there were patrolling tow trucks to help people stranded along freeways. There weren't patrolling Santa sleighs, or even helicopters, to help people stranded on housetops.

"The bread's nearly done, Carrie," said her mother. She was plump and several inches shorter than Carrie but had been surprisingly helpful hanging the indoor Christmas decorations. "Would you like me to—"

The timer on the stove began to buzz—just as the doorbell rang. Carrie turned first toward the range, then toward the door. She stopped, took a deep breath, then smiled ruefully. "You take care of the bread," she said to her mother. "I'll get the door."

Heading down the hall, Carrie took in the way her home looked. Wonderful! All the clutter had been safely socked away. Festooned with candles and fragrant wreaths, golden garlands and angels, the house looked glittery and festive, full of the spirit of the season.

But the tree would have to wait. Carrie liked beautiful, bushy, fresh-cut trees, and she decorated hers on Christmas Eve.

Then there were the eaves of the house. They remained nearly bare. Carrie's favorite decoration, the large Santa and reindeer, still rested against the house in the backyard.

One day she'd get up the gumption to return to the roof to complete the job she had started. She would. She really would.

It wasn't as if she would fall again the way she had, as a kid, from a scaffold against a neighbor's house—along with two gallons of the neighbor's gray paint.

And now that Elliot wasn't around to tell her how dangerous things were, she had to learn to do them herself.

Carrie patted her hair, then looked at her hand to make sure she hadn't powdered herself with flour. It was clean, thank heavens. She stepped toward the door as the bell sounded again—a rendition of "Jingle Bells," programmed into the musical doorbell for the season. "Ouch," she said, for the system was right by her ear. She pulled open the front door.

There, in a pretty red maternity dress with a matching bow in her long blond hair, stood Leanne. Behind her was a black-haired man. Carrie felt her eyes widen. She looked around, in case there was another male nearby who could be Leanne's brother.

There wasn't.

"You—" she said angrily, then stopped herself.

"Carrie," Leanne said, "I'd like you to meet my brother—"

"Brother Greg," Carrie managed. "Mr. Sam Di*Greg*orio. Mayor Sam . . . we've met."

Chapter Four

"Sorry, Carrie, a baby's not a house pet. You don't get one just so you won't be alone." Sam DiGregorio sat across from her. His tone was light, but his meaning bore down heavily on her shoulders: he did not want her to have this baby.

"I'm sorry you look at it that way, Your Hon—Mr. Mayor—Greg—er, Sam," Carrie said, irritated at her stumbling. What was the protocol for begging a politician to have a heart?

She had tried hard this evening not to look at him—much. He had dressed up for the occasion; she had glanced at him enough to note how handsome he appeared in his dark suit and patterned necktie.

"Getting a pet is not my sister's intention, Sam," said Joey, beside her. "If it were, she'd buy a dog."

Carrie appreciated the way her brother spoke up for her. "I was simply trying to be candid," she explained, "about why I want this child. I expect a baby to be a baby, not a pet. Not perfect, not a creature to be trained to speak or do tricks, but a child with all the wonderful and frustrating dimensions children have. I love kids; I teach second grade, you know. My husband died a year ago. Since I lost him and won't be able to have babies of my own, adoption sounded ideal. And when I met Leanne, and she was eager to make sure her baby got a good home, it seemed like fate."

They were finishing the meal of turkey tetrazzini, penne pasta, fresh green beans, and home-baked bread that Carrie had worked darned hard to prepare. She'd started what she could early in the morning, then bolted home after the three o'clock bell to complete dinner. But even with all her work, were her guests enjoying it? She wasn't the world's greatest cook. Elliot had been tolerant, but he had told her often that—

"You're a lovely young woman." Sam was looking at *her*. Upset that she felt herself flushing at his compliment, Carrie was nevertheless glad she had put on one of her favorite blouses and a long skirt. She began to thank him—until he finished his thought. His tone was almost belligerent. "You'll marry again."

"That's what I keep telling her," said her mother, who sat on Joey's other side.

"No, I won't," Carrie said firmly. "My husband— Elliott—spoiled me for any other man."

"He spoiled you, all right," grumbled her brother.

"Joey!" Their mother's raised voice was a chastisement. Carrie just sighed. She'd known what Joey thought of Elliott. But her husband was gone, and this was not the time—

Leanne chimed in. "Some people marry only once, Greg," she pointed out. "Unlike our mother." She looked at Carrie. "That's why we have different last names. Mom had Greg first, then divorced. She married again and had me—same story. Only she . . . she died when I was little, when Greg was in college. He took care of me."

Carrie glanced at him. Sam DiGregorio was young for a mayor—thirty, she'd read in the papers. Leanne had to be eleven years younger. He had probably been about Leanne's age when faced with raising his little sister. He had been a product of a one-parent home, then had been turned into a quasi-parent himself, when he should have been a rowdy college kid. Carrie could not help admiring the man for that.

No wonder he was worried about this baby. But he needn't be. Not with Carrie as its mother. She'd cherish it. But how was she going to convince them—Sam and his sister—that this adoption would be right?

Maybe she didn't need to convince *them*, but *him*. Carrie sensed that Sam ran his own small family as he ran the City of Calridge. "Okay, Mr. Mayor, you want reasons why I, as a single mother, should raise this baby? I'll give you reasons."

She had thought this through. Oh, had she ever! She began a rundown of the list she'd created. "Though I'll want to go back to teaching eventually, I'm financially independent for now. I still have an interest in my husband's car dealership, plus his insurance money. My mom"—she glanced at her mother, whose return smile was endearingly encouraging—"has promised to care for the baby when I work, and to help out in general. So has Joey, so there'll be a masculine influence in the baby's life."

She didn't bother to say that her brother might have little more maturity than the infant. But he'd grow up with the baby.

"I know about kids," she continued. "I teach. As far as two-parent households—well, some of my students would be better off with just one instead of a squabbling duo. And one of my kids would be better off with *neither* of the parents he's got. It has nothing to do with how many parents a child has; it has to do with quality. I'd make a great parent. And I'd be delighted to let Leanne remain in the baby's life. You, too, Sam." She hesitated before posing the query at the forefront of her thoughts. "This isn't my business, Sam, but since you're so concerned about the baby's welfare, did you consider raising it yourself?"

His expression froze; he glanced at Leanne, then back at Carrie. She braced herself for his answer. Would he berate her for her brashness? The answer was important. It might give her insight on how to get past his apparently immutable opposition.

"Yes," he said slowly. A look of suffering sketched wrinkles into his handsome forehead, and Carrie wished she could cram the question back down her throat. "I thought about it. I decided against it for both Leanne and the baby. I didn't want my sister to feel compelled to give up her dreams for the child, for she'd have insisted on helping me. And since I'm not married, I wanted to spare this child the misery of growing up in a one-parent household."

Carrie's already flimsy hopes started to flutter away. He clearly had no conflicting opinions about one parent raising a child. Still, it was too early to give up without a fight. She placed her chin on her hand and rested her elbow on the table. In as mischievous a tone as she could muster, she said, "Well, Mr. Mayor, I've always heard that good politicians keep open minds on the issues. Are you a good politician?"

"The best," he replied, his sparkling blue eyes daring her to contradict him. "But that doesn't mean—"

"Well, I'm just going to lobby you 'til you're on my side."

On her side . . . a pleasant thought, Sam realized.

Unlikely, though. He had to think of Leanne and the defenseless baby she carried. And Carrie Ritenour had admitted that she intended to be, forever, a single parent.

Then there was that little escapade up on the roof. What kind of a mother would she make?

A darned good one, piped up an ornery little voice at the back of his mind. Leanne certainly thought so. Carrie had shown herself to be caring and a determined advocate. She'd doubtless stand up for her child against all the wickedness of the world.

But she would still be a single parent.

He said, "Just how do you plan to conduct this lobbying effort?"

"Well," she said, "first I'm drafting you to help with the dishes. You'll see how I'd teach my child to do chores."

"All right," Sam agreed, to his own surprise. His sister even raised her sandy eyebrows at him; she knew how much he detested doing dishes. "In the interest of giving Ms. Ritenour a fair opportunity to lobby me," he explained.

"That was a great dinner," Sam said as Carrie handed him an apron. He put it on over his shirt and trousers, well aware of her hands at his back as she tied it for him.

"Really? Did you think so?" She sounded surprised. She moved to face him, her brown eyes huge. "I was worried about the sauce, but . . . I'm delighted you liked it."

The sauce had been excellent. The meal had been excellent. And Sam wondered why Carrie had seemed so incredulous at his compliment.

He noted that she had decorated the kitchen as she had the rest of her charming cottage-style house. Silver garlands dripping with pine cones hung along the tops of the walls.

"So," he said as Carrie turned toward the sink, where pans soaked in soapy water. "Tell me more about why you want to adopt this baby."

She pivoted again toward him, her small chin raised boldly. "How much has Leanne said about me, Mr. DiGregorio?"

"Sam," he reminded her. "She didn't say much more than you explained over dinner; she said you lost your husband before you could start a family, and that you were considering adoption even before you met her."

Sam now knew more about Carrie, of course, than his sister had mentioned—had even known. He had done some digging, had learned that Carrie had been married to Elliott Ritenour. He'd learned that Ritenour had died in an unfortunate accident at the local car dealership that he and a partner owned.

And he'd learned that Ritenour had been under investigation for fraudulent dealings when he died.

"That's right," Carrie said softly. "My husband, Elliot, was a wonderful man. I miss him. He'd never have allowed me to get stuck up on the roof where you found me yesterday." She stopped for a moment. "You were here to check me out, weren't you?"

"Well, sort of," Sam began as he searched for the most innocuous explanation.

But Carrie didn't wait for further response. "Don't judge me by that fiasco. I'm usually not careless.

Elliott would never even have let me go up there—too dangerous."

Sam directed his scowl toward the dripping pot she handed him. He hadn't liked Carrie's comment earlier that her husband had spoiled her for other men. Nor did he like the pang that went through him now; surely he couldn't be jealous of a man he had never known—a dead man.

But Ritenour had apparently inspired deep devotion in his wife. Sam had the impression that, to Carrie, Elliott had seemed a saint. Sam, however, had reason to believe he was a sinner.

"Now that he's gone, I'm still going to get those Christmas lights hung," she said with conviction.

"Sure," Sam agreed, "but get someone reliable to help out." *Like me.*

"Like you?" she echoed his thoughts.

"Well . . . sure." Now, that certainly sounded enthusiastic.

"Thanks for the offer," she said, picking up another pot, "but if—when I go back up there, it'll be on my own. It's something I want to do."

Have to do, was what he heard. He admired her guts.

And that was not all he admired about her, he realized, as he watched her slender body—clad in a pretty white blouse and long, deep-red skirt beneath the apron tied at her waist—as she scrubbed the dirty cookware.

"But you wanted to hear more about why I want to adopt Leanne's baby." She changed the subject adroitly. "I've explained why I think I would be a good parent. I agree that the right two-parent family is the ideal, but one that's not always achieved. I could create a wonderful one-parent family. Oh, Sam, I'd love to have a little one to come home to."

And I, Sam thought, would love to have someone as loving as Carrie to come home to. . . . Now, where had that thought come from? His tone too gruff, he retorted, "But what about the baby? You've said you won't marry again. Would the child be happy coming home from school to mama and grandma, but no daddy?"

Carrie looked stricken. "I'd make it a happy home my child would want to come home to," she whispered, her voice breaking. "I really would. At least I would try. . . . Do you think I'm just being selfish?"

Sam had not intended to hurt her. She did, after all, seem like a nice person. A very nice person. He said quietly, "I hear a lot about what this baby would mean to you, but—"

"But honestly, Sam, I'm not just thinking of myself." She had regained her composure quickly. "I couldn't. Particularly not at this season, when giving is so important. Yes, I need someone in my life, but it's more than that. There is a baby on his—or her—way. A baby whose mother can't keep him. A baby who should never worry about being alone or unwanted. That baby needs someone, too. Someone to love him. To be a family to him. And that someone should be me."

He was silent for a moment, trying to think what to say. She was a lovely, lonely woman who wanted a baby—for what might be all the wrong reasons.

Despite the fact that he found appealing both what she said and who she was, this was his sister's baby they were talking about.

Carrie obviously realized she had not won him over.

"I had a lot of love growing up, so I know what it feels like." She sounded desperate. "I can give that wonderful feeling to this child, I swear it."

"And I know what it feels like to come from a one-parent home," Sam blurted out. "I don't want that for my sister's baby."

He saw sympathy war with sorrow on her lovely face. Damn! Despite Leanne's revelations, he hadn't intended to say anything personal. He didn't want to explain further, but now he had to.

"Look, Carrie, my parents divorced when I was five," he said. "I lived with my mother. My father stayed in touch but wanted nothing to do with her—and little to do with me until I was older. But I grew up determined to be a policeman like him."

Carrie's smile lit her face. "All kids want to be like their parents; I hear it all the time from my students. But instead, you grew up to be mayor."

"No, at first I *was* a policeman." Now he realized it had been his method of trying to get closer to his dad. It hadn't been right for him. And that was why today he was a politician.

But his father had taught him a lot about making sure he knew people. *All* about them.

Which was why he had decided to check so closely into the woman who wanted to adopt Leanne's baby. And how he had found out about her husband.

"Then how did you get to be mayor?" Carrie had stopped placing dishes into the dishwasher and watched him with puzzlement.

"We're supposed to be discussing you," he reminded her. "And the baby."

"And one-parent households." Her voice was softly sympathetic. "It hurt you."

He didn't want to talk about it anymore. "It hurt Leanne, too, though she won't admit it. But what we went through doesn't matter. This baby—"

"So, do you have it all figured out?" Leanne waddled into the kitchen, followed by Maude and Joey Fells. "I'd like to get home, if it's not too rude to eat and run." She looked exhausted.

"No, that's fine," Sam said, but the look Carrie shot him was frantic. She knew she had not yet persuaded him.

She couldn't persuade him; Sam was certain of that. Still, he hated the sorrow that turned her large brown eyes into deep, sad wells.

"I think, though," he said, "that Carrie might want to continue our discussion another day."

The big, grateful smile she turned on him was worth all his discomfort at having his own childhood dissected.

And somehow he didn't think he would mind at all another meeting with Carrie Ritenour.

Chapter Five

"I hope you don't mind a mall expedition." Sam DiGregorio's deep, smooth voice washed over Carrie a few afternoons later as she held her kitchen phone receiver to her ear. "I don't have a lot of time right now, and if I can get some Christmas shopping done while we talk, it would be helpful."

"Sounds fun," Carrie said. "I still have a few things to buy, too."

While managing to teach thirty kids who were enthusiastically chattering about their upcoming Christmas pageant, she had wracked her brain for an excuse to get together with Sam. For her "lobbying," of course. Even if she had enjoyed his company and their verbal sparring, the only reason they had to see each other again was to discuss the baby.

No good plan had come to mind, though she had

intended to phone Sam anyway and improvise. But he had called first.

A mall outing? Why not! Carrie would have agreed to go on a snowboarding expedition in her bathing suit to keep their dialogue going.

"I'll pick you up at six this evening," Sam finished.

Carrie hung up the phone, then stared at it. Six was only a couple of hours away. She needed to think.

The house had felt empty as Carrie walked in the door, emphasizing how alone she was—this afternoon, and most of the time. How she needed someone in her life to come home to. Someone who needed her.

She had to convince Sam that her someone was his sister's baby.

Her mother had left a note; she was out grocery shopping. Carrie was glad. It would give her time to organize her thoughts.

She found a pen and some lined paper, the kind she used to teach her students how to write. Sitting on her living-room sofa, surrounded by sparkling and fragrant Christmas decorations, she readied herself to jot down all the reasons she thought she could be a wonderful mother. Column A: all her good points. Column B: all her even better points.

But her pen refused to write anything at all.

Couldn't she be a great mom? Or was Sam right? Did she want Leanne's baby for purely selfish reasons?

The last time they had been together, she had showed her uncertainty to him for a moment before catching herself. With Sam, she just had to be certain—and strong.

But what if she just *wasn't* right for this child? She would only find out when it was too late.

Her mind slipped to Elliott. If he were here, he'd

have told her exactly what he thought. But if he were here, she would not be in this predicament.

"I don't know, Carrie," she could hear him say in his most serious tone—the one he'd always used while considering her request to do something different. He would be standing in front of her, gripping her shoulders. He had been taller than her five-foot-five by a couple of inches. She could see him shaking his head, his light hair cut short, his narrow lips in a tight line. *"You've never been a mother before. You've had a lot of trouble with that recipe for turkey tetrazzini when I haven't been there to help. I just don't know how well you would handle a baby."*

"But I got the recipe perfect a few days ago," she responded aloud earnestly, trying to whisk away her disloyal wish that her imagination would not be as blunt as Elliott.

"Well, if you've made up your mind," he would have said, turning away so quickly that she would get a whiff of his strong deodorant soap that sometimes made her sneeze. *"There's nothing I can do to stop you."* Those words had never been more true than they were now. Still, they, and his turning away, *had* always managed to stop her.

Are you right, Sam DiGregorio? Carrie asked herself desperately. Maybe she should call the mall expedition off. Maybe she should just stop the whole lobbying effort, for the sake of the baby.

Glendale Galleria was the largest shopping mall in the area, though it was not the closest to Calridge.

"I hope you don't mind going there," Sam had said when he picked Carrie up promptly at six.

She had not made up her mind by then whether to call the evening off, and so she was going by default.

And she was going by Sam DiGregorio's side, in his sport utility vehicle, a GMC Yukon. He was dressed in a charcoal long-sleeved shirt that looked great with his black hair. It managed to make the blue of his eyes stand out, too.

In fact, he looked wonderful. And she liked the way he had smiled at her from the moment he met her at the door. The guy certainly had Christmas spirit. His presence even lifted her spirits. She could do this. At least she could survive the evening.

She was glad she had picked out a pretty jade pantsuit. It didn't clash with what Sam was wearing. In fact, she suspected they looked rather nice together.

Not that it mattered. This was not a social event. *You understand that, don't you, Elliott?* her thoughts inquired. *I'm not being disloyal to you. This is a crusade.* Wasn't it?

"Glendale sounds fine," she said. She didn't mind the mall. What bothered her was the idea of trying to convince Sam of something that she herself had diminished confidence in.

"Glendale's big enough to have the best selection," he explained. "And we'll have more privacy in the crowd there than at Calridge Plaza."

A pang of nerves shot through Carrie. "Do the media hound you the way they do other politicians?" she asked. Would the fact that the baby she wanted to adopt was the mayor's niece subject her to investigative reporters' inquisitions? She had enough things to worry about without "film at eleven" being among them.

"Not unless I do something that's actually newsworthy," Sam replied. "I stay low-key unless there's an issue the public needs to know about. My private life usually stays private; I'm not nearly as interesting as the president or even the mayor of Los Angeles."

Thank heavens, Carrie thought, sighing to herself. But would the media find this adoption interesting enough to bring Sam out of the background?

Sam had to drive around the parking lot for ten minutes before finding a space. Then they went inside.

The mall was full of chattering people with brimming bags. Trees and ornaments abounded, and Christmas carols filled the air. "Where shall we begin?" Sam asked.

"It's your expedition," Carrie said. "You choose."

Would the perfect mama, in Sam's eyes, have been more decisive? "On the other hand," she continued, "I need to go to a toy store. I want to pick up some small presents for my students." There. Now just let him think she didn't love kids.

"I don't have anyone I need to buy for at a toy store," he said. "Would you like to go there first, then meet me?"

Drat! The whole idea of going with him was to stick near him, sway him to see her excellence.

"I can do it later," she said. "Where do you need to go?"

"Let's start at Macy's. I want to get some things for my father and Leanne and I haven't any ideas. Maybe you can think of something."

Oh, no! What if this was part of the test—was she intuitive enough to understand other people's tastes? She knew Leanne a little, but probably not well enough to pick a perfect present. And his father, the policeman . . .?

"I'll be glad to try," she said, smiling with gritted teeth.

They had come in through the center of the mall and had to walk to one end for the department store. The crowds were dense, jovial, and jostling, and more than once she got separated from Sam—till he firmly tucked her arm beneath his.

He was much taller than Elliott had been; her shoulder fit snugly beneath his. She liked the feeling of another human being so close. It was the time of year, she told herself, a good time not to be alone. Few people, as she looked around the mall, were by themselves. She was entitled to be with another person, too. Staving off loneliness didn't make her disloyal to Elliott or his memory.

And if that nearby person was one she had to impress, well, she could hardly pull away.

"Let's stick together," Sam said, looking down at her and smiling. "We've got lots to talk about, after all."

"Yes," she said. "We do." She groaned inside. Here it came—the barrage of questions that would make or break her chance at motherhood.

She had to respond correctly. Sure, she was steeped in doubts about whether she would be the right mama for Leanne's little one, but now was not the time to dwell on them.

"What do you want most for Christmas?" Sam asked, raising his voice to be heard above the crowd.

"Besides a baby?"

He nodded. "Besides a baby."

Carrie looked at him. "Is this a trick question?"

He laughed. "No, I just thought the answer might help me get to know you a little better."

It *was* a trick question. Should she answer "Peace on earth, good will toward men?" Or tell him about those fuzzy bunny bathroom slippers she'd had her eye on all year?

"Tell me what *you* want first."

He raised his thick, dark eyebrows along with one

335

corner of his mouth. "All right. I want the bright red long johns and matching nightcap I saw in a sporting goods store near the skiing equipment."

She laughed. "You're kidding."

"I never kid," he kidded.

"Well, I'd love to see your long johns and nightcap beside the fuzzy bunny bathroom slippers that I want most."

"So would I." His grin was the most engaging smile she had seen for a long time.

Carrie realized what she'd just implied. His body-hugging nightclothes beside her slippers . . . If he looked so good in his everyday clothes, she had no doubt he had the kind of body those nightclothes would hug well. Her face grew hot. "Er," she said, "they're the kinds of things a store might put near one another to sell, don't you think? That's what I meant."

"That's not necessarily what I meant," Sam said. But before Carrie could protest, he pointed. "Here we are. We've reached the store."

For the next hour, Carrie walked side by side with Sam where the crowds allowed, studying clothes and accessories and gifts by the gazillion. She asked questions about his father's and Leanne's tastes, then made suggestions. Some Sam shook his head about, sometimes dislodging a dark wave of hair that slipped over his forehead. When that happened, he shoved it back impatiently.

Carrie had an urge, now and then, to push it back herself, more gently, so it would stay. But that would not have been appropriate. She hardly knew Mayor Sam DiGregorio.

With her consultation, Sam bought for his father a handsome pullover shirt in a dressy knit, along with a coordinating sweater, since the old man enjoyed impressing ladies when he took them out in the evening, especially this time of year.

Leanne was more of a quandary. Clothes were out; she wouldn't be in maternity garb much longer, and size would be a problem thereafter. She wasn't dating now, and she planned to go back to school the following term. "Jewelry!" said Carrie, suddenly inspired.

Leanne had pierced ears, and Carrie helped Sam pick out an adorable pair of cat earrings with a matching pin.

And then she saw it, hanging alone on a display rack—a gold Christmas pendant, a Santa and sleigh. "Oh!" Carrie exclaimed before she had time to think.

"Oh?" Sam asked.

Carrie shrugged. "Oh, I just saw a necklace like one I lost a long time ago," she said. She pointed to the pendant. "I dropped it up on the roof when I was stringing Christmas lights."

Sam cocked his head in question. "When was this, and how did you avoid getting stranded?"

Carrie laughed, then grew somber. "About five years ago, when . . . when Elliott and I were just dating. I was afraid of heights then, too, but that didn't stop me. But I always considered the pendant good luck. And then I lost it, and Elliott and I got serious and he didn't want me going back up, so I never found it. I was hoping that this year I'd see it, but I didn't. Yet."

She looked at him defiantly, daring him to demand that she not return to the roof. But he didn't.

"I can see why getting back on the housetop means so much to you. And I can also see why your Elliott didn't want you going; if I had someone like you in my life, I'd want to protect her from dangers like that, too."

Carrie stared at him, all the while feeling as though warm apple cider flowed through her veins. His eyes captured hers, and his lips were open just a little, as though he intended for more to come out of them.

No. Being here might not be disloyal to Elliott, but looking at this man this way, flirting with him . . . She just couldn't do it.

"So," she said with a forced smile, "don't you think we ought to find a salesgirl so you can pay for the pin and earrings for Leanne?"

"Yes," Sam said softly, without pulling his gaze away. "I guess we should."

After he had finished his purchase, they meandered through other stores. In a puzzle shop, she challenged him to pull two pieces of metal apart. He couldn't, but she knew the trick.

"Hey!" he said. "I'm impressed."

"And I'm smart. Don't forget that. There's a lot I could teach a baby."

The teasing in his eyes disappeared. "Yes," he said, "I'm sure you could. But this baby . . ." He let his voice taper off as he turned toward another puzzle.

Carrie sighed and looked at the floor. What would it take to convince him? *Could* she convince him?

As they left the store, Carrie changed the subject. "Any idea how many stores there are in this mall?" she asked.

"No, but I doubt my feet will stand visiting them all tonight!"

Good. They were back on a lighter note once more. Maybe that was the key to his good graces.

This time, Sam took her hand to keep them from getting separated. She enjoyed his firm grip—the better to keep them together for her lobbying, she told herself.

In the middle of the mall, Sam ducked his head toward Carrie as he dodged a man carrying a wrapped pair of skis.

His face was nearly touching hers. His lips were so close . . . Carrie felt herself tremble. Would a good mother step firmly back? Would she allow herself to be kissed, here in the middle of a mall?

She didn't move. Didn't even breathe. She felt the heat from Sam's face on hers, and—

Someone jostled her from the side. The moment was over. She did not need to decide whether to kiss or flee. Thank heavens.

And what if someone had seen them—gotten a photo, even. That would look just great in a local paper: "Mayor of Calridge Kisses in Mall Without Mistletoe." She looked up, just in case. No, no mistletoe dangled from the mall's ceiling high above.

"It's getting late," Carrie said softly. "I have to teach tomorrow. Would you mind if we started home?"

If the muddled expression in Sam's eyes was any gauge, he was as confused as she felt. "But you haven't bought any presents yet."

"That's okay. There are still twenty or so shopping days till Christmas."

She was not so certain how many days there were until Leanne gave birth. What had she been doing? She had been acting inappropriately with this man instead of convincing him of her mothering abilities.

At least she wasn't questioning them herself—not at this moment. Why had she listened to Elliott before in her mind? She didn't really know what he would say in this situation. Maybe he'd cheer her on.

"So," she said as they braved the crowd to head toward the car, "what else can I tell you to persuade you to let me adopt Leanne's baby?" Enough teasing; she was running out of time.

He shrugged his large shoulders without looking at her.

"It's not up to me."

"No, Leanne has to decide," Carrie agreed. "But she'll listen to your veto. So how do I persuade you to abstain from any vote at all?"

"You don't want me to champion your cause?"

"I suspect, Mayor DiGregorio, that to hope for that would be a *lost* cause."

He smiled, then grew serious. "All right, then. One reason I think a two-parent family is better is because one parent can support the family while the other cares for the children. I know you said you could handle the expense for a while. I also know it's not always fashionable these days for a mother to stay at home, but it's at least possible when the father works."

"You don't think I should teach ever again if I get this baby?" Carrie heard the hoarseness in her voice. She loved teaching. It was the one thing she had remained adamant about when Elliott had told her to quit working since he made plenty of money to support them both.

Sam answered her question with one of his own. "You're the expert; isn't it better for a child to have a stay-at-home mother when he's in grade school?"

"No," she said with conviction. "But I could stop working that long, if it would sway you. Even after the insurance runs out, I'll still have an interest in my husband's business."

"And are you active in that business?"

"Absolutely," she said, sure that showing him an alternative, ongoing source of income was imperative. "I consult with his partner a lot, even give him instructions."

Now what was that strange, searching glare Sam gave her? It disappeared in an instant. "I see."

But Carrie didn't. For the first time that evening, she was certain that she had said something that Sam considered wrong.

She had no idea what it was—but she was afraid that she was farther away than ever from getting his approval to adopt Leanne's baby.

Chapter Six

The evening had been a dismal failure, and Carrie didn't know why.

Oh, Sam was pleasant on the way home, but she could tell something troubled him.

"What kind of toys do you intend to get for your classroom of kids?" he asked as they passed a local toy store.

"Ones that'll fill their little hearts without emptying my wallet," Carrie replied with a grin.

Sam's return smile appeared more polite than genuine. "Sounds like a tall order. Any ideas?"

She shook her head. "Something will come to me." But gifts for kids were a long way off from a lifetime gift for her: Leanne's baby. Would some way come to her to win over this mystifyingly solemn mayor beside her?

They reached her house. Should she ask him in for a nightcap? Hot chocolate, of course; he had to drive home. "I had a nice time," she said diplomatically, though she felt confused.

"So did I." But his tone belied his words.

"Yes, well . . . " She turned toward him. He watched her expectantly, obviously eager for her to vacate the car. The blueness of his eyes stood out in the otherwise neutral colors of the night. His dark beard beneath his untanned skin had begun to grow during the day, and his stubble was emphasized by the shadows inside the car.

He was a nice-looking man, much more mysterious looking than Elliott's beach-boy blond openness. Mayor Sam was nice-acting, too—most of the time. He had saved her from the roof. He had his sister's and her baby's best interests in mind.

But why, oh why, couldn't he understand they coincided with Carrie's best interests, too?

As his outstanding eyes continued to regard her in the increasingly uncomfortable silence, her mind raced back to the mall. To the moment he had bent toward her—had been pushed, rather. To the moment she had thought he was going to . . .

An impulse impelled her toward him. She gave him a kiss, right on his wide, sensuous lips.

For a moment, it was one-sided. She nearly drew back in embarrassment. But then his warm mouth responded. He kissed her back.

And, oh, what a kiss it was! Carrie's toes hadn't been particularly cold in her comfortable flat walking shoes, but all of a sudden they were blazing. Not to mention the rest of her. She felt a volcanic glow in parts of her that had long lay dormant, since Elliott had been gone. And perhaps even before . . .

No, she would not be disloyal to her husband.

But hadn't she been, by initiating this kiss? She drew back, immediately missing the feel of Sam's fantastic lips. It was all right, she told herself. She had done this in the interest of her future—hers and the baby's.

"I'll lobby you again soon," she said, her light tone belying the heavy emotions swirling sensually inside her. She quickly got out of the car.

She turned at her doorstep. His Yukon still stood at the curb. She waved and went into the house.

In the blackness of her bedroom, Carrie's eyelids flew open. That didn't surprise her; her eyes had been opening every few minutes since she'd gone to bed three hours earlier.

What did surprise her was that this time she had actually fallen asleep. Begun to dream.

About that kiss. And Sam DiGregorio.

Even after all the mental flogging she'd laid on herself since that moment when she planted her lips on Sam's.

It would have been all right if the dream had been similarly self-chastising. But it had been pleasant. *Too* pleasant.

In it, Sam had kissed her first. And she had enjoyed it.

"I'm so sorry, Elliott," she whispered into the dark.

She could nearly hear his response. "*I understand, Carrie,*" he would say in the stiff voice he used when she'd hurt him. She had hurt him often at first, by not heeding what he said. "*You're alone now. You're entitled to a life.*"

"I have a life, Elliott," she whispered, stroking the cool sheet. "A nice life, though I'll always miss you. But I want that baby so much. That's the reason I kissed the mayor. It was part of my lobbying effort, to get on his good side so he'll allow his sister to let me adopt her baby."

Never mind, continued her disloyal thoughts, that the kiss had rocked her right through to her most scandalously torrid fantasies of candlelight and champagne, warm fingers on hot skin.

That kiss had led her to wonder what if . . . what if she hadn't decided to remain true to her sweet, departed husband? What if Sam DiGregorio had more interest in her than as the woman who wanted to adopt his sister's baby?

What if they had ripped each other's clothes off, right in that car, and—

"Stop your disgraceful notions right now, Carol Cornelia Fells Ritenour!" Carrie demanded aloud in the darkness.

She wanted a baby, that was all. To care for, to love her as she would love it. She didn't want complications—like a relationship with the baby's uncle.

Relationship? "One kiss doesn't mean a relationship, Elliott," she said into the emptiness. "I promise." And it wasn't just out of loyalty to Elliott that she would stay alone. She just wanted no other man after losing him. He had been good to her. . . .

"But you still want that baby?" Now the tone in her head was his most accusatory, and she winced.

"You're gone, Elliott, and I'm lonely." She swallowed as her voice broke.

"You can hardly take care of yourself, Carrie." There was his cajoling, convincing tone. *"How could you handle a baby?"*

"You haven't seen me lately, Elliott," she pleaded with the darkness. "I can take care of a baby."

She realized she was arguing with a man who wasn't even there. Not anymore. But a man who had always had her best interests at heart.

But he'd broken her heart by dying. And now she

was trying to mend a corner of it. His objecting wasn't fair. Especially when she only imagined what he would say.

She sat up and folded her arms. "I don't want another man, Elliott," she said, her back to his side of the bed. "But don't interfere with how I need to handle the rest of my life. Do you hear me?"

There. She'd stood up to him. She had hardly ever done that when he'd been around to argue back.

There was no answer, not even in her head. She sighed and lay back down.

She could be a wonderful mother. She *would* be a wonderful mother. Despite Elliott's doubts . . . for they couldn't be her own, could they?

In any event, she might never know *what* kind of mother she would be. Not unless she convinced Sam DiGregorio.

Chapter Seven

The next day, a sleepy Carrie pointedly ignored her bloodshot eyes in the bedroom mirror. She picked up the phone to call Leanne to check on the progress of her pregnancy—and her own progress with Leanne's brother.

That kiss had wreaked havoc with Carrie's state of mind. But maybe it had turned the tide with Sam.

She doubted it. A kiss, even a good one, did not correlate with superhuman abilities as a single parent.

And then there was Sam's inexplicable retreat at the evening's end. Carrie needed to understand why.

Leanne lived with her brother now. She doubtless saw a lot of him. Had Sam mentioned to her his trip to the mall with Carrie? Or anything else about last evening?

"I'm fine, thanks," Leanne responded to Carrie's initial question.

"And Sam . . . How is he? I mean," Carrie amended hastily, "has my lobbying worked? Does he agree yet that my adopting your baby is a wonderful idea?"

"Well . . ." The way Leanne drew out the word spoke volumes.

"Did he tell you about our shopping expedition? I thought it went okay." Until she had confused matters further by her impulsive kiss. Had that been what had driven Sam to become so distant? She sighed aloud.

"Yes, he mentioned your mall trip. He said it was very nice."

Nice? thought Carrie. Nice was someone's maiden aunt. Nice was a slightly stale oatmeal cookie. It wasn't an auspicious evening of persuasion. It wasn't a soul-shaking kiss . . . or its indecipherable aftermath. "That's all? It didn't change his mind?"

"I'm sorry, Carrie," replied Leanne. "But . . ." That one hesitant syllable sent tears to Carrie's eyes. Not that she had expected anything different. Not really.

"Guess my days as a lobbyist are just beginning." She wished she felt as cheerful as she made herself sound.

It took Carrie nearly a week to get up the nerve to call Sam for a date—for strictly political reasons, of course.

Not that they were completely out of touch. Oh, no.

Sam called now and then, politely asking how Carrie was doing with her Christmas shopping. He mentioned once that he had seen some small plush bears at a local store that might make good presents for her students. He mentioned his sister and her good health. He mentioned nothing else, not even that kiss.

Carrie called Sam, to let him know she had seen a picture of him in the paper lighting the lights on the

Calridge Christmas tree, near City Hall. To let Sam know she had picked up the plush bears he had found, to thank him again for the idea. She mentioned his sister a lot, so Sam would know that Leanne and the baby were foremost on Carrie's mind.

That was the only reason, of course, that Sam, too, remained on Carrie's mind.

She did not tell him she had bought him the red long johns and nightcap, just because . . . well, just because she believed everyone should get his fondest Christmas wish. She most certainly didn't tell him she had wrapped it immediately to avoid her imagination's dressing him in the skin-tight, muscle-hugging outfit.

In any event, their polite palaver was not enough. What excuse could she use to get together with him next? She supposed she could insist that he accompany her on another shopping expedition, one for her. But she wanted something different to pique his interest, if not his immediate agreement about the adoption.

Everyday she worried about her lack of progress, even as she rehearsed her students for the Christmas pageant.

The Christmas pageant! That was it, she realized as she drove home one afternoon. What would better convince unconvinceable Sam DiGregorio that she would be a wonderful mother than to get him to see her mothering some kids? Thirty of them. All at once.

The school extravaganza was the following Tuesday night, not quite a week away. Only a week before Christmas.

After dinner that evening, Carrie squirmed in her plaid overstuffed chair as she watched the evening news with her mother.

"Something bothering you, dear?" asked Maude Fells. She put the Christmas scene she had been embroidering down on her lap and regarded Carrie quizzically. Her hair was silvery, her form rotund, and she reminded her daughter at this time of year of no less a personage than Mrs. Claus.

"No, I'm fine, Mom," said Carrie. And lucky, she thought, even without her missing sleigh pendant. She had always had her mother around to help her through troubled times. Her dad, too, till three years ago. She had been brought up in a loving, two-parent home.

Unlike Sam DiGregorio and his sister Leanne Dutton.

But that didn't mean that one parent couldn't give all the love a baby would need. Especially with a loving grandma around to help. And an uncle who, if not always the most thoughtful of men, still cared a lot.

But Carrie had to convince Sam. She could delay no longer.

She rose and gave her mother a hug. "Thanks, Mom," she said.

"For what, dear?"

"For being here."

"You're inviting me where?" Sam DiGregorio asked incredulously.

"My school's Christmas pageant," Carrie said. Was she actually giggling into the phone at his reaction?

He wished he could see that. She hardly even smiled when he was around, let alone laughed.

He just might risk an evening at her school, in the hopes of getting her to laugh again.

The last time they were together—nearly a week ago—he had been the party-pooper. He'd been unable to stop his repulsed reaction when reminded of the fraudulent dealings at her husband's car dealership. The fact that Carrie still owned an interest, took an active role in the business, did not help.

What if she were involved? How would the head-lines read in his next campaign—"Mayor Squires Swindler's Wife." Or, worse, "Mayor Squires Swindler."

Worst of all: "Mayor Kisses Swindler."

But that kiss of Carrie's—it had been unexpected. It might have been calculated to capture his attention, but he doubted it. Seduction was hardly the way to convince him she'd be the best mother for his sister's baby. Besides, it had seemed impromptu.

And it had been incredible. It had been on his mind all week.

"You promised me an opportunity to lobby you. What do you say, Sam?" The voice at the other end was sweet, mesmerizing—and it reminded him, as so much had lately, of her kiss.

He wasn't mesmerized when he answered. He knew what he was doing—didn't he?

"Lobby away, Carrie," he said. "I'll be there."

Was he there?

Carrie hadn't had much time to look out at the growing audience in the school auditorium. Not that she expected to be able to pick out one person among all the proud parents.

"Will you tie my bow, Mrs. Rit'nour?" piped a tiny voice. Carrie looked down to see little Benjamin Brattlethwaite staring up hopefully, his thick red ribbon in hand.

"Sure, Benj." As she bent down, she smiled to see that the seven-year-old had dressed in the dark pants and white shirt that she had requested. The child smelled sweetly of peppermint.

Standing straight once more, she looked around the classroom that was the pageant's staging area. Most of the kids had arrived. And most had fortunately followed her instructions regarding the evening's attire.

They looked cherubic in their big red bows, everyone's hair combed above huge Christmas smiles. She wanted to hug each of them.

But she couldn't relax now—not until she got through the evening's ordeal—getting them all out on stage and through the class's Christmas song.

A knock sounded on the door. Carrie looked up. "It's your turn next, Mrs. Ritenour," said Erma Sheldon, the thin assistant principal. She was clad in a bright green dress with a twinkling star in her hair.

"Thanks, Miss Sheldon," Carrie said. She clapped her hands, to get the attention of the thirty kids skipping merrily about. "Time to line up, everyone."

Five minutes later they were all on stage, tallest on the top tier of the platform, shortest at the bottom. Little bodies swayed, little mouths giggled, but everyone was in place, in the beam of the spotlight.

Squinting, Carrie tried to see beyond the lights into the crowd but could make out no one—not till she looked along the wall to stage left. There, near the front, stood Sam DiGregorio. He smiled up at the stage.

At the children. Not at her. She reminded herself of that. But he had come.

Okay, kids, she prayed. Make me look good.

Make me look like I could be one of the mamas out there who are watching you.

The pianist struck a chord. Carrie raised her hand, then brought it down.

The kids started singing. Not exactly on key, not exactly in rhythm, but they belted out the Christmas carol she had chosen—"Up on the Housetop."

Chapter Eight

Leaning against the wood-paneled auditorium wall, sandwiched among beaming parents, Sam chuckled. "Up on the Housetop." What other Christmas carol would Carrie have chosen?

He watched her sway at the side of the stage. She was clad in a red knit dress that matched her kids' bows—and draped most becomingly over her show-stopping form. One hand waved the song's rhythm in an attempt to keep the kids together. A not-very-successful effort, but it didn't matter. All the little angels stood there singing about how reindeer paused and how dear old Santa Claus jumped out. Nearly in unison they raised their hands and tried to snap their fingers: "click, click, click."

Two other choruses followed, about little Nell's stocking being filled with a dolly, then little Will's with a hammer, tacks, ball, and whip. Not politically correct these days, Sam thought, always mindful of what was PC. What if little Nell wanted tools or a ball?

Cute, though, he opined. Very cute.

Too soon, the song was over. Carrie hustled her brood offstage. Sam thought about trying to find her, then realized it would be impolite to leave before all the students had sung.

Just as he was aware of what was PC, he had learned through grueling campaigns that politicians could not afford to be impolite.

He wished he had ignored that rule, though, when the concert was finally over and he was immediately accosted by Phoebe Briggs, a reporter from a local TV station, trailed by her photographer. "Mayor DiGregorio, what brought you to the Calridge Elementary School Christmas Pageant?" A microphone was thrust into his face by the attractive, camera-ready woman with perfect makeup and hair.

Just then he spotted Carrie, wending her way through the crowd of hugging parents and beaming children. She stopped a distance away, a wary frown on her lovely face.

Something told him she did not like reporters. Guilty conscience? he wondered, his thoughts briefly lighting on the bait-and-switch scheme at her husband's car dealership. So far, that had not been made public. And he wasn't about to blow the whistle—together with any official police investigation. It was enough that he knew about it.

Besides, he didn't like reporters much, either—though he'd never hesitated to call self-serving press conferences around election time. He couldn't afford to be rude to one in any case.

"Mayor DiGregorio?" The reporter sounded more insistent. "Is there a special child you've come to hear?"

No special child, he thought, but a special adult, one waging a one-woman campaign to convince him she would be a wonderful single parent. Not that he could tell the reporter that. And not that he was convincible.

He made himself smile into the camera. If he gave Ms. Briggs a sound bite, maybe she'd go interview some kids. They were better looking than he was, anyway. Besides, he suspected little ones were her human interest assignment du jour. " ' 'Tis the season to be jolly,' " he quipped, "and no better place to get into the holiday spirit than spending it with our country's future leaders, don't you think, Phoebe?"

"Of course, Mr. Mayor. Thank you." After a few more meaningless exchanges, she hurried away as he'd hoped, microphone outstretched and photographer in close pursuit.

He watched until she was ensconced in an interview with a tiny caroler before turning back toward Carrie.

She wasn't there.

He looked around in time to see a woman with dark, wavy hair and a red knit dress exit the auditorium at the top of the rising aisle. "Excuse me," he said several times, feeling like a matador as he dodged through people to hurry after her.

By the time he reached the lobby, she was gone. He scanned the departing crowd to no avail. Damn! he thought. All the pleasant pre-holiday glow he'd felt from hearing the kids flew out of him, leaving him deflated.

"Sam?" At the soft, feminine voice, he turned—and the smile he'd lost returned to his face. There she was, her head cocked quizzically as she looked first to one side, then the other. "What happened to your friend?"

"The reporter? She found someone more exciting to

grill—a kid with big ideas who just might oppose me for office some day."

Carrie smiled. "What did you think of the show?"

"It was great. Where'd you go? I couldn't find you."

"I had to help one of the kids find his brother in another homeroom." She hesitated, then stuck out her chin with attitude. "So?"

"So . . . ?" he repeated.

"So, how did you think I did managing all those kids?"

"Couldn't imagine anyone doing any better." And he couldn't. She'd looked perfect up there, shepherding her crooning flock. "But—"

"But you don't think that's enough." Her chin fell, and the light left her eyes. "What will it take, Sam?"

He was jostled from the side by a running imp in a green elf hat and nearly bumped into Carrie. He took her arm. "For tonight, it'll take a cup of coffee," he said, "so we can discuss it."

"It isn't you." Sam sipped his coffee. His eyes were on hers, and though they looked apologetic, Carrie thought his expression disturbingly firm.

She had suggested a Denny's restaurant several miles down the main Calridge Street—far enough away that it was unlikely to be frequented by the spill-over from the school pageant. Though it was busy, Carrie did not see anyone she knew. Thank heavens.

What if she began to cry?

Cry? Her? Not in this life. She wouldn't just give up like that.

A tenor voice in her head contradicted her. "*It's all right, Carrie,*" said her imagined Elliott. "*Since I can't take care of this for you, it isn't worth doing.*"

"You're wrong!" she retorted much too loudly.

Then she blinked at the amazed expression in Sam's brilliantly blue eyes. She laughed, then said more quietly, "You're wrong about me, Mr. Mayor. And wrong about most of the single parents in the world. How many do you think there are right here, in Calridge, your constituency?"

"Probably a lot," he conceded. "But their kids—"

"Their kids are doing fine. You certainly turned out great, and you came from a single-parent household."

He cocked one of his thick black brows at her. There was a look in his eyes that went far beyond curiosity—and way into the realm of sensuality. It sent surges of soaring temperature all through her.

"You think I turned out great?" The proud rumble of his deep voice seemed to make her vibrate sympathetically.

She inhaled, trying to cool her thoughts. "Of course," she said with a bright, breezy smile. "Not just because you're an excellent mayor. You're an even better big brother." Not to mention a superb kisser—but she was hardly about to bring that up.

"Really?"

He sounded so pleased with himself that Carrie started, sure that he'd read her thoughts.

But when he continued, he spoke of his skills in brothering, not kissing. "Before Leanne went away to school, it was she and I against the world. I practically raised her after our mother died. She knows it, and I think she appreciates it."

"I know she does," Carrie said. "That's why she probably won't go against you in this. But did you ever ask her why she considered my adopting her baby in the first place? Call it women's intuition, call it whatever you like, but Leanne knows I'd make a damned good mother."

"*Damned* good?"

"Damned good," Carrie repeated. "Though you can be sure I'll watch my tongue in front of my own child. I'm great about curbing it in my classroom."

Sam laughed. "I'm sure you are." And then his deep blue eyes bored into hers, unnerving her with earnestness. He reached across the table and took her hand.

His was warm. It was firm. His fingers began to stroke her palm with a sexiness that almost made her forget about her mission.

"But Carrie, keeping a rein on swearing, teaching kids to sing Christmas carols—they're useful, I'll grant you, but they aren't the skills one would need to be two parents to one kid." He looked incredibly caring. And sincere.

And infuriating—despite the fact that, a moment before, she had been so distracted by his hand that she'd wanted to test whether his kiss was as spectacular as she remembered.

But not now. Definitely not now.

Carrie yanked her hand away and set it firmly in her lap. Her dander rose. And so, inside her, did the words she had been badgering herself with for months. The words that had kept her going—even if she had never before allowed herself to believe them.

Elliott hadn't believed them. . . .

But Elliott wasn't here.

She blurted, "There's nothing I can't do, Sam DiGregorio. If I decide to be a perfect mother, I can do it. I *will* do it." She leaned across the Formica table toward him and made her voice sink lower, though she could still feel the stares of people at nearby tables. "I can teach, I can watch my tongue, I can even hang those damned Christmas decorations on my roof, even if you don't believe any of it. And I sure as heck can be the right mother for Leanne's baby."

"I'm not saying there's anything you can't do." Sam's voice was tinged with exasperation. "But there are some things that are better to do with more than one person. Hanging Christmas lights, especially up on your roof, is among them. So is parenting."

"Well, I'm going back up on my roof tomorrow, Mr. Mayor, to finish hanging those lights, and I'll do it myself. Perfectly. Just as I can raise a baby."

Sam shook his head. She could see his irritation in the straight line of his lips. "Don't do something foolish just to try to make a point, Carrie. You can't go back up on your roof on your own."

"Just try and stop me!" she retorted.

Chapter Nine

Sam didn't try to stop her from going back on the roof. But he did insist on helping.

She put off her mission for a few days, hoping he'd forget. Or change his mind.

He didn't. He called each day to ask about her plans to return to the roof. Now and then he would stop by. They'd have coffee together, or he would take her out to eat. She was glad for his concern. Wasn't she?

She was definitely glad for his calls and visits. They let her continue lobbying. She reminded him often of how well she handled her students. How much she looked forward to caring for Leanne's baby. *Her* baby, after the adoption.

She had to think positively.

She didn't tell him how she lay awake nights thinking about him. No, no—it was about how lonely she would be if she didn't get this baby to love. To love her.

She needed this tiny one, and it would need her.

Carrie would shelter and teach and impress the baby, as it grew, with her knowledge. There was a lot she could give to a baby. And that a baby could give to her.

She would be a good parent. She *would*.

But lobbying, a voice inside kept niggling, was not the only reason she looked forward to Sam's nightly call. She was getting too used to it. It would stop, no matter how things turned out, after the baby came. It had to, for she had promised herself to let no man into her life after Elliott left it. She needed no other man. Ever.

But the baby's arrival loomed not far ahead. So did Christmas. On the Saturday before the holiday, Carrie told herself that she could put her task off no longer. It was time to return to the roof.

"Call Joey to help," her mother said as Carrie dragged the Santa and reindeer back to the base of the ladder.

"He was a big help last time," Carrie replied.

"Well, I've an appointment at the beauty salon." Her mother patted her platinum hair.

"Then go."

"I can't leave you alone," her mother protested.

Secretly, Carrie agreed. She did not want to get stranded again. But she said, "I'll be fine, Mom."

Just then the phone rang. Her mother went inside. "It's for you, Carrie," she called.

It was Sam. "I just asked," he said without ceremony. "Your mom said you're about to go up the ladder. Wait fifteen minutes, and I'll be there."

Carrie did not need to obey him. She did not have to wait one minute, let alone fifteen.

She returned to the rear of the house. The ladder stood where she had left it. She tested it. The wide metal shoes seemed steady enough on the ground. In the cool winter sunlight, the ladder's side rails and rungs cast a patterned shadow against the white frame of the house.

Carrie stared at the black-on-white design as she took a deep breath. Then she lifted the Santa and sleigh, a metal framework for blinking Christmas lights. It wasn't heavy, just bulky. She positioned it over her arm—just as she heard a car pull up out front. Hurriedly, she took two steps up the ladder.

"Carrie?" her mother called. "Sam's here. I'm leaving now."

In a moment, Sam came out the back door. He wore worn jeans and a blue pullover sweater that did marvelous things to his already marvelous eyes. Carrie fought her own smile of happiness at seeing him—and lost. Though he smiled back, his raised brows hinted of exasperation. "I told you to wait," he said.

"I can hang the lights myself," Carrie grumbled, taking another step up the ladder.

"I know," he replied. "I have every confidence in you. I just want to steady the ladder."

Carrie blinked as a wonderful sense of warmth traveled through her. He believed in her. He only wanted to lend a hand.

Maybe. She needed to test his forbearance. She climbed another rung, then another.

True to his word, Sam merely held the ladder. At the top, she gingerly clambered onto the roof.

"Are you all right?" Sam called.

362

"Fine." But Carrie wished she could have banished the shakiness from her voice. She went about her business, draping the lights she had left up there around the remaining dormers and eaves. When she was finished, she fastened the Santa, sleigh, and reindeer in front. Then she was nearly done.

She maneuvered her way to the rear once more. "I'm going to toss down the plugs," she told Sam. "There's an extension cord with four outlets near the back door. Would you plug them in? I need to make sure everything works."

Happily, it did! Though not easy to see in the sunlight, the waterfalls of lights turned on. So did the array of blinking lights creating Santa, his sleigh full of presents, and a complement of reindeer, including Rudolph of the red nose. Up on the housetop, her housetop, reindeer had paused—and now, so could Carrie.

"Did you see, Elliott?" she whispered. "I did it."

"*Good, Carrie,*" the voice in her head replied. The tone was a touch incredulous, darn him. "*But you still need to get back down.*"

She looked at the ground. It looked so far away. She shuddered. She *did* still have to get back down. But not, fortunately, immediately.

She crawled to the back once more. "How does it look from there?" she called to Sam, way below, shouting to drown out the tremor inside her.

"Wonderful. But I'll go around the house to check things out—unless you're ready to come down."

"Not quite yet," Carrie said. There was something important she hadn't done last time she was here.

She saw Sam step back, squint up at the lights and at her, shielding his face as he assessed the decorations.

She smiled. She'd done all the work herself, yet she had felt wonderfully, warmly safe—for she knew Sam was there if she needed him.

"I'm okay, Elliott," she stated to the heavens. "See?"

While Sam was busy looking around, so was Carrie. She crawled along the shingles toward the gutter. She had stuck a trowel in her back bluejeans pocket, and she pulled it out. The gutters needed to be cleaned anyway; the neighbor's eucalyptus trees rained leaves everywhere, including here.

She scraped out the detritus in the pipe along part of the house, then examined it. Dirt and leaves, that was all.

"You all right up there?" Sam called again.

"Yes." She felt herself grin. So what if she hated heights? She had faced her fear and won—at least for today. She continued around the roof, cleaning the gutter, examining what she removed . . . and then, there it was! Five years after she had lost it, filthy and covered with caked-on mud, the gold Santa, sleigh, and reindeer pendant and chain that she had lost was finally in her hands. "Oh, how lucky!" she said softly. She squeezed the necklace gently, then stuffed it down deep in her pocket, followed by the trowel.

Now, it was time to get down.

Carefully, she crawled back toward the ladder. Sam was not in the backyard.

"Sam!" she called, suddenly afraid. What if he had pulled a Joey and jumped ship? She had to get down. Now.

"Here, Carrie." He emerged from the side of the house where the fruit trees were. "Everything looks great from here," he said. "Are you ready to join me and look?"

"Yes," she said fervently.

"Okay, then. I'm holding the ladder. Come on down."

Carrie stilled as she reached the ladder. She recalled how afraid she had been the last time, and how Sam had helped her down.

She knew he would do the same now. And that was why she didn't need him to.

With determination, knowing she had her lucky pendant in her pocket and Sam below, she swung one leg around, followed by the other. In a minute, she was on the ground.

"You did great," Sam said. He was beaming, as though he were as proud of her accomplishment as she was.

"Yes, didn't I?" Carrie practically purred.

And then her glance met Sam's. He wasn't smiling anymore. Instead, his gaze, straight into her eyes, was intense and arousing. Carrie suddenly felt as though he touched her everywhere with his stare.

"Sam." Her voice was a hoarse whisper. She wanted to thank him, then tell him to leave.

No, that wasn't at all what she wanted. She shivered, wishing for him to touch her. Everywhere. And not merely with his stare.

"You did great, Carrie," he said again, his voice a whiskey-smooth murmur that intoxicated her. He put out his hand. She did not have to think; she took it.

And then she was in his arms. The kiss they had shared before was mere prelude to the sensation of his lips devouring her, and not just her mouth. He nipped gently at her earlobe, the most sensitive areas of her neck, her throat. "Oh, Sam," she murmured.

She couldn't. She shouldn't. But she took his hand and led him into the house.

At the base of the stairs he swept her into his arms and carried her. She was hardly aware of showing him which was her bedroom.

She stilled when he gently placed her on the bed. This room was filled with ghosts. She had lived here with—

"Are you all right with this, Carrie?" Sam asked gently. "I want you, but I don't want to hurry you."

"Hurry?" she replied, her unsettled gaze focusing on his eyes. They were hooded with desire, mirroring her own soul-stirring passion. She'd need to roll up in a carpet on the floor if he failed to quickly put out the conflagration within her. "Yes, Sam. Please hurry."

With no further delay, Sam gently pulled her T-shirt over her head and unfastened her bra, and she moaned as her breasts spilled into his seeking hands.

"Lovely," he whispered, and bent over her. She gasped at the sweet sensation as he took one nipple into his mouth, then the other. His hair tickling her neck, she inhaled the scent of shampoo, and a wonderfully masculine aroma that was strictly Sam's.

She arched into his touch as he unhooked her jeans and slid his hand inside. His fingers curled momentarily in the nest of her hair, then quested farther down until they touched her where her aching had grown nearly unbearable.

He drew away, and she protested without words. In a moment, he drew her jeans and panties from her, then began his incredible stroking once more.

Carrie felt as though she would scream. Or explode. But as incredibly mad as the sensations drove her, they were not enough.

Her turn. Quickly, fumblingly, she started to undress Sam. She stared through half-closed eyes at the wonders she bared. Mayor Sam was no flabby, pork-barrel bureaucrat. His chest, with its mat of dark hair, was hard, brawny, incredible. The bulging muscles of his arms flexed as he drew down his own jeans.

He knelt on the bed, and she took in the phenomenal sight of Sam DiGregorio in the raw. Yet nothing felt as raw as her own emotions. She looked him unabashedly up and down, feeling his eyes devour her with equal ardor. His erection was large and powerful. She had to touch it.

He moved even as he groaned. He reached to the side of the bed, and she heard the crackle of cellophane. She couldn't help it; she had to assist him with the condom.

And then he positioned himself over her and plunged inside.

Carrie was carried away by the rhythm that started slowly and built to a booming crescendo. "Oh, Sam," she cried as she felt the world explode.

Chapter Ten

Carrie lay still for a long minute, utterly reveling in the sensation of being sated. She snuggled against Sam, her cheek on his heated, hard chest. She enjoyed the way his heavy breathing made her head move up and down.

His lovemaking had been wonderful. No, it had been outstanding. Superlative. She couldn't ever remember feeling this way before.

Ever. . . .

She bit her lip. She had already been untrue to Elliott's memory by this stolen episode of sexual indulgence. She shouldn't compound it by comparing Sam to her poor dead husband.

But how could she help it?

"Are you all right?" Sam whispered beside her.

"Fine," she answered. "More than fine." But she knew her tone turned her words to courteous untruths.

A horrible thought struck her. *She* was having tardy second thoughts, but what about Sam? Elliott had always told her just what to do, how to touch and stroke and kiss so she wouldn't disappoint him.

But Sam had given no such instructions. What if he had hated it?

She groaned and moved away, though she allowed her backside to remain against the wonderful warm body in bed with her.

"What's wrong, Carrie?" Sam's voice was kind. Maybe he was too polite to tell her how unsatisfying she had been.

"I didn't . . . I mean, did I . . . ?" She stopped. There was no easy way to ask. And she had been teaching herself to do what was necessary, no matter how hard. "Did you enjoy yourself, Sam? I mean, what did you think of . . . what we just did?"

His laugh was a deep, sexy rumble that shot shivers through her everywhere. Could it be that she hadn't been too bad? Or was he just—

"Oh, Carrie," he said. "What did I think? I thought it was great. *You* were great." He stopped. When he spoke again, there was something in his voice that she could only interpret as vulnerability. "Did you ask because you didn't enjoy—"

She broke in. "Oh, Sam, no!" She turned to face him. "What we just did here was the most incredible experience I've ever had." She felt herself turn red. She bit her bottom lip. She wanted to bite her tongue. *Oh, Elliott*, she thought. *My disloyalty to you today is utterly unforgivable.*

Sam's deep blue eyes darkened. "Tell me about him," he said.

"Who?"

"Your husband," Sam said. His voice was remote.

"Were you thinking about him when we made love?"

"No," Carrie said hastily. But she wanted to be honest. "Not 'til after. But it wasn't what you think."

"What? You weren't comparing us?"

Carrie broke her gaze from his, and it landed on their bare bodies still pressed together on the bed. She sat up to reach for the sheet, then covered them both.

A question was still pending. Did she have to answer?

Yes, she realized. It would be unfair to Sam if she didn't. "I . . . I did make a comparison of sorts. Elliott was the only man I had ever made love to. He was my husband, and I cared deeply for him. But what we just did . . ." She hesitated.

"What we just did . . . ?" Sam prompted.

"You have to realize, it's been a long time since I'd been with Elliott. He died more than a year ago. But from what I remember, well . . . this was so much better than anything I recall."

Sam laughed again, then said kindly, "To give your Elliott his due, you may be right—that long abstinence may have colored your recollection."

Carrie smiled and burrowed closer to Sam beneath the sheet. He smelled wonderful: earthy, sexy . . . not the perfect and political Sam. She liked him this way. "Maybe it did."

"But I don't know how you could have asked whether it was good for me. It—"

"But you didn't tell me what you wanted," she blurted out.

Sam seemed startled, then said, "I see." He was quiet for a long time.

To fill the empty air, Carrie began an explanation. "Elliott told me what he needed, and I tried to comply.

But sometimes—" She stopped. She was saying too much. *Much* too much.

Sam put his arms around her in a gesture that seemed protective. She nestled her head beneath his chin. "Your Elliot . . . " Sam finally said. He sounded as if he spoke through gritted teeth, and Carrie pulled back to look at him. There was anger in the tilt of his thick, dark brows. She shook her head slightly, wondering what he was thinking.

"My Elliott what?" she urged, though something inside her had suddenly gone from wonderful heat to iceberg cold. Something told her she shouldn't have asked.

"Your Elliott was not perfect," Sam finished. He sat up suddenly and put his feet on the floor. She studied the expanse of his perfect, broad back. His skin was so taut, so masculine . . . she wanted to touch it but didn't. Not now. There was something going on that she did not understand.

"I know he wasn't perfect," she said finally. "But he loved me. A lot. He took care of me. He told me what to do to keep me from making a fool of myself. And—"

"Carrie, he didn't let you breathe." Sam sounded exasperated. "Your Elliott smothered you. He made you—"

"Don't you criticize him," Carrie cried, hands pressed against her hot cheeks as moisture flooded her eyes. She felt as fragile as if she were a balloon being poked with a pin. "You have no right. You didn't even know him. He was wonderful. He was good to me. He was—"

"A thief." Sam shouted, drowning out whatever words she had fumbled for. "He defrauded people. Did you know that his car dealership was under investigation for its bait-and-switch selling techniques?"

Linda O. Johnston

In the moment of ensuing silence, Carrie felt her stomach churn. "No. No, that's impossible."

Sam turned to face her. She refused to let her gaze drop to his devastatingly delicious chest—the sight would only confuse her more.

She saw him take a deep breath. "I'm sorry I yelled at you. I'm sorry I criticized Elliott. But Carrie, before there can be anything more between us, you should know the real reason I came to your house a few weeks ago. I knew Leanne and you had been talking about your adopting her baby."

Carrie forced herself to smile, though her breathing had grown haphazard. "You've already admitted you were trying to find out something about me."

"But there was more. I was investigating you. And Elliott."

Carrie felt her eyes widen, her stomach drop. "What do you mean?" she asked in a hoarse whisper.

"I wanted to make sure, in case Leanne let you adopt her baby, that you had nothing in your background that would keep you from handling things well. That's how I found out about the pending charges against Elliott. But then he was killed in that accident at the dealership . . . and you inherited his interest. You said you deal with your partner actively, give him instructions. And as far as I've been able to ascertain, the bait-and-switch is still going on."

Carrie stood up abruptly, hardly aware of her nakedness. "You—you—" she sputtered. "You had no right to look into Elliott's company. And for you to even imply that I have had anything to do with something shady, without even knowing my side of things—" She stopped, suddenly realizing that her chest was heaving, and Sam was having a difficult time not watching the rise and fall of her breasts. She blinked in fury, strode to her closet and pulled out a robe.

When she had put it on, she said, with all the dignity she could muster, "I think it's time for you to leave, Mr. Mayor."

"I think," said Sam DiGregorio quietly, "that you are right."

Chapter Eleven

Carrie made herself drive the legal speed along Calridge's main street, despite her urgent desire to be at her destination. Her entire future might depend on her impending lunch.

She hardly noticed the Christmas decorations hanging from the streetlights, the pretty displays in store windows, the carols playing softly on the radio. Her mind rehearsed the script she'd prepared to present to Leanne.

"I'm the right mother for this baby, Leanne," she said aloud. "Your brother may not believe in single parents, but he doesn't really know *me*. He made up his mind before he even met me. Did you know he even stooped to investigating not only me, but my dead husband?"

Oops. That last question wasn't in the script.

What if Leanne responded to the real spiel by saying that Sam had called Carrie a few times in the past week, to try to get to know her better—but that Carrie had not spoken with him?

He *had* called, but Carrie never answered, never returned the messages left on the machine and with her mother. There was nothing he could say to make things better. If he'd called to pass on more dirt he had allegedly unearthed about Elliott, she didn't want to hear it. If he had called to apologize—which he surely hadn't—she wouldn't believe him anyway.

She hadn't yet returned the much-too-intimate long johns and nightcap. She would wait until after the holidays, when crowds had thinned, to take them back. Meanwhile, she had hidden the box at the back of her closet. To see the ill-fated gift would remind her of Sam, his beautiful body—and his treacherous mind.

There. She had reached the restaurant. She pulled into the parking lot and took a deep breath. This was it. This lunch would make or break her.

She had to convince Leanne. She *would* convince her. She was perfectly capable of making an irrefutable argument. Of showing what a perfect mother she would make. Of—

"Oh, my poor little Carrie," came a voice in her mind as she reached for the car door. *"Don't you know better than that? You can't take care of yourself, let alone a helpless baby. I've told you that before."*

"Yes, you have, Elliott," Carrie whispered. "And once I might have believed you. Or at least I wouldn't have argued. But now . . . You stay out here, understand?"

She didn't wait to hear any reply. No more well-intended but painfully pointed questions from Elliott; no more trying to convince others of her capability when she could not quite convince herself. No more room for the slightest self-doubt. Carrie had a mother-to-be to charm. She hustled from the car and into the restaurant.

Mangini's was a charming Italian place, decorated with checkered tablecloths, Chianti bottles and Christmas lights. In their phone call setting up this meeting, Leanne had mentioned that she craved pizza lately. Mangini's had immediately come to Carrie's mind.

She didn't see Leanne. She sat at a table for two and ordered a soft drink.

Ten minutes later, she still sat there alone. Her thoughts roiled. What if Sam had convinced Leanne not to come? Would he do such a nefarious deed?

Of course he would. He had been investigating Elliott. He had been investigating *her*. And he had thought Elliott was embroiled in an illegal scheme.

Worst of all, he thought Carrie was, too.

She took a quick swig of her Coke, wishing for a moment it was a glass of Chianti. Or something stronger.

No, she couldn't and wouldn't drown her sorrows that way—no matter how much she hurt. For she did hurt. Miserably.

After all, she had made love with Sam, the man who mistrusted her. The man who thought her capable of breaking the law, and incapable of raising a baby by herself.

The man whom, despite all that, she had realized she had begun to love.

She felt tears in her eyes, but blinked them back. She wouldn't cry. Whether or not Leanne showed up, she wouldn't cry.

"Hi, Carrie."

Carrie looked up. There was Leanne! She looked

wonderful in a Christmasy red-and-green plaid maternity top that adorably stuck way out in front.

"Sorry I'm late. I just take so much longer to get ready these days."

"No problem," Carrie reassured her. "I've just been studying the menu." In fact, she had not looked at it at all. Her nervousness had eaten away her appetite.

Carrie ordered nevertheless—angel hair pasta with marinara sauce. Maybe she could attract a little luck if angels had anything to do with her lunch. Instinctively, for luck, she fingered the Santa and sleigh pendant she had hardly removed from about her neck since the day she found it. The last time she had been up on her roof. The day Sam and she . . .

Cut that out, she commanded herself.

"Is something wrong?" Leanne asked.

Carrie shook her head. "Not at all." She smiled brilliantly—the way she hoped a prospective adoptive mama might.

"That's a wonderful necklace," Leanne said. "Is it new?"

"No," Carrie said. "But I'd lost it for a while." She waited as their server put bread on the table, then plunged into her practiced speech. "Leanne, we need to talk about your baby, and why it's important to all of us for me to adopt him—or her."

Leanne's pretty blue eyes looked pained. "I don't know, Carrie."

"I know you don't." Carrie made herself sound upbeat, ignoring how downhearted she felt at the girl's words. "But listen." She reiterated all the rational arguments she had advanced before, added more for good measure, and finished, "I can even supply letters of reference from fellow teachers and my students' parents. As many as you'd like. Honestly, Leanne," she finished, "I'd be perfect."

"You'd still be a single parent," the girl said with a sigh.

Carrie closed her eyes and breathed deeply. Then she looked straight at Leanne. "You're going to listen to Sam, aren't you? Even though you don't feel as strongly about the issue as he does. But he doesn't know everything, Leanne. He's simply biased against single parents."

"Carrie, I know you're aware of our childhoods."

Leanne stopped for a moment as the server placed a zesty-smelling small serving of pasta before Carrie and a large pizza in front of Leanne. *She's eating for two,* Carrie thought. *For herself and for my baby . . . it* has *to be my baby.*

"It's no wonder Greg—er, Sam's biased," Leanne finally continued. "Can you imagine how it was for a guy just twenty to raise a ten-year-old sister? That happened after our mother died, while Sam was still in college. He knows what it's like to be a single parent, Carrie. He thought about adopting my baby himself but decided it was wrong for all of us. Now, he's protecting you as much as the baby." Leanne looked accusingly at Carrie. "What happened between you? Greg won't say, but when I've told him to call you to make peace, he says he's tried but you won't respond.".

So that was why Sam had been calling. All the more reason Carrie shouldn't have answered; he was calling to satisfy Leanne, not because he wanted to. Speaking of pain . . . but Carrie shrugged it off. Or at least she tried.

"I've just been busy," she said lightly. She leaned toward Leanne. "I know you love your brother." *So do*

I, insisted an insidious voice inside that she ignored. "But please, Leanne, trust your own judgment." She took a deep breath, preparing to bare her soul for a final shot. "I want this baby, partly because I'm lonely. But the most important thing should be that the little one is loved. Leanne, please believe me—even as a single parent, I'd have love enough for two."

Fingering her pendant, hoping against hope, Carrie stared into Leanne's eyes. Or at least she tried to, for the girl wouldn't meet her gaze.

"I'm sorry, Carrie. I can't decide, not right now. I'm so confused. . . . "

And with that Leanne called over the server to pack up the rest of her pizza. She was ready to leave—and Carrie was, after all her best intentions, ready to cry.

Chapter Twelve

As Carrie got into the hospital elevator, her heart pounded. This was it! Leanne was in labor. And she had called Carrie to request that she come.

It was early evening, Christmas Eve. Carrie had dropped everything, leaving her mother and brother to finish decorating the tree.

She pushed the button for the sixth floor, grinning at the elevator's other passengers. She was about to become a mother!

She shouldn't allow herself to hope like this. But Leanne had invited her. Surely that meant good news.

The elevator reached the sixth floor and Carrie rushed off. She asked a nurse at the reception desk where to find Leanne. She was not yet in a delivery room; Carrie wasn't too late!

Reaching Leanne's room, Carrie took a deep breath

and knocked on the closed door. "Come in," a female voice called.

Carrie shoved open the door. "Leanne, thanks so much for inviting me," she said. She drew close to the girl on the bed, who was clad in a standard-issue skimpy hospital gown. "How are you getting along?"

"Fine, they tell me. But I think it's going to be a while—" Her blue eyes grew huge, and she gasped aloud. Her face paled. Beeping monitors beside the bed seemed to speed up. She reached out, and Carrie took her hand. Leanne clutched hers so tightly that it hurt, but it didn't matter.

"Shouldn't you be breathing differently?" Carrie asked, remembering films of Lamaze childbirth techniques from television. Leanne looked at her gratefully, then began panting. Carrie found herself panting along with her.

"Greg's . . . my . . . coach," Leanne managed between breaths. "He . . . had to make a phone call . . . but he'll be back."

Not too soon, Carrie hoped.

Leanne's blowing slowed. "Wow," the girl said in a minute, letting go of Carrie. "That was one strong contraction." She attempted to smile. Her pretty cheeks were flushed and moist, and Carrie smoothed her damp blond hair back from her face. "But they tell me it's not going to be quick."

"Is there anything I can do?" Carrie asked. Like adopt this baby for you right this minute, she wanted to say.

"Not really." Leanne paused. "I had an ultrasound a little while ago. The baby is a couple of weeks early, and they wanted to see how ready she was to be born."

"*She?*" Carrie felt her face light up.

Leanne nodded.

Impulsively, Carrie reached around her own neck and pulled off her precious Santa and sleigh necklace. "This is for her." She pressed it into Leanne's hand.

"It's beautiful, Carrie. But it's yours. I've seen you wear it."

"No, it's the baby's now." Carrie took it from her. "I'll put it with your clothes so you don't forget it." She opened the door to the small closet and found a pair of Leanne's jeans. She put the pendant into the pocket, with only the tiniest pang of regret; she only hoped she had not given away her last shot at good luck, when she needed it most. She turned back toward the bed. "Please hand it to whoever the baby's mother will be, to give it to her when she's old enough. You know, of course, that I hope I'm the one you'll return it to."

"Carrie, you need to understand—"

The door to the room opened, and Leanne pasted a mock pout on her face. "Good thing Carrie was here to help, Mr. Mayor, or I'd never have made it through that last contraction. Some coach you are."

Sam looked even more handsome than Carrie remembered. He wore a burgundy sweater over gray slacks—casual time for the mayor. He smiled lovingly toward his sister. "You're tough, kid. You handled the last bunch just fine without my doing a lot. You're much better at heavy breathing than I am."

"You're right!" Leanne laughed. "So why don't you two just get out of here? I have the call button in case I need a nurse."

"I'll stay," Carrie said.

"Carrie, please come with me."

Carrie looked into Sam's blue eyes. They looked tired. They looked pleading. She tried nevertheless to be strong. "I'd rather—"

"Go with him, Carrie," Leanne said, her voice tired but insistent. "He wants to talk with you."

Carrie started as Sam took her arm. In moments, she found herself out in the hall with him.

He wanted to talk to her. Why? Had he been given the job of hatchet man? She supposed hardened politicians handled such things well. Was he going to make sure she understood why they would not let her adopt this baby?

She went icy inside as hot tears rushed to her eyes.

No, even if that were his mission, she wouldn't cry. She would take it, with dignity.

"Mind going to the coffee shop?" Sam said. "Poor kid's been at this for a while, and neither of us got breakfast or lunch."

"That's fine," Carrie said, though she knew she could not down anything. She walked silently beside him through hospital corridors with gleaming white walls and sparkling linoleum floors. The place smelled, not unexpectedly, medicinal.

She heard clattering dishes before she spotted the cafeteria. She got a cup of coffee to be polite. Sam insisted on paying for it, along with his turkey sandwich. He led her to one of the many available tables in the nearly empty cafeteria.

"So," Carrie said brightly, "what did you want to talk about?" No use beating around the bush. She might as well get socked right away with the bad news.

Sam's gaze riveted hers. "My investigation, Carrie."

She felt her heart sink. He was going to point out all the problems, then puncture her dreams. Well, she would beat him to it. "You don't have to tell me. I'll tell *you*." She took a sip of coffee for fortification, then looked Sam straight in those gorgeous blue eyes. His cheeks were dark and shadowed; he could have used a shave, but oh, how the rugged look became him.

Carrie made her mind return to the business at hand. "I didn't know about the bait-and-switch, Sam."

"Carrie, you don't—"

"Let me finish. After you told me, I went to Elliott's partner—*my* partner now—and insisted that he stop. He promised he would, in memory of Elliott—and to prevent me from drop-kicking him out of the dealership on his derriere. I don't believe Elliott was aware, but even if he was, the dealership won't do it anymore. I'll make sure. My partner knows I will. We've hired a lawyer to negotiate with the district attorney, and my partner will pay any fine out of his own pocket. And I've told him to make restitution to any customers who were treated badly." She glared at Sam. "You didn't need to accuse not only Elliott, but me, too."

"I'm sorry, Carrie," Sam said, his voice humble. "I let my reasons for wanting you not to adopt the baby get in the way of good sense. I shouldn't have started the investigation in the first place, and I most certainly should not have jumped to conclusions. Please accept my apology."

She hesitated. But holding grudges would not help her now. Not that she could anyway, against Sam.

"All right, Sam. I know you had good intentions, at least toward Leanne and the baby." But she wasn't through. "You have to understand, though, that I loved my husband." She watched Sam wince. Why? Did he care? Hardly. "Elliott wasn't perfect. I knew it. So did he, though he would never admit it. He tried to make up for his faults by taking good care of me. And not letting me take good care of myself."

"Carrie, you don't have to—"

She needed to finish. "It was wonderful to be cared

for that way—and terrible." She let Sam reach across
the table toward her and take her hand. What she was
trying to say was not easy. She appreciated a little
emotional support, even if it wasn't entirely sincere.
"The thing is, I don't want to be the woman who was
Elliott's wife anymore. I can't be. I became afraid I
couldn't do things myself—not without Elliott's per-
mission, or his help. But I've been proving to myself
that I am someone. That I can accomplish lots on my
own. That's why I want to raise Leanne's baby alone.
I can do it. I really can, Sam. Please let me have the
chance."

"It's not my decision, Carrie," Sam said gently.
"And that's what I wanted to talk to you about."

Carrie felt her heart plummet to somewhere far
beneath her shoes. Here it came—the kind but
absolute refusal. She would not become mother to this
baby.

She raised her eyes to look straight at him. She
would take it. She could handle anything.

"I talked to Leanne about what I'm going to say,
and she's agreed."

Carrie did not turn away. She did not even pull her
hand back, as Sam stroked it comfortingly. She needed
a little comfort now.

"Carrie, I love you."

Carrie felt her jaw drop. She shook her head
slightly, as though to clear it. She was hearing things.

But Sam had not stopped talking. "I think I fell in
love with you that first day, when I had to help you
down from the roof. You were so sweet, so lovely, and
so determined to get back up again by yourself. And
then I spent time with your family, with you at the
mall. I saw how you were with your students—and
how you did, at last, brave your fears again and get

385

back up on the roof. And that day, when we made love—"

Carrie felt herself color. She tried not to react to what he was saying. Was she imagining it? And if she wasn't, then how could he possibly be so cruel as to deny her this baby? Or was he just trying to let her down in a way meant to be kind, but which could turn out to be the most devastating blow of all?

"—it was more wonderful than anything I could have imagined. But I spoiled it. I would hate to think I spoiled everything that could have been between us."

"Sam, there's—" Carrie wasn't sure what she was going to say. It didn't matter, for he didn't let her continue.

"Before I finish, I want to give you something." He reached into his trouser pocket, and his hand came out with a small box wrapped in red paper. "Open it, Carrie. Please."

She did. Inside was a gold pendant with Santa and his sleigh—very much like the one she had just given Leanne for the baby. "Oh, Sam, it's wonderful. But—"

"It's the one you saw in the mall. It's yours, no matter what you say to the idea I'm going to suggest." He rose and fastened the clasp around her neck. She felt the warmth of his hands at her throat and closed her eyes, soaking in the wonderful sensation.

But what was his idea?

He sat again. "Carrie, as far as I'm concerned, if anyone can be a good single mother, you can. I know there are plenty of women who do a fine job. And if you want this baby for yourself, I'm going to tell Leanne that I vote yes."

"Oh, Sam!" Carrie felt tears course down her face. "Thank you. Thank you so much. I'll take wonderful care of her. You'll see."

"I hope to see," he agreed. "Carrie, I've come up with what I think is the most ideal solution for all of us—Leanne, the baby, and most especially you and me."

She frowned through her happy tears, wondering what he had in mind. "What's that?" Was he about to take away the wonderful news he had just delivered? No. Sam wouldn't do that.

To her surprise, he got down on one knee on the cafeteria floor. "Marry me, Carrie," he said. "I want you to because I love you. And if you do, we'll both adopt Leanne's baby. She'll see her little one grow up, and the baby will have a wonderful two-parent home."

She looked around frantically. All eyes in the restaurant were on them. "Mr. Mayor, what if someone from the media is here?"

"Then if you refuse, I'll look pretty silly. To everyone. 'Mayor Sticks Foot in Mouth in Hospital Cafeteria.' Sounds unsanitary." His smile was mischievous, but the lines in his forehead told her that his wait for her answer was hurting him.

She didn't want to hurt Sam, but—

"Mr. DiGregorio? Ms. Ritenour?" Carrie turned to see a uniformed nurse standing beside them, staring at the mayor, who was still on his knees. "Leanne sent me. It's time."

Chapter Thirteen

Leanne was panting like crazy in the delivery room when Carrie and Sam joined her. After the contraction was over, she turned to them expectantly.

"Well, big brother?" she managed, though still breathing hard.

He looked at Carrie. "I don't know yet. She hasn't answered."

He sounded sad. He sounded worried.

"Don't keep us in suspense," Leanne demanded.

Carrie cocked her head as she regarded Sam. "Do you promise that I can take care of you as much as you take care of me?"

"Count on it," he said, looking a tiny bit more hopeful.

"And you'll be honest and forthright with me, and trust me?"

He nodded. "Always."

"Oh, Sam! I love you." Carrie threw her arms around his neck, kissing him fervently and blissfully.

"Is that a 'yes'?" asked Leanne from behind them.

"Yes." And Carrie laughed as Sam beamed a warm and loving smile down at her.

"Wonderful," Leanne exclaimed, clapping her hands, though when Carrie turned toward her future sister-in-law, she could tell Leanne was being careful not to dislodge the IV. "Perfect."

Leanne had another contraction soon thereafter. They were coming frequently now, and the delivery room was bustling with doctors and nurses. Carrie clutched Sam's hand as they watched all the activity together.

And then someone said, "There's the head!" It did not take long after that before the baby came out, stretched, cried, and turned pink.

Leanne was laughing and crying. So was Carrie, hugged tightly in Sam's arms.

After a while, the nurse holding the cleaned and swaddled baby took her to Leanne. Leanne held her for a minute, then said wistfully, "Carrie, here. She's yours."

The most beautiful words in the world, Carrie thought as she took the baby from Leanne. But—

"No," she said. "She's ours."

Besides, they had been only the second most beautiful words. "I love you, Carrie," Sam whispered as she held the baby. *They* were the best words of all.

"I love you, too." Carrie smiled at Sam over their daughter. Then she glanced down. "She's beautiful," Carrie said, watching the sleeping, red-faced bundle with black peach fuzz on top. Her nose was tiny but perfect; her mouth was small and pursed. "What shall we name her?" she asked Sam.

"We'll figure that out," he said. "All three of us. Your mother and Joey can make suggestions, too. We're all going to be a family."

Carrie smiled, thinking of the beautiful tree that her mother and brother would have decorated by the time Sam and she returned home with all the wonderful news.

Home. Her home, with the Santa sleigh and lights on the roof that she had hung herself. The roof where she had met Sam and found love . . . up on the house-top.

LEIGH GREENWOOD
The Independent Bride

Colorado Territory, 1868: It is about as rough and ready as the West can get, a place and time almost as dangerous as the men who left civilization behind, driven by a desire for land, gold . . . a new life.

Fort Lookout: It is a rugged outpost where soldiers, cattlemen and Indians live on the edge of open warfare, the last place any woman in her right mind would choose to settle.

Abby: She is everything a man should avoid—with a face of beauty and an expression of stubborn determination. Colonel Bryce McGregor knows there is no room for such a woman at his fort or in his heart. Yet as she receives proposal after proposal from his troops, Bryce realizes the only man he can allow her to marry is himself.

Dorchester Publishing Co., Inc.
P.O. Box 6640   _____5235-0
Wayne, PA 19087-8640 $6.99 US/$8.99 CAN

Name: _____

Address: _____

City: _____ State: _____ Zip: _____

E-mail: _____

I have enclosed $_____ in payment for the checked book(s).

For more information on these books, check out our website at www.dorchesterpub.com.
_____ *Please send me a free catalog.*

A Texan's Honor
Leigh Greenwood

Bret Nolan has never gotten used to the confines of the city. He'll always be a cowboy at heart, and his restless blood still longs for the open range. And he's on his way back to the boundless plains of Texas to escort a reluctant heiress to Boston—on his way to pick up a woman destined to be a dutiful wife. But Emily Abercrombie isn't about to just up and leave her ranch in Texas to move to an unknown city. And the more time Bret spends with the determined beauty, the more he realizes he wants to be the man in Emily's life. Now he just has to show her the true honor found in the heart of a cowboy.

LISA KLEYPAS
LISA CACH * CLAUDIA DAIN
LYNSAY SANDS

Wish List

Dear St. Nicholas—
What we'd really like for Xmas this year is:

An Irish Estate
A Family
~~Mountains of Sugarplums~~ (Too fattening)
A Quiet Elopement
Someone to ~~burn~~ close down all the London clubs (like White's)!
Marriage to a Man who is Honest, Loving, Sexy, Handsome, and Titled.

But we know there aren't enough of those to go around...
are there?

—Respectfully,
Four Hopeful English Ladies

- -

CLAUDIA DAIN
DEE DAVIS
EVELYN ROGERS

SILENT NIGHT

Snow falls, but this is no ordinary white Christmas. There's no festive cheer, no carolers, no mistletoe. Three women are running for their lives: a college student home on break, the wife of a murdered DEA agent, a Denver widow. They're frightened and alone.

And Lindsay Gray, Jenny Fitzgerald and Tessa Hampton *are* in peril. A desperate snowmobile chase through the forest; a raspy, anonymous telephone call; a bloody stranger by the side of the road—every step seems to lead farther from safety . . . but toward what? Who waits in the darkness? Friends? Lovers? And on a cold, silent night, when do you call for help?

Darlene Gardner
snoops in the city

Tori Whitley is possibly the world's worst snoop. Who else would fall for the man she was investigating? As a favor to her private-detective cousin, she agrees to tail Seahaven businessman Grady Palmer. How hard can it be—especially following a man with such a cute rear end? But checking out Grady proves easy on the eyes and hard on her heart. He's packing charm, intelligence, and too many secrets. Tori has no choice but to discover the truth—by going undercover instead of going under the covers. And all the clues lead to one conclusion: To be a successful private eye, sometimes you have to follow your instincts . . . and hope you bag the man of your dreams.

ROBIN WELLS

THE BABE
Magnet

Holt Landen is in trouble. He's been left with a six-month-old child he never knew he had, and while he's attracted plenty of babes in the past, they were always the kind in high heels and garters.

Stevie Stedquest dispenses parenting advice on a radio talk show, but she doesn't have kids. And though she wants a child of her own, Mr. Right is nowhere on the horizon.

Baby Isabelle needs a mother in the worst way. A temporary marriage between her newfound father and Stevie would solve the problem, but they seem terribly mismatched. Fortunately, Isabelle has two aces up her diaper: opposites attract, and her daddy isn't the only babe magnet in the family.

Dorchester Publishing Co., Inc.
P.O. Box 6640
Wayne, PA 19087-8640

___52536-4
$6.99 US/$8.99 CAN